W9-BIN-861

HEART OF THE HARBOR

HEART OF THE HARBOR

by

Katrinka Blickle

DOUBLEDAY & COMPANY, INC.,
GARDEN CITY, NEW YORK
1979

ISBN: 0-385-15181-0
Library of Congress Catalog Card Number 78-22755

CONTENTS

HEART OF THE HARBOR

I'll catch the impetuous darkling (Cain), at his first re-
coil. And temporize his hatred to my wish!

Fratricide
J. Ross, 1773

1

Windows on the World

"That's the man I'm going to marry," I said.

"Beg your pardon?"

"What? Oh." Too late, I realized that I had spoken the words aloud. To Victor Bacall, of all people. "Oh," I repeated lamely, "nothing—I was just remarking on the scenery. We're lucky to have such a clear night." I turned to the window to consider the pointed tip of New York City far below us, then New York's long upper harbor with the Statue of Liberty's beacon twinkling through the November dusk settling over Manhattan.

It was exciting to be sitting so far above the city, but I could have been looking out at a brick wall for all it mattered. Sipping a glass of sherry in the highly polished bar on the 107th floor of the World Trade Center was the last place I wanted to be. And entertaining Victor Bacall, up-and-coming fashion designer, was the last thing I wanted to do. But Alix had insisted, and business being business, I had agreed. Now, Alix was late, and here I was stuck with her new "find." Worst of all, I was bored.

"I say. I do believe that's young Van der Hoek," Victor said suddenly.

I twisted my head to look where Victor was pointing. I flushed. It was the very same tall, lightly tanned restless-looking man I had been watching when I had made my unfortunate remark. He stood by the dimly lit entrance, a lock of brown hair falling artfully over his high forehead, his arms casually folded, as though trying to decide whether it was worth the effort to descend the few steps to the lounge. Now, as I looked at him again, it seemed that he was content to remain where he was, surveying the room through half-closed eyes. It had been that aloofness that had attracted me, the challenge a personality such as his would mean. Then our eyes met, and I thought I saw a half-smile play across his mouth. Oh no, I thought, had he, too, heard what I had said? Even more embarrassed, I turned back to Victor. "*Young* Van der Hoek?" I asked. The man appeared to be several years older than Victor.

"Well, yes. To distinguish him from his father, don't you know," Victor replied.

"No, I don't know." But my reply was unheeded as Victor jumped up and went over to Mr. Van der Hoek, who continued to stand where he was. He showed no great pleasure at being greeted by Victor, yet he moved toward our table amiably enough.

"Here we are. Quite a crush for a Thursday night. Gretel darling, this is Pieter—with an 'i'—Van der Hoek! The illustrator. We were at school together, only one year though. I couldn't stick it out and ran away to Seventh Avenue. Pieter, this ravishing creature is Gretel Drew. She's the art director for *Milady*, that wonderful magazine that is, I hope"—Victor paused to wink broadly—"going to feature some of my little things in one of their fabulous issues. Gretel is so clever, Pieter, I just know she'll make my designs look wonderful. No, no, Gretel, it's true. I've been meaning to tell you how much *Milady* has improved since you started working there. Now the magazine has a real concept, a very classy look."

"Thank you, Victor, I'm sure." I smiled tightly, resisting an impulse to kick him. I was the one and only art director that *Milady* had ever had since its inception two and a half years before. I turned a genuine smile on Pieter Van der Hoek, but before I could speak, a whirlwind descended upon us. Alix Silverstein, the thirty-two-year-old fashion editor of *Milady* magazine, had finally arrived.

"Oh, darlings. I am so sorry. But you have been enjoying the view, haven't you?" This last was directed appealingly to me. Alix knew full well what I thought of Victor Bacall. She also knew what I thought of meetings that were more productive when held in my office.

"It's been delightful," I answered. "What happened? Were you caught in traffic?" *Milady's* offices were also in the northeast tower of the World Trade Center, fifty floors down.

"What? How could I have been? You know better than that, Gretel—oh, I see. Well, I did have to wait for the elevators. But the phone rang every time I tried to leave my office, and then Madame Mavis called me in to chat. And you know how she can be. One thing after another. It's a miracle I'm here at all. Who is this interesting-looking person?"

Introductions were made; two empty chairs found and dragged up to the circular table. Somehow, we were all seated, new drinks were ordered, and when the dust had settled, I found myself squeezed next to Pieter Van der Hoek, while Alix and Victor entertained each other on the other side of the table.

"I hope you didn't feel pressured to join us," I said, breaking the awkward silence between us.

"Not at all. I enjoy meeting new people," Pieter said, rolling his glass between his palms.

"Are you meeting someone here?" I asked.

"No," said Pieter.

"Then you came up by yourself." I hated to state the obvious, but pulling words from this man was as difficult as silencing Alix. I was reminded of those painful conversations I had had in junior high school, with boys so embarrassed when sitting next to a girl that they could no more than mumble.

"Yes. I'm here by myself," said Pieter.

"Have you been here before?" I wondered if he were really shy. I wouldn't have thought it from the way he had surveyed the lounge from his position by the door, leaning nonchalantly against the wall, his head tilted slightly back so that he seemed to be looking down his long, sharply defined nose.

"No. This is my very first time up here. These slick places don't usually attract me." At last, I thought, he has volunteered some information.

"Don't you like the decor?" I asked.

"I've only seen the elevators and this part so far, so I really shouldn't comment," said Pieter.

"Well, I think this is the nicest area," I replied. "The bars are much cozier than the restaurant proper. By the way, this is called the Statue of Liberty Lounge, for the obvious reasons." I waved my hand to indicate the tiny lighted figure in the now completely dark harbor below. "She looks minuscule from up here."

"It's vulgar," said Pieter.

"What? What is?" I asked.

"This. All of this," he replied. "The Statue of Liberty was not designed to be looked down upon, to be reduced to a toy for bourgeois amusement."

"Then I take it the view displeases you?" I asked.

"No. I can admire it. But I prefer things in their proper perspective," said Pieter.

"Then why are you here?" I asked in exasperation. "Surely not as a tourist?"

"No. I've been commissioned by the Port Authority to do a series of paintings of the various views from the top of the Trade Center towers. I spent part of the afternoon on the observation deck in the other tower. I stopped in here to catch the sunset, to fortify myself against the trip home."

"Don't you live in New York City?" I asked.

"Oh yes. Born and raised. Right over there." Pieter leaned forward to point around me in the direction of the harbor.

"Staten Island?"

"No. Hoek Land." I looked at him suspiciously to see if he were joking, but Pieter appeared perfectly serious. "It's near Staten Island, in the Narrows, but I'm afraid you really can't see the island from here. It's too dark."

"I've never heard of Hoek Land," I said. "Ellis, Liberty, Governor's, and Staten. No more and no less."

"I assure you that it does exist," said Pieter.

"Hoek Land? Named for you, I suppose?" I was still unsure whether or not he was teasing me. He didn't seem the type for practical jokes. Yet a privately owned island seemed so unlikely.

"No indeed. I haven't that much conceit," said Pieter. "No, my great-great-great-great-great—well, I'd have to look it up—grandfather had that honor. Fredericks Van der Hoek. The island was given to him by Director-General William Kieft, for bravery shown during the Year of the Blood, 1643."

"Now I know you're making the whole thing up," I said, hesitantly.

"It was called that because of all the Indian massacres. My noble ancestor was personally responsible for the elimination of a troublesome Indian village on Staten Island," said Pieter, loftily. "And Kieft, being an Indian hater, gave him the island out of gratitude. It's been in the family ever since."

"Well, it's a very romantic story, but . . ."

"I see you're the type that needs proof," said Pieter.

"I suppose you have a snapshot in your wallet?" I asked.

"No. I meant substantial proof," said Pieter.

"Such as?" But any reply that Pieter might have made was interrupted.

A white-coated waiter bore down on us with what seemed a laden-to-overflowing tray. Fresh drinks were put before us (though I had barely touched the one I already had), and two steaming plates of hors d'oeuvres appeared almost magically in the center of the table. Tiny sauce-covered shish kebobs were arranged symmetrically on each plate.

"Oh, don't these look interesting!" Alix squealed, delicately picking up a skewer between two immaculately manicured fingers. "Don't be bashful, Gretel, take one. I'm sure you must be positively starving after all that conversation." Alix's almond-shaped eyes crinkled mischievously.

"Thank you," I said. "When did we order these?"

"Victor and I did," she replied. "Of course, you two were so deep in conversation that a bomb could have exploded and you wouldn't have noticed!" Alix licked her fingers daintily. It was amazing, I thought, how a usually gross gesture became exquisite when Alix made it. We were both five feet ten but I always felt awkwardly oversized next to Alix. "And now," she continued, "now that I've captured your attention with food, perhaps you can help us. Victor thinks his designs look their best if they're presented this way." Alix handed over some scribbled-on sheets of paper. "But I think it'll cost too much. You know how careful I've had to be. Now, Gretel, be super and think of some way we can do what Victor wants without Madame going into a tizzy over the expense."

I sighed and dragged myself from one fantasy world (Pieter's island) to another (*Milady's* fashion pages). I would have preferred to continue discussing the former—and finding out what Pieter's substantial proof was—but, alas, duty called.

I scolded myself. It was duty that had brought me here, after all.

Pieter remained silent while we talked—with us and yet not with us—sipping his drink. Although he was out of my line of vision as I huddled over sketches with Alix and Victor, I was very aware of Pieter's presence. I felt that if I turned around quickly I would catch him staring at me with those hooded eyes whose heavy lids did nothing to mask the energy that flashed darkly there. And, sure enough, when our discussion ended, and I sank back against the curved back of my chair, I turned to find Pieter's dark eyes on mine.

"Are you ready to be proved wrong?" Pieter asked, picking up our conversation exactly where we had dropped it almost an hour before.

"Ah, you're about to produce your substantial proof," I said.

"It's not exactly something that can be produced," said Pieter.

"Ah-hah! Then your island doesn't exist," I said triumphantly.

"Oh yes it does. And I intend to convince you," said Pieter.

"How?" I asked.

"By letting you see for yourself," said Pieter. "That should do it."

"I agree that it would," I said.

"Shall we go then?" asked Pieter.

"Now?" I looked out at the black night. "But I shouldn't be able to see anything at night."

"Ah. But at night, Hoek Land is at its best," said Pieter cryptically. "A peacefulness descends, the gentle slap of the water against the dock, the chug-chug of the Staten Island Ferry, the lights of the noble city that surplant the stars, the . . ."

"Stop! Enough!" I cried. "I hope the pictures you make with paint aren't as corny as the ones you make with words."

"Once you are there you will see that I do not exaggerate. Are you ready?" said Pieter.

I bit my lip, worrying it with my teeth. I looked across at Alix and Victor, immersed in the world of fashion gossip. We had planned to eat dinner here, but I felt no guilt at leaving them. I slid my eyes to look at Pieter. Since the conversation had turned to his island, he had become a different person—animated, attractive. If I refused to accompany him (even on what I was certain was a wild-goose chase), I might never see him again. And Pieter Van der Hoek was someone I definitely wanted to see again. He might not be the man I was going to marry, as I had stated so matter-of-factly earlier this evening, but I wasn't about to let a chance to know him better slip through my fingers.

"All right. All right," I said slowly. "Yes, I'll come see your island." Yes, I thought, I'll call your bluff, Pieter Van der Hoek. "Alix," I said, slipping my purse over my arm, "I hope you and Victor don't mind, but we've decided not to go on to dinner with you after all."

"That's quite all right, Gretel," answered Alix, her eyes appraising each of us in turn.

"But we haven't . . ." Victor began, but Alix put her hand on his arm. He stopped. I knew from experience just how persuasive those fingernails of hers could be.

"Now, Vicky, you know Gretel and Pieter don't want to listen to us gossip the night away," Alix said silkily. "It's always so boring if you don't know the people. Run along, Gretel, I'll see you tomorrow."

We escaped gracefully (although I knew Alix would tease me mercilessly the next morning). Pieter started up the steps to the lobby, but I caught his arm.

"No. If you've never been here before, we should go out this way," I said. "Then you can see the rest of the bar and the restaurant."

"You seem very familiar with the Windows on the World," Pieter said as we threaded our way through the bar. I led the way, keeping to the windows as much as possible.

"Since *Milady*'s offices are in this tower we come here a lot. At first, it was the novelty, but now it's become habit. As a matter of fact, one of our editors calls this place the 'Annex.' There she is now." I waved, but didn't stop. One co-worker's teasing would be enough.

We reached the end of the bar. I pushed through the swinging green doors into the hallway. "Do you want to see the restaurant?" I asked. So far Pieter hadn't seemed at all impressed with his tour, nor with the twinkling panorama of city lights.

"Of course," he replied, so once again I led the way.

The restaurant was directly across from the bar. One of the omnipresent white-coated young men (who served as ushers, waiters, and busboys) stood at the entrance ready to direct those who were lost. I saw his eyes widen as he looked at Pieter. I was puzzled for a moment, and then I realized that Pieter was dressed casually. He wore no tie. I wondered how he had gotten past the polite but firm young men who stood on guard in the lobby, scrutinizing those who stepped off the elevators for breaches in dress. But then, I reflected, few would have the nerve to stop Pieter Van der Hoek from going where he wanted.

We glanced quickly about the restaurant and then headed out. "What do you think?" I asked.

"Early 747," said Pieter.

"What?" I said.

"I am reminded of a very elaborate plane," said Pieter. "What the first-class area would look like if there were no limitations on weight and space."

"Oh, I see. I always think of a ship," I said. If Pieter was making a joke, I wanted to share in it. But he spoke as if he were deadly serious. "All that brass tubing, and the levels and the boys in their white steward's coats. A huge luxury liner, very impersonal," I added.

"Oh my God!" Pieter's muttered exclamation made me look up. We had climbed the stairs that ran around the outside of the bar and had entered the last hallway before the elevator lobby—a glittering passage that was virtually a hall of mirrors. Walls, ceiling, even the floor—though the burnt-orange carpeting that was in the other rooms continued in here also—reflected us endlessly. I would have lingered, for the room has always amused me, but Pieter took my arm and hurried me through. I started to laugh, and Pieter joined in, saying, "If I stay here one more minute, I swear I'll smash every bloody mirror in the place."

* * *

A few minutes later, my ears still buzzing from the ninety-second ride in the oversized elevator, we were at the bottom of the World Trade Center. We quickly clattered through the now-deserted plaza —almost a city in itself with its shops, restaurants, and banks—to the harsh outside where the brisk November wind whipped through man-created wind tunnels. Pieter gallantly took my arm to steady me against the gusts. "I prefer to walk, do you mind?" he asked. But it was only a formality. We were off before I could agree or protest.

The streets that comprise Lower Manhattan are a veritable rabbit's warren. I wasn't sure where we were walking. I have always prided myself on being a good walker, but Pieter's long legs moved more rapidly than mine—imprisoned on fashionably unpractical high heels—cared to. I thought we should go on forever, but after about fifteen minutes, I could see we could go no farther. We were at the edge of the Hudson River, at one of the piers that line the west side of Manhattan. Never breaking his pace, Pieter led me up some rickety wooden steps, along the pier's edge, and then down a wooden ladder, into a launch that bobbed merrily on the water.

It was a handsome boat—old and kept in beautiful condition. Its dark-wood interior gleamed magnificently in the dull moonlight. But I was scarcely aware of its details as I seated myself gingerly on one of the wooden seats—the one closest to me. I was beginning to think that Pieter was completely serious about living on an island in New York City's harbor. I was also very, very cold.

"Here, this should help," said Pieter as he clambered down after me, busying himself rummaging about the boat, wiping dew off the seats and windshield. He pulled a blanket from a storage bin and placed it over my shoulders. I accepted it gratefully.

"And, for heaven's sake, don't sit there," said Pieter. "You've picked the worst seat on the boat. You'll freeze. Here, move up front, where the roof and the windshield can protect you." I got up quickly, too quickly. I gasped as the boat rocked, and just as quickly, I sat down again.

"Oh, don't be a silly goose. It'd take a lot more than your weight to tip the *Stuyvesant* over." I must have looked puzzled, for he smiled and said, "This noble craft is the *Stuyvesant*." Taking me by the shoulders, he half-carried me to the front of the launch. "There. Haven't you been in a boat before?"

"Not too often," I admitted. "And certainly never dressed like this."

"That's all right," said Pieter, obviously relishing being in charge, "you don't have to do anything more than sit tight and enjoy the trip. All set? All right then, hang on!"

Pieter eased the *Stuyvesant* away from the pier, turning the wheel with casual skillfulness. It was very dark. The boat's headlights and the pier's lights did little to dispel the gloom. But then we pulled away from shore, sliding past the ink-black shapes of the other boats docked for the night, and there was all Manhattan to light our way. We glided along the tip of the island, the two towers of the Trade Center standing sentinel, past the wide expanse of Battery Park and out into the open harbor, picking up speed gradually. I had been in the harbor before, but only on the ferries that serviced Staten Island and carried tourists to the Statue of Liberty.

It seemed entirely different in a small launch. New York's harbor is best thought of as an enormous funnel. The mouth of the funnel stretches ten miles across, fed by the Hudson River on the west side and by Newark Bay on the east. The walls of the funnel are shaped by Brooklyn on the right and Staten Island on the left. The tip is marked by the Verrazano-Narrows Bridge, twelve miles as the crow flies from the World Trade Center towers. Through the Narrows is the Lower Bay, which becomes in turn the Atlantic Ocean. But this is to think of the harbor from high overhead. Down inside a speedboat, one feels small and insignificant.

I felt more insignificant a few moments later when Pieter swerved the launch to the right, toward Ellis Island, away from our original direction. Looking about, I found the reason. The Staten Island Ferry was bearing down upon us. Seen this close and from this perspective, it was as intimidating as it was stately, steaming southward toward Staten Island.

Pieter slowed the launch as he veered out of its route, then quickly sped up, cutting sharply to the left and across the wide wake left by the ferryboat. As we hit each deep furrow, we were tossed high in the air. I was certain we would be thrown out of the boat or that the *Stuyvesant* would shatter from the punishing impact of the waves. I gripped the sides of the boat and squeezed my eyes tightly shut, only once opening them to sneak a look at Pieter. He was certainly calm enough, his hands poised lightly on the small steering wheel, lips pursed slightly as though annoyed at having to yield the right of way, hooded eyes appraising the dark waters as they had earlier appraised the crowd in the Statue of Liberty Lounge. Once free of the ferry's wake, Pieter turned the launch into our original direction, increasing our speed even more. I relaxed my grip slightly (chagrined that I hadn't even bumped my head on the boat's roof), but I still maintained a firm hold. I didn't like at all the way the lights of the city were receding, nor the way the Statue of Liberty (no longer toylike, but reassuringly majestic) seemed to flash by.

We slowed once again, this time to pass a line of huge ships anchored off Governor's Island, headquarters of the Coast Guard. I guessed that the military took a dim view of speeding. Once again I felt tiny beside the great ships, but I was glad for their bright lights. Then they were behind us, and we were in the widest part of the harbor, heading straight at the Verrazano-Narrows Bridge, brightly outlined in green against the black sky. Good God! Was I being carried off into open sea?

I continued to watch the man who guided the launch so expertly through the dark waters. What did I know about him? Just a half-baked fairy tale about an island. No one could possibly live on an island in New York City's harbor. It was all too fabulous. I had only Victor Bacall's word for it that Pieter was an illustrator, a person of repute. That wasn't much word to go on. Pieter said he had been commissioned to do paintings from the Trade Center towers, and that he had spent the afternoon on the observatory deck. Yet he had no portfolio with him, nor anything remotely resembling a sketch pad. Not even a camera slung over his shoulder. How then could he have been working? Was he planning to do the paintings completely from memory? All right, Gretel, I thought. He's not an illustrator; he was in collusion with that fool Victor to meet you this evening. All for the nefarious purpose of getting you into a motorboat for a joy ride in the middle of the night, the coldest night so far this year. But why, I asked myself, why? The answer was, obviously, for no reason. Because everything Pieter says is true, and you're being silly about ulterior motives and mysterious islands and serendipitous adventures. All the same, I reminded myself, the man at the wheel of this boat is an inscrutable stranger. I would be a lot happier when Pieter turned the boat around and headed for the city. I had had enough of adventure for one night.

The boat slowed. Pieter touched my shoulder and pointed to our right. I turned in my seat, wriggling closer to the windshield to peer into the darkness. We were in the Narrows, the wide, riverlike passage that joins New York's upper and lower harbors. At first, all I could see was the massive shape I knew to be Staten Island. But as we neared, I thought I could make out the edges of a smaller island. Then, suddenly, we were there, and Pieter was maneuvering the wheel of the launch with the fingertips of his left hand, leaning back to grasp the edge of a small dock with his right as automatically as if he had been doing it all his life. Since I now had to believe all he had told me, he probably had.

"Welcome to Hoek Land," said Pieter, on the dock already. With one strong swift movement, he bent and, grasping my hands, lifted me bodily onto the slippery boards beside him. He was much stronger than I would have guessed from his rangy build.

"Pieter, I owe you an apology," I said.

"What for?" Pieter swiftly tied the boat, coiling the rope neatly before turning to smile politely.

"Because, until this moment, I didn't believe this island of yours existed," I answered. "In fact, I'm still not sure, I'm not absolutely convinced that this isn't an extension of Staten Island."

"Turn around and you'll have proof enough," said Pieter.

I did as he instructed. We walked along a path that passed the ramshackle boathouse by the water's edge. I saw that, indeed, we were a mile or more from Staten Island. "My goodness. Well, then I must apologize once again."

"Nothing to apologize for," said Pieter. "I sometimes find it hard to believe myself. It seems a fantasy."

"How nice that some fantasies come true," I said quietly.

We turned to climb some uneven brick steps. Except for a lone light at the end of the dock, the path so far was unlit. Only the moon's glow saved me from tripping all over myself, though Pieter's steadying arm saved me from more than one bruise.

"Not to worry," Pieter said cheerfully. "Just a few steps more and then it's level again. I suppose I should repair these steps, but I never seem to have the time."

We continued walking. The path was smoother now, and we seemed to be coming to a clearing of some sort. The pine trees that lined the path were more sparse. Suddenly, Pieter stopped. As my eyes were fixed firmly on the ground, I thudded into him. Pieter seemed not to notice.

"Up there," he said quietly but clearly, "is the house." I fancied I heard triumph mixed with pride in his voice.

"Oh," was all I could say.

We neared a building of some sort, dimly outlined against the sky. A faint light glowed at one end.

"That is Hoek House," Pieter announced. He showed no interest in going nearer.

"This is where you live?" I asked, trying to make out the details of the building.

"Oh yes. I was even born here," said Pieter. "As was just about every member of every generation of the Van der Hoek family. Since 1661."

"I thought you said your ancestor was given the island in the 1640s," I said, wondering if I had caught him out in a mistake. Though I was now seeing it with my own eyes, I was still skeptical.

"I did say that," said Pieter quickly. "I'm pleased that you paid attention. You see, the problems with the Indians made it impossible for anyone to live here safely for some time. That was the same year that a permanent settlement was finally established on Staten Island."

"You seem well versed in New York's early history," I said.

"Well, not really. Only where it coincides with the Van der Hoeks' early history," said Pieter. "At any rate, the man who won the island, Fredericks, did not survive to live here. It was his son, Adrian, who built the first house. But he only lived in it a few years."

"Why?" I asked.

"Because, three years later, on September 8, 1664, New Amsterdam was surrendered to the English and renamed New York," Pieter explained.

"Was Hoek House destroyed in the war?" I asked.

"Oh no. It was a peaceful surrender. Most of the Dutch were pleased with the change. But some of the land titles were in question, so Adrian moved his family back to the mainland," said Pieter.

"But he returned," I said.

"Nine years later. The Anglo-Dutch Wars thrust the city—again peacefully—under Dutch rule in August 1673. This time, they called the city New Orange. Anyway, Adrian again made Hoek Land his home, and rebuilt his house, which had been partially burned by the Indians." Pieter paused for breath. "Then, a year later, the city went back to the English and became New York again. But this time, Adrian refused to move, saying he had had enough of seesawing back and forth. He had built his house twice, that was enough for any man."

"What happened?" I asked.

"Nothing," replied Pieter. "What with all the changes in government, nobody knew what belonged to whom. I doubt that they ever figured it out. And by then, no one could remember a time when the Van der Hoeks didn't live on Hoek Land. No one's questioned it or bothered us since. But I do have the original document signed by Director-General William Kieft himself, locked away in a fireproof, burglarproof safe. Just in case," laughed Pieter.

"Well, it ended happily for Adrian," I said.

"Actually, no. Two years after moving back to the island, Adrian drowned in a boating accident," said Pieter.

"Oh," I said quietly. I felt sorry for the man who had built such a magnificent house, but never enjoyed it. I said as much to Pieter.

"Actually, the original structure was added to and changed so many times by succeeding generations that I'm sure old Adrian would have trouble recognizing his home. One thing has remained unchanged," said Pieter, pointing up, "that chimney."

I looked up to where Pieter indicated to see a large chimney rising over the pine trees. What a wonderful fire that would make, I thought, longing to be inside. But Pieter still seemed content to remain where he was. I sunk my chin deeper into the collar of my coat and tried not to shiver audibly.

"You live here by yourself?" I asked, shifting to lean against a tree. As I did so, I thought I saw a glimmer of light far to the left.

"Yes," Pieter answered. "I live here alone."

I turned my head toward the glimmer. Yes, it was definitely a green light. At first I had thought it was a boat, for the waving pine boughs made it flicker and dance, but as I continued to watch, I determined it was stationary, on this island. "What is that green light over there?" I asked.

"Oh," said Pieter, not turning to look. "We have a dock at the other end of the island. That's the light on the pier, similar to what we landed at."

"Why two docks?" I asked.

"Why not? No, seriously, it's for . . ." But what Pieter had been about to say was interrupted by the sound of a very powerful speedboat starting up from Hoek Land.

"What's that?" I jumped. "Do you have trespassers?"

"Always a possibility," Pieter said quickly, then he slowed his speech: "More likely it was my brother, Dirk. He lives in the boathouse by the other dock. It's a more elaborate structure than the one you saw."

"Your brother?" I said. "You said you lived here alone."

"I do. Let's go up here." Pieter took my arm brusquely, and led me toward the house. Was it my imagination? Or had Pieter's exuberance disappeared with the mention of his brother? He was once again the aloof Pieter Van der Hoek that I had first seen. But any puzzlement vanished as I anticipated entering Hoek House. Perhaps Pieter would build a roaring fire in the fireplace Adrian had built. Perhaps . . . but no, we were not going inside the house. Pieter led me to a terraced area, paved with smooth bricks arranged in concentric patterns. It was an extension of a large porch that opened off one side of the house, the end whose entire wall was given over to the massive chimney. Pieter jammed his hands in his pockets, sighing deeply and contentedly.

"This was one of my favorite places as a boy," he said. "I sat here for hours, no matter what the weather, watching the harbor, the lights of the city."

I went and stood beside him, looking away from the house, over the island. It was a spectacular view. A few feet from us, the island fell away sharply, forming a small cliff. There was a break in the pine trees, giving an unhindered view of the harbor, still now but for the slapping waves. In the distance, seemingly farther away than it really was, was the island of Manhattan. The twin towers of the World Trade Center stood self-importantly at the tip, dwarfing what came before and behind. Even though the hour was late (how late? I wondered), the city shone brightly, powerfully. I could readily understand how a small boy could stand here, fascinated for hours on end. With the slightest encouragement, I could stay there forever.

"How wonderful," I breathed. Oh, why oh why couldn't I say something less inane! "Now I know why you weren't so terribly impressed with the view from the top of the Trade Center. You've had this to look at all your life."

"Yes," said Pieter. "And now I hope you see what I meant about the proper perspective. Everything looks as it should. Even those ridiculous towers."

"Do you really hate them?" I asked, laughing.

"No. But they're silly. The view was nicer before, the city leading up to the Empire State Building gradually. Are you cold?" Pieter suddenly asked, as though he had just realized that it was not the middle of August.

"Well, I don't really like to complain," I said, hesitating slightly, but not too slightly. Perhaps now I would get to sit in front of the fire.

"Well, here. We should get back to the boat." Once again I was dragged off into the darkness. In no time, it seemed, I was once more aboard the *Stuyvesant,* wrapped in a coarse blanket, snuggled up close to the heater, which, despite its age and small size, gave out a great deal of warmth. I sighed happily. I was disappointed that we hadn't gone inside the house, but at least I was warm. I was rocked by the gentle slap-slap of the waves. I was also very, very hungry.

"Thought you might like this," said Pieter suddenly. As if by magic, he produced a bottle, two paper cups and a brown paper bag that contained a roast-beef sandwich. I didn't know how old or stale it was. I didn't care. It was without a doubt the best half of a sandwich I have ever eaten. Pieter then handed me one of the cups, filling it to the brim with whatever was in the bottle.

"Brandy," Pieter said. "The best thing in the world to wash down a sandwich. I'm sorry I didn't think of this before."

"So am I," I agreed. I took a gulp of the brandy, choking slightly. Now, I felt wonderful.

"It's just that if I'm not hungry, I assume that no one else is either," said Pieter. "Bad habit I have. From living alone."

"You couldn't have always lived on the island alone," I said.

"Oh no," Pieter answered. "For the past three years. Since my father died."

"I'm sorry," I said.

"Thank you, but he was sixty-one and had a heart condition, and if it hadn't been for . . . well, he just had one shock too many." Pieter paused to refill our glasses.

"He was a painter, too, wasn't he?" I asked.

"Yes. He used to like to say we were the New York Wyeths," said Pieter. "My grandfather was also an artist. Unfortunately, the Van der Hoeks haven't achieved the fame of that other painting dynasty. But we've survived."

"Is your brother also an artist?" I asked.

"Oh no. Dirk spends his time on more important things," Pieter replied, his mouth turning up slightly. I guessed that I had stumbled upon a family feud. I tried to think of another topic of conversation, but couldn't.

"Tell me about yourself," Pieter said abruptly. "You've told me nothing."

"There's not all that much to tell," I began, but Pieter snorted disbelievingly.

"Surely there must have been something interesting that occurred in the what—twenty-five, twenty-six . . ."

"Twenty-eight next February," I interjected.

". . . years that Gretel Drew has been alive," Pieter finished. "Gretel. A most unlikely name. You should have fat rosy cheeks and golden braids wrapped over your ears. Instead . . ."

"Instead, I'm deathly pale and this"—I lifted one unruly brown lock—"this needs a good brushing. But, my mother always liked the name, and so, I got stuck with it."

I told Pieter as quickly as I could about myself, warming to his apparently sincere interest. I honestly hadn't thought there was all that much to tell, but it seemed as though I talked forever that night. Of my childhood—growing up in the suburbs of New York, my parents, my fraternal twin brothers Philip and Carson (now the troublesome age of sixteen). Of my four years at Manhattanville College and my subsequent seven years working in New York City.

"And here I am, the perfect career girl," I finished, somewhat embarrassed.

"Why don't you like talking about yourself?" Pieter's question caught me off guard.

"Why, I do. I don't. I mean, oh, I don't know. It's as I said, there's nothing very exciting," I answered. "Certainly not a centuries-old family and a romantic house on an improbable island."

"Yet, I envy yours," said Pieter.

"How can you?" I asked.

"Because, you, uh, you had a real family."

"My brothers might say otherwise," I replied, laughing. "But surely, your parents . . ."

"Were divorced when I was six and Dirk barely a year old," said Pieter.

"Oh," I said. "But you stayed with your father."

"No. Actually not," Pieter replied. "Father sent us to live with his sister in the city. We did come out here on weekends and vacations. He thought it best we grow up in a 'normal' environment."

"What happened to your mother?" I asked.

"She left us," Pieter said with a finality that closed that subject forever.

"Oh." What could I say? "But then you did come back here to live permanently."

"Actually, only five years ago. I was at Yale, stayed on to get my master's—God knows why—then I did come back to the city, but in my own apartment in the Village. One of those romantic, sky-lit, roach-infested, six-flight walk-up studios I couldn't really afford. Yet I wanted to be on my own. It wasn't until my father had his first heart attack that I came to the island to live. I felt he should have someone here with him. By then, I'd begun to establish myself as an illustrator. We had a good two years working together. Pity one waits until it's almost too late to fully appreciate one's parents." Pieter fell into a reverie. I didn't wish to disturb him from it. It lasted only a few moments. "Well," he said, shaking his head slightly. "I didn't mean to get into that." He ran his fingers through his tousled brown hair, before pouring us yet another cup of brandy. "But again, that comes from being alone. Though I do have a ghost for company."

"A ghost!" I said, instantly alert.

"Well, it's more a family tradition than a ghost," laughed Pieter. "One of my less-than-illustrious ancestors, by chance also named Pieter. Though I am not his namesake, I assure you. He met a foul end in the basement of Hoek House."

"Murdered?" I asked.

"Suspected, but never proved," said Pieter. "His wife had a lover, whom she preferred to her husband. One night, on a trip to the cellar, Pieter fell and broke his neck. The bereft widow mourned a month and then left Hoek Land forever."

"And did she marry her lover?" I asked.

"Alas, no," said Pieter. "It seemed she liked being a merry widow, and saw no need to rush into another alliance. He had served his purpose, so off he went."

"Served his purpose?" I asked.

"The steps to the cellar are brick," explained Pieter. "After the accident, it was discovered that the supporting bricks had been removed, or, at any rate were missing. From a stairway that had been repaired six months before."

"Oh. When did all this happen?" I asked.

"In 1811, or thereabouts. I assure you that the stairs have been repaired since then." Pieter stood up and stretched, rocking the boat gently. I thought of doing likewise, but I was too comfortable to stir.

"Well, Gretel, you're in for a treat," Pieter announced. "The sun rising over New York City."

"What!" I sat bolt upright and looked around. Without my realizing it, the night had gone. It was morning. A beautiful clear morning. Somehow, we had talked to sunrise. Even more incredible, I—who always collapsed by midnight—was not in the least tired. Perhaps it was the constant sipping of brandy, the novelty of my surroundings, the excitement of a late-night adventure. More likely, I thought, it was the company of this young man whom I had known only twelve hours, who seemed to have told me all about himself yet had actually revealed nothing, who seemed interested in me yet had not even tried to hold my hand. It had been the most curious evening of my life, and, although I knew I would pay for it later in the day when the lack of sleep caught up with me, I didn't regret a single moment.

Unfortunately, it had to end. "Pieter, it is lovely, but I have to leave. I have to go to work today, and . . . oh, what a pity," I added quietly.

"We've plenty of time," Pieter said, slipping into the driver's seat to turn on the ignition. "Where do you live?"

"The West Village," I replied. "Greenwich Street."

"Good. I can ferry you to the Christopher Street pier and get you a taxi. Nothing could be easier," Pieter finished in a take-charge tone of voice. While the motor idled, Pieter untied the launch. Then he climbed back into the boat and deftly eased it away from the dock. As he did so, I looked up at Hoek Land, seeing it clearly for the first time: the dwarfed but handsome pine trees, boughs waving in the brisk breeze that hummed about us; the sparkling blue-gray of the water and cloudless sky; and Hoek House. I could see diamond-paned casement windows glittering gold in the sun's light. The pattern of the bricks stood out clearly, the jigsaw work that framed the dormer windows gleamed white and brave. I think that if it were possible to fall in love with a house at first sight—especially a house that one has never been inside—I fell in love with Hoek House that instant.

The harbor was alive with early morning traffic. The first commuters crowded the Staten Island Ferry. Cars filled the bridges leading into Manhattan. A new day was beginning, but I wanted no part of it. I wanted to sit in this boat and ride forever, feeling the rhythm of the waves, the occasional spray of water against my cheek. It was a wonderful free feeling that had invaded me. I had never felt so alive, I . . .

"Here we are, Gretel," said Pieter.

The *Stuyvesant* slowed. We pulled up to the pier. It was over, my adventure of the night. It was time to re-enter the real world.

2

Terror!

"Oh, wow! Did you pick a morning to goof off!" The lisping voice of my secretary, Maggie, followed me into my office. Barely five feet two, she should have had a hard time keeping pace with me, but in the six months she had worked for me, Maggie had never once shuffled. I sank into the stuffed brown armchair she had pulled out from beneath my long glass-topped desk, grabbed up the steaming cup of black coffee she had waiting for me, and prepared myself to listen to my messages. From the number of pieces of pink paper Maggie waved, it had already been a whopper of a morning.

"First of all, *they*"—with a jerk of her head to the left, Maggie indicated the senior editors—"have been pacing like tigers, because the ten o'clock meeting has been held up. I said you had called in with an emergency dental appointment. Try and talk like you had a Novocaine shot. Then the printer called. One of the presses broke down overnight. They're not going to be able to finish the run until tonight at the *earliest*, which means the February issue might be delayed two days in getting trucked to the West Coast. I switched that call over to Arthur in production, but thought you should know. The type house called. They don't have the typeface you specified for that wine article, and Susie said there might be changes anyway. Roger"—Maggie jerked her head to the right, indicating my assistant—"Roger has asked me to make an appointment with you for him. Said he'd only need about fifteen minutes. Sometime this afternoon? I think he's going to ask for a raise. He has his suede vest on. And, Melissa Cossinni called. Said to tell you it's of 'earth-shaking importance' that she talk to you, and that she was worried 'half out of her mind' because she tried to call you all night and you weren't home. And"—Maggie raised her head to look at me—"I guess you weren't. I hope it was worth it." Maggie shook her head maternally.

"That bad?" I gulped at the bitter black coffee, trying to open my eyes wider.

"Well, let's just say you won't have any trouble selling that toothache story," said Maggie.

"Oh well. Okay, Mags, in order of importance. If Melissa calls again, while I'm in the 'Roundup,' tell her I'm available for lunch. I have to talk to her, too. Have, uh, Laurie call the type house. They're crazy. Tell them to check their catalogue, before they say they don't have something. You're absolutely right, let production worry about the printer, though if Arthur calls and wants my opinion, the printer shouldn't be allowed to get away with anything that delays our schedule. Madame would be furious—she prides herself on the timeliness of her editorials. And, oh yes, Roger. Tell him I can see him"—I made a show of glancing over my calendar—"at ten to five. That should teach him. And"—I gulped the last of my coffee down—"if anyone should ask, I'm on my way to the Friday meeting."

Patting Maggie's shoulder gratefully, I slipped out of my office and went quickly down the dark-brown carpeted hallway that separated my art department from the editorial offices. I paused outside the editor in chief's office until her secretary, Ollie, with an arched-eyebrowed nod, gave me the go-ahead. I felt immediately annoyed. What business was it of hers what time I chose to enter or leave Milady's offices. Fortunately, the door was open. I eased inside inobtrusively.

". . . And, as I'm sure you all know by now"—I winced at Madame's pompous intonation—"with the January issue, Milady is increasing her circulation to one and a half million. Not bad for two and a half years." There was some slight applause. "And so, in light of this fact, I think that we should become a bit more serious in our approach. All right. So we're not the new kid on the block anymore. We've had our fun. We've been brash and outrageous, but now we're going to take ourselves seriously so that others will take us seriously. We've proved that there's a need for our sort, let's capitalize on it. I'm sick and tired of . . . oh, good morning, Gretel. You're just in time for my weekly tirade. Sorry about your tooth. I understand it happened suddenly."

"Very suddenly," I said.

Alix, as usual, sat in the corner. Her almond eyes glinted at me mischievously. I grimaced back.

"Yes, Alix said she saw you last night, and you were fine."

"I was fine then," I said.

"All right then. Now, as I was saying . . ." continued Mavis Hollosoll, the editor in chief of *Milady* magazine. I knew she really didn't doubt the truth of my fabricated story. She just pretended to suspect me (as she had others before) out of principle. It was one of her methods of controlling her large, vain, energetic staff. I just wished that this morning I could feel as self-righteous as I had other times. Yet I acted as if I did. Pretense, I thought, all pretense. Pity one has to work this way, but with Mavis, there was no other way to work. A thin, slightly faded, dark-eyed blond beauty in her late thirties, Mavis ran her staff the way a high-strung teacher runs her schoolroom—sometimes imperially, sometimes tyrannically, sometimes (but not often) familiarly. The office nickname of "Madame" suited her perfectly. There were moments when I wished that I had Alix's knack of cajoling Mavis into her way of thinking. But Mavis and I were too wary of each other for so subtle a relationship.

Having settled into my accustomed seat (all the staff had their unofficial places) by the window, I relaxed. I had trouble following Mavis's speech. I knew I didn't have to concentrate—it was the usual Friday pep talk, what she had come to term her "Weekly Roundup" lecture—and so I cuddled against the dark-pink cushions that were scattered over the wide window seat that ran along two walls of Mavis's office. (Naturally, as the most important of us all, she had a corner office.) My gaze was automatically drawn to the Hudson River, some fifty stories below. Had it really been last night that Pieter and I had motored up those waters? My tired body told me it was, as had Alix's knowing glance. But it seemed so long ago, as though in another time and place. I smiled to myself. I had thought those same words the night before. If Pieter called me tonight, as he had promised before saying good-bye, then I would know it was not a dream. That what had happened could continue in the real world—another thought from the night before.

The real world. This morning, the Hudson was so peaceful, so little trafficked. There was just one lone barge chug-chugging its way south to the harbor after a night spent at Pier—what? Obviously nearby, since it wasn't moving very fast. But then, they seldom did. And this one seemed especially weighted down. Pity, as Pieter had noted, that I didn't know very much about boats, or I might actually be able to identify what it was. Well, I scolded myself, enough of this. I really have to listen to *some* of what Mavis is saying. There might be a quiz afterward. But just one last look. I wonder what it's like on Hoek Land this morning. Does the water sparkle as it does here? Is the water as smooth? The harbor as lazy? The . . .

BOOM!

"Oh my God! I don't believe it!" I shrieked, as the long windows shuddered.

"What? What is it! Gretel, what's the matter?" The others crowded about me, startled and confused by the ear-splitting and terrifying noise.

What had been a quiet wide ribbon of gray-blue was now a veritable inferno. A brilliant, mushroom-shaped fireball shot three hundred feet straight up. Then, mountainous clouds of black smoke edged with orange fire billowed up toward us, obscuring our view and shadowing the river. Once I had recovered from my initial surprise, I saw that it was the barge I had studied earlier that had exploded. It was burning—what little of it I could see—at a fierce rate. Surely, it must sink, I thought, but it continued to move slowly down toward the harbor with its newly acquired cargo of flame and smoke.

"Must be an oil tanker, nothing else would burn that much and not sink immediately," said Verna, our fiction editor, who was obviously relishing the spectacle below.

"It'll never be noticed with all the pollution," replied Barbara Guarrera, the managing editor.

"Is it one of ours? Or one of the Arabs'?" asked Ollie, who had rushed into the room at the sound of the explosion.

"How could such a thing start? Those tankers aren't very safe if they can suddenly burst into flames like that," Alix's concerned voice chimed in.

I was barely aware of the commotion, for I had begun to worry that Pieter might be on the river. Everyone on the floor seemed to have crowded into Mavis's office for a better look. Even Mavis had been torn away from her speech and was gazing as open-mouthed as the rest of us. It was a spectacular sight.

After just a few moments, the first fireboats motored toward the scene; some were prepared to pump huge streams of water, others to spread layers of chemical foam. Then, helicopters began to buzz the barge, darting in and out of the thick smoke like vultures circling a doomed, crippled animal. At first, there were only police helicopters, then, inevitably, they were joined by the helicopters of the television stations—identifiable by the logos painted boldly on their sides: CBS, ABC and the abstracted N of NBC. They were soon joined by the local networks—WNEW, WPIX, WOR—who were anxious not to lose out to their bigger, more powerful rivals.

The arrival of the newsmongers set up a cry for a radio. Ollie reluctantly left her perch on the window seat, returning almost immediately with my assistant Roger's radio in her arms. The entire art department trailed behind her. Mavis's office was now chock-full, and everyone strained closer to the windows. I would have gladly relinquished my spot, but it was physically impossible. I tried to curl up even smaller.

There was much fuss as Ollie tried to find a free outlet to plug the radio into. Roger hovered about her, torn between keeping an eye on the spectacle of the burning barge outside and the spectacle of Ollie commandeering his possession inside. Finally, the radio was plugged in, turned on, and its static and insistent hum added to the confusion. Roger regained control of his radio, and twisted and fiddled with the dials, trying to find a station with information. It was useless. All the newsmen could tell us so far, with all their on-the-spot reporters, was that there was indeed an explosion on the Hudson River. An explosion that could prove very dangerous if it were not brought under control soon. Pooh, I thought to myself, pressing my forehead against the cool glass. I could have told them that.

The piers below us, meanwhile, filled with the helpful and the curious. Other launches were now on the river, keeping a respectable distance from the flaming wreck. Occasionally one would dart in, then just as quickly dart out again. I hoped that the reason was to rescue a floundering survivor, not to gain a front-page photo.

The tanker seemed to be sinking now, but the oil it left behind continued to burn, spreading out to create a pool of fire. We continued to watch, paralyzed by horrid fascination as more and more thronged to the scene. I was sure all traffic in Lower Manhattan had come to a complete standstill (as had all work in the offices of *Milady*), and I smiled at the thought of a city of rubbernecks—a smile that froze abruptly as I thought: My God! What if this burning keeps on? What if it spreads throughout the harbor—causing other boats to fire up, buildings, piers? Hoek Land! Pieter's house could be in danger! Suddenly, this fire became a very real menace, not an isolated blaze.

Time passed. Fascinating as it was, I was too tired to continue watching the catastrophe unfold. (And, as the amounts of black smoke increased by the minute, there was less and less to see. The white waterfalls pumped by the fireboats had had little effect on the blaze.) Since it was clear that Mavis's meeting was not going to continue, I returned to my own office.

I sank gratefully back into my chair and absent-mindedly swiveled gently around. But the sight that greeted me—the gray haze of smoke hanging over the Hudson and now the entire harbor like a dark canopy, beginning to drift between the twin towers of the Trade Center—caused me to return to my desk and the paper work that awaited me there. I sighed and took the first bill up, only to be interrupted by the intercom. Saved by the bell, I thought, pressing down the lever.

"Yes?" I said, taking the call. Maggie had remained in Mavis's office along with everyone else.

"Melissa Cossinni is calling for Gretel Drew," said the switchboard operator. There was a touch of exasperation in her voice. I gathered that she was annoyed to be missing out on the excitement. And to take messages for everyone into the bargain!

"Okay. Put her through on ninety-one. Thanks." I picked up the phone on the first ring.

"Gretel! Did you see that? Wasn't it frightening? My God! I thought that we were going to go up with it!" The law offices Melissa worked in were on the eleventh floor. She would have had an excellent vantage point to watch the explosion.

"I certainly did. I was in Mavis's office," I said.

"Do you know what it was? I was in the firm's library when it happened. Naturally, I had to be in the one place where there aren't any windows. By the time I got back to my office it was all smoke. You creative types always have radios, did you hear anything?"

"Nothing much. It was a barge that exploded, a tanker carrying oil," I replied.

"An oil tanker," Melissa exclaimed. "Good God! One of the supertankers?"

"No. Besides, I don't think one of those things could fit on the Hudson," I said.

"Oh. But imagine if it had been. The whole city would have exploded!" Melissa seemed more pleased than frightened by the prospect. "Did they say anything about the cause?"

"No. It was too early. It'll be on the news tonight and in all the papers tomorrow and the day after that, till we're bored to death."

"Well, I shan't be bored," Melissa announced. "Being down here, I got the you-are-there treatment! Anyway, since it's sure to be a mess around here for some time—you know the way disasters always attract large crowds, I was thinking of having a sandwich sent up to my office. Care to join me?"

"Of course. I've got lots to tell you," I said.

"I hope that includes where you were last night."

"Maybe, maybe not, Miss Nosy. Wait and see. What time's good for you?"

"One?"

"One it is. See you then." I replaced the receiver and with a last glance at the hectic scene far below, I returned to the papers on my desk.

Melissa Cossinni and I had been best friends since the second grade, when, on the first day of school we both wore the same dress. I can still remember it: a floral print on a chocolate background, cap sleeves, white Peter Pan collar, a straight bodice with a dropped waistline that opened into a flared skirt. (Melissa swears the dress was red.) Had we been ten or twenty years older, the situation would have been disastrous. But we hadn't learned enough about fashion and femininity and we thought it was fun. From then on, we would wear "our" dress on prearranged days.

Having survived that first great test, our friendship went on to survive many more: braces (I had them, Melissa didn't); a crush on the same soccer player in high school (Melissa dated him, I didn't); our choosing different colleges, different careers; sharing an apartment our first years in New York; Melissa's marriage, and, most recently, her divorce. I had been delighted when her law firm rented space in the same tower of the World Trade Center as *Milady* magazine. I had always felt better when Melissa was nearby for confidences.

Melissa's secretary, Debbie, was on the phone when I arrived at her office, but she waved me through with a friendly smile. As a result, I caught Melissa in the midst of doing sit-ups. Her back was to the door and I stood watching her for a moment, before clearing my throat self-importantly. She whirled around, mouth open and eyes wide, her already red-from-exertion face turning even redder from embarrassment.

"Oh! It's you! What on earth do you mean scaring me like that. Debbie's supposed to buzz me before letting anyone in. I'll have her hide!" Melissa jumped to her feet, smoothed out her skirt with her right hand while running the fingers of her left through the tousled curls of her short brown hair.

"Debbie was on the phone," I said. "Besides, she knew I didn't matter. Since when did you start exercising in the middle of the day?"

"Since I stepped on the scales this morning. Lunch is over here." Melissa opened up a large paper bag on her desk. "I forgot to ask what you wanted, so I ordered tuna fish for us both."

"Fabulous." I took the sandwich from her, setting it on a paper towel Melissa had supplied as a plate. We munched for a while in companionable silence. Melissa's office was not large (as befitted a very junior member of a prestigious law firm), but it was cozy. Books lined one wall. A few prints and Melissa's law school degree decorated the others. Her windows took up almost another whole wall, opening, I knew, onto the Hudson River. But today the plum-colored drapes were drawn—I guessed against the explosion and its aftermath—making the room seem smaller than it actually was.

"All right, Gretel, fess up." Melissa wiped an imaginary crumb from the corner of her mouth and curled up catlike in her chair. "Where were you all night that you didn't answer your phone at midnight? And still didn't answer it at six-thirty this morning?"

"What were you doing calling me at six-thirty in the morning?" I countered. "You know I don't get up until eight."

"Oh, never mind. You weren't home to answer it anyway. Your office dinner couldn't have gone on *that* long." Melissa folded her arms with an air of expectancy.

"What am I—on trial?" I asked, not actually upset.

"No," Melissa replied. "It's just that as your best friend I expect you to keep me up to date on events in your life. Begin."

"All right, all right," I said, laughing and throwing up my hands. "As it turns out, I've been dying to tell you all about it." I proceeded to tell Melissa the events of the previous evening. ". . . So, this morning, instead of sleeping peacefully in my bed, I was ferried up the Hudson River in grand style. We docked at the Christopher Street Pier. Pieter put me in a cab. I went home, changed and barely made it into the office. I'm totally exhausted, and I think I'm coming down with a cold, but it was worth it. Oh, Melissa, it was so wonderful. A real adventure."

"And you're in love," said Melissa.

"Well, I don't think I'd say that," I protested.

"You are," Melissa said firmly. "I've seen you like this before. You had that same starry look in your eyes when you told me about that photographer. Whatever happened to him anyway?"

"He moved to Chicago," I muttered.

"Oh. But not so long ago it was the passion of the century," Melissa reminded me. "And now it's some illustrator. Heavens, Gretel, can't you find someone with a *real* job? Just a joke, a joke. I found someone with a job and look what good it did. Divorced at twenty-seven. But really, Gretel, don't you find it a little strange?"

"What do you mean, 'strange'? Unusual perhaps," I said defensively.

"Highly unusual." Melissa unfolded herself from her chair and began pacing back and forth in her best lawyer style, her fingers counting out her words. "Now. Let's go over this whole thing, point by point. Yet meet this Pieter, Pieter Van der Hoek, at a restaurant. He invites himself into having dinner with three strangers. . . ."

"He knows Victor," I corrected. "Victor brought him over to the table."

"Not much of a recommendation from what you've told me of Victor," said Melissa, her eyebrows arching sharply. "Don't interrupt. Then, he tells you he owns this island in New York's harbor. An island that you've never even heard of, much less seen. So, trusting little you, you leave the restaurant with this Pieter Van der Hoek and walk, in the coldest night so far this season, to a pier, get into a boat and motor out into the darkness. After a suitable length of time, you arrive at another pier, that he claims is on *his* island. You then walk around for a while, he points out a building that he claims is *his* house. What did he call it?"

"Hoek House," I answered. I could see where Melissa was heading, but I was powerless to stop her.

"Oh yes. On Hoek Land," said Melissa, lending added emphasis to each word. "Oh, Gretel. What a lot of fairy tales. A family ghost, famous Dutch ancestors, a weird brother that you didn't meet. Oh, boy, did he hand you a line."

"Now see here, Melissa," I protested. "I felt that way, too, at first. I didn't believe it either, not until we got to Hoek Land. And even then, as you say, I just had Pieter's word for it. But it was the way he told me, not what he told me. If you could meet him, hear the pride that creeps into his voice, see his eyes glow when he talks about the house and the island. Nobody's that good an actor!"

"Maybe. Maybe not. You've been fooled before." Melissa sounded unconvinced. "But why didn't you go into the house?"

"Because . . . Pieter said it wasn't fixed up and, well, and, so, I didn't ask," I finished lamely, hoping she'd believe me. She didn't.

"Feeble excuse that. You didn't go into the house because Pieter doesn't have the key to it. Because it wasn't his house!" Melissa concluded triumphantly, pounding one fist into the other.

"We, the jury, find the defendant not guilty," I retorted. "But seriously, Melissa, why would he have a motorboat if he didn't live on the island?"

"I don't know," she said. "Maybe he lives on Staten Island, and prefers using his boat to the ferry."

"Why are you so sure Pieter lied?" I asked.

"Because it's"—Melissa paused to seek inspiration from the ceiling —"it's all too fantastic! And I'm sure it's impossible. But mainly, because I'm worried about you."

"Worried about me?" I asked, barely suppressing a smile. What was this?

"Yes, I am," Melissa replied, as serious as I had ever seen her. "One night with this guy and you accept everything he tells you. I've seen this happen to you before. And I've seen you hurt by it. You're too reticent. There's nothing wrong in asking questions. No one's going to be insulted. That was your whole problem with Geoff," Melissa continued, mentioning a man I had almost married four years before. "You never questioned him, you left him alone, let him go where he wanted, never got jealous and look what happened: he's now married to someone else!"

"Good riddance!" I snorted. "Melissa, I may be wrong, but I want the man I love to accept me the way I am, so I have to accept him the way he is. We're each individuals. I don't have to know or share every aspect of his life as long as the life we do share is special and wonderful. And, since I've known Pieter for less than twenty-four hours, it's ridiculous to be talking like this."

"I don't think so," Melissa answered. "I just want you to be cautious, that's all. I know that I'm the last person who should be giving romantic advice, but the one thing I've learned is to be careful. You can be sure that if I ever get involved with anyone again, it's going to be someone I've checked out thoroughly."

"We might not have anything to worry about if Pieter doesn't call me."

I got up and went over to the window, parting the drapes to look down at the river. The fire raged on and there was still much activity on both sides of the river. It seemed to me that there was an unusually high number of police vehicles, as opposed to the fire department vehicles, present. But then, perhaps that was commonplace at catastrophes of this magnitude.

"Not to worry. He'll call," Melissa said.

"What makes you so sure?" I asked, turning around and letting the curtain fall back into place.

"Because, if *you* came away from last night's encounter all ga-ga, Pieter couldn't have been unaffected," Melissa said patiently. "Even if, as you claim, he didn't make a pass at you. No, he'll call. All I hope is that he makes a clean breast of it all and confesses that he made up the whole idea of living on an island."

"I still believe that he does live there," I said stubbornly, but not from any real conviction.

"Oh! Why didn't I think of this before!" Melissa clapped her hands and began to rummage through her bookcases. "Oh," she said disappointedly. "It isn't here."

"What isn't?" I asked, puzzled.

"The phone book. He should be listed in the phone book." Melissa grabbed her phone off the hook, pressing the intercom button decisively. I cringed for her secretary's sake. "Debbie? Bring in a Manhattan and Staten Island phone book. Thanks."

Melissa and I took turns going through both the books, but neither of us turned up a listing under "Van der Hoek, Pieter," or "Hoek, van der, Pieter" or any other combination we could think of.

"No matter how he spells it, he's not listed," Melissa said finally.

"Well, at least we've found nothing to disprove what he told me," I answered, determined to be cheerful.

"True, but we've found nothing to prove it, either," Melissa said.

"Isn't it strange that an artist doesn't have a phone listing? How can he get called for work?"

"Hmmmm? Oh, he probably has an agent or a manager who handles the business details for him. It's quite common," I said to reassure myself as well as Melissa.

"Oh. So the artist can keep his hands pure for creating," Melissa said.

"What?" I wasn't in the mood for sarcasm.

"You know, Gretel," Melissa persisted, "untainted by the details of mere mortal existence."

"Oh." I preferred to ignore her. The fact that Pieter wasn't listed in the phone books did distress me. Not for Melissa's reason—that neither Pieter nor his island existed—but because there was no way I could reach him. I would definitely have to wait for him to call me. And wait, and wait, and wait, I added glumly to myself. I thought Melissa's certainty that Pieter would call me tonight the most farfetched thing she'd said that day. But, oh, my God. What if he didn't call?

"Hey, Gretel." Melissa touched my shoulder, causing me to start. "Are you really upset? You should know after all these years not to pay attention to anything I say. I tease like mad. In fact, you know, I'm very jealous of your mysterious island. It's, he's, what every girl dreams of. You've found him."

"Don't be so sure," I said slowly. I found this speech the most farfetched of all. "It was only for one night."

"That's all Romeo and Juliet had."

"Yeah," I said, remembering their fate.

"Well," Melissa frowned, momentarily disconcerted. "All the great love affairs had to start someplace."

"And end someplace," I bitterly replied. "Melissa, I appreciate your trying to cheer me up, but it's really not very tragic. If nothing else, I had a great time last night. Perhaps such things are better left alone. It was a peculiar evening. To try and repeat it could be a mistake."

"Gretel?" said Melissa, her eyes blinking in puzzlement.

"Sorry. I guess it does sound silly." I pushed back the sleeve of my sweater to look at my watch. "I've got to get back. Duty calls."

Melissa and I quickly cleaned up the remains of our lunch. I went to the window, pulling aside the rough-textured drapes.

The pandemonium had quieted somewhat. Lunchtime was over,

and many of the spectators had undoubtedly returned to less spectacular sites. The charred superstructure of the barge still smoldered in the middle of the Hudson, the charcoal-gray smoke now drifting lazily in the still air. Other boats circled the wreck, not daring to close into the heat of the fire storm, even though the fireboats were continuing to hose it thoroughly. Dark-coated officials lined the shore on both sides, poking and prodding through the debris at the water's edge. I guessed they were looking for some clue that would determine the cause of the explosion. As Melissa and I watched, one of the men on the New Jersey side bent suddenly, then waved to those behind him. He was joined by someone with a large plastic bag, and together they gingerly lifted something—it was impossible to tell what—into the bag.

"I wonder if they'll be able to salvage anything worthwhile," I mused.

"I shouldn't think so," Melissa replied, laughing. "Anything pulled from *that* river is bound to be grease-coated and corroded beyond all recognition. Ugh-disgusting!"

"And it will probably all end up on the bottom of the river anyway," I said, pointing to the barge, which had lurched lower into the water.

"I just hope no one was hurt," murmured Melissa.

"Well"—I yawned, turning away from the window to stretch widely—"speculate all you want, I've got to get back upstairs."

"Want to take in a movie tonight?" Melissa asked.

"Oh, no thanks, Mel. I'm exhausted. All I want to do is sleep," I said.

"All right. I'll call you over the weekend."

* * *

After the excitement of the morning, the afternoon was anticlimactic. No work was done. All anyone could talk about was the explosion—especially in the art department, where there was a radio. Any other time I would have at least made a fuss—for I really shouldn't have tolerated the four people that comprised my department (even diligent Maggie) buzzing about the windows when all the layouts for the next issue were due the following Monday—but in my present mood I was grateful for the diversion. My lack of sleep had caught up with me. More than once I dozed off in my chair.

Fortunately, I jerked myself awake before anyone came in to catch me. But even when I was awake, I felt in a stupor.

Maggie came in hourly to repeat the radio bulletins. From what did filter through my fog, I gathered that nobody knew very much of anything, only that arson was suspected. *That* was from a source who refused to be identified. But as soon as details were known, they would be announced to the public. I yawned sleepily and waved Maggie out of the office.

Other people entered and left my little office that afternoon, but I paid them scant attention. As a result, as I left, I had the terrible feeling that I had promised Roger a twenty dollar a week raise, agreed to attend a fashion breakfast on Monday morning with Alix, and promised Mavis that the art department would work the Friday after Thanksgiving if that were necessary to finish up the March issue. Perhaps I had actually refused to do all those things. There was only one person who could have broken through my haze that long Friday afternoon. Pieter Van der Hoek hadn't called.

As I waited in the hallway for the elevator, Maggie came rushing out of the art department.

"Gretel! I'm glad I caught you. Someone brought these for you!" she called out. In her arms was a large straw basket filled with miniature red roses and baby's breath. A large red bow decorated the handle.

"What on earth?" I said. Pieter, I thought. I poked through the bouquet, but there was no card. "Who brought them?" I asked.

"They were left at the front desk," answered Maggie, shrugging. "They're gorgeous."

"Yes, but near impossible to carry," I laughed, shifting my briefcase to my left hand and seizing the basket in my right. It wasn't heavy, but it was awkward. Just then, the elevator came. "Good night, Maggie, have a good weekend."

"You, too, boss," she called after me.

Burdened as I was, I wasn't up to coping with the subway, so I used the western exit and headed for the taxi stand. But the lines were impossible and I decided to try my luck on the street. But not too surprisingly, every cab that passed was either already taken or off-duty. Getting a taxi during the Friday-afternoon rush hour was never easy. The confusion and crowds from the morning's explosion now made it impossible. I walked along Liberty Street to an intersection where I might have better luck. The latest edition of the

New York *Post* had arrived at the corner newsstand bearing the headline "TERROR STRIKES CITY!" I bought a copy to read later, tucking it under my arm while I continued to search desperately for a cab. It was futile. Exhaustion slowed me down, and two prospects were stolen from me by importunate dark-suited executives. I cursed them both, ready to cry from frustration. The one time I really needed a taxi, I couldn't get one! I stamped my foot, turning it and stubbing my toe awkwardly on the curb. Damn! Dropping my paper and briefcase, I hopped around clumsily, clutching my foot with my free hand. Just then, it started to rain gently—a thick mist, actually, and I really did start to cry. I would never get a cab now. My flowers would be ruined. The satin bow was already bedraggled. I picked up my briefcase and now-dirty paper and dejectedly turned in the direction of the subway. Maybe, now that it was later in the rush hour, it wouldn't be suffocating. No, I decided miserably, with my luck, it would be horrible.

"Hey, lady! You want a taxi?" a low, Spanish-accented voice called out. Unbelieving, I looked out into the street. Yes, a man was leaning out of a dark, shabby sedan, waving at me. "I'll take you where you want to go!" he yelled again. I hesitated slightly. It wasn't a proper Yellow Cab. It was what is known as a "gypsy cab." Unable to afford their own hack licenses, and unwilling to work for the large cab fleets where they'd have to share their earnings, many people had taken to driving their own cars as "car services." It was legal as long as the driver responded only to telephoned requests for a taxi. Picking up customers on the street was illegal. But the Taxi Commission seemed to wink at this practice because the gypsy cabs serviced the poor, unsafe areas of the city where legal Yellow Cabs often (illegally) refused to go. It wasn't complicated, it was New York City.

I was surprised to see one of these cabs so far downtown, out of its turf. I stared in a daze at the cardboard "Car Service" tag stuck in the window.

"Hey, lady, you wanna taxi or not? I ain't got all day! Plenty other fares waitin', ya know?" The driver was right. Several other prospective fares were eying the car covetously. It was raining harder. Never look a gift horse in the mouth, my girl, I said to myself.

"Okay," I called back, gripping my briefcase and basket and stepping out into the street. The back door swung open and I stepped inside, settling back against the patched, lumpy seat gratefully. As I arranged my belongings, someone leaned across me to close the door and the car roared off. I looked over, startled to see someone in the back seat beside me.

"Wait a minute," I said, pounding on the dirty plastic partition that separated the front and back seats. "You already have a passenger! You can't pick up another fare!"

"It's okay, lady," the driver hissed back in such a thick accent that I couldn't believe it was real, "he's my cousin. I'm takin' him home. I'm through for the day, but I do you a favor and take you where you wanna go. Where you wanna go?"

"The corner of Jane Street and Greenwich," I answered, deciding against revealing my exact address. I could walk the extra block. I relaxed a little bit. The driver's story sounded plausible. Certainly, I was unfamiliar with the ways of Puerto Rican gypsy-cab drivers. There were two men in the front seat, but the partition was so dirty that I could see neither of them clearly in the glow of the streetlights.

The three men bantered back and forth, mostly in Spanish, occasionally directing a remark at me. I ignored them. It would be, thankfully, a short ride, I thought. I concentrated on being out of the rain and cold.

"Hey, lady, what do ya think of this?" my companion in the back seat asked, nudging me and holding up my *Post*. "Pretty big bang, huh?" He grinned. I nodded. The last thing I wanted to do was start up a conversation with these people. I was being a snob, true, but I couldn't help it. They seemed eager to become over-familiar with me. I shifted slightly, leaning toward the door. We should be nearing Jane Street, I thought, looking out the window. But we weren't. I had no immediate idea where we were. I pounded on the partition again.

"Driver, where are you going?" I said forcefully. "I want Jane Street. You should have turned on Canal. West, west." I pounded again. Stupid, I thought. Stupid, stupid, stupid. I should have known better. I should have known these people wouldn't know the West Village. But then, as the driver continued to drive what seemed to be north and east, I began to think maybe we weren't lost, maybe I was being abducted. I thought quickly and defensively. I hadn't gone to the bank today. I had only about forty dollars on me. That might not be enough to satisfy them. I'd heard stories about scenes like this. I panicked. I pounded again. "Stop! Stop this car! Let me out here! I'll walk! Stop!" I yelled. I hoped they'd believe I was as tough as I acted.

"Lady, relax, it's okay," the man in the back seat said. In the shadows, he appeared to be leering at me. I shuddered. I looked out the window. My hands were ice. This is so stupid! I was so stupid! But what, in God's name, was I going to do?

"Okay, lady, here's where you wanted to go," the driver growled, stopping the car. I looked out. We were indeed pulled up to the northwest corner of Jane and Greenwich streets. I sat stunned, feeling as if I were re-entering the real world from the fantasy of my fears. I opened my briefcase, fumbling for my purse.

"How much is the fare?" I asked, hoping they wouldn't notice my embarrassment. (There are usually no meters in gypsy cabs.) The man beside me again reached across and opened the door.

"No charge, Gretel," said the driver. "I said I was doing you a favor."

I stepped out, shaken, and looked at the car. The driver's window was cranked open. The driver slouched against the seat, a faded Mets cap pulled low on his forehead, its brim touching a pair of oversized sunglasses. He was bearded. All I could see of his face was a wide nose. "I said I'd take you where you wanted to go," he growled accusingly. He had realized what I had feared. He was offended, but in a condescending way, as if he'd expected no better from me. He was also acting very familiar with me. Had he really said my name? I couldn't remember. I wanted to apologize. I couldn't find the words. It probably would have offended him more. He'd been gallant, if unorthodox, and I'd been bigoted. I was ashamed. I finally said:

"Thank you very much," stumbling over the words, even more embarrassed. To my relief, they didn't linger. The driver rolled up his window. The car roared away in the rain. I watched for a few moments, then turned to cross the street and head for home. It had been an ugly scene, but it was over. I would never see those people again. A typical New York City incident, I thought. It wasn't all that important. I checked my mail (more bills!) and slowly climbed the five, long flights to my apartment. I unlocked the door, slipped inside, quickly relocked its three locks, found a vase for my roses, turned on the television, and, after exchanging my wet coat and clothes for my bathrobe, sank down onto my couch to watch the early evening news. I promptly fell asleep.

I was awakened by a heavy weight on my chest and a roaring in my ears. I cautiously opened one eye and was confronted by an indignant yellow-eyed glare. When Samantha, my once-sleek but now decidedly chubby cat, knew I was awake, she leapt down from my stomach with a grace that belied her bulk and ran to her empty dish just inside the kitchen door, sitting in front of it expectantly. Samantha had not been fed since early morning, when I had dumped the last of her cat food into her dish. I had promised myself to buy her some food on the way home, but I had forgotten. I was not about to drag myself down and up five flights of steep steps for one overweight cat. I made no move. She ran back to me, once more jumping up. This time she uttered an outraged meow before scampering back to her empty dish. This could keep up for hours, I knew, so I sighed and went into the kitchen, opened the cupboard, and reached up for the one and only can of tuna fish in the apartment, one I had planned to eat myself. The only other food in the apartment was three eggs. I could eat those. Samantha didn't like eggs.

Purring loudly, Samantha rubbed herself against my ankles as I opened the can, jumping up on the counter, and, putting her pink nose dangerously close to the electric can opener, then jumping down to eat from her dish before I had finished filling it. I left her to her one passion—food—and went back to the television set, which had been on the whole time I was asleep.

The eleven o'clock news was just starting. I heard the anchorman say, "Lower Manhattan was struck by terror today when a deserted oil barge burst into flames on the Hudson River. A newly formed terrorist group, believed to have Latin American connections, took credit for the explosion.

"Nothing is known about this organization which is thought to be a sister organization to another group, the self-styled F.A.L.N. terrorists—a Puerto Rican organization responsible for bombings here in New York and in several other major American cities. This new group apparently has no real name, but their leader was referred to as 'El Condor' in a phone call made this afternoon to the mayor's office.

"No demands have been made, nor was any reason given for the explosion.

"The barge was completely destroyed, harbor officials reported, but some pieces of the wreckage were salvaged. They will be examined for possible clues. No one was injured during the explosion.

"There will be a special report on this and other recent terrorist activities immediately after our regular news broadcast."

I turned down the sound of the set as the commercial started. So, I thought, it's another terrorist group. One that I had never heard of, and hopefully, now that some publicity had been gained, one that would never be heard of again. Out of curiosity, I decided to watch the special report.

Then I remembered I was hungry, and went back into the small closetlike but cozy space my landlord insisted was an eat-in kitchen. Samantha, now purring quite loudly, had finished the tuna fish and was industriously licking her paws to clean her face. However, when I opened the refrigerator door, she leapt up on the counter top to peer inside inquiringly.

"No, Miss Greedy," I said firmly, holding the three eggs in my left hand, shutting the door with my right. "This is for me. You ate. Remember? But what am I talking to you for?"

I had just slid the eggs into boiling water and was watching anxiously for cracks when the phone rang.

Melissa, I thought automatically, slouching back into the living room. I rehearsed the conversation. No, Melissa, no phone call from Pieter. Yes, Melissa, I was right after all.

"Hel-lo, Me-liss-a," I answered the phone in my best nasal singsong.

"Is Gretel Drew there?" a somewhat taken-aback male voice said hesitantly.

"Oh. Yes. Speaking. I'm sorry, I thought . . . who is this?" I asked. I hoped it was Pieter, but I didn't want to be wrong twice.

"It's Pieter. Pieter Van der Hoek. I'm sorry to call you so late, but . . . well, I took a chance you'd be home," said Pieter.

"Oh, yes," I laughingly assured him. "I've been asleep all evening, recuperating from last night."

"Yes. I slept most of the day also," said Pieter.

"Oh. Then you missed the explosion," I said. "It was spectacular! We saw the whole thing from our office windows. I suppose you couldn't have seen it too clearly from Hoek Land."

"What? No. I don't know. I wasn't there today," Pieter answered.

"But," I began, then stopped. I had no desire to cross-examine Pieter. Besides, it sounded very noisy where he was. He had undoubtedly misunderstood my question.

"They say on the news that some terrorist group—a new one—was responsible for the explosion. It's terrible that things like this hap-

pen, isn't it?" I hated to keep talking about the incident, but I couldn't think of anything else.

"Senseless taking of life is always terrible," Pieter agreed.

"But they said no one was killed," I said, again confused.

"What?" said Pieter quickly. "Oh, I was talking generally. People have died in other bombing incidents. Listen, Gretel, I'm in a phone booth and there's someone waiting. Are you free for dinner tomorrow night?"

Was I? I would be. "Yes," I answered firmly. "Oh, and thank you for the flowers," I added.

"Flowers? Oh, have to go. I'll pick you up at eight-fifteen," said Pieter.

"In a boat?" I asked, but Pieter had already hung up.

What a strange man Pieter Van der Hoek is, I thought as I slowly replaced the receiver. Did he always make his appointments on the quarter hour? And he had sounded so distracted. He really hadn't been paying attention to what either of us were saying. Nevertheless, I hugged myself, he'd called! He'd asked me to dinner! And if he did it from a rowdy bar while he was with some other people, who cared!

"Heigh-ho," I sang to Samantha, who was now seated precariously on a window sill, staring out into the black night with great interest. "Pieter asked me out to dinner."

She looked at me round-eyed for a moment, then turned back to the window. I was about to scold her for her lack of enthusiasm when a strange crackling noise reminded me of . . .

"The eggs!" I moaned. I had forgotten all about them. The shells were blackened and stuck to the bottom of my one good saucepan; wide cracks revealed a congealed yellow mass. I turned the burner off and thrust the pan under the faucet. It sizzled noisily when the rush of cold water hit it.

"There goes dinner," I announced to myself, picking gingerly at the now rubbery yolks. Rummaging in the cupboard, I found a handful of stale saltine crackers. Armed with these and a glass of port (the only beverage I could find), I went back to the television set where the special report on El Condor was under way.

". . . And the authorities are certain that this group, this El Condor, is in no way connected to the F.A.L.N." Several men were seated about a low round table, while footage of the oil barge's explosion played on a screen behind them.

"That's right, Jack. It's possible that they might be a splinter group, but that's all," replied a TV news reporter whose name I'd forgotten.

"And the name of the group *is* El Condor?" said Jack, a burly, forceful man.

"It's assumed so," answered a third man. I knew him to be an investigative reporter for *The Village Voice*. "At least, that's the name the leader of the group calls himself. No other title has been given in the communique received this afternoon. I should emphasize that this is a brand-new terrorist group, one that has not been heard from before. So if we sound vague, that's the reason. We just don't know that much about this particular group."

"They seem to have chosen a rather dramatic way of introducing themselves," said the burly man.

"According to their statement, that seems to have been their point." The TV announcer turned toward the camera and began to read excerpts from a statement that had been found in Central Park, taped to the base of the statue of José Marti, the Cuban revolutionary.

"'We are prepared to engage in a war of nerves against Yanqui imperialism,'" the statement read. "'Today's action was merely to demonstrate the discipline and strength of our organization. We shall annihilate you as you have tried to annihilate the Puerto Rican nation. The multinational corporations are our true enemies and our ultimate targets. They have caused the problems of Puerto Rico and Latin America. They choke us with their colonial yoke.

"'Imagine if you will that today's target—a deserted oil barge— had been a supertanker, filled with precious, expensive oil. The explosion would have created a mushroom cloud as immense as that of any A-bomb. Every window in Manhattan would have shattered instantly. The whole of New York's harbor would have been immobilized by a fire that would have raged for days. Imagine this, and you will know what we are capable of.

"'Manhattan is at my mercy. I shall circle this island until it's as dead as its soul!'" The statement finished with a bang.

"Wow," said the *Voice* writer, visibly impressed. The others considered the statement in silence.

"That's a very powerful statement, Carl," the burly man said slowly. "But interestingly enough, El Condor does not seem to be making any demands."

"Actually, he, or they, seem to be threatening punishment for crimes committed against the Third World and Latin America in general and Puerto Rico in particular," the Voice writer interjected. "It's a completely different pattern from the F.A.L.N., who have always made some sort of demands: the independence of Puerto Rico, the freeing of the Puerto Rican nationalists who wounded five congressmen and tried to assassinate President Truman in the 1950s."

"Perhaps demands will come later, once the group has established itself as a force to be reckoned with," suggested the TV news announcer, now identified as Carl.

"I'm sure you're right, Carl," said the Voice writer. "In addition to the statement, there was also a poster found taped to the statue in Central Park. It consisted simply of a very interesting graphic, I think it's coming, yes, it's on the screen now. It seems to depict the city of New York, you can identify the twin towers of the World Trade Center, and the outline of the Empire State Building, being overshadowed by a large birdlike creature, which, I suppose"—here he laughed, a little nervously, I thought—"is meant to represent a condor."

I studied the poster intently, for it was a very sophisticated design, simply but clearly rendered. Although the winged creature hovering over the city—one wing tip just touching the World Trade Center— was portrayed in silhouette, it was impossible to mistake the ruthlessness it symbolized. It was a powerful, threatening image.

The rest of the newscast consisted of the mayor reading a prepared statement calling for the return of the death penalty as a deterrent to terrorism; the governor of Puerto Rico reading a prepared statement denouncing the terrorists and asking us not to judge the people of Puerto Rico by the acts of a few maniacs; and a brief history of the Puerto Rican liberation movement. It ended with the announcement that a special hotline number was being set up for callers with information about the explosion.

I turned the set off and went to bed. I fell asleep to dream of the very first time I had flown high over Manhattan. But this time I had the sleek plane all to myself.

*　*　*

I woke Saturday midmorning energetic and refreshed. Spurred on by Samantha's insistent meows, I dressed quickly and clattered downstairs to the crisp gray morning air. I did my marketing, bought the morning paper, and then, on purest impulse, splurged on a bunch of long-stemmed yellow chrysanthemums on my way back. Then it began to rain, the large drops hitting my face, and I ran home as best I could, juggling flowers, paper, and groceries. Ordinarily, such an effort would have put me into a foul mood, but not today. I could laugh at the ridiculous sight I must have presented, could laugh that the check-out girl had put my coffeecake at the bottom of the slightly damp bag and that it was now bent out of all recognizable shape, could laugh (almost) that the freshly ground coffee I had purchased had been leaking all the way from the store. I put away the groceries, brewed a huge pot of coffee, heated up the flattened cake, fed Samantha, and settled down quite happily to read the New York *Times*. The rain was now pounding heavily against the windows, but the flowers dispelled the weather's gloom. My little kitchen looked as cheerful as I felt.

The only sensational news, of course, was the explosion. There were the usual reports by eyewitnesses, the usual editorials denouncing terrorists, and the usual spectacular pictures of the blaze. The communique from El Condor was reprinted alongside the poster. It was even more striking reproduced in the smudgy black ink of the newspaper. Without really knowing why, I clipped the design from the paper.

Idly, I perused the rest of the paper. In the back, buried in the Metropolitan Briefs, was the item "Starr Mills Believed Found." My goodness, I thought, after all these years. I read the disappointingly brief story. It was terrible and expected.

Starr Mills was two years older than I, and had made a splash in society as the brightest and richest debutante of her season. Melissa's cousin had also been presented that year, and the stories she told us kept us entertained for months. Starr's season had ended rather abruptly after a huge party at her family's summer home in Newport, Rhode Island. The guests had grown rowdy. The police had had to be called, and, in the end, damage had run into the thousands. In the fall, Starr left for Berkeley—sent into exile, we all gossiped.

Several years later, Starr Mills made headlines once again. She became a prominent participant in the radical student movements of the late sixties, speaking out against the Vietnam War and other excesses of the "establishment." She associated with the more violent groups, of course, dropping out of college during her senior year to demonstrate full-time. Since the early 1970s, she had been wanted by the FBI in connection with an explosion that had destroyed an apartment building in New York City. She was said to be living underground.

How coincidental that Starr had turned up the very day of the barge explosion, I thought. Or rather, that her body had.

A woman's body, partially clothed and streaked with oil, had been found washed up yesterday afternoon on the Statue of Liberty Island (Bedloe's Island)—a woman's body believed to be that of Starr Mills. The police coroner was quoted as being unsure of how long the woman had been dead. The effects of exposure had made his task difficult. The presence of oil was obvious, he'd said, since the waters of the lower Hudson and the harbor were coated from the explosion of the oil barge. The police and the FBI refused to comment any further on the reappearance of Starr Mills, as it could hinder their investigation and search for the few remaining radicals still with the underground.

"Who would have thought Starr Mills would end up like that?" I announced to Samantha. I had seen her once some ten years before, and had been impressed by her glamour. She had even been a beautiful revolutionary (much to the indignation of some of her fellow militants and much to the delight of the media). How tragic. A life had been taken after all. For I did not for a moment believe that the explosion and Starr Mills's death were unrelated. I had read too many detective novels to believe in pure coincidence. (The summer I was ten, I had seriously considered changing my name from Gretel to Nancy Drew. I had been crushed to learn I would have to wait eleven years.) Starr Mills would have been an asset to any terrorist organization. She had been one of the few remaining stars the radical movement had, for, as they had grown older, most of the leaders had resurfaced to state their desire for a normal, "straight" way of life.

I yawned and looked at my watch. Melissa always slept late on Saturdays, but I didn't hesitate to call her. I wanted to tell her about Starr, to speculate about her connection with yesterday's explosion. Most of all, I wanted to tell her about my dinner date with Pieter.

3

Caribbean Honeymoon

"Gretel, there's something, uh, something that I've been meaning to ask you," said Pieter.

"Ask away then," I replied dreamily. I was sitting cross-legged several feet away, before the tiny brick fireplace in my living room. I had just poked another log onto the fire and was enjoying the lick and jump of the flames. Even more, I was enjoying the warmth, since my apartment was its usual chilly self. My landlord was generous with the heat six months of the year. December wasn't one of them.

"I can't with your back to me. Lovely though it is," Pieter added, poking me with his foot. I sighed, reluctantly turning away from the heat.

Pieter sprawled casually in my overstuffed armchair, which, in its shabby splendor, was also Samantha's favorite scratching post and roost. Pieter seemed the perfect idler—head carelessly cocked to one side, long legs stretching over my one ottoman. He caressed Samantha's tummy with his left hand, scratched her head with his right. Samantha lay there, purring up a storm. Her attachment to Pieter amazed me continually. From the outset, with Pieter's first visit to my apartment six weeks before, Samantha had favored him not only with her presence (she usually hid from visitors), but also with her person. How she craved Pieter's attentions. Almost as much as I do, I giggled to myself.

"Well," I said. "Here I am. What is it you wanted to ask me?"

"This," said Pieter, suddenly lifting Samantha from his lap and coming to sit on the floor beside me. Nonplused, Samantha resettled herself in the chair, proceeding to lick herself energetically. I, however, was startled, and crossed my arms, hugging them to my chest defensively.

"I've been waiting for the right moment," continued Pieter, "and though I'm not sure this is it, I thought I'd give it a try. I'm not very patient."

"What? What?" I said.

"What?" said Pieter, mimicking my tone. "Why, waiting for the right moment to ask you to marry me."

I must have gaped. I don't remember behaving in a dignified manner. I sat still.

"Don't look at me like that," chided Pieter. "Shall I take it back?" He reached out his arms to drape his hands over my shoulders. "Gretel, you know I love you. Very much. You're wonderful. Wonderful to me and for me. Now, will you marry me?"

I continued to stare into the eyes of a man I barely knew. He seemed very serious, enough so that he also seemed extraordinarily vulnerable, as if he were afraid of rejection. He commanded me to answer. How could I refuse? How dare I refuse? He, too, was wonderful—an exciting enigma that had made my life an exciting, exhilarating adventure. But marry him?

"All right," I whispered.

"What?" said Pieter. "I didn't hear you."

"Yes," I said firmly. "I said yes. Pieter Van der Hoek, I will marry you."

"Certain?" said Pieter. "You won't change your mind?"

"No," I said quietly. "Will you?"

"No," said Pieter. "And to prove it, I remembered to bring this." He then produced a small navy-blue velvet box. "Go ahead. Open it. It's for you."

My fingers trembled. I fumbled with the catch. Finally, the lid popped up to reveal a ring nestled in the white-satin lining. It was a slender gold band, with delicate filigree work on the top. In the center was set a single, soft-white pearl.

"It's beautiful," I said.

"Go on. Let's see if it fits," said Pieter, taking the ring from the box, taking my left hand and sliding the ring over my finger. I held my breath. It fit perfectly! "It's something of a family heirloom," Pieter continued. "But, more importantly, it's a family tradition. All the Van der Hoek brides wear this as their betrothal ring. I think it was my great-great-something who had it made for his wife."

"It's lovely," I said, holding up my hand to admire the ring in the fire's glow. How warm and cozy the room seemed now! "I shall treasure it all the more. Family histories fascinate me."

"Well then," said Pieter, laughing and drawing me to him. "Before you go on, there's an unhappy history here as well."

"What?" I asked.

"Every bride who has ever worn this ring has had a tragic end to her marriage."

"No," I protested.

"Yes," said Pieter. "Two died in childbirth. My grandmother succumbed to influenza in her early thirties. And, my mother, uh, divorced my father."

"Are you trying to scare me?" I asked.

"No, no, not at all," said Pieter. "I just want you to know everything."

"You made it up, then," I accused.

"Me? Lie?" said Pieter.

"Well, regardless," I said confidently. "My answer is that I will be the exception that proves the rule. This is one Van der Hoek bride who . . . Samantha! No! Oh, Pieter, get that box away from her before she . . . oh, Samantha!"

* * *

I called Melissa the next morning, which was—fittingly, I thought —the last day of the year.

"Oh, Gretel. How are you?" Melissa greeted me breathlessly. "I've been up since *dawn*. Well, it seems like dawn. I swear to God I'll never give another New Year's Eve party, but as Ed would say if he were here—thank God he's not—I say that every year. So, Gretel, why are you calling? Oh dear, you're not calling to say that you and Pieter won't be able to come?"

"No, I'm not," I said. "We shall definitely be there. With bells on. Especially now that I've got something to show off."

"Show off? Gretel, what are you talking about?"

"Oh . . . a present from Pieter," I said casually.

"I've already seen the shawl," said Melissa.

"*This* present is at this moment adorning a finger on my left hand. It's gold and round, and has a stone," I said, moving the phone away from my ear in anticipation of Melissa's response.

"You didn't!" shrieked Melissa. "You're not! Oh, Gretel! Stay right where you are. I'll be right over."

Ten minutes later, just as I had brewed a fresh pot of coffee, the front-door buzzer sounded. I buzzed back, and a few more minutes later, I admitted a breathless Melissa.

"Why is it," she gasped, "that you insist on living at the top of an ungodly set of stairs? You should have more consideration for your friends." Melissa lived in a fashionable elevator building. "I'll admit that this place does have character, though not much heat."

"Come and sit by the fire," I said. "Have some coffee. Catch your breath."

"Brandy is what I need," answered Melissa, shrugging off her silver fox (the one present from Ed that she hadn't given away after the divorce). "Or perhaps champagne would be more suitable. Oh, Gretel." Melissa caught me in a giant bear hug. "Did your Flying Dutchman really propose? Let me see the ring! How lovely! Now, tell me everything! When did this all happen?"

"Just last night," I said. "You're the first to know. After mother, of course."

"I should hope so. Were you at dinner?"

"No. Here, sitting on this very floor. He took me completely by surprise."

"No, it wasn't to be expected," agreed Melissa. "After all, you've only known each other what—a month?"

"Six weeks," I snapped.

"That's a short time!" said Melissa. "Are you sure about this?"

"Sure about what?" I said. "That Pieter and I are engaged?"

"No, silly. Sure that you're doing the right thing. Six weeks is a *very* short time," said Melissa, sipping her coffee. I held mine between my hands, but did not drink.

"It's long enough," I replied evenly.

"Oh, Gretel, don't go getting huffy," said Melissa, moving to the couch. "If *I* can't say these things, who can? I care very much about you. I want to be sure you're doing the right thing. I don't want you to make a mistake like I did."

"I know you mean well, Melissa, and I'm grateful. But I *am* sure.

Very sure that I love Pieter and that he loves me. I'm not a love-struck kid, I'm twenty-seven years old!"

"Cheer up. When I turned twenty-eight last week, I gained three new wrinkles," said Melissa with mock despair.

"Oh—you! You don't look a day over twenty, uh, twenty-six. Hey! Watch where you're throwing that!" I ducked as Melissa took aim with her teaspoon. "Seriously, though, Pieter has passed all the tests. We've been together almost constantly since we met. He was home with me at Christmas. He got along great with them all. Even the terrible twins! And, most important of all, Samantha adores him."

"What, that fat old thing?" sniffed Melissa.

"*Pieter* says she's elegant!" I protested.

"*Pieter* is being obvious," Melissa countered. "So, when's the wedding going to be?"

"As soon as possible," I said. "Mother has to check her schedule. We'll have the wedding there, but it will be very small. That's Pieter's one condition. So it won't need much preparation. Just family."

"And me," said Melissa.

"And you," I agreed, laughing.

"Speaking of family, you've never met any of Pieter's, have you?" asked Melissa suddenly.

"No. But there doesn't seem to be much to meet. His father is dead. His mother might as well be. He did mention an aunt once, I'll have to ask Pieter if we should invite her."

"I thought you said Pieter had a brother," said Melissa.

"Yes, Dirk," I replied.

"You've never met Dirk," continued Melissa, her brows arching delicately.

"No," I said as casually as possible.

"Even though he lives on the island with Pieter?"

"Well, actually . . ." I began.

"Actually, you haven't been back to the island," Melissa finished for me.

"No. Just that one night," I confessed.

"Don't you find that a little strange? Have you asked Pieter? Or have you respected his privacy too much to ask?"

"Actually, I did ask," I said.

"I don't believe it," Melissa murmured.

"But Pieter says," I continued, ignoring her remark, "that it's bad luck for a fiancée to enter Hoek House before the wedding. It's a family tradition," I continued as Melissa rolled her eyes.

"Then you are going to live there once you're married?"

"I imagine so. We haven't really discussed the details, Melissa. Last night we were more interested in other things."

"I know. I know. God forbid you should discuss details! I'm not here to play the voice of doom, believe me. I like Pieter. He's handsome and charming. But I think that before you become Mrs. Pieter Van der Hoek, you should find out about a few things first—namely, the mysterious invisible brother and the house you may or may not live in. Am I wrong?"

"No, not wrong," I said sullenly.

"But not right, either," said Melissa. "There are some things you are going to have to face. Like, one, how is Pieter going to support you? Two, where are you going to live? Do you really know what he's like? What does he expect from you? Maybe the two of you should live together first," she finished, shrugging her shoulders.

"Trial marriage?" I asked. "No, thanks. I believe that you marry for love. I have the rest of my life to get to know Pieter, but I love him *now*. We're not going to starve. We'll live on his island. And, he expects me to be wonderful." I paused for breath, continuing, "My mother knew my father for two weeks before they got married, and then he went off to war, and they've been happy for thirty years! We should be so lucky."

"All right, all right. You're right, I'm wrong." Melissa laughed. "What do you want me to say?"

"Happy New Year," I said.

"Don't say that now, say it tonight. And don't change the— tonight!" she repeated, jumping to her feet. "Oh, my God! My party!" Melissa grabbed her coat, hugged me quickly, and disappeared out of the apartment, clumping loudly down all five flights of steep stairs.

* * *

Two quick weeks later I became Mrs. Pieter Van der Hoek. My parents, my grandfather, my two brothers, and Melissa and her parents were the only guests at the quiet ceremony in the very same quiet chapel I had been baptized in. Afterward, we held a reception at my parents' home, where the neighbors could offer their congratulations and appraise the man "little Gretel Drew" had married.

There was no one present from Pieter's family. When I had asked, he had said his aunt had died several years ago and that it would be "inconvenient" for either his brother or his mother to attend.

It was a cozy, austere wedding, but traditional in every way. As I walked down the red-carpeted aisle, I wore a bright-blue gaudy garter, with a yellowing piece of lace from my grandmother's wedding gown sewn onto the collar of my own floor-length, cream-colored velvet dress. My mother's emeralds, borrowed for the occasion, twinkled at my ears.

Later, at the reception, Pieter and I together (his large bony hand covering mine) cut the first slice from the three-layer, ornately decorated cake. But I drew the line at spooning it into my new husband's mouth. And then, after a suitable time had elapsed, I slipped upstairs to change into the red and charcoal-gray suit my mother had insisted on buying for me. Pieter and I posed for one last picture while I tossed my bouquet, which I aimed at Melissa—only to have her duck at the last moment. It ricocheted into the plump arms of Mrs. Phillips, our minister's wife. We raced to the shiny yellow Volkswagen bug we had rented for our honeymoon, and drove off jerkily, the obligatory noisy tin cans and white crepe-paper streamers trailing gaily and embarrassingly behind.

"Whew!" I sighed happily, leaning my head against the seat. "I don't know why, but I'm exhausted."

"Becoming Mrs. Pieter Van der Hoek is very exhausting work." Pieter smiled, reaching over to take my hand in his. "Any regrets?"

"None. None whatsoever," I answered, returning his smile. How odd, I thought. Melissa had asked me that very same question. Rushing up for one last hug, she had whispered, "Are you happy?" into my ear. A wide Hollywood smile had been my reply.

"I'm glad to hear it," Pieter replied, suddenly pulling over to the side of the road. He kissed me fiercely, then before I had quite recovered, he leapt out of the car to strip away the cans and bunting. "We'll have no more of that sort of nonsense," he announced, climbing back into the car.

We were to spend the night at a quaint inn an hour or so north of New York City, and then drive to the airport in the morning to board a plane. But for where? The question had maddened me for days. The wedding trip was all Pieter's doing, all Pieter's planning, and all Pieter's surprise. And here it was, the night before we were due to leave—with a lovely full honey of a moon shining down upon us—and I still had not tricked the information about my own honeymoon from him!

"*Now* will you tell me where we're going?" I asked bluntly as I plopped in the middle of the double bed we were to share, waiting for Pieter to emerge from his shower.

"You'll see when we get there," Pieter called through the closed door, evading the question as he had so often the past week.

"But how can I be sure to have the proper clothes?" I asked, as I had so often the past week.

"It's all taken care of. I packed for you!"

"You did? How can you be sure to have got the right size," I said, trying to remember if I had noticed anything missing from my closets. "And I didn't see my suitcase." I had only brought my small overnight case into the inn.

"Don't worry. I packed everything in my bag, so it would be easier to carry. And," he added, opening the bathroom door to let out clouds of steam, "I'm an excellent judge of sizes. Especially yours."

"Well, husbands and wives are supposed to share things, not keep things from each other," I stated, sulkily pulling the covers up to my chin.

"I disagree," Pieter responded, coming out of the bathroom, a towel wrapped around him. "I think husbands and wives should have certain secrets from each other. It keeps the marriage interesting."

"Only if they're good secrets," I began, determined to have the last word. But any further conversation was swallowed up in Pieter's embrace.

*   *   *

The next morning, early, too early, I was brutally yanked from bed by a wide-awake Pieter, who hurried me through dressing, forced me to gulp a scalding hot cup of coffee while I longed for the sumptuous breakfast the other early risers at the inn were enjoying. Then he bustled me into the car. We were on the New York State Thruway before I was actually awake. Within an hour we pulled into the large parking lot at Kennedy International Airport, parking the car, grabbing our one locked suitcase (Pieter having foreseen my desire to "peek"), checking in at the airline ticket counter.

"Your plane boards in ten minutes." The uniformed attendant

smiled brightly. "Enjoy your flight." Pieter thanked him and headed off toward the boarding gates.

I glanced at the information board. There were two flights leaving in thirty minutes. One to Miami and one to San Juan, Puerto Rico.

"Puerto Rico?" I guessed, trotting to keep up with him. "We're going to Puerto Rico?"

"For a week or thereabouts. Surprise!" said Pieter.

"But . . . why?" I said, stunned a little. Stunned a lot. Of all the places I had guessed this past week, Puerto Rico had not been one of them.

"Have you ever been there?" Pieter asked.

"No, as a matter of fact, I haven't."

"Reason enough," said Pieter.

"But you didn't, uh, I mean, we never discussed, uh, you didn't know I hadn't been there, did you? You haven't been there, have you?" I stammered.

Pieter's puzzling smile was all the response I received. Oh, Gretel, I scolded myself. Just be glad you're going south in January and stop worrying about the whys and wherefores. Oh! Won't the gang at *Milady* be jealous when I show up tanned and healthy! Deciding that Pieter just liked surprises, I calmed down and decided to enjoy the flight.

I have always loved to fly, but this flight seemed truly magical as the vacationer-filled 747 transported us from a gray New York winter to gloriously bright sunshine and sparkling deep-blue waters. To make the flight even more perfect, Pieter and I were able to fly first-class, champagne and all, as one of the stewardesses guessed we were honeymooners and surreptitiously moved us up from the coach section to two empty first-class seats.

As the plane began its descent through the clouds three hours later, I couldn't restrain myself. I squealed like any child on her first trip as I caught my first glimpse of the Caribbean—miles and miles of glistening sea, and then the island of Puerto Rico, and its intensely green expanse. The last few minutes of the flight seemed as long as the first few hours, for I was impatient to be there, to lie on the narrow beaches with the gently swaying palm trees overhead. Pieter, though smiling indulgently at my excesses, avoided my mood. He stubbornly insisted on making sketches of some of the more bizarre passengers ("Tacky Touristas") throughout the trip. Even, much to my chagrin, during our in-flight movie, a poignant love story that I thought seemed especially chosen in our honor. Pieter put his sketch pad away only after the plane had taxied to a complete halt.

I danced off the plane, danced through the surprisingly (to me) large and modern airport. My light wool suit was immediately uncomfortable. I wanted to tear it off! I had to be merely satisfied with shedding the jacket, while Pieter dealt with the reclaiming of our single suitcase. He then deftly steered us to the taxi station. Being one of those clumsy people who is hopelessly lost when traveling (and hopelessly embarrassed when lost), I was grateful that Pieter seemed one of those deft travelers who unerringly know which direction to take. He took charge effortlessly. I was happy to trot obediently beside my husband of twenty-four hours, thankful at long last that I had someone to take charge of my life, and to take charge of me—even if it was only something as minor as finding a taxi.

"So where's San Juan?" I asked, as the taxi pulled away from the airport. We seemed surrounded by vast fields of tropical grass.

"The downtown area is about half an hour away," Pieter replied.

"San Juan is larger than I thought," I added as the taxi picked up speed, turning onto the four-lane highway that would eventually take us into the city proper.

The city of San Juan is built upon a narrow piece of land on the northern coast of Puerto Rico. The highway runs along the ocean front, past the large apartment buildings, shopping centers, and luxurious hotels that decorate the shore. These buildings, that looked as though they had all been built within the last ten years, were sadly mingled with grimy dwellings and unkempt dirt yards. The scene was made more hideous by the windows—shuttered tightly against the hot noonday sun. They gave the buildings an abandoned air. I noticed that the buildings were closer now, when suddenly I had to laugh aloud.

"What is it?" asked Pieter, slightly irritated, I thought.

"Just look!" I sputtered, pointing to the familiar signs we had left behind. "MacDonalds, Grand Union, Chase Manhattan Bank, and Kentucky Fried Chicken! They're all here! It's as if we'd never left home." Although I knew that Puerto Rico was part of the United States, I had assumed it would be, well, more foreign. I stifled another giggle.

"Yes, the island has become quite Americanized," Pieter said. "Especially in the cities. San Juan most of all."

"It's not at all what I imagined," I answered. "Except for the

signs, it's as though we were still at home. And"—I laughed again—
"many of the signs in New York are also printed in Spanish."

"You'll find the old part of the city more what you expect," Pieter
said. "It's fairly authentic, although very tourist-conscious. And, then
of course, many parts of the interior remain unspoiled—even by
modern plumbing. This is a very, very poor country, despite the sky-
scrapers and shopping centers you've been ogling," Pieter added,
turning to gaze out the window. We were now obviously in the
downtown section. The city was crowded with modern white buildings, many of them unfinished (as were parts of the express highway
we were traveling). We had to stop more often now to allow for the
heavy midday traffic. San Juan was indeed a large urban sprawl.

"You shouldn't let me do that," Pieter said suddenly, turning back
to face me.

"Do what?" I asked, puzzled.

"Drift into moodiness when what I should be is happy," he said.

"One can't be happy *all* the time," I said quickly, rushing to his
defense. I had been put off by Pieter's mood, but I didn't want him
to know.

"This is not *all* the time, this is our honeymoon," Pieter replied,
first kissing then licking my ear so vigorously that it tickled. From
then on, Pieter was as attentive a husband as any bride could wish.

We had driven through what seemed all of the modern downtown
section of San Juan before the driver slowed. The buildings—still
relatively new highrises—were sparser now, and again, the hotels
along the sea edge dominated. What a city of hotels, I thought. I
had not heard Pieter give directions to our driver, and I did not
know where we would be staying. But it seemed to me that we had
passed all of the large hotels that would be our logical choices: the
Holiday Inn, the Sheraton, El San Juan Towers—all the places I had
seen advertisements for and heard about.

Now we turned off the highway, pulling away from "hotel row" to
race across a long sea wall—actually (I would learn later) a bridge
connecting the old and new sections of San Juan. We turned off the
main highway, motored a few more feet, then came to a complete
stop before a large, white building.

"Normandie," the driver muttered, turning to accept the fare
Pieter handed him.

Smartly uniformed porters waited at the doorway, waiting for a signal from the doorman to seize our luggage. I stepped from the cab to survey our home for the next few days.

All the hotels I had seen on our ride from the airport had been modern, luxury hotels of the type to be seen at every resort—the ubiquitous, boring, multistoried building, every floor bedecked with identical rectangular terraces. But not our Normandie. The Normandie appeared to be a hotel from a more glamorous, stately, bygone era. It was a large ocean liner-shaped building—much like the pictures I had seen of the *Queen Mary*—swelling slightly in the middle then coming to a point overlooking the sea. It was wider than it was tall (another rarity in modern San Juan), being only seven stories high. Each window was protected from the sun's rays by a large, dark-green, scallop-edged awning, though I thankfully spotted a concession to modern times: huge Fedders air conditioners appeared haphazardly below the windows. They were obviously a later addition. However, despite its old-fashioned design, the hotel appeared freshly built, almost brand-new. Perhaps it was new, I thought, and was only aping an older style. Unlikely. I was amused to notice that the building was gaily decorated—multicolored streamers hung from the windows, swaying in the sea breeze. The doors were similarly festooned. I thought perhaps they were left over from the Christmas and New Year's holidays. I whispered to Pieter that perhaps the hotel knew of our wedding and our arrival.

"A pleasant thought, but unfortunately, no," Pieter answered.

We followed the smartly uniformed bellhop to our room in silence. I reveled in every detail: the obviously new carpeting (for how could pale green stay immaculately clean?), the pristine white wicker furniture, the slow-moving large-bladed fans overhead, the primitive, gaily colored paintings hung on the cool white walls. Pieter seemed oblivious to his surroundings.

Once again I had been impressed with Pieter's ease and air of command while checking in. The hotel employees had actually seemed to defer to him (or his air of majesty). "The hotel was just reopened this week," Pieter said as we were swept into an elevator and up to the top floor. "And all"—he waved his hand impatiently— "that you see is in honor of that gala occasion. We were very lucky to obtain a room. They are very much sought after. The reopening of the Normandie has been a long-awaited event."

"Then how did you manage it?" I asked. "And on such short notice, too."

"I have my ways," Pieter answered, closing his eyes to form mysterious slits. Then he laughed at my puzzled expression. "Besides, Gretel, you should know by now that when I want something, I get it. I wanted to stay in the Normandie."

"And you wanted to marry me," I said playfully.

"Precisely," he said. "You didn't stand a chance."

Any thought of a reply was forgotten as I stepped out of the elevator, through the pastel-green hallway and into our room. It was light and airy, and almost entirely decorated in white. The oversized furniture was white wicker, with one delightful chair in rattan. The green I had seen in the lobby and the hallway was echoed here in the dark, almost forest-green carpeting. The bedspread was a cream color; the gay, raucous pillows casually (but artfully) strewn across the white headboard were the only real notes of color in the entire room. We were on the top floor of the hotel and thus in one of the few rooms to have its own terrace. I immediately passed through the french doors with gently billowing white-cotton gauze curtains to admire the view of the sea directly below us. To our right stretched the towering section of San Juan we had driven through; to our left—largely hidden by gently swaying palm trees—was the crowded old section of the city. Directly below us was a semicircle of golden beach, surrounding the transparent blue waters of the bay that the Normandie shared with the Hilton hotel complex next door.

"Well, do you approve?" asked Pieter, coming up from behind to hug me tenderly.

"Oh, it's wonderful! Everything that I could have dreamed of," I answered, sighing happily. "Oh, look!" Breaking free of Pieter's embrace, I dashed over to the long white table next to the overlarge double bed, where a golden pineapple sat in the center of a white china platter. The fruity sweet aroma filled the air. "How lovely! It's so fresh, it melts in your mouth." The fruit had already been sliced up; a colorful plastic toothpick pierced each section. I eagerly slurped at the fruit.

"It seems to be more on your chin than in your mouth." Pieter laughed, stepping behind me to take me in his arms once again. "Now, what do you say we get, uh, organized. Then we'll go down to the beach."

* * *

The next two days passed lazily but quickly. I felt as though I were living a tropical dream. There were no demands on our time, no decision more difficult than whether one side of my body had had enough sun, time to flip over, apply some more tanning oil and cook some more. I reddened as Pieter browned, a fact that bothered me more than I let on. A fair Dutch Scandinavian had no business tanning while an olive-complexioned Celt burned to a crisp. But Pieter was delightfully attentive, complimenting me on my various shades of red, warning me when it was time to move into the shade. When I complained of being parched, Pieter popped up to trundle off to the bar, returning with one exotic rum cocktail after another. When I would ask what they were, Pieter would smile mysteriously and urge me to drink up. The sun's warmth, the rum's potency, and Pieter's love. A deadly combination, and I willingly became its victim.

But Pieter had become bored by the sun after our second day, so he brought his sketch pad to the beach. With a few strong, quick lines, he would catch the idiosyncrasies of those sunbathing near us. Each time he chose a subject, he'd spin some fantastic, often sarcastic, tale of their vocations, educations, natures, and ambitions. His drawings were, more often than not, accurate but slightly cruel caricatures. Nevertheless, a few of Pieter's subjects, noticing what he was doing, offered to buy them at what I thought were outrageously generous prices. One distinguished-looking man with a bride much younger than he, offered Pieter two hundred dollars for a sketch of the two of them sitting side by side. Pieter turned him down (several times) and then gave it to his wife, who obviously didn't really want it. I put down my paperback novel—a classic British murder mystery —to ask Pieter what that was all about.

"She married him," Pieter replied curtly, starting immediately on another sketch, this time of some children playing tag in the breakers.

"I don't understand," I said.

"Rich men think they can have whatever they want. This time he couldn't. But then, I thought she should see what she had done to her life," Pieter said casually.

"Don't you think that's a bit harsh?" I asked.

"Life is harsh," said Pieter, finishing his drawing of the children, waving them over to show them. They loved it, of course, giggling as they recognized themselves. Soon their mother ("Governess, more like," muttered Pieter) appeared to ask after the drawing. Pieter handed it to her with a laugh. She thanked him profusely. He did a quick study of her, gave it to her, finally took ten dollars for it, then popped up to dash across the beach and up onto the pier. I thought he must have gone mad. When he returned, I asked him what he'd done.

"Made an investment," replied Pieter.

"With ten dollars?" I asked.

"Sure. A future deep-sea diver needed some fins," said Pieter.

I again put down my book to look over to the pier where Pieter had gone. A Puerto Rican boy, about ten years of age, was flopping around awkwardly in a pair of brand-new shiny black flippers. He was parading up and down on the other side of the railing separating the hotel's beach from the small, littered public beach that hooked to a point formed by an abandoned fortification. Because of the distance, I couldn't be sure, but I guessed, asking Pieter:

"Did you buy that child flippers?"

"What boy?" said Pieter, engrossed in a new sketch.

"Aha!" I said. "Got you!" But Pieter merely smiled blankly. "Oh, I see. You're embarrassed. Is that it?" I challenged.

"You're beautiful when you try to be clever," said Pieter, winking broadly.

I had to laugh off Pieter's escapade. My husband, playing out his own version of Robin Hood. Obviously, Pieter believed in taking from the advantaged and giving to the disadvantaged. The wealthy sunbather had disgusted him too much for Pieter to deal with him in any fashion. But the "governess" had bartered fairly for Pieter's talent. Rather than pocket the money he'd earned but didn't want, Pieter had purchased a gift for a child who never could have enjoyed such a luxury unless he'd stolen it. Pieter was noble but eccentric. I liked him for it.

And that night at dinner, in the Normandie's open-air restaurant on the first floor, which Pieter much preferred to the air-conditioned, rather formal dining room upstairs, Pieter again displayed his eccentric chivalry.

While we dined exquisitely on fresh-caught, succulent lobsters and chilled-to-perfection dry champagne, three Puerto Rican musicians circled the tables, serenading the diners with popular tunes that ran the gamut from "Vaya Con Dios" to "Blue Moon." Pieter cringed each time they neared us, but I quite openly enjoyed the romance of it. Finally, when our main course was cleared, and while we waited for dessert, it became our turn. The musicians glided to our table and launched into a long, melancholy song about unrequited love. I sat enchanted while Pieter sat patient. When they finished, the lead singer bowed, then started to move away. Pieter stood, thanking the men in (as far as I could tell) perfect Spanish, and surreptitiously handing their leader some money. I couldn't see how much it was. The man took it with an odd, almost astonished look on his face. I was puzzled. Other diners had tipped them, although admittedly not so formally, so half-apologetically. Pieter sat down again, saying, as if by explanation:

"Those men have to support families on this, can you imagine? They're great musicians, and they support families on . . . on tips." He almost spat the last word.

"I'm sure the hotel pays them well. It is run by the Hilton company," I said, lamely.

"Yeah, Hilton. A great socialist. That's why he owns the world," Pieter chuckled mirthlessly.

"Just hotels around the world, Pieter," I said.

I could see Pieter didn't think me clever. He seemed sincerely perturbed. I admonished myself for not taking Pieter's politics seriously before this. He was a genuine iconoclast, hence his remarks about the World Trade Center, the tourists on our flight, the flipper incident on the beach. He disliked wealth. I decided to draw him out. "Pieter," I began, "what is it that irks you about the way these men work?"

"They have so little while others have so much," said Pieter.

"Is it that simple?" I said.

"No, unfortunately it's not, Gretel." He sighed. "I don't mean to seem abrupt, but can we drop this? I spoke out of turn. Hotheaded, you know?" Pieter smiled broadly. "How about some guava with cream for dessert?"

"Fabulous," I said.

* * *

By noon of our third day, I was sunburned, and Pieter was restless. Our solution, after a light lunch and two light-headed rum confections, was to tour Old San Juan. It seemed a good decision, as I realized that I'd been in San Juan for three days and hadn't yet toured the most famous castle in the New World, El Morro.

We set off cheerfully. I was all for taking a taxi; I still felt lazy from the morning's sun. More importantly, I worried that my crisp white-linen sundress would wilt in the afternoon's heat. But Pieter would have none of such luxury.

"Oh, for heaven's sake, Gretel. It's less than half an hour by bus," said Pieter firmly, steering me from the taxi stand with equal firmness.

"But the taxi'd cost less than two dollars. I asked a clerk in the hotel," I protested vainly, trotting to keep up with his long, measured strides.

"And the bus costs a quarter." Pieter seized my hand to cross the street. There seemed to be no stoplights. We raced across quickly. "Really, Gretel," Pieter continued once we were safely on the other side, "sometimes you're too New York City for your own good." I stuck my tongue out cheerfully at him for reply.

We walked for the bus down Ponce de León Avenue, a modern three-lane highway that ran from the old city through the new city to the airport and beyond. We stood on the edge of a lush green park, near what Pieter explained was the Supreme Court Building. Soon the bus pulled up, and I began to fish in my purse for the exact change, but Pieter stopped me, saying with a grand flourish, "My treat."

It was a short ride along the avenue, the park on our right, the harbor on our left. Soon we pulled into a large square, the Plaza de Colón. "This is the end of the line," Pieter announced, jumping up to join the other passengers. Once we were off the bus, I rummaged in my bag, this time to find a map of the city I had picked up at the hotel, but Pieter took my arm. We crossed the street before I had even had a chance to find out what street we were crossing.

"Wait a minute," I said. "Let's find out where we are first. We'll get lost!"

Pieter paused, looking as if he were about to speak. Then he shook his head, smiling to himself, and continued up the street. I had no choice but to follow. And follow I did, while continuing to rummage in my purse. I finally found my map. I decided to use it surreptitiously, for peace of mind if nothing else.

We had taken Calle O'Donnel out of the plaza, turning left on Calle Luna, then turning right again. The street we were now on wasn't important enough to be mentioned on my map, but it was obvious we were heading toward the sea. And in the opposite direction from the walking tour suggested by the map. I shrugged my shoulders and trotted obediently in Pieter's wake.

We were now walking along the city's edge. To our right stretched the sea, as far as we could see, a vast expanse of dark blue, merging far in the distance with the light blue of the sky. I sighed with pure happiness, my petty worries about our direction forgotten.

"I'd thought you'd like this," said Pieter, waving his hand. "It'll be much nicer than trying to make our way through crowded narrow streets. This road will take us directly to the castle." (A quick glance at my map verified this.)

The road curved around the city. The ground fell away to our right, forming a gently sloping cliff to the sea. The ancient wall of the city ran along the sea's edge, all the way to the castle. As did, much to my surprise, the slums of the city. Fragile-looking shanties had been built along the wall, looking out to sea, a few feet of grass and sand separating them from the water. I was astounded that such conditions could exist just a short distance from a tourist attraction and some of the oldest, loveliest homes in the city. Perhaps as it was outside the walls, it didn't matter. I looked questioningly up at Pieter, indicating the hovels below, but the only answer I received was a shrug of the shoulders.

We passed through the stone gates that marked the entrance to the castle, and into the wide green park that was El Morro's grounds. We walked along the tarred, two-lane drive that led at angles up to the castle, a low gray-stone structure pointing out to sea. The drive was lined on both sides with Australian pine trees, bent into graceful shapes by the constant sea winds. It was a peaceful, busy spot. Cars passed us continually, tourists strolled the close-cropped lawns, joggers circled the outskirts of the gently sloping park. We continued up the path, crossing a stone bridge before entering the main gate of the castle. We paused a minute to admire the eighteenth-century coat of arms placed centrally above the arch to the main entrance. We passed through a dark tunnel that opened onto a large triangular courtyard, its walls painted a dull gold while the arches and windows were outlined in white. There seemed to be some renovation work going on.

I started vaguely off across the yard, but Pieter pulled me to the right.

"First things first," he said, opening a door which I obediently stepped through. "You'll appreciate the tour a lot more if you know what you're looking at. And something of its history."

I opened my mouth to complain, but I promptly closed it again. Pieter seemed too serious. We suddenly were in a recently built museum, filled with artifacts and historical panoramas detailing the history of Castillo San Felipe de Morro, as the castle is properly called. The exhibits were arranged sequentially, so that one could follow the castle from its earliest beginnings (a tower built on the sea's edge in 1539) to its present-day renovations and excavations.

One historical panel caught my attention. In 1625 a Dutch fleet, under the command of General Bowdoin Hendrick, entered the harbor, captured the city of San Juan, and laid siege to El Morro. The Spanish finally drove off the invaders, although the Dutch burned the city as a farewell gesture. Thinking to amuse Pieter, I called him over to the sign. He appeared to be familiar with the incident.

"Oh yes. There's a monument outside, we passed it on our way in, dedicated to the memory of the leader of the Spanish, Don Juan de Something or Other, for valiant heroism displayed in the battle." Pieter paused to take a breath, looking around admiringly at the low vaulted walls. "This is an impressive fortress. Others tried to conquer it, including Sir Francis Drake. He defeated the Armada, but not El Morro."

I listened to Pieter with some surprise. He seemed almost proud of the Spanish who had successfully defended El Morro against foreign attackers, including his own ancestors. After examining gleaming suits of armor and deadly looking swords, we went back into the bright sunshine.

We had great fun scrambling over the many levels of the castle, walking along the parapets, poking our heads into each and every musty sentry box. Pieter seemed to know a great deal about the castle. Of El Polvorin, the arsenal—how it was built in 1783 with a slanted lead roof (so that bombs would roll down it). Of the different names the areas of the castle had—the Austria Bastion, the San Augustin Battery. He even knew that the lighthouse had been constructed by the Coast Guard in 1906. I accused him of studying up at night while I was asleep, but his blank look assured me that was not the case. I shrugged my shoulders, deciding I had wed a secretive eccentric, and listened to his next monologue.

As we left the top levels to explore the cellar, I excused myself to use the facilities, saying I would catch up with Pieter down below.

On my way back, I decided to buy some postcards to send to my family. There wasn't much of a selection, but I did find some of the suits of armor that I knew my brothers would enjoy. As the clerk rang up my purchase, I wandered over to the tiny, barred window set deep in the stone wall. It afforded a view of the very tip of El Morro. I could see the blue-green sea crash against the rocks. I could see the tourists taking pictures of each other standing on the wall. I could see Pieter, leaning casually against a massive black cannon, one hand jammed deep in his pocket, the other patting the iron. He seemed to be contemplating something. I fancied I could see his lips move as if he were reciting some epic verse to himself. Then he turned his head and I could see that he was talking to a squat, plump Puerto Rican clad in a baggy white suit. If Pieter was casual, his companion was not. Every few seconds the man would take his hat from his head, a bandanna from his pocket, mop his brow, and replace both hat and bandanna. I watched in fascination, wondering what on earth they could be talking about. Whatever could Pieter have to say to a man who looked a Graham Greene caricature?

"Señorita?" The clerk held my cards and change out patiently. I flushed, realizing he had been waiting for me, took my purchases, and hurried outside. I wanted to rejoin Pieter as quickly as possible.

A long, steep ramp (once a gun ramp) led to the lower level, with a narrow staircase on either side. It was so narrow, in fact, that the traffic was one-way. I waited impatiently, as some red-faced climbers struggled up. Then I clattered down the stone steps. At the bottom, I turned and bumped into someone who was in as much of a hurry as I. I moved back, smiling an apology. My smile froze. It was the very man Pieter had been talking to. He bowed slightly, never raising his eyes higher than my waist, before rushing up the stairs. I watched him for a while. He was very agile for a fat man. He smelled of cheap after-shave and even cheaper rum.

I found Pieter standing next to a huge artillery piece that was much more modern than the others. He turned as I called his name, smiling sunnily as the day.

"Pieter, who was that man?" I asked.

"What man, Gretel?" said Pieter.

"The one you were talking to. The fat one. I saw you when I was buying some postcards."

Pieter turned to look up where I was pointing. "Oh," he said, his eyes narrowing to dark slits. Then he turned back to me. He looked ingenuous, his eyes wide open and unclouded. "Oh," he repeated, smiling a little. "He was asking directions. I couldn't help him much." Pieter then called my attention to some historical detail. I paid scant attention. Pieter had lied to me. I was certain. He hadn't wanted me to know about his conversation with the fat nervous Puerto Rican. That was also certain.

*   *   *

That night, after dinner, Pieter seemed more restless than usual. When he suggested a tour of the gaming tables, I readily agreed, thinking him already bored by resort life.

The Normandie's casino was as tropically elegant as the rest of the hotel: oversized rattan furniture, tall dark-green palms in the corners, crisp straw matting underfoot. To reach it, we descended a wide sweeping thick-carpeted stairway, then passed through glistening glass doors held open by a portly uniformed attendant who bowed us through. Formal attire was obligatory and, although I saw a few wrenched-open collars and jacketless gamblers, most of the guests complied with the rule. At first glance it was a handsome crowd— men in their dark tuxedos or gleaming-white dinner jackets, the ladies in chiffon confections, stoles casually tossed over an arm or the back of a chair. I wished I had worn something other than a long cotton dress. A quick glance at Pieter, however, reassured me that he was the handsomest of all, the plain almost severe lines of the formally cut black suit he had worn at our wedding suited him better than any frilled shirt front or pleated cummerbund.

We sashayed through the three large rooms that comprised the main casino—Pieter leading, I following—surveying the various tables. I recognized most of the games (blackjack, craps, and the whirling roulette wheel); but, as I had no knowledge of the rules themselves, I soon tired of watching the tables. I took to watching the players themselves. What startled me most was their lack of emotion. Certainly, the male and female croupiers seemed impassive as they dealt the cards or spun the wheels. Yet, most of the players were equally expressionless, moving cards and chips around noiselessly, losing and winning with but the flicker of an eyelash. The exceptions, I soon understood, were the novices—the giggling girls who bet together (one dollar at a time); a young man trying to impress a voluptuous señorita. I decided I liked them the best, for they, at least, seemed to be enjoying themselves. The rest seemed grim.

"Well, which do you want to try first?" said Pieter of a sudden.

"What? Gamble?" It hadn't occurred to me. I had assumed we were bystanders.

"Of course," Pieter responded, his eyes racing across the room.

"But I never have. I don't like to gamble," I said.

"Everyone gambles when the stakes are right. Now," Pieter continued, "what shall it be?"

I realized that Pieter had set his mind on trying the casino for fun. I didn't want to disappoint him. It would just be for this once. It was our honeymoon. "Oh, I don't know. The roulette wheel, I guess."

"I knew you would choose that. A woman's game."

"It's the only one where I'll know what's going on," I laughed. "It seems the simplest."

"It's also the one where the odds favor the house the heaviest, but that's all right. I don't imagine you plan to gamble away your life savings," said Pieter.

"No indeed!" I said.

"Here, then. I'll stake you to ten dollars. After that you're on your own." Pieter settled me at one of the long, green felt-covered tables, then turned as if to leave.

"Aren't you staying?" I asked. It wasn't going to be nearly as much fun if I were alone.

"No. Well, all right. Just to get you started off right." Pieter stood behind my chair, his hands resting casually on its back.

Pieter did stay with me, and his presence was invaluable. He explained the various technicalities of the game: the split, the straight, what the split was; what each bet paid: low—even, square—eight to one, straight—thirty-five to one. Pieter even calculated in his head the amounts I could win if I was daring: $110 if I bet $10 on the street, $50 if I bet $10 on the quarter, and (the one Pieter urged me to bet) $350 if I bet $10 on the straight. Throughout it all, I smiled, placing my chips where Pieter pointed. But I steadfastly refused to bet such a grand sum as $10 all at once.

"Well, Gretel, the lure of the dice," Pieter said after an hour, jerking his head at a nearby craps table. He deposited a pile of plastic chips in front of me. "Don't spend it all in one place," he whispered as he left.

I sighed. Then, determined to make the best of it, I turned my attention to the game. I watched for a few turns of the wheel before placing my next bet. Then, when the bouncing ball had fallen into a red slot three more times, I placed one of my precious dollar chips onto the black. I held my breath as the dealer spun the wheel, not breathing until the ball had tumbled into a black slot. (Black pays even.) I smiled at the dealer as he slid another chip across. He ignored me. Oh well. I took that chip away, leaving the original. I decided to "let it ride." Black must be my lucky color. Alas. After two more such spins, the fickle ball went back to red, and my original chip was swept away. I watched the game some more, learning which bets made more money consistently (as Pieter had tried to teach me), which combinations turned up most often, and which players made the most money. I bet cautiously, but consistently, never repeating myself more than twice, frequently covering myself by betting several combinations ("odd-red-low" or "even-black-high") at the same time. At the end of another hour, I had doubled my original stake of chips—$20. (My elation was tempered somewhat by the knowledge that if I had won every bet I had made, I would have ended up with five times the amount.) Nonetheless, I had had enough. I began to look around for Pieter, for surely he, too, would be ready to leave.

I found him at the noisiest, smallest craps table. His dark head bobbed above the rest of the throng. There were only men here, whereas women dominated the blackjack and roulette games. Pieter was not, as I had guessed he would be, just having fun. No, he was in the very thick of things. I squeezed through the crowd to stand next to the table at the opposite end from Pieter. I was mostly puzzled, but a little frightened by what I saw. Pieter was the one rolling the dice, making an elaborate production of every throw. First, he blew on them, cradling them in his long fingers, then he shook them, tossing them from hand to hand as if deciding which hand he was going to throw with. Then he gracefully drew back his right hand, and with a movement as exquisite and as sure as that of any pitcher he threw the dice over the table. Over and over they tumbled, until they bounced against the far edge and ricocheted to a stop. All eyes had been on the dice. All hands had been motionless. The only sound heard was a barely breathed encouragement. But now, the crowded table burst into activity. The dice were raked in with a long thin stick and handed back to Pieter. Chips were alternately raked in and shoveled back out. The players moved their chips about on the table, adding or subtracting from their piles. Pieter performed again.

It was on his second throw that I spied the stacks of chips in front of Pieter—multicolored stacks that seemed enormous. If he saw me, he took no notice, but I unabashedly stared at him. This was a Pieter I didn't know. The hooded eyes, the finely drawn mouth, all had taken on a menacing appearance. The face had set into hard lines, only one cheek muscle twitched faintly to show his concentration. Pieter's eyes were fixed on the dice that tumbled and fell, and the black spots they showed. He scarcely noticed the chips, moving them automatically with his left hand while he cradled the dice with his right. I felt sudden tears start to my eyes. But why was I upset? Pieter was winning.

I walked away. I needed to think, to relax. Perhaps it was just the smoke and the din that bothered me. There was a row of soft armchairs on one side of the room. I moved over to sit and wait for Pieter. A waiter silently appeared to take my order. Suddenly famished, I ordered a ham sandwich and coffee. But when the food came, I couldn't eat it. I stared down at the sandwich morosely, idly picking at the soft white bread with my fingers. I felt sorry for myself.

"Gretel."

I started from the chair to find Pieter bending over me. "I guess I was daydreaming," I said, somewhat embarrassed as I picked the sandwich from the floor. I realized that I had been asleep. Fortunately, I had put the coffee to one side. I looked at my watch. It was three in the morning!

"I'm sorry I deserted you." Pieter sank wearily into a chair beside mine. "I'm afraid I got carried away. It's been a problem with me when I'm playing a game."

I thought "playing" too mild a word for Pieter's attitude toward gambling, but I was too sleepy to say so. Besides, it was his honeymoon, too. The Pieter that sat beside me now was the Pieter I knew, the Pieter I loved.

"Can you forgive me?" he asked, wrinkling his brow in mock anxiousness.

"Of course," I said softly. I was just glad to have him back at my side. "I didn't realize how much you enjoyed this. I was watching you at the tables."

Pieter frowned, looking away. "It's something that I tend to be very good at." Pieter raised his hands, dropping a shower of chips into my lap.

"My goodness!" I said. "This makes my winnings silly in comparison. Do you always win this much?"

"No. Only when the conditions are right. The right location, the right"—he leaned to kiss me on the nose—"people in the room. Dear Gretel, you must be exhausted. Let's cash in our chips, and get to bed."

*   *   *

Despite Pieter's seeming contrition, our next night in San Juan was also spent in the Normandie's casino. Again, Pieter won dramatically. I wanted to complain, but felt I shouldn't. Everyone has at least one vice, I reasoned, and Pieter's is gambling. It could be worse, I told myself, he could be losing each time.

Pieter again played craps. It was up to me to amuse myself as best I could, for, once Pieter became involved in his game, he was oblivious to all else. Again, I sat at the roulette wheel—placing my bets cautiously, sometimes winning, sometimes losing. It didn't really matter to me. Again, I wandered the rooms of the casino, observing the people who gambled. I soon realized that the veneer of glamour offered by the casino was just that—a veneer. The eyes of the beautifully coifed generally middle-aged women who haunted the blackjack tables were dead. They numbly watched the cards flip and turn over, slide out across the green felt only to be pulled back. The players at the slot machines were the saddest. They stood in front of the machines for hours, a paper cup filled with quarters clutched tightly in one hand, while with the other they pulled the machine handle like machines themselves. Barely had one turn been completed before the next was started. Once or twice I saw someone hit the jackpot. They calmly scooped the quarters up and methodically returned them to the machine one by one. These people puzzled me. I couldn't understand why they gambled. Least of all could I understand my own husband's yen.

The next night we made a third visit to the casino. As usual, I sat at the roulette wheel, making my small bets. As usual, I ambled around the other tables, watching the other gamblers. As usual, I ended up at Pieter's table. But I discovered I couldn't watch him. It was too—I hated to use the word, but could find no other—terrible. Melodramatic as it sounded, Pieter became another person when he rolled the dice. I didn't know why. Pieter had said everyone gambled if the stakes were right, if they were important enough. But what was so important here to make Pieter spend night after night at the craps table. And on our honeymoon!

I turned away. I was tired and had a slight headache from being out in the sun all day, a headache that was growing steadily worse. I decided to leave. I looked back at Pieter, but I didn't disturb him. He was totally engrossed. Gamblers are said to be notoriously superstitious, and I didn't want to be held responsible for breaking his concentration and thus his winning streak.

So I returned to our room alone. I slipped off the brown silk-chiffon dress Pieter had bought for me that morning. It fell weightlessly to the floor. I left it there. I slipped into bed, the smooth fresh sheets cool against my skin. I stretched luxuriantly into the bed's comfort, enjoying the view through the french windows—I had not drawn the curtains—the silvery moon shone over the now black sea, an occasional feathery wisp of a cloud straying over its gold-white surface. I fell asleep, wishing Pieter beside me.

The door burst open, shattering the peace of the room. Pieter rushed into the room, gathered me up roughly into his arms. I groggily protested, but I quickly stopped. Pieter was murmuring over and over how panic-stricken he had become when he had realized I wasn't in the casino, how a thousand fearful thoughts had run through his mind, how he had raced up to our room (not waiting for the picturesque but tediously slow elevator) to make sure I was safe. I was flattered, but thought his concern excessive. I told him so.

"I should never forgive myself if something happened to you," Pieter answered, stroking my hair.

"But what could have happened?" I laughed.

"Oh," Pieter paused, then grinned boyishly. "Oh, you could have been captured by pirates and held for a king's ransom because your father is really the King of New York!"

"Oh, you silly!" I laughed, kissing him on the nose.

"Perhaps I am, but I did wonder where you had got off to," Pieter said, the boyish grin gone. "Promise you will always tell me where you're going."

"But I didn't want to bother you."

"You can't ever bother me. Gretel, I'm serious. Promise me to always let me know where you are," said Pieter.

"I promise," I said.

* * *

The next day, after lunch, Pieter suggested we tour San Juan's other fortress: Castillo San Cristobal. This time, we took a taxi, which deposited us in a small parking lot at the foot of the long curving ramp that led into the fort. Once again, Pieter astounded me with his knowledge of Puerto Rican history.

Begun in 1634, San Cristobal's purpose was to defend the city from land attacks and to protect the north coast, along which it was built. The building of the castle was part of a project to surround the city with walls. The English and Dutch attacks had shown the need for total defense of the city. El Morro guarded the harbor entrance only. The San Cristobal fort was finished in 1783, and since then had played a large role in the defense of San Juan from would-be invaders—especially in 1797, when its powerful artillery had successfully controlled the eastern approaches to the city, driving off the British once again.

Its artillery was also famous. There was a huge plaque commemorating the firing of the first shot of the Spanish-American War in Puerto Rico. That first shot had been fired at an American battleship, just outside the harbor, under the command of Admiral William Thomas Sampson. Pieter seemed to find all that amusing. He chuckled as he recounted the details.

"It was a moment of glory for Puerto Rico," he explained. "How many times since then, I wonder, have Puerto Ricans wanted to fire on the American empire."

"What?" Pieter never ceased to amaze me.

"Oh, I was just being fanciful. Actually the great majority of Puerto Ricans are content to remain a U. S. Commonwealth. Ah, now here's something interesting." Pieter moved on to another historical sign.

There were many other people roaming the thick castle walls that afternoon, mostly tourists like ourselves. But I soon became aware of one man who stood leaning casually against a parapet. There was nothing casual in the way he watched us. And he was watching us, I was certain of it. He was a Puerto Rican, and wore a broad-brimmed straw hat against the sun. It also threw his face into shadow. I began to think (I lived in New York City, after all) that he was a thief and was sizing us up. I clutched my purse tightly to me, and thought of calling Pieter's attention to the man. But then, the man took a bandanna from his pocket. Pushing back his hat, he mopped his brow before returning the bandanna to his pocket. I gasped, staring at him openly. I was sure it was the man I had seen at El Morro, the man Pieter had denied talking to. Pieter had left my side to admire the sea view, a few feet away. Pieter stood between me and the man, within speaking distance of us both. As I came up to Pieter, I saw him glance flickeringly at me. Then he gave a slight shake of his head, raising his hand as though in a warning. Almost immediately, the man in the hat turned away. Pieter turned to me, looking as though nothing unusual had occurred.

"Who was that man?" I demanded immediately. "You seem to know him."

"Who? What man?" Pieter asked. In answer, I turned to point. The man had disappeared.

"He was just here," I said, my voice rising nervously. "He was wearing a hat. He was watching us."

"Perhaps your dark tan becomes you." Pieter tucked my hand into his, patting it as he did so. "No, I certainly didn't notice anyone," he said firmly. I started to tell him that I had seen the man before, but Pieter put his finger on my lips. "How about a long cool drink before starting back to the hotel?"

A few minutes later, I was sitting on a tall stool at the bar of a quaint, dimly lit restaurant, sipping a chocolate frost—a wonderful concoction made of cream, ice, chocolate, and coffee-flavored liqueurs. As I lost myself in it, I decided I was forcing my opinion. They had been two innocent, quite different men.

*　*　*

That night at the casino, I decided to try my hand at blackjack instead of my usual roulette. I wandered through the rooms, looking over the tables and the dealers, trying to find one that wasn't too intimidating. I finally chose one that was on the far side of the smallest room in the casino, as far removed from where Pieter was as it was possible to be. It was almost quiet here. The dealer was a pudgy man in his late forties who looked fatherly, although his surprisingly slim fingers moved with lightning speed. I stood to one side —not wanting to get too close and annoy the other players—while I waited for a chair to become vacant.

There were some large potted palms against the wall, and as I stood there, they must have covered me, for all of a sudden Pieter was standing not five feet away. He was talking to a man whose back was to me, but Pieter faced me fully. I smiled at him and half raised my arm to wave. He didn't see me. I let my arm drop back to my side. I decided I didn't want Pieter to notice me. As he alternately talked and listened, his face wore the same expression it did when he gambled, a severe look I did not want turned on me. Who could he be talking to, I wondered? To my knowledge he knew no one in San Juan.

A spot at the blackjack table opened up, but still I did not move. The longer I watched Pieter, the more certain I became that I didn't want him to see me. Then, at last, the conversation was over and Pieter walked away without shaking the man's hand. It was safe for me to emerge now. As I came out from my hiding place, my mind was on Pieter and not my direction. I walked headlong into Pieter's acquaintance—if that's what he was. He didn't seem to recognize me, and after a muttered apology, he continued on his way. I had certainly recognized him.

As I watched the man Pieter had been talking to disappear through a side door, I knew I had not been wrong this afternoon. Nor had I been confused. The man that Pieter had talked to at El Morro, the man I had seen at San Cristobal, and the man I had just bumped into were all the same person. He had arranged a meeting here in the casino with Pieter so that they could talk unnoticed. Talk about what? I asked myself. It was disturbing and very mysterious. I changed my mind about investigating the mysteries of blackjack. I had a mystery of my own to mull over. Shivering slightly, I went to my favorite armchair in the lounge to sit and wait for Pieter.

I did not have long to wait. Pieter came over almost as soon as I had sat down. Once again his "gambling face" had disappeared, and he was smiling warmly at me. He pulled me to my feet, kissing me lightly on the forehead as he did so. My doubts of a few moments before began to seem silly as I returned his smile.

"Had enough?" he queried as we went to the cashier's window.

"Yes. I'm afraid I don't enjoy the casino as much as you do."

"I meant San Juan."

"Oh. Well. I guess so. We've seen most everything, haven't we?"

"We have indeed."

"But I'm not ready to return to cold weather."

"Neither am I. I'm suggesting we merely shift westward, to Mayaguez," said Pieter.

"Mayaguez?"

"Mayaguez. It's a large, lovely city on the west coast. We'll rent a car and drive there tomorrow morning. It'll make a nice change."

"But"—we were in the elevator now and I lowered my voice—"when did you decide all this? And how do you know about Mayaguez?"

"I decided just now. The existence of Mayaguez is not exactly a Puerto Rican state secret." Pieter unlocked the door to our room and ushered me inside. "Now, sit on the bed and study the map and see where we're going. I'll order us a snack." Pieter went to the phone while I did as he told me. But my mind was on other things. Should I embarrass him by telling him I'd discovered his lies? No, it seemed the wrong time. Pieter was being sweet and loving. It could be innocent after all. Pieter was my husband, but, as an individual, he did deserve to have his own affairs and keep his own counsel. It hadn't been a woman he was meeting on the sly, I thought, amused at my own sly logic. I opened the map to find Mayaguez, Puerto Rico.

4

Casa Flor

The sky seaward was overcast the next morning at seven when I slipped quietly from bed, leaving Pieter to snore softly without me, and tiptoed out to our little terrace. I'd hoped to catch some last rays before we left, but there seemed no hope. What sun was left was quickly disappearing into thickening haze as huge cumulus clouds, black and ominous, closed in from the north. I took that as a good omen. Otherwise, I should have regretted leaving a sunny beach for a stuffy car. I contented myself with staring at the darkening sea below, thinking over the past week's happenings, coming to this happy conclusion: even with its few mysterious uncertainties, my life had vastly improved since I became Mrs. Pieter Van der Hoek.

Pieter reluctantly rose at nine, demanding in mock anger to know whose idea this venture was. I reminded him it was his. "That figures," he muttered, going off to wake up under a hot, stinging shower. It was nearly ten when we finally ate breakfast. I was ravenous. I was also anxious to be on our way. Without sun, beach resorts quickly became tiresome. As we ate on the hotel's wide terrace overlooking the beach, we chuckled at the guests below us—lying in rows along the beach, coated with tanning lotion even though the sky threatened rain at any moment. I decided that I'd had enough of beach life; I was ready for more adventure.

I finished spooning up my papaya while Pieter checked us out of the Normandie. Together, we strolled to the parking lot where, after some searching, we located our rented car—a bright red compact. Pieter put our luggage in the trunk and walked around to the passenger's side. I watched him in surprise.

"You *do* drive," Pieter said, bending to open the door.

"Of course, I do," I retorted.

"Well?" Pieter nodded at the driver's seat.

"I enjoy driving, but, well, it's just that I haven't driven very much since I moved into New York City. There's been no need," I said. I refused to approach the car, continuing to remain where I was.

"Then you'll do very well." Pieter came over to where I stood and ushered me gently, but firmly, into the driver's seat. He then shut the door and went back to the other side. "Besides," he continued, shutting his door and fastening his seat belt, "I don't like to drive."

Pieter opened up the glove compartment, took out the car manual, and proceeded to read through it aloud as if we were about to take off in a jet plane. He did it so methodically that I relaxed and let him finish without protest.

"What are you, our navigator?" I asked, half-teasing, half-annoyed.

"I just want to make sure we know what we're doing," Pieter answered.

"All right," I said, turning the key in the ignition. "But I don't want any criticism of the way I drive."

"Don't worry. I won't be a back-seat driver," Pieter promised solemnly, although the corner of his mouth twitched suspiciously.

Truth to tell, it soon became apparent that I was a better driver than Pieter was navigator. After familiarizing myself with the car's controls, I maneuvered us out of the parking lot and onto the main highway with a minimum of difficulty. Soon we were on the modern expressway, speeding through town, watching for the exit Pieter had designated as ours. Twenty minutes passed, and I began to think we had made a mistake. Ten more minutes and Pieter agreed we should turn around. We went speeding back toward town. We passed the Normandie, circled onto the highway once more, and this time exited correctly.

"It was the rental agent's fault," Pieter said as I breathed a sigh of relief. "She distinctly said *not* to take the exit marked 'Bayamon.'"

"We're not," I replied, pointing to the left. The route to Bayamon was clearly marked to our left. We continued straight on the road heading due south.

"Well, at least you got a chance to see more of San Juan," Pieter replied cheerfully.

Pieter was not so cheerful a half hour later when I made another U-turn, and drove through a medical complex before returning to the highway. But I ignored his sputterings. We hadn't *really* been lost, and if Pieter had been a proper navigator—his chosen role, I gently reminded him—it wouldn't have happened. Serendipitous detours were all part of the fun and excitement of travel.

In spite of ourselves, we managed to find the superhighway that ran from San Juan south to Ponce on the opposite coast. The four-lane highway that cut through the mountains had recently been completed—in our honor, Pieter jokingly maintained. Eventually all the major cities of Puerto Rico would be connected, greatly reducing the travel time throughout the mountainous island.

And, in spite of myself, I began to relax about the driving itself, although it would be some hours and many miles before I became used to being passed on both the left and the right, usually at the same time. Even though I went no slower than the speed limit. I soon formed a low opinion of the—to my mind—reckless Puerto Rican drivers.

As we drove across the irregular oval that is Puerto Rico's shape, I soon realized that the urban sprawl of San Juan is atypical of the island's culture. Small towns and clusters of shacks spotted and clung to the mountains—one-room, dirt-floored hovels I was certain had no sanitary facilities. It was amazing to me that this could exist less than an hour's drive from the city. I began to realize why so many Puerto Ricans had emigrated to New York City. Even the poorest housing the city had to offer them would have had electricity and hot and cold running water. But my God, I thought. It was so beautiful here. How could anyone bear to leave? If the choice were mine, I thought confidently, I would rather be poor in a warm sunny country than poor in a strange cold city where no one spoke my language. I said as much to Pieter.

"You're right, and many do remain. Or return here after a short time. But I don't think you realize just how poor this country is, Gretel. The unemployment rate here is forty-five per cent, while the cost of living is twenty-five per cent higher in Puerto Rico than in any state in the United States. Seventy per cent of the population is on food stamps. Puerto Rico," Pieter continued, drawing a deep breath, "is a perfect example of the colonization process gone wrongheaded. It both produces for and buys from the United States, an impossible situation. Puerto Rico cannot begin to develop its own economy."

"Surely there's a way to reverse the damage done?" I asked while negotiating a particularly nasty curve. A black sedan was tailgating impatiently.

"Once Puerto Rico had a great potential—in its agriculture. Nowhere else was there such a combination of climate, arability, and land structure."

"Then the land *can* be developed?" The black car finally pulled around me. I relaxed.

"No. Pollution has made that impossible. The factories and refineries have destroyed too many resources. One third of the oil brought from the Middle East is refined here in Puerto Rico. It is the largest producer of pharmaceutical goods in the world. And, it's the fifth largest consumer of American goods. Fairly staggering for an island of three million. When you consider all this, it's not surprising that some things—clean air, clean water, arable land—have to be sacrificed. Puerto Rico is more a machine than an island."

Throughout his recital, Pieter's voice had remained cold and unemotional, as though he were reciting a laundry list, not speaking of a Great American Tragedy. I wished I could have looked at his face, but we were climbing the mountains of central Puerto Rico now, and the driving took all my concentration as the road curved through the steep hills. The little car provided by the rental agency, although certainly adequate, was not very powerful. Even with my foot pushing the accelerator all the way to the floor, it could only maintain a steady chug-chugging. I winced every time another car came up behind us.

Nor could I enjoy the passing scenery, which from the few glimpses I had stolen I knew to be spectacular. Yet, what Pieter had just told me had taken some of the pleasure from the tropical beauty, and so I did not suggest we stop.

Pieter must have sensed this, for he suddenly cut short his litany of the trials and tribulations of Puerto Rico, saying:

"Gretel, I've warned you not to let me do this. It's not fair to you. Or to me, either. We're on our honeymoon. We're on vacation. We're not sociologists collecting research data. I don't know why I ran off at the mouth like that. I get started and then I can't stop. It's your duty," he added, turning toward me, "as my loving wife, to stop me. It's no fun having a bore for a husband."

"Don't worry," I chuckled. "If you ever do bore me, I'll let you know. But I was interested in what you were saying. I had no idea of what Puerto Rico is like, of its history. I'm glad you're telling me. But is there truly nothing to be done?"

"Well, there are those that think independence is the answer. But the problem there is, of course, will Puerto Rico be able to survive as an independent country? It was the tax advantages that brought the big corporations—and their jobs—to Puerto Rico after the war. The tax benefits were part of Operation Bootstrap, which has become the backbone of Puerto Rican economy. A lot of people are doubtful about Puerto Rico's future if she becomes an independent country."

"What do you think?"

"Oh, I'm not sure." Pieter shrugged and turned back to the window. "But there's a lot to be said for the old argument that you'll never know unless you do it. I . . ."

But I didn't let him finish. We had climbed to the top of the tallest mountain—2,500 feet—and were beginning our descent to the southern coast. The view in front of us (which even the driver could enjoy completely) was breath-taking. The sky above us was still cloudy, but to the south and west the clouds were breaking up and I could see the rays of sunshine stretching to the sea. It was as though we were heading for a golden land.

The drive became truly enjoyable. The car was more than content to be traveling downhill. I shared its pleasure. As we approached Ponce, we had glimpses of the sea, sparkling to our left. But alas! It was at Ponce that the highway ended. We had to turn off onto a two-lane road.

It was on this and the other back roads that I truly appreciated the (although ordinary by American standards) expressway. I quickly got a taste of what traveling in Puerto Rico must have been like before it was built (and what it unfortunately was still like in many areas). The route we had to follow was badly marked, frequently with the wrong route number; it went where our map said it didn't, and it wasn't there when our map said it was. The latter quickly became apparent an hour out of Ponce, when the road suddenly and abruptly terminated in an empty cane field. There had been no hint that this would happen; in fact, there was a speed-limit sign not ten feet from the edge of the highway. I glared at Pieter as I swung into a harsh U-turn. "Some navigator," I muttered under my breath.

"So, the map's a bit optimistic," said Pieter. "*It* says there's a road." He thrust the much-folded map under my nose. There was indeed a red line. A broken red line. I pointed this out to him.

"Now we know what that means," he cheerfully replied. "A road that isn't there."

"Well, let's aim for the roads that *are* there."

We made several more U-turns, though we took them in our stride, and there was one long nasty uphill stretch that was all curves and blind turns. I positively breathed a long loud sigh of relief when we passed the sign welcoming us to Mayaguez. It had been only three and a half hours since we had set off from San Juan, but because of the challenges of the drive, and the fact that I was unaccustomed to being behind the wheel of a car (much less a strange car), it had seemed twice as long. My arms and neck ached with the effort of concentrating on the road. It had been a beautiful, but scary drive. And while I envied the other drivers their daring as they whizzed about the hairpin curves, ignoring the sheer cliffs just below, I would have been much happier without them there, showing me up. Every time I had begun to feel the least bit confident about driving, and dared to sneak a look at the scenery, another car had swooshed by, throwing me off balance. My fingers were stiff from gripping the wheel too hard.

"So, where's the hotel?" I asked Pieter as we drove through the town, which so far seemed unremarkable. "I can't wait to dive into the swimming pool."

"We're staying at the Hilton," Pieter replied, consulting the little map the rental agency had given us. "And it should be coming up on the right any time now. It's right off Route Two on the north side of town."

"That map's been wrong before," I muttered as we continued driving without sighting a sign for the Hilton. "There. We have now driven through the entire town. Now what?"

"I remember seeing a large villa-type building in the hills, that was probably the hotel. I guess we'll have to . . ."

"I know," I interrupted, turning up into a side road. "We'll have to turn around." We turned around, and after a few more twistings and turnings we came to the Mayaguez Hilton. "You know," I said, as I pulled into a parking space, "there were times that I was certain we'd never arrive."

"But we did, and you did a marvelous job of getting us here," Pieter replied, patting me on the shoulder.

"Pity I can't say the same for your navigation," I said, quickly adding, "Only kidding." Pieter glared in mock anger. "Now, let's check in and go swimming. I feel as though I've melted into the seat!"

The hotel was much smaller than the ones in San Juan. Only fifty rooms to the Normandie's 150. It seemed more of a country club than a resort hotel. It was set high in the lush tropical hills overlooking the city and the harbor. It was blissfully, peacefully quiet, and our room had a perfect view of the ocean.

"Oh, Pieter," I sighed happily later as we splashed in the pool, "this is so lovely, I wish we had come here straightaway. This is what all of Puerto Rico should look like—green, lush, oh! Look! There's a lizard scuttling into the grass."

"You sure it's not too quiet? You won't get bored and feel lonely?" Pieter asked.

"You're all the entertainment and company I need," I replied. "Besides, honeymooners are meant to be alone in romantic hideaways. This certainly is that. Thank you for bringing me here."

"At your service, Mrs. Van der Hoek," Pieter responded, giving me a watery kiss.

We spent a quiet evening, dining in the hotel on freshly caught lobster, and then walking around the grounds with only the moon to light our way. There was no trace now of the "other" Pieter—the hard-eyed Pieter I had glimpsed at the gaming tables in San Juan. It was as though he had never existed. I found myself thinking that perhaps I had overdramatized Pieter's gambling fever; that, because I was puzzled and caught off guard, I had made more of it than it deserved. My wifely concerns seemed silly here in this tropical paradise. There was certainly nothing to fear from a man who clasped me as tightly in his arms and kissed my lips as tenderly as Pieter was doing now.

* * *

As usual, I awoke before Pieter. After surveying the morning dew steaming up in the already strong sunshine, I decided to go for an early morning swim. At that hour, I had the pool to myself, and I gloried in it. I could almost believe that the hotel was here solely for my pleasure, and daydreamed about what it would be like to live like this always—completely happy and secure, spoiled by beauty and luxury. I suppose, I reminded myself, that one could become bored. But wouldn't I love to have the chance, I chuckled as I pulled myself out of the pool.

"Well, you certainly sound cheerful this morning," said Pieter. "I had no idea I was getting a mermaid for a wife."

I shook the water out of my eyes to find Pieter squatting beside me. "Good morning," I said. "I hope you don't mind that I slipped away for an early swim, but it's such a gorgeous morning, I couldn't resist. It's wonderful. Join me."

"No thanks," said Pieter, holding out a towel. "I don't believe in swimming on an empty stomach. I'm famished."

"So am I." I took the towel from him, rubbing myself vigorously. My whole body tingled, and I couldn't remember when I had ever felt so alive. I slipped into my beach dress and sandals, twisted my hair into a knot at the nape of my neck. Then Pieter and I walked hand-in-hand to the veranda tables.

"Now," said Pieter, buttering a piece of toast. "We have to decide what to do with the day."

"Sun. Swim. Then some more sunning and more swimming," I answered gaily.

"Well, yes, but I can't have my wife getting too lazy, can I?"

"There is no such thing as too lazy."

"Hmmm. Well, you can sun and swim all morning, but I thought that it would be nice to do some exploring this afternoon. See the sights of Mayaguez and all that."

"Oh, Pieter, I really don't want to do any driving today," I began, but Pieter held up his hand.

"Not to worry," he said cheerfully. "I shall pilot. All you'll have to do is admire the sights."

"There's a lot to admire from poolside."

"You'll see much more interesting things during our drive," Pieter answered firmly. "Now, go have another swim and then we'll be off. You'll enjoy yourself, I promise you."

* * *

An hour and a half later, we were in the car. Pieter drove confidently, without hesitation, as though he knew exactly where he was going—although I was certain that was impossible. We drove north from Mayaguez, following the twisting side roads of a residential district which I guessed to be an upper-class suburb no more than a half hour from the center of town. It was lovely here, the tropical growth was luxurious and hid many of the homes we passed, offering only tantalizing glimpses of white and pastel stucco walls and elaborate grillwork. How wonderful to live here, I thought again, to be in the middle of a beautiful jungle of flowers, with nothing more ferocious than a quick-moving lizard to share it with. I was just wondering what the homes themselves were like when suddenly Pieter swung the car into what at first I assumed was a public road, but what I quickly realized was a private driveway. A black iron-grillwork gate framed the entrance; the words "Casa Flor" were intertwined into a delicate floral pattern.

"I would have thought you had had enough of U-turns after yesterday," I said, my chuckles turning into a squeal of surprise. Pieter wasn't turning around, he was driving steadily ahead. "What are you doing?" I asked, somewhat alarmed. "We can't go through here. This is private property."

"I can safely assure you that we won't be arrested for trespassing," Pieter answered, one side of his mouth drawn up into a crooked grin. There was a suspicious twinkle in his eye.

"That's all very well and good, but why are we here? Do you know the people who live here? Is this a museum or something and not a home? Where *are* we going? Where are you taking me? I do wish you'd stop smiling like that and tell me!"

"Typical, always asking questions. Really, Gretel, you disappoint me."

I was about to retort angrily, but a glance at Pieter told me he was baiting me. He was now smiling broadly. "Oh, you're impossible," I said. "All right, have your little mystery if it makes you happy. You men. You'll do anything to feel superior."

I would have died rather than admit it now, but I was desperately curious as to where we were going. It was such a beautiful place, the drive wound through banks of hibiscus, trimmed to form colorful hedges. The brilliant green lawn beyond was meticulously manicured. I saw two straw-hatted men pushing lawn mowers. Obviously the grounds were constantly cared for, they had to be to look this perfect. In this humid heat, even one day's neglect could mean inches of unruly tropical growth. I began to think that indeed this was some sort of public park when Pieter deftly maneuvered the car around one more turn, bringing the car to a stop with a flourish that sent gravel flying in all directions.

We were parked in front of a private home. It was not large, but it was impressively designed. A wide row of stone steps led from the drive to its ornate front door. Pieter bounded from the car and came over to my side, opening the door for me. I sat motionless.

"Well, come on, Gretel," he said impatiently, taking my arm and pulling me out of the car. He then closed the door and directed me, with surprising urgency, toward the steps. I was now even more mystified, but remembering Pieter's teasing remarks, I asked no questions and followed willingly enough. Pieter must know what he's doing, I thought. At least I hope he does, I added to myself as we trotted quickly up the steps. My high-heeled sandals clattered noisily against the stone.

A large veranda circled the house, encased in the by now familiar black grillwork which served double duty in Puerto Rico—it allowed air and light inside, providing security all the while. A gleaming brass bell hung next to the door. Pieter rang it twice, briefly but insistently. I felt the beginnings of a blush creep up my neck. What would these people think of us? I was soon to find out. Within seconds, a woman silently appeared on the terrace, gliding toward us gracefully.

She was tiny. I could not guess her age. The long hair pulled tightly back into a braided coil was jet black. Her olive-skinned face was unlined. Then she came out into the light, shading her eyes to look up at us, and her face broke into a thousand tiny lines as she smiled at Pieter. She threw her arms about his waist, and began babbling in Spanish so rapidly that I could not make sense of what she was saying. She seemed to be alternately scolding and praising Pieter, and he endured her verbal torrent with a tolerant smile. Finally he spoke.

"Enough, *basta*, Maria. My Spanish is not what it should be. Besides, there's someone you should meet. Maria, may I present Gretel Drew Van der Hoek, my wife."

Pieter's announcement caused another spate of words to emerge, but this time I was included in the hugging and the admonishments. Then, sighing deeply but happily, the little woman turned to lead us inside the house. Too startled to ask what was happening to us, I stumbled after her, grateful for the reassuring hand Pieter had slipped into mine.

The house was bright and airy; all the rooms opened in some way onto the terrace. The walls were white, with little to decorate them. What furniture there was was bright, modern, and—even to my unpracticed eye—expensive. I was looking about so much that I didn't realize it when our little procession came to a halt. I bumped into Pieter unceremoniously. When I looked up, I saw that we had entered a cozy, white-walled oval-shaped room in the center of the house, lit gloriously by a skylight framed by plants. A white couch filled one side of the room. Bright orange and red pillows were scattered over it and in the exact center sat a striking-looking woman dressed in emerald green, a large white flower tucked into her glistening blue-black hair her only ornament. Her complexion was creamily pale, her ringless fingers long and tapering, her head was tilted gracefully upon a long swan's neck. I guessed her to be in her early fifties, though she could easily pass for forty. She was one of the most elegant women I had ever seen.

I suddenly realized that I had been staring, and quickly looked up at Pieter, who looked back at me with thinly disguised amusement. Then, clearing his throat self-importantly, he said:

"Gretel, I should like to introduce you. Gretel, this is my mother, Isobel Van der Hoek."

I'm afraid that my mouth dropped open. I know I felt the impact of Pieter's words physically. His mother! Anger crowded out surprise. How dare he do this to me! I was ready to die from embarrassment and longed to run from the room, from the house, from Puerto Rico if that were possible. Pieter just stood there.

"I fear that my son has behaved very badly, Gretel," said Isobel Van der Hoek. "But he has always enjoyed making his little surprises." She rose from the couch and came over to me, taking both of my hands in hers and pressing her cool cheek against mine. The scent of gardenia wafted toward me. "Welcome to Casa Flor, my dear. Come and sit with me and tell me everything. Pieter, of course, has told me nothing. Maria." She turned to address the little woman who stood by the door wiping her eyes dramatically on the corner of her snowy white apron. "Maria, Pieter and Gretel would like some refreshment." Maria slipped from the room.

"Maria was Pieter's nurse when he was small," Isobel explained. "She returned to Puerto Rico with me. So she hasn't seen Pieter very often." Isobel spoke excellent English, only slightly but charmingly accented. I was enchanted with how she spoke my name. I had never thought it attractive, but upon her lips, it seemed musical.

We sat and chatted for an hour. As usual, I was uncomfortable speaking about myself, but I soon spoke easily, prompted by Isobel's genuine interest. I found myself opening up to my new mother-in-law as if I had known and loved her all my life. Pieter had withdrawn so silently that I had not even noticed. When I commented on his disappearance, Isobel said it was a tactical maneuver so that we could become better acquainted.

"How long has it been since you left New York?" I asked when I felt as though I had exhausted my own history. An hour earlier, I would not have dared to pry, but emboldened by Isobel's warmth—and Maria's excellent daiquiris—it seemed a natural question.

"Oh, many many years," Isobel said, smiling down at the floor through the smoke of her freshly lit cigarette. It was her fifth since we had started talking. Perhaps, I thought, she, too, was nervous. She continued speaking after a slight pause. "Pieter was still a little boy, although already very independent of course. I had no fears about him. A survivor is my Pieter."

"But Dirk was a baby," I said quietly to myself, trying to decide if Isobel was being complimentary or not to Pieter.

"I'm sorry, what did you say?" Isobel said, stubbing her half-smoked cigarette out awkwardly.

"Dirk. Pieter's younger brother. He was very young at the time of your divorce." I suddenly felt foolish.

"Oh yes. Of course. Yes, *very* young. It was my one regret. Perhaps, if Nicholas and I had . . ." Her voice drifted off. "But then"—she smiled brittlely and lit another cigarette—"'The saddest words of tongue or pen.'" She laughed. "You must forgive me, Gretel, your coming here has thrust me back into the past. No, no," she added swiftly, "it's not your fault by any means. There are many good things in the past worth the remembering." She paused again, adding, "Do you like the house?"

"I've only seen it once," I replied and I recounted the story of my one and only visit to Pieter's home.

"And you've never been inside the house?" Isobel asked, laughing when I shook my head. "Oh, Pieter is naughty. Much like his father. It's another Van der Hoek tradition. The bride never crosses the threshold until she is a bride. I'm a believer in traditions, but that was one that annoyed me. I can't bear not to know where I'm going. It is a lovely house. You'll enjoy living there."

"It seems a very romantic place," I said. So Pieter had told me the truth about that custom. I couldn't wait to tell that to Melissa!

"Oh yes, that it is. I was very happy there, in the beginning."

"What happened between you and Pieter's father, that is, if you don't mind my asking?"

"No, Gretel, I don't. For if Pieter is anything like his father, he's told you little or nothing about his early life. Though you've probably had your fill of ancestral stories! I thought so."

"He's always saying there's not much to tell," I admitted.

"And then will go on for hours about the old Van der Hoek ghosts," said Isobel, shaking her head. "Well, with Nicholas and myself, it was a mistake. Pure and simple. My family had been against it from the start. They didn't approve of their only daughter marrying off this island. I had gone to New York to be educated. It was in my senior year at Barnard that I met Nicholas, Pieter's father. He swept me off my feet, as the storybooks say. I was never happy living in New York. Too cold and dirty. Nicholas couldn't live anywhere else. I left and came home."

"Why did you leave your children?" I said.

"Pieter resented it for many years, I know. But there was no question of his coming with me. My mother would have been horrified at a visible reminder of a mésalliance. It's silly, now. We are even sillier for sitting here talking about it. Pieter and I have made our peace many times over. He's been to visit me many times."

"And you will come to visit us?" I said.

"We shall see. Perhaps on the occasion of the birth of my first grandchild," she said, chuckling. "For, of course, Maria will never forgive you if you deliver without her being there to supervise."

"Well," I answered, much embarrassed. "There's plenty of time before we have to worry about that. In fact . . ." I broke off abruptly as Pieter re-entered the room.

"Have you two ladies run out of things to say yet?" Pieter asked, his eyes twinkling under the heavy lids that were so like his mother's. "I should have warned you, Mama Isobel, Gretel can talk with the best of them."

"What?" I demanded.

"Don't worry, I like talkers," Pieter replied, patting me on the head. "Well, I hate to be the one to say it, but we should be getting

back to the hotel. We have to make an early start in the morning.
I've got us booked on a late afternoon flight to New York."

"Oh, we're going back," I said quietly. I had hoped we could
spend a few more days in Mayaguez visiting with Isobel. This was
the first I'd heard of our having reservations.

"It had to happen sooner or later," Pieter agreed cheerfully.
"We've the house to get ready, and you have to move from your
apartment. And remember, you are a working woman."

Under Pieter's prodding, we said our good-byes quickly and
painlessly, and I promised to write. In no time at all we were whizz-
ing away from Casa Flor. What an amazing day, I thought to myself; I acquired a mother-in-law I never even knew existed. Which
reminded me . . .

"Why didn't you tell me we were going to visit your mother?" I
demanded. "I felt positively scruffy in this old T-shirt."

"What's the matter, don't you like surprises?" he said.

"No, and you wouldn't either if you were on the receiving end."

"Oh, I am never surprised," Pieter replied. "But you have to
admit, Gretel, that you would have been beside yourself if I had told
you where we were going. Right?"

"Yes, yes. You're right. But I do wish we could stay in Puerto Rico
longer."

"That's the best time to leave, when you wish you could stay
longer."

"But why didn't you ever tell me about your mother? That you've
visited her? I had assumed you hadn't seen her since you were a
child."

"Obviously that assumption was wrong. Ah, here we are. Now,
why don't you get in one last swim before we have dinner?"

* * *

I had the pool to myself, as Pieter showed no inclination to join
me. But for once I didn't mind his not being there; I was glad to
have the time to swim and think. Although I liked Isobel very much,
I was more content when I had thought Pieter never saw her. His
reasons for not discussing her were obvious then. But now, now that
I knew he had a mother—one who was alive and well and whom he
visited somewhat regularly—his reasons for not mentioning her
were unclear. He had a reticency that Isobel told me he had inher-
ited from his father. But she had been fairly reticent herself on cer-

tain subjects, I thought, turning over on my back to kick the length of the pool. Odd, how she hadn't wanted to discuss Dirk. I kicked harder, churning the water into sparkling white foam.

"Hey, Chicken-of-the-Sea!" Pieter's voice called over my splashes. I quickly paddled over to the pool's side.

"Can I buy a lady a drink?" he asked. I laughingly agreed that he could and ran up to our room to change.

I was feeling extraordinarily romantic and dressed in my flimsiest, daringly (or so I thought) see-through sheer white-cotton dress. Its hemline floated delicately about my ankles. I towel-dried my hair and twisted it into a knot at the nape of my neck. A pair of long silver earrings—and I felt exotic enough to take on the world.

The dinner lived up to my expectations. We got pleasantly drunk in the bar beforehand, then went into the dining room next door for a wonderful meal of fresh red snapper washed down with champagne. Lots and lots of wonderful, beautiful, bubbly champagne, as I said repeatedly to Pieter.

"Can it be that my bride is a little bit tipsy?" Pieter asked as we went—slowly, carefully—up to our room after dinner.

"Sssssh! People can hear you. Think of my sterling reputation!" I replied, leaning heavily on Pieter's arm.

"I am. Anyone who could consume that amount of liquor and still remain sober is definitely no good."

"Pooh. It's wasn't all *that* much. And you egged me on."

"I like to see you enjoying yourself. You're quite adorable when you've one glass of champagne too many."

"I have not had one glass too many," I protested firmly. "It's more like four too many."

"Well, get into bed and you'll feel better." Pieter carried me over to the bed and, pulling back the spread, slipped me between the sheets. I held my arms over my head obediently while he lifted my dress off carefully.

"Aren't you coming to bed?"

"Yes, darling. I just want to take a shower first."

I fell asleep to the sound of water hitting the tiles.

*　*　*

Some hours later I jerked awake. The effects of the champagne had vanished. I felt clear-headed and wide awake. I looked over to Pieter's side of the bed. It was empty. I flicked the light switch on, expecting to hear his "What's wrong?" from the bathroom, but there was nothing. It was as though he had never come to bed at all. Only my turnings had disturbed the covers.

I got out of bed and padded about the room. No Pieter. There were evidences of his taking a shower: wet towels were flung carelessly on the bathroom floor, the clothes Pieter had worn that day were tossed into a corner. He had changed and gone out. Undoubtedly he couldn't sleep and had gone to the bar for a drink, I thought. In which case, he'll be back shortly. I went back to bed to wait.

A half hour passed, and still no Pieter. Restless, though not so wide awake, I went to the window to look out. The moonlight played eerily over the pool and the garden below, creating dancing shadows although actually nothing moved. Or did it? No, it was the tropical breeze moving the giant leaves to create the wavering darkness. I went over to flick the light back on. It didn't work. None of the lights worked. I looked out the window again to see no lights—in the hotel or even in the sleeping town below. I shrugged, thinking it a periodic blackout, as the bell captain had told us sometimes happened. I sighed and got back into bed.

*   *   *

Sometime later, an hour or two—I couldn't be sure—I woke once again. But this time Pieter was beside me, breathing deeply, one arm flung awkwardly out, the other resting across my waist. I turned and snuggled contentedly against him, falling once more into a deep, dreamless sleep.

5

Hoek House

"Pieter, aren't you going to carry me across the threshold?" I asked, a bit more sharply than I had intended. But I was sleepy and cranky after the flight and the bother of driving from the airport to the docks of Lower Manhattan, getting the *Stuyvesant* out of storage and Samantha out of the vet's, and then motoring out to the island.

"What?" said Pieter. He had already unlocked the door and was several feet inside before he turned.

"Aren't you going to, you know, carry me inside your, *our* house?" I whispered. I knew I was being childish to insist upon this old tradition, but I was determined. I had gone to a great length in order to set foot in Hoek House.

"Gretel," said Pieter, impatiently.

"Pieter," I said with marked exasperation. I set the cat carrier down on the brick steps just outside the door, folded my arms, and waited.

"Oh, all right." Pieter laughed. He stepped quickly to my side, scooped me up with one swift movement, and deposited me with a thud six inches inside the door. "There, my bride of eight days, welcome to Hoek House." Pieter bowed low, sweeping off his cap, knocking over a lamp in the process. "So much for grand gestures," he said, righting it and turning on the light.

The room we had entered was the kitchen, shaped in an overlarge rectangle, with old-fasioned quaintness that would have been charming if it had been clean. Piles of dingy dishes stood stacked in an enormous white tub of a sink; the crumbs of a meal (perhaps several meals) rested on a round table covered with a grease-stained vinyl cloth. I surveyed the room open-mouthed, resisting the impulse to demand we return to my cozy and *clean* apartment on Greenwich Street. Seemingly oblivious to the mess, Pieter went to a cabinet, opening it to reveal a well-stocked liquor supply. He selected a bottle of brandy. He then grabbed two glasses from another cabinet, and cradling the bottle under his arm, carried them over to the table, handing one to me. Dubious of its cleanliness, I inspected the tumbler. To my surprise, it was spotless. Pieter sloshed a generous amount of brandy into it, and, raising his own in a toast, again announced:

"Welcome to Hoek House."

I smiled up at him over the rim of my glass, sipping my drink. The kitchen began to seem less dingy.

"I apologize for all this," Pieter said, waving his hand to indicate the room. "Although I'm a terrible housekeeper, I didn't remember it as being this bad."

"We'll have it gleaming in no time," I lied cheerfully.

"No. Tomorrrow morning, I'll see about getting some help. It's not fair to you. You shouldn't have to clean up after my—" Pieter gulped the rest of his brandy and poured himself another glassful. "When I was little, we had Mrs. Ballantine in to clean, but after my father died, she stopped coming. She was getting old anyway. She only stayed on as long as she did out of loyalty to my father. She's retired, living with her daughter in Hackensack."

"Oh," I said. I didn't want a housekeeper, but that decision could wait. What concerned me was Pieter's abrupt change in topic, his volunteering information about his childhood.

"Well, Gretel, would you like to see the rest of the house?" said Pieter.

"Uh, yes. Of course I would. After all, it's my home now." My sleepiness was forgotten with the adventure of a whole new world.

"That it is," Pieter said, reaching over to hug me to him. "All right. First of all, this is the kitchen. It wasn't part of the original house, but an ell added during the eighteenth century. It was modernized around the turn of this century, but it hasn't been touched since. As long as it works there's been no need. Now, for the house proper."

Pieter turned and led the way up a small flight of brick steps, opened a door, and ushered me into what I guessed to be the dining room. There was an immense fireplace in one corner, which Pieter said had once been used for cooking. The room was plainly decorated, with a long trestle table in the middle and two chairs pulled up to it the only furniture. The walls were paneled, giving the room a dark appearance which I doubted even the brightest sunlight could brighten. There were only two narrow, diamond-paned windows. Pieter opened a door, and we went into a small book-lined library that I admired briefly. He showed me two other rooms quickly, both as starkly furnished as the first and seemingly unused. He then led me across the black- and white-tiled front hall into one of the largest rooms I had ever seen. Its size was all the more emphasized by the small rooms we had just passed through.

"This is, or rather was, the most used room in the house," said Pieter. "It was big enough so that we could all be here in front of the fireplace and each doing something different without fear of disturbing the others. Yet we were all together." Pieter fell silent. I walked about the room, pausing to admire the great fireplace. This was the magnificent chimney that Pieter's ancestor, Adrian, had built in 1661, the chimney Pieter had proudly shown me on my only other visit to the island. Now, looking at the great gray stones, I pictured many cozy evenings sitting before it with *our* family.

"There's still the upstairs to see," Pieter called from the hallway. I tore myself away from my fancies, thinking that I would have the rest of my life to linger before the fireplace.

I clattered across the living room's bare floor and into the hallway where Pieter was already climbing the impressive flowing staircase to the second floor. The rooms here mirrored the ones they were built on.

There was a large—ridiculously so—bedroom over the living room. The same chimney ran through both, almost covering the entire north wall with its handsome stone pattern. Next to this room, at the top of the stairs, was a comfortable bathroom—the only modern touch, Pieter said, in this part of the house. There were four other bedrooms, two small, two not so small. In all of them, the ceilings sloped sharply; the windows were dormers that poked through the red-tiled roof.

All the rooms were as sparsely furnished as the rooms downstairs, containing only the barest necessities—an unmade bed, a table, sometimes a chair. All the rooms looked equally unused, including the largest, which I guessed would become ours. Obviously, Pieter had not lived in any of the rooms I had just seen. We were disturbing layers of dust that had rested unmolested for years. It was understandable, of course. It was much too big a house for one person.

But I wondered at the lack of furnishings. What little there was was of good quality, and some of it, even to my unpracticed eye, was valuable antique—family—pieces, lovingly preserved through the years. But surely the Van der Hoek generations had required more than what I had seen. What had happened to the rest? Could it be in storage? Had it been sold? Pieter had said once that the Van der Hoek artists, although not famous, had done well enough. Had selling the family possessions helped?

We made our way slowly back to the kitchen. I wondered where we would sleep that night. None of the beds were made up. I hadn't thought to bring any linens from my apartment, as we would be moving my things out later in the week.

"There's still one room you haven't seen," said Pieter, interrupting my thoughts.

"What's that?"

"The most important room of all," he replied.

"Oh! Of course! Your studio. Where do you work?"

"On the other side of the kitchen," said Pieter.

I had not realized that the ell extended beyond the kitchen. Now I saw that it extended a great deal. We entered a room that was the equal in size of the kitchen. And especially light and airy, even in the late afternoon sunshine that filtered softly through the pine trees. There were windows on all three sides, with a large bay window cut into the north wall. At the height of the day, this room would be as bright as the other rooms were dark.

It was a cluttered room of artist's clutter: canvases, rags, jars half filled with different-colored waters, brushes of all sizes standing in old coffee cans. There was a narrow bed in one corner, a corduroy coverlet pulled over what were undoubtedly rumpled sheets. Pieter lives here, I thought to myself. He lives in this room and in the kitchen, ignoring the rest of the house.

There was little wall space left about the windows, most of it covered with work and nonsense. Drawings—perhaps studies for larger canvases or a moment's thought jotted down—were thumbtacked helter-skelter, as were book jackets, pages from magazines, even an

advertisement for an expensive brand of whiskey. All gave evidence
of an illustrator's career. But nowhere did I see a trace of the assignment to draw the World Trade Center and its environs—the assignment that had caused us to meet. I shrugged my shoulders. Pieter
must have finished the drawings and already delivered them. I inspected the rest of his work avidly. It was the first time I had seen
any of it, aside from the sketches he had made on the beach at San
Juan.

As I inspected his life, Pieter stood silent, either in disinterest or
embarrassment. I didn't know. There was one beautifully framed
sketch in the room, and as I went to examine it, Pieter also moved
toward it. It was a rough pencil sketch of a man's head, a man that
could almost be Pieter in another twenty years. It was unsigned, and
I wondered if Pieter's father or grandfather had drawn it. It was impossible to tell from the shapeless garment draped over the subject's
shoulders what period the drawing represented. It was definitely an
old drawing, however. But how old? I tried to examine the quality
and texture of the paper.

"You've discovered the family treasure," said Pieter.

"It's a lovely drawing, but what . . ."

"And also the family conceit," finished Pieter.

"And a family mystery?" I asked.

"Well, perhaps in one sense, but not as far as the Van der Hoeks
have been concerned. The drawing is believed to be a study for Jan
Van Eyck's A Man in a Red Turban, which was painted in 1433. I
have a reproduction in a book around here someplace, and the like-
ness is quite apparent. At any rate, the drawing has been in the family for centuries. Not that the Van der Hoeks are such connoisseurs
of art, but because the drawing has resembled so many of us. I've always liked it, and so I moved it in here. It could almost be a portrait
of my father."

I studied the drawing with new intensity. The large heavy-lidded
scrutinizing eyes, the long crisply defined nose, the thin-lipped
mouth—there was no emotion in that face. Whoever had sat for that
portrait guarded his feelings well. I then looked at Pieter, whose casually combed brown hair softened but did not hide those same features.

"Yes, I see the family resemblance. Do all the Van der Hoek men
resemble the drawing?"

"No, not all." Pieter had obviously done with the tour of his studio. He flicked off the electric light and opened the door to the kitchen. Once there, Pieter again poured out generous amounts of brandy.

"Well, what do you think?" He seemed anxious.

"It's a lovely, lovely house," I replied honestly.

"Yes, but it should be lovelier. Unfortunately, that would take time and money. And, although we've always had plenty of the former, the Van der Hoeks haven't ever been able to hold onto the latter."

"Could your brother help?" I asked.

"Dirk isn't interested in Hoek House."

"But he does live on the island."

"Only because it's rent-free. It suits him and his work."

"What *does* Dirk do?" I asked. I knew as little about Pieter's brother as I did the first time I met Pieter.

"Oh, he writes. God knows *what* he writes. He's yet to have anything published. He claims to be working on the first great novel to come out of the Woodstock generation. By the time *he's* finished, the flower children will be collecting social security."

"How old is Dirk?"

"Twenty-six. How about dinner?"

You're evading me again, I thought to myself. Oh well, there was time. My questions would be answered soon enough.

We had brought food with us, and, while Pieter set about building a fire in Adrian's chimney, I set about clearing enough of the kitchen to broil a steak. We ate in front of the fire, and later, as we sipped wine in the flickering light, I felt that my dreams had come true.

* * *

One week. I had given myself one week to accomplish the move to Hoek House, to settle in at Hoek House. I hadn't realized exactly what that would mean.

I estimated it would take three trips to move everything from my apartment to the island. The *Stuyvesant*, sturdy though she was, could carry only so much. And in the five years I had lived on Greenwich Street, I had accumulated a surprising (depressing) amount of possessions. Pieter refused to have anything to do with the business of packing. He would lift and carry and drive the boat back and forth to Hoek Land. It was up to me to decide what should or should not be transported. I recruited Melissa for the task, persuad-

ing her to take one day out of the office to help me. She agreed readily enough, wanting to hear all the details of my honeymoon.

"What a dump!" Melissa quoted when she saw the chaos I had
created in my apartment.

"That's the 'take' pile. That's the Salvation Army pile. That's the
'it's-yours-if-you-want-it' pile," I said, peeking around the door of the
hall closet I was rummaging through. "What should I do about
these?" I asked, holding up a pair of jodhpurs I hadn't worn since
my freshman year in college.

"Salvation Army. You're aquatic now, remember? I don't suppose
there's a cup of coffee in this place. Whew! One good thing about
this marriage of yours, Gretel, I won't have to climb five flights of
steps to visit you!" Melissa collapsed dramatically into an armchair
(Salvation Army).

"No, just walk on water," I said, dislodging Samantha from my
lap. She slunk off and I went into the kitchen to check on the status
of the boiling water. "Melissa, I really appreciate your coming over."

"Don't be too appreciative. You know how rotten a packer I am."
Melissa laughed ruefully. I had been the one to organize her apartment for her.

"Well, thanks for the moral support anyway," I answered. The
water ready, I poured it into two mugs, handing one to Melissa, who
wrinkled her nose.

"Instant?" she sneered.

"Oh, Melissa, you only pretend to be able to tell the difference." I
passed by her to survey the living room with its untidy piles and half-
packed cartons. "You know, this is harder than I thought it would
be."

"Shedding one's skin is never easy, kid." Melissa hugged me
briefly. "You're not having second thoughts, are you?"

"Oh for heaven's sake! No!" I hooted, returning to the closet.
Melissa joined me. We gossiped while we worked.

I told her about our trip to Puerto Rico (leaving out the episodes
of the sinister man in San Juan, which I now regarded as coincidence), and how I had met Pieter's mother in Mayaguez. Melissa
stopped in her task of wrapping newspapers around my wineglasses
to stare open-mouthed.

"Well," she breathed, sitting back on her heels. I took the glass
she was holding just as she was about to drop it. "Well," she repeated. "*That* was a bit of a shock, wasn't it!"

"But a pleasant one," I agreed. "Mostly," I confided, "I was annoyed at Pieter for not telling me. Can you imagine? When he introduced me to this beautiful woman he casually announced was his *mother!* Oh, I felt like such a fool! I'm sure she thought me one, too. I must have stared at her for a good ten minutes."

"I wonder why Pieter did that?" Melissa asked. She had recovered from the shock of what I had told her, and was now fascinated. "I mean, not tell you about his mother."

"Oh. I don't know." This was something I, too, had tried to puzzle out, but to no avail. "Boys will be boys, no matter what their age."

"Hmmmm," said Melissa.

"Well, anyway, I was delighted to meet her. We became good friends in just one afternoon, and she may come to visit in the fall. You'll like her, she's totally charming."

"She certainly sounds infinitely preferable to my ex-mother-in-law, if only because she's in another country. Imagine," Melissa added, shaking her head, "Pieter's being Puerto Rican. I certainly never would have guessed it. He must take after his father."

"Yes, Pieter's a Van der Hoek."

"What about Dirk?" Melissa asked.

"What about Dirk?"

"Whom does he resemble? Mother or Father?"

"I don't know," I muttered, becoming interested in the contents of my closet once again. Blast Melissa's memory, I thought.

"You mean, you *still* haven't met him? Even though you now live on the island?" Even without looking up, I could tell that Melissa was shaking her head in disbelief once again.

"No. I haven't met him. He and Pieter don't get along. Dirk doesn't live at the house."

"Is the island *that* big?" asked Melissa.

"No, but apparently Dirk just stays in the boathouse when he's on the island, which isn't that often, according to Pieter. I think I heard a boat late last night," I said, groping for details.

"Of course, you could take a stroll down to the boathouse to pay a sisterly call. Then you could see for yourself what Dirk is like," said Melissa, her eyes lighting up mischievously.

"Oh, sure," I answered. "That would go over real well." I shuddered at the thought of Pieter's reaction.

"Pieter wouldn't like it."

"Pieter definitely wouldn't like it."

"Would Pieter have to know?" asked Melissa hopefully.

"Melissa!" I replied.

"Oh, you're right," she sighed. "It's just that it would be *so* tempting."

"Well, I shall have plenty of things in the house itself to keep me busy for the next year. I wouldn't have time to get into trouble even if I wanted to."

"It's a wonderful house?" she asked, hooked by Hoek House.

"It's a wonderful house," I assured her, happy to be off a dangerous subject. I described Hoek House for Melissa (skipping over the sorry state of the kitchen), the flat area of ground where I hoped to start a vegetable garden, my decorating plans. "I was thinking of doing the bedroom in browns and reds—it'd be so cozy with the brick. And the kitchen *has* to be painted white, definitely white. *All* the rooms will probably need to be painted," I sighed, "but I'm just going to worry about the kitchen and the bedroom first. I want to live there awhile. Get the feel of the place. I don't want to make any mistakes. Why don't you come to dinner Saturday night? We should be reasonably under control by then, Pieter'd love to see you, and that way you can make some suggestions."

"I'd love to! I never thought you'd ask. I've been dying to see this island of Pieter's. And this ancestral home you say is so fantastic."

"Oh, it *is* fantastic. I can't even begin to describe it properly," I answered.

"You know, Gretel." Melissa laughed. "If you love Pieter half as much as you love his property, you're going to have a wonderful marriage!"

*   *   *

By Wednesday I was struggling hard to make Hoek House my home. My bentwood rocker—the very first piece of furniture I had ever bought with my own money—fitted neatly in a corner of our bedroom. A quilt my grandmother had made covered our bed. Melissa's welcome-home gift—an immense bouquet of yellow roses— bloomed in the large blue vase I had captured at a country auction three years before. Samantha, totally bewildered and disgusted by the move, had taken over the wide sill of the bay window in Pieter's studio. She curled up there every day, purring in the sunshine and refusing to budge. Everywhere I looked, in every room, there was some-

thing that belonged to Gretel Drew Van der Hoek. But the rooms
did not belong to me.

It was not that I did not love them. I did. I had never cleaned and
polished so affectionately, nor fretted over the placement of a lamp
or a clock so tediously. It was just that I was too conscious of the
generations of Van der Hoeks who had lived here for all those years.
Dozens of them for hundreds of years. I felt more a curator or a cus-
todian than a resident.

There you are, being fanciful again—I scolded myself. This is your
house, yours and Pieter's. I listened to my more rational side, shrugging my shoulders. This was only the first week, after all. Given
enough time, it would seem as though I had never lived anyplace
else. Hoek House would become as much mine as it had been any
Van der Hoek bride's. Or would it? Had this sanctity I sensed helped
drive Isobel back to Puerto Rico? Had she finally realized that she
could never truly belong in Hoek House? That she could never truly
become a member of the Van der Hoek family? There I went again,
conjuring up a romantic unrealistic version of the facts. I decided
that a brisk walk would clear my head.

The late afternoon sun shone beautifully but palely overhead, giving no warmth. I pulled the collar of my coat closer about my neck.
There was a dusting of snow on the ground—just enough to cover
evenly, but not enough to make walking difficult. I picked up a
broom leaning against the wall just outside the kitchen door to
sweep the brick courtyard. It seemed best not to allow it to freeze
overnight. As I swept, I chuckled to myself, remembering where I
had been walking a week before.

Pieter was in his studio. I could see him bending intensely over his
drawing table. I scooped up as much snow as I could gather, formed
it into a lumpy mound, and threw it against the large bay window.
But either it was a sorry excuse for a snowball or Pieter was lost in
concentration, for he didn't look up. I threw another, this time drawing an indignant stare from Samantha, curled up cozily on the wide
window sill. She turned her back and proceeded to lick away the in-
sult. Still no response from Pieter. I blew a kiss at his back and
moved down the hill toward our dock.

The harbor waters seemed cheery, a bright blue that grayed as I
neared the pier. Pollution, I muttered to myself. There would undoubtedly be unsightly trash that had floated onto our minuscule

beach that would have to be cleared away. I wondered if there was a rake in the boathouse.

I came to an abrupt halt. I was certain I had heard a noise, but perhaps it was the crunching of my feet upon the half-frozen ground. I paused, not moving, listening carefully. Yes, I had heard something. A clanking noise that came from the boathouse. A rustling and a bumping noise. Perhaps some animal was inside, I thought—a badger, a beaver, or a skunk had gotten in and now was unable to get out. All I had to do was slip quietly to the door, unlatch it, and free the animal. I took a step, but stopped short again. There was a crash, silence, and then a sound that no animal could ever make. I had distinctly heard someone, a man, swear. A trespasser! I crouched lower, wishing that I had worn my dark-brown coat instead of my bright-red plaid hunter's jacket.

I thought of turning to run and getting Pieter, but then it occurred to me that instead of being an unwelcome trespasser, the person clumping about in the boathouse might be Dirk. I would feel pretty foolish if that were the case. I decided to wait and see. I felt sure I could recognize him and, if it was Dirk, then I would introduce myself and invite him up to the house for supper. It was time the brothers ceased their feud, undoubtedly over something boyish and prideful. I smiled happily, picturing the scene of two brothers reunited—because of me, Pieter and Dirk. . . . Another crash startled me. What if it wasn't Dirk? Well, then, I calmed myself, I would quietly slip up to the house to warn Pieter. But what if he catches you? Bah! I answered myself. I had totally convinced myself that the person in the boathouse was Dirk.

It wasn't Dirk. But neither was it anyone that I felt I had to be afraid of. The door to the boathouse opened, and an old man appeared back first, awkwardly dragging out a large box. I decided to investigate.

"Hello! What are you doing? Need some help?" I called out, waving my hand.

The man stopped and slowly straightened, shielding his eyes. As I neared, his thin craggy face broke into a gap-toothed grin. With a decidedly salty Irish brogue, he said:

"Bless, if I didn't think you were the Cellar Ghost himself, missus, I'm that near-sighted. Clyde's the name. Pleased to meet you. You be the new Missus Van der Hoek?"

"Why, yes," I answered, surprised. "Gretel Van der Hoek. But

how did you know? You don't"—I looked around me doubtfully—
"you don't live on the island, too, do you?"

"Me? Not bloody likely." Clyde chuckled to himself. He was a
small, wiry man in his sixties, with a quick nervous habit of jerking
his arms about when he talked. He moved them now, continuing:
"As if anyone but a Van der Hoek would ever live *here*." I wondered
how he meant that. He must have sensed this, for he paused to smile
again and say kindly, "Nah, missus, 'twas nothing bad I meant. Just
that no one but Van der Hoeks have the right. I live over to South
Beach." He jerked his head toward Staten Island. "And I'll bet
you're wondering what it is I'm doing here."

"Well, yes, I am rather. I must say I didn't expect to see anyone.
You gave me quite a start. I thought you were a trespasser," I said,
smiling back. Though I wasn't sure that he wasn't one. "What was
it you thought I was? A ghost?"

"Aye. The Cellar Ghost."

"What's that?" I asked.

"A Van der Hoek got himself killed by his wife one night in the
cellar of the old house. After it were done, she shut up the house and
left. When they found him, he was just a pile of bones and rags.
They buried him, but by then it was too late. Already a haunt. Legend is that he roams the island. His revenge."

I listened avidly. This was a version of the story Pieter hadn't told
me. "His revenge?" I prompted.

"It was a woman who done him in. It's women that he hates. He
only rests when there are no women on the island. But when a Van
der Hoek takes a bride, then the Cellar Ghost walks." Clyde paused,
realizing to whom he spoke. "Beg pardon, missus, don't take it serious myself."

"That's all right. I'm certainly not afraid of ghosts." I laughed.
"You do seem to know a lot about the history of Hoek Land."

"Aye. I've been coming to this place since I was a boy—sixty year
and more. Aye, in my time, I've been mechanic, gardener, carpenter.
Hoek Land would have washed to sea without Clyde to put it together. Why, I even used to help Master Nick stretch his canvases."
He puffed his chest out.

"You work here," I said awkwardly.

"That's what I said, missus. Course now, I can't do much more
than tidy up about the place. It wouldn't seem right not to come to

Hoek Land. It's fine that Master Pieter married. Ain't good for a house to be empty."

"You must know a lot about the family," I said. I sat down on an old wooden crate on the dock, hugging my knees to my chest. Clyde was indeed a find. I forgot the cold afternoon in my eagerness to hear about the traditions I had married.

"Oh yes. Master Pieter and his father," said Clyde, busying himself in the boathouse again, but obviously eager to talk, rather, gossip, with me. "Master Nick and I used to fish together when we were boys. I remember when he brought the dark one here to live. The smart-looking one. After she left, all he did was work. But we'd get together and do some drinking now and again. That man could drink!" Clyde chuckled appreciatively. "That reminds me," he said, reaching into his grease-stained khaki coat. He pulled out a pint bottle of whiskey, opened it to take a swig, then handed it to me. I took a brief drink before handing it back. It seemed to make a bond between us.

"Knew Master Nick's father, too—old Mister Adrian. I was feared of him, I was. For all that he was artistic." Clyde sneered the word. "He'd howl like a banshee if anyone bothered him during his work. I gave him a wide berth, I can tell you. Don't remember his wife, Nicky's mother. There's seldom been a happy woman on the island."

"What was Pieter like as a child?" I asked, ignoring his unfortunate remark.

"Don't right remember. He didn't live here after the Missus Nicholas left. Quiet sort of kid, I guess. Spent most of his time there, the studio. Didn't play much." Clyde took another swig of whiskey.

"And Dirk?" I asked.

"Who?" he said.

"Dirk, Pieter's brother. He was a baby when their parents divorced."

"Aye. I do remember a babe. It died."

"Oh, no. That's impossible. Why, Dirk lives on the island now. In the other boathouse."

"Must have been thinking of someone else," he said, flustered at his lapse. He shook his head. "I've seen a lot, known a lot, and remember most of it, I do. I'd be willing to wager there ain't nobody who knows more about these waters than Clyde. I've lived on the harbor all my life. Ain't nothing I don't know."

I murmured something. I don't know what. I wasn't nearly as in-

terested in the history of New York City's harbor as I was in the
history of the Van der Hoek family. But Clyde relished having an
audience, and I was content to listen. He gave up his fussing and,
lighting a well-chewed cigar, began to talk. He seemed especially to
relish disasters. I heard about the sinking of the *General Slocum* on
June 15, 1904, in which 1,021 lives were lost; about the fourteen
ships that were ice-bound during the winter of 1917; about the burning of the liner *Hanseatic* on September 7, 1966, berthed at Pier 84
in the Hudson; about the explosion of the tanker *Black Sea*, off
Bayonne, New Jersey, on February 23, 1927. This last disaster reminded me of the tanker explosion I had witnessed. I asked Clyde if
he, too, had seen it.

"Oh, aye. Wished I'd been closer. I was doing the lock on the
boathouse here when she went. All I could see was the black smoke
straight up to the sky. Made them two towers look small, it did. Aye,
that was something all right. Smoked all day. Could smell it days
after." Clyde took another swig from the bottle, but I refused.
"What a time we had cleaning the *Stuyvesant* that afternoon, when
Master Pieter drove it home. Looked like he'd been in the thick of
it, but I guess the smoke spread over the entire harbor. If it had been
me, I would have waited it out. The Master said he'd already started
out for home."

"Oh, really?" I asked. Pieter had never said anything about being
in the harbor during the explosion. In fact, as I recalled, Pieter had
been particularly vague about his whereabouts that day.

I shivered. We'd been talking over an hour. The sun was low and
the dark shadows long. I stood up, staggering slightly from having sat
so long. Pieter would be wondering where I was. More important,
he'd be wondering where his dinner was. I thanked Clyde for his stories. His reaction surprised me. He grabbed my hand and shook it
hard, saying he was happy to have a woman like myself around now,
assuring me heartily that if there was anything I needed done—no
matter how onerous or trivial—he'd be only too happy to oblige. I
promised to call on his services at the first opportunity and watched
as he climbed into his small outboard to put-put back to Staten Island. There goes a genuine character, I chuckled to myself. I quickly
climbed back up to the house. As I neared Hoek House, I could see
nothing had changed during my absence. Samantha still snoozed in
the window, and Pieter still hunched over his work.

"Hel-lo," I called as I entered the kitchen. I removed my coat before tiptoeing into the studio. Pieter was putting the finished touches on something—I couldn't see what.

"Hi," I repeated. "Miss me?"

"Huh? Oof, my back." Pieter straightened with a grimace. "Dinner ready? I'm starved!"

"Uh—in about half an hour or so," I answered, remembering thankfully that there was a steak already defrosted. "You know," I continued, "you should really paint Samantha, she spends so much time here."

"Done!" said Pieter with a bow, turning his afternoon's work about for my inspection. There, upon his easel, still wet, was a watercolor of Samantha at her best: asleep, one paw curled daintily under her extended chin, her long tail draped gracefully over the window sill.

"Pieter, it's wonderful! Oh, you've captured her very personality. We must get this framed, uh, as soon as it's dried." In my eagerness I had picked the painting up.

"Don't worry, I can fix that smudge. Yes, Samantha looks quite good here. Good enough to eat," he added with a meaningful leer.

"Okay, okay." I laughed. "Dinner coming right up. I get the hint. Fix the smudge and before you're through, I'll have dinner ready."

By mutual agreement, Pieter and I had chosen to eat our meals at the large round table in the kitchen rather than in the more formal but austere dining room. I think we both felt more comfortable. I know it was easier. In three days, I had accomplished the impossible and made the kitchen a pleasant, habitable, *clean* place. I wanted to make new curtains, of course, and replace the refrigerator, but those alterations could come later.

"So," Pieter said, after a flattering few moments of eating in silence, "so, what did you do this afternoon? Not more cleaning, I hope?"

"No. I declared a holiday." I smiled back. "I decided to wander about, and quite by chance, I met Clyde."

"Clyde Brennan?"

"I guess so. I gather he's done odd jobs for your family for years. Anyway, he seemed to know a lot about the Van der Hoek clan. Including"—I lowered my voice to a stage whisper—"the Cellar Ghost."

"That old nonsense."

"You might have told me," I said.

"What? And have you accuse me of trying to scare you?" Peter asked in mock alarm. "You thought I was crazy enough claiming to live on an island, never mind an avenging family ghost."

"You're right," I agreed reluctantly. "Still, it's a great story." I was already anticipating telling Melissa what I had learned about the ghost, but *after* she was on the island.

"Well, old Clyde tells wonderful, romantic tales when he's feeling good. He's usually good for nothing, of course." Pieter shrugged. "But I let him come here out of loyalty and tradition. He putters about the dock. Actually," he added, "I don't think I could stop him if I wanted to."

"He had an interesting tale about you," I said, beginning to clear away the dinner dishes and heat water for coffee.

"Oh? What was that?"

"That apparently you were right in the El Condor explosion. You know," I added, as Pieter looked puzzled, "the barge on the Hudson. The oil tanker that blew up. I watched the whole thing from my office. You remember."

"What about it?"

"Clyde said you were in the harbor when it happened. That he had a hard time cleaning the *Stuyvesant* afterward."

"Clyde's gone fuzzy again," said Pieter indignantly. "It must have been Dirk. I know I was nowhere in the area. Clyde, you see, he's always had a few drinks by afternoon."

"That's for sure. You know he actually told me that Dirk had died years ago?" I shook my head, then I asked, "Do you and Dirk look alike?"

"There's a family resemblance. He likes the Mets, I like the Yankees." The water was boiling; I jumped at the kettle's whistle. Pieter measured out spoonfuls of coffee, poured the water into the mugs, and brought them over to the table. I had set out a chocolate cake, but neither of us touched it.

"But would Dirk have been driving the *Stuyvesant*?" I asked, idly stirring my coffee with a spoon. I didn't think Clyde could have confused the boats. He had most definitely said it was the *Stuyvesant* that he had cleaned up. But then, he had most definitely stated that Dirk was dead, and that was certainly not true.

"Oh, for God's sake, Gretel. Leave it alone, will you? One comment from an old drunk and you charge at me like a crusading district attorney!" Pieter stood up from the table, throwing his napkin down in disgust. "For the record, ma'am, to the best of my recollection, I was working at home the day of the explosion. Dirk could have stolen the house from over my head without my noticing it. Now, if you'll excuse me, I've got some details to attend." Pieter tousled my hair and returned to his studio, shutting the door behind him.

I sighed, staring morosely into my coffee. No wonder it tasted funny. I had forgotten to put cream in it. I got up, went to the refrigerator, opened the door, and shut it again without getting the cream. I decided that what the coffee needed was a dash of brandy, not cream. Thus fortified, I returned to the table. Lover's quarrel, my mother would have said. Pieter being weird about Dirk again, Melissa would have said. I would just have to learn how to talk about Dirk without making Pieter angry. I decided to call my mother for a long, daughterly chat about the house, and to state again that I didn't need her help, and to insist again that she wasn't to visit until Hoek House was as near perfect as I could make it.

*   *   *

Thursday morning, our quarrel forgotten, Pieter left right after breakfast, saying he had some supplies to pick up in town. For our groceries and common household items, we went to Richmond, the chief district of Staten Island, but Pieter said he had to go to Manhattan, so not to hold lunch.

That was fine, I agreed. Pieter was the sort who demanded three "real" meals a day—soup and sandwiches would have been frowned upon. That meant I had the whole morning and perhaps part of the afternoon to set a plan in motion. I wanted to prowl the attics and closets of Hoek House for photographs, diaries, clippings—anything that might yield information about the Van der Hoeks. Especially Dirk Van der Hoek. It was such a wonderful old house, with just the right kind of nooks and crannies to tuck away memorabilia in.

I decided to begin my search at the top and work down. As soon as Pieter had left I went quickly up the sweeping staircase to the second floor. The part of the house we didn't use was closed off, and for a tense moment I thought the door leading to the hallway might be locked. It opened easily. I peered inside, looking for the light switch. I hadn't been in here since Pieter first showed me around. His tour had been so swift that I didn't remember any of it.

There were four bedrooms in this half of the house, two medium-sized, two little more than closets. None was locked. But my search proved fruitless. The closets were as bare as the rooms themselves. Even the two bureaus that I found were empty. I pulled their drawers out jerkily, hoping that some scrap of paper—a laundry list, *anything*—had fallen down behind, but there was nothing. Then I remembered Pieter's telling me about the Indian attacks during the early years of colonization. Surely a house built during that time would have tunnels and secret passages in its walls, or at least a small hidden closet to hide away in. I felt about the bricks of the fireplaces in two of the rooms, hoping to find the spring that would release an invisible door. Again, I found nothing. All I was getting from my efforts was dirty. My jeans and T-shirt were streaked with dust. I regarded myself with disgust. The other two bedrooms could wait, all I wanted now was a long hot soak in the tub.

Minutes later I was luxuriating in the large, claw-footed tub that took up most of the only bathroom, on the second floor. Pieter had given me some bubble bath for Christmas, and I had measured out more than I should have. As a result, I was surrounded by mounds and mounds of sparkling white bubbles. I sighed happily and turned on the hot-water tap with my toes, sending the bubbles even higher.

"Aha!" said Pieter. I poked my head over the bubbles. He was standing in the doorway, arms folded casually, a wide grin on his face. "So this is what you do when I turn my back. I can see if I don't watch you closely, you'll turn into a fat lazy hausfrau. Shall I bring up the television so you can watch the soap operas?"

"You shouldn't have given me this stuff if you didn't want me to use it." I stuck my tongue out at him. "And either come in or get out. You're causing a draft."

Pieter came into the bathroom, shutting the door behind him. He pulled over a stool to sit beside the tub. "You must have been fairly dirty," he said, "if those are any indication." Pieter pointed to my jeans, which I had left tumbled on the floor.

"Yes, I was investigating the other bedrooms. They're very dusty." Since I had found nothing, I felt no need to hide my morning's activity from Pieter. "This bath has taken care of me, but not my clothes. What do we do for laundry on Hoek Land?"

"I usually go to one of the laundromats in Richmond," Pieter replied. "But we can install a washer and dryer here if you like. There's room in the basement."

"Can we afford it?" I asked. I didn't want Pieter to feel he had to spend money on my account. Indeed, I had vetoed the hiring of a cleaning woman as an unnecessary expense.

"There's never been anything I wanted that I couldn't afford," replied Pieter. Then with a smile, he pulled up the tub's plug.

"Hey! What are you doing?" I protested at having my bath cut short.

"Can't have you turning into a wrinkled prune, my dear. Besides," Pieter added, going toward the door, "there's something I picked up in town that I want to show you."

I watched the soapy water drain out. In a few short days, I would have to return to work and my chances for long, lazy soaks in the tub would be few and far between. I dressed quickly, pulling on slacks and a bulky turtleneck. The air felt chilly after the hot water. Humming, I went down to the kitchen where Pieter stood waiting by the outside door.

"Well?" I asked, looking about.

"It's outside. Down at the dock," Pieter answered, handing me my jacket.

"What is?" I asked.

"You'll see" was all the reply I received.

We moved quickly down the hill to the dock. I could see the *Stuyvesant* bobbing peacefully up and down beside the ramshackle pier. Clyde may have been worth his weight in gold once, I thought, but—as Pieter had intimated, he was certainly worthless as a handyman now. I thought of saying something to Pieter when what I saw next drove all such thoughts from me. There, bobbing in counterpoint to the *Stuyvesant*, tied to her stern, was a gleaming-white beauty of a motorboat. It was sleek and low next to the more solid older boat. I skipped down the path to catch up to Pieter.

"Well, what do you think?" asked Pieter, casually leaning against the boathouse.

"Think?" I echoed, still staring at the boat.

"Yes. If you don't like her, say the word and"—Pieter snapped his fingers sharply—"poof! She disappears."

"Oh no. What do you mean, if *I* don't like her?" I passed by him to go onto the wharf. It was a *neat* little boat.

"Because she's yours," said Pieter.

"Mine?" I turned to stare up at him.

"Yours. Really, Gretel, your sudden lack of comprehension is appalling. Yes, yours," he repeated firmly, coming onto the wharf. He took me by the shoulders, shepherding me to the very edge, turning me around to face the boat. There was a bright red bow affixed to the brown steering wheel. A manila tag peeked out from its folds. Pieter bent me over almost double. "Read," he commanded.

" 'For Ms.' Ms.?" I cocked an eyebrow quizzically at Pieter.

"Read," he commanded.

" 'For Ms. Gretel Drew Van der Hoek'—aha! Couldn't get it all on one line, could you?"

"Read," he commanded. Was there or was there not a distinct edge to Pieter's voice. I decided to finish quickly.

" 'For Ms. Gretel Drew Van der Hoek, with love, from Mr. Pieter Van der Hoek.' That's nice," I sighed happily.

"Nice?" asked Pieter.

"Yeah, nice. The nicest thing you could have done," I answered, reaching up to kiss him softly.

"Okay," he said, mollified. "Happy commuting, Ms. Art Director."

"Oh, commuting," I sighed, less ecstatically this time. What had once seemed a wonderfully long vacation was now nearly ended.

"It'll be a snap in this." Pieter hugged me to him. "She's a beauty, all seventeen feet of her, with all the power of a cruiser. Want to try her?"

"Me?" I looked up at him, eyes bulging. "Me, drive this . . . this . . ."

"That is the idea," Pieter said.

"Yeah." I nodded my head. "Okay. It's now or never." I smiled tightly.

I climbed into the low-slung Chris-Craft, seating myself gingerly on the wide coffee-colored vinyl seat. I gripped the steering wheel while Pieter untied it from the *Stuyvesant* and the wharf. He then climbed in, sliding onto the seat next to me, and handed me the shiny keys. The motor caught immediately. We were off! The boat responded deftly. In minutes we had shot past Hoek Land, swooped under the Verrazano-Narrows Bridge toward the ocean. I was exhilarated by the speed. I ignored the icy spray that splashed up on the boat and, occasionally, on us. Above the noise of the inboard motor and the rush of the growing waves, Pieter gestured me to turn back. Reluctantly, I did so. The seventeen-foot Chris-Craft had never been meant to travel in the open winter sea (and certainly not under my inexpert guidance!). With a flourish of foam, I pulled up at our wharf. I sat, cradling the steering wheel while Pieter climbed out onto the pier.

"What do you think?" he asked.

"Fabulous. Oh, she is a dear little thing. And all mine!" I almost hugged myself.

"So"—Pieter leaned down to help me out of the boat—"what are you going to call her?"

"Call her?"

"It is customary," laughed Pieter.

"Oh." I frowned, pursing my lips. "I'll have to think about that. It shouldn't be rushed into." A hundred names rushed into my mind—*Harbor Queen, Empire State, Manhattan Mermaid*—but none of them seemed right. "It should be relevant," I said. "Let's see, she's low, long, and quick. She's silver. *Quicksilver, Silverfish?* No, that's a nasty insect."

"How about the *Silver Fox?*" said Pieter.

"The *Silver Fox?* Yes, I like the sound of it. But why?"

"Because it suits both of you," said Pieter, reaching over to pull a hair from my head and dangle it in front of me. It was silvery white.

"The *Silver Fox* it is then." I laughed.

"All right," said Pieter. "Now," he continued, climbing into the *Stuyvesant*, "after I put her in the boathouse, do you think you can ease the *Silver Fox* in next to her?"

"Is there room for both?"

"Of course. What do you think Clyde was doing the other day? He was cleaning it out so there'd be extra space."

"Oh," I said.

"Yes," Pieter continued, "I was worried that he had spoiled my surprise." Idling the motor, he eased the *Stuyvesant* in to the boathouse. A few moments later, I brought the *Silver Fox* to rest alongside.

* * *

The next day, Friday, I spent exclusively in my beautiful new boat. Fortunately, the weather was pleasant—warm for late January. I wanted to learn the route to Manhattan by heart, so that I could feel comfortable come Monday morning. The first trip I made, Pieter went with me. After that, I was on my own.

New York City's harbor, containing the third largest port in the world, is never quiet. I saw every kind of boat. Huge transatlantic

liners berthed in the Hudson, barges, tugs, cutters, fireboats, ferry-boats, the dredgers that keep the harbor free of debris—I encountered them all. I practiced turning and churning. I learned the best side of the Staten Island Ferry to pass or be passed on. I searched out the calmest waters to ride.

Although I had traversed the harbor many times with Pieter, it was different now that I was by myself. I realized that I had never really paid attention—I had been too dazzled by the experience itself, and by Pieter. Now I learned and explored every inch. The docks and piers that lined the shores of Staten Island, Brooklyn, New Jersey, and Manhattan. I have read that there are 1,630 piers in New York's harbor, and I passed by them all. I passed by the hills of Staten Island, the oil refineries and naval port of Bayonne, New Jersey; I kept track of the hour with the Colgate clock of Jersey City, one of the largest in the world. I circled Bedloe's Island, staring up at the colossal Statue of Liberty that guards the harbor, and the nearby, slightly larger Ellis Island, with its low buildings that had once housed millions of immigrants and was recently refurbished as a museum. I glided past the 120 acres of Governor's Island, with Castle William, built in 1812, at its tip. As my confidence grew, so did my daring. I passed under the spider-webbed structure of the Verrazano-Narrows Bridge to discover two small islands in the Lower Bay. (Later I learned they were Swinburne Island and Hoffman Island, once used as places of detention for passengers on arriving ships carrying infectious diseases.) But the Lower Bay, two miles from the Narrows, was as far as I dared go alone.

I made new acquaintances, too. The pilots of the Staten Island ferries waved whenever I passed, as did those of the ferries to the Statue of Liberty. In fact, the pilot of every boat I passed, large or small, waved a cheerful hello, and I eagerly returned the salute. But the most enthusiastic wavers were the uniformed young men aboard the Coast Guard ships anchored off Governor's Island.

*　*　*

When it came time to fetch Melissa for dinner Saturday afternoon, I volunteered to make the trip. I was dying to show off my newly acquired boating skills and my newly acquired boat. Pieter agreed readily, it meant he could work a bit longer in his studio, and sent me off with a kiss and a caution against showing off with daredevil stunts.

On the way in, I kept to the right to avoid both the Staten Island Ferry and a determined-looking tugboat heading toward the Hudson River. I came closer to Governor's Island than I had before, within shouting distance of some of the Coast Guard ships. A young, smartly clad officer was leaning against the railing of a cutter. As I passed within fifty yards, he waved and called a greeting. He then shouted something else, but I couldn't distinguish the words. I brought my boat about and to a stop directly alongside.

"Hello!" I called up, putting my hand to my face to shade my eyes from the sun.

"Hi," the officer called back. "You're an adventurous sailor. I watched you yesterday. It's not exactly the time of year I'd pick for pleasure boating."

"You're right," I answered. I wondered if he was flirting or acting in his official capacity as a guardian of the harbor. "It is fairly cold. I've just moved to the island over there. I'm learning my way about the harbor," I added.

"That little island?" he asked, pointing toward Hoek Land. I nodded. "I've seen lights and an occasional boat. I wondered whose it was. I never would have guessed it was owned by so lovely a sailor. My name's Michael, by the way, Michael Dragon. Ensign Dragon, at your service." He bowed slightly, touching his white cap in a smart salute.

"I'm Gretel. Gretel Dr—uh, Gretel Van der Hoek," I corrected myself, realizing that this was the first time I was introducing myself since my wedding.

"Oh, you're a genuine Dutch settler," said Ensign Dragon.

"Oh no, not really, but I'm . . ." I started to explain, but Ensign Dragon had turned away. Then he turned back with an apologetic smile.

"Sorry, I'm wanted below. Hope to see you again, soon. The Coast Guard is always anxious to serve." He waved cheerfully and was gone. I powered up and speeded toward Manhattan and a Melissa who was undoubtedly waiting most impatiently.

She was. As I pulled up to a dock off Battery Park, I found her jumping up and down on the cold stones, hugging her long fur coat tightly to her. I held onto the dock while she scampered down and slipped shivering in to sit beside me.

"Only for my best friend would I do this," she muttered through clenched teeth.

"Oh heavens," I said, laughing, "it's not that bad. So, tell me, how do you like it?"

"Like what?" asked Melissa, her face still buried in her furred collar.

"This. The *Silver Fox*. My wedding present." I gestured with my hands.

"The *Silver Fox*? Oh, you mean the boat." Melissa came out of her silver fox to look around. She turned to me round-eyed. "Pieter gave you this boat? He bought you this boat?" I nodded happily. "Wow," she said. "I'm impressed. Do you know how much these things cost? They're at least ten . . ."

"Ssssh," I answered, starting the motor. "I don't know and I don't want to know. I love my little boat and I don't want to feel guilty about Pieter giving her to me." As I pulled away from Manhattan, I ran down her virtues: her 225 horsepower inboard engine, the soft, padded interior and fiberglass sole, even the teak drink holder for the use of my passengers.

"They may need it if more things like that happen," squealed Melissa, clutching the grab bar. To avoid a looming barge, I had swerved to the left directly in the path of a speeding cutter. I quickly swerved back again, sending a fine spray onto the windshield. "Is it always like this?" asked Melissa, still holding on tightly although we were once more on a calm and straight course.

"It's no worse than the West Side Highway," I said. "Relax and enjoy the sights." But Melissa barely glanced at the things we passed, even though I chattered gaily of my new-found knowledge. She stared straight ahead, as if willing us safely to our destination. She did relax enough, however, to be properly appreciative as we approached Hoek Land, though I sensed some of her enthusiasm stemmed from setting foot on solid ground. When we reached the house, I took pity on her and advanced the cocktail hour slightly. Melissa accepted her drink gratefully, and I took her on a tour of the house before dinner, and showed her her room. I had fixed up one of the other bedrooms, lighting a fire earlier that afternoon to take off the chill of years. Now, the coals glowed cheerily behind the protective screen I had set in front of the fireplace, and Melissa was charmed.

We had plenty of time before dinner, so I gave Melissa the complete tour, showing what I had done and what I hoped to accomplish.

"Of course, at my pace, it will take years before it's the way I want. Right now I'm concentrating on just getting it clean." We were in the hallway and Melissa was admiring the carving on the staircase.

"I could have a field day in a house like this," she said, fingering the paneling.

"I hardly think of you enjoying housework."

"Heavens, no! I meant exploring. A house this old is bound to have secrets," said Melissa.

"If so, they're well hidden," I said, thinking of my unproductive search a few days before. But I didn't tell Melissa of my theories about secret doors and hidden passageways. I knew if she knew of my suspicions, she would insist on going over every square inch of wall herself tonight. "Come on," I said, taking her by the arm. "There's still one room left to tour. And that's the kitchen. I'm getting hungry."

As it was the first time we had had a guest to Hoek House, I made it a special occasion, even if it was—as Pieter had teasingly reminded me several times—only Melissa. I prepared my most spectacular, fattening meal: coq au vin, topped off by my favorite dessert, floating island.

"Well, it's everything you said it was. And more," Melissa announced. We were having an after-dinner brandy in the living room, before the fireplace that Adrian built. Pieter was outside, cutting some more wood for the fire.

"It's absolutely gorgeous, just gorgeous," Melissa repeated. "I must say, I do envy you." She paused to reach over to squeeze my hand. "But," she added with a twinkle, "I certainly don't envy you that ride across the harbor. Brrrr!"

"Oh, it's not so bad once you get used to it," I said. "And, if you're bundled up properly."

"But suppose you have an accident? You could drift for hours and freeze to death."

"Unlikely. But in that eventuality, I've already an admirer in the Coast Guard who would be more than happy to come to my rescue." I told Melissa about Ensign Michael Dragon.

"Dragon?" she asked.

"Dragon," I replied.

"Where do you find them?" she said, rolling her eyes.

6

Milady *Magazine*

"Hey, boss! You look fantastic!" Maggie gave me a bear hug the minute I entered the art department. "You look so healthy!" she squealed, releasing me only to hug me even tighter. I had nearly forgotten my recently acquired sun tan. There was little enough left.

It was disorienting to be back, to glide through the air-controlled carpeted halls, to relax at my unusually clean desk. It seemed a world that belonged to someone else—an unmarried girl named Gretel Drew.

I hadn't been sure what to wear this morning. What was suitable for an office job was not suitable for an open motorboat. I would just have to keep a collection of shoes in the office, I decided, looking down at my sturdy, bright-yellow, fleece-lined rubber boots. Thank God the rugged, outdoorsy look was "in" this year. I shouldn't look too out of place in my denims and bulky down-filled jacket. I dismissed the trivial problems of wardrobe from my mind and set to work.

Two weeks is barely adequate for a vacation, but in the trendy world of magazines, it's a long time. The April issue of *Milady* was on its way to the printer; the May issue of *Milady* was well on its way to completion; and there was a meeting this afternoon to discuss the June issue. We had been buried in the newest spring coats when I had left for Puerto Rico. Now, in a few hours, I would be discussing the latest in beach wear. I closed my eyes—dizzy from the whirl-wind that calls itself Fashion.

"You okay?" Maggie entered, bearing two weeks' worth of messages. I hadn't realized that I knew that many people.

"Oh, fine." I smiled. "It's just the first-day-back blues."

"It sounds as if you had a wonderful time. We sighed over your postcard," said Maggie. "Rumor has it you drive a boat to work?"

"Yes," I answered, describing the *Silver Fox* as briefly as possible. I wanted to plow through my messages and mail before gossiping. But after an hour, I'd returned only five phone calls out of fifty. Everyone—photographers, salesmen, friends—wanted to hear about my marriage, my trip and my new home (Was I *really* living on an island?), before relating the various crises that had occurred during my absence. Another half hour and I sank back into my chair with a sore neck from cradling the phone. A knock at my door roused me.

"Welcome back!" Alix, *Milady*'s fashion editor, sang out. "You look wonderful." Alix came over to kiss my cheek. "To think, I'm the one who introduced you." Smiling smugly, she slid gracefully onto the chair next to my desk. "Now, I hate to do this to you, Gretel, but I must talk some business."

I sighed inwardly. "Yes, business," I said, nodding my head.

"I'm really afraid," continued Alix, "that we'll have to reshoot some of the evening wear. These pictures don't show off the clothes. How is a reader going to know what the dress looks like from *that?*" Alix held out a color slide. It was a pretty picture of a model twirling on her toes. The full-skirted dress swirled about her knees—a blurred confusion of colors. I handed the slide back to her.

"No, Alix. The picture is lovely. And it's being used full-page. We have neither the time nor money to do it over, and there's no need. If you want, you can write some extra copy describing the dress in more detail. It's the mood that's selling the dress, not the fact that it has eighteen buttons. We're not a department store catalogue. Our reader sees the picture, she knows that she's going to feel pretty in that dress, she's going to feel like dancing in that dress, she's going to . . ."

"Enough, enough." Alix laughed. "You're right. It's just that the merchandising is so important to the manufacturers. They *hate* blurry pictures."

"It's not blurry. It's photographed with a romantic, soft focus," I answered, trying with difficulty to keep my face serious.

"Oh, you and your soft focus," retorted Alix. "I should switch the manufacturers' representatives over to you when they call. Well, now that that's settled, tell me all about your trip. Don't you dare leave anything out."

I did tell her (as I would tell so many others that day) about the wedding and the trip. The scenes were familiar enough, so that Alix nodded throughout, often interjecting anecdotes of her own travels in the Caribbean. Yet when I mentioned meeting Isobel, her eyes brightened with suspense.

"You mean, his mother is Puerto Rican?" she asked.

"Yes," I said flatly.

"Pieter's Puerto Rican?" she asked.

"Yes," I said again, adding, "well, half."

"My goodness," she said.

"Why?"

"Well, I mean, it's so, uh, unexpected. That Pieter Van der Hoek should be Puerto Rican. My, my. Were you shocked?"

"Well"—I shouldn't confess to that, I thought, it would sound disloyal to Pieter—"meeting my mother-in-law was unexpected. Pieter planned it as a surprise visit."

"Men," said Alix, shaking her head. "What won't they try! 'Surprise' indeed. *I* would have belted him. So, tell me about your island. That sounds romantic. Is it?"

"Yes," I answered fervently. "The house, our house, is over three hundred years old. Can you believe it? There's this mammoth fireplace . . ." I spent nearly half an hour singing of Hoek House. Alix listened attentively, even asking me to repeat certain descriptions. Flattered by her interest, I told her all I could.

"Fascinating," she said finally. "To think that it could be right here, in the harbor. I never would have guessed. A little gem of a picturesque island. You know, Gretel," Alix's tone altered subtlely.

"Know what?" I asked.

"I've been looking over the figures for the last six months. We're dreadfully over budget in our fashion pages."

"What? That's impossible," I snapped. If there was one thing I monitored closely, it was the budget.

"'Fraid so. Especially in our location shootings. The ski-wear section last November did it," Alix sighed dramatically.

"You would insist on Lucerne!" I reminded her.

"Where else was I going to find authentic snow in July?" she asked innocently.

"There are closer mountains than the Alps."

"You're still sore because you couldn't come along," Alix pouted. "Besides, you know what these shootings are like. I can't function without a hotel suite. Meetings, all those clothes, all those changes!" Alix shuddered delicately at the memory. Perhaps Alix was right, I thought. I had wanted to go with them. And I had been overly critical of the results. It was my contention that an art director was absolutely necessary on fashion shootings.

"Anyway," Alix continued, "I'm sure that we'll have to do the next six months in the studio. All my beautiful clothes photographed against boring old no-seam paper!"

"We'll think of something." I was not in the mood to join in her melodramatics. Alix was, of course, exaggerating wildly. Why, I couldn't guess.

"We can talk about it at this afternoon's meeting," Alix said cheerily. "I'll leave you to your catching up. It is good to have you back." With a click-clatter of high heels, Alix was gone.

Looking at my watch, I was surprised to find that it was past noon. Instinctively, I phoned Melissa. Thirty minutes later we were poking through the bread basket at a table in a small restaurant on the main floor of the World Trade Center.

"You're looking rugged," said Melissa, glancing at my apparel.

"A motorboat ride at eight o'clock on a February morning," I answered, "is not what you'd think."

"I can guess. Hey, I'm honored that you chose me for your first lunch hour. Or did somebody stand you up? You called awfully late."

"No, no. I didn't realize what time it was. I have to readjust to a schedule."

"How is it?" asked Melissa, crumbling a hard roll between her fingers.

"Okay. But I'm awfully glad to be with someone who isn't asking me about my trip and my wedding."

"Ummmmmmm. Nine days' wonder. Do you like being back?" Melissa put down her menu and signaled a waiter.

"I feel different. I expect, in two days, it will be as though I'd never been away."

"Aye. More's the pity." Melissa turned to the hovering waiter and began to order.

"Actually," I said when the waiter had gone. "It's beginning to feel more natural."

"How did Pieter take your going off this morning?" asked Melissa.

"He didn't mind," I answered. Silly question, I thought to myself; Melissa had once been a newlywed. "He gets up at six every morning to paint. He says it's the best time to work."

"Every morning?"

"Every morning so far," I said. I decided that what Melissa was curious about was not the married state, but a happy marriage. Perhaps that was why Alix had asked so many questions about Pieter and Hoek House. She, too, was divorced.

"Well," said Melissa, "if Ed had insisted on getting up at that ungodly hour, I would have packed my bags and left."

"You did," I said, smiling.

"Yes, but not soon enough," said Melissa. We ate for a while in silence, thinking of marriage—what it was and what it could be.

* * *

I spent that entire afternoon at the editorial meeting. Editorial meetings had always seemed to me a necessary bother. But I would have preferred to spend the time with the art department, catching up with any problems and progress that had occurred in my absence. As I sat, trapped in Mavis Hollosoll's office, I kept telling myself that in two weeks no serious crisis should have arisen that couldn't wait until the next day. I made a mental note to have Maggie arrange for a morning meeting with my own department.

"Are you with us, Gretel? Or are you still in the Caribbean?" said Mavis, her sweetly sarcastic voice forcing my attention.

"Sorry." I flushed. I felt like a schoolgirl being scolded by her prim-lipped English teacher for chewing gum in class. I didn't like Mavis enough to accept her reprimand, no matter how silly.

"I was making lists," I explained needlessly.

"We've delayed this meeting three days so that you could be with us," Mavis said before returning to the discussion of the June issue. Alix winked at me broadly, rolling her eyes. I stifled a giggle.

For the rest of the meeting, I paid strict attention, listening as each editor submitted her ideas. Mavis liked theme issues. The obvious theme for June was weddings. There was to be a short story about a girl's anxiety on the night before her wedding; an article on the elements that contribute to a successful marriage; a quiz to determine whether or not "you are ready to walk down the aisle." The food editor submitted recipes for a do-it-yourself reception. The home-decorating editor planned to devote her section to decorating that "first" apartment. She wanted to show five different apartments, but Mavis cut her down to two, one in a modern style, the other more traditional, dismissing her protests with an airy wave.

"Young marrieds can't afford anything anyway. They're stuck with what their parents give them. Older couples have already made their decorating decisions. Now, I think that takes care of everything. Except"—Mavis smiled tightly—"the fashion and beauty pages." She nodded in Alix's direction. She smiled in return, sliding her eyes to glare at the articles editor, Rosemary Tyler. Every month Rosemary tried to grab a few more pages for her section. And every month Mavis refused, saying that she had no intention of turning *Milady* into a *Redbook* or a *McCall's*.

Alix and I remained with Mavis as the other editors filed out. Mavis preferred that just the three of us discuss the fashion section.

Alix briefly outlined what she wanted to do. They were fairly obvious ideas: dresses for the wedding party; a section on etiquette—what to wear at an afternoon or a morning wedding; and a few pages devoted to casual occasions. Alix refused to spend much energy on the bridal issue. It was her contention that wedding gowns always looked the same no matter how or where they were photographed. The fashion pages were already budgeted to be shot in a photographer's studio, so there was not even the excitement of going on location. I, on the other hand, found the assignment interesting. It was an exciting challenge to take something usual and turn it into something unusual. Anybody (well, almost) could make a location shooting look good. The scenic pictures could overcome the lack of good design and imagination. But a studio shooting demanded imagination and talent. I was already envisioning a stark-white issue—the clothes photographed against white backgrounds using only white props. In the food section we would use only white china, white tablecloths and napkins. It would be more difficult in the home-furnishings section, but I would talk to Suzanne about that. A compromise could be worked out. I sighed contentedly. As Mavis liked her theme issues, I liked to make the issue hold together visually.

"Well, Gretel?" Mavis looked at me with her direct stare. Her smallish black eyes had the trick of intensifying her gaze.

I quickly outlined my ideas, growing more enthusiastic as I did so. I had learned that if one was excited about an idea, others soon would be, too. As I talked, Alix nodded, only interjecting occasionally to mention some accessory or prop we might consider using. Her lack of intense interest was a mixed blessing. Although she would not work as hard on this issue, her mind already on the next more challenging ones, she would interfere less. I could (well, almost) do exactly what I wanted with the fashion section.

"Well, then." Mavis leaned back in her overstuffed armchair to light a cigarette. "That's settled. Gretel, you get together with the individual editors to determine which artists or photographers you will use. It looks like the issue will be all right. A traditional bridal theme, but with a few surprises among the lace." Mavis puffed for a few moments in silence. Alix and I remained seated, not moving. We had not been officially dismissed.

"Well, then," Mavis repeated through the bluish smoke. Her gaze was calmer, more genuine. We had obviously finished discussing business. "You look fabulous, Gretel. A walking advertisement for marriage. I shall fear an epidemic at *Milady*." I smiled to myself, remembering my thoughts over lunch. It was indeed going to be a challenge to be a happily married woman with everyone commenting on it. Manhattan was definitely the island of the not-so-gay divorcee.

At Mavis's urging, I again related the past two weeks, although in a highly abbreviated version. After all, Alix had already heard. Alix sat still, seemingly fascinated, especially as I described Hoek Land.

"Can you imagine, Mavis?" she interjected. "Living on your very own island? In New York City's harbor nonetheless! And so picturesque and unspoiled. Why Gretel says it's something right out of the seventeenth century. Isn't that so?" I agreed.

Alix then deftly turned the subject of conversation to the upcoming fall fashions that we would be featuring in the August issue, the "back-to-school" issue. We would be concentrating, as usual, on the girls just going off to college, and the recent graduates who were starting their first job; the changes in wardrobe these new life-styles would demand.

"I've seen a few previews," Alix continued, "and it really seems a more traditional approach this year. An up-dated, old-fashioned look. A classic look. Hemlines are shorter this year. We shall have to scout

out a traditional location, I think, something with a touch of class. Oh, but I'm *so* bored with some bucolic campus, or some plastic fantastic office. Everybody does that, from *Glamour* to *Essence*, every year, over and over. Aren't you all bored with it, too?" Alix asked, but didn't wait for a reply. "If only . . ." She paused. "Oh, I've the most wonderful idea. If only, oh, but it's too much to ask." Alix looked over at me, biting her lower lip delicately. It was all I could do to keep from laughing. Whatever else she was (co-worker, gossip, friend), Alix was not a convincing actress.

"Oh, Gretel," she went on. "I know it's a lot to ask, but do you think, since it's so *romantic*, do you think it would be possible, but only if you want to, do you think that we could possibly, just possibly, do the fall shooting at Hoek Land?"

"What?" I hadn't been expecting this.

"Use Hoek House for the location. Definitely the exterior, perhaps the interior. Depending on what we want to do, of course. Oh, it'd be so wonderful, so different. And, of course"—Alix turned to smile at Mavis—"so inexpensive. No traveling, no hotels. No more costs than doing the whole thing in a studio."

"That is appealing." Mavis nodded. I felt trapped.

"But, of course, Gretel, only if you want to." Alix turned the full battery of her charm on me. I was trapped.

"Well," I began, faltering. "Perhaps it's not what you—we—want. I do have a tendency to make it sound like a paradise. But I am prejudiced, of course."

"An authentic, seventeenth-century Dutch house? With bricks and diamond-paned windows and a gigantic chimney? And a courtyard? And a dock? And trees? It's what we want!" Alix insisted. "Why we can do everything there—from sports clothes to evening wear. If we searched the whole Northeast, we'd never find anything so ideal."

"Have you seen it?" asked Mavis, lighting another cigarette.

"Well, no," Alix admitted.

"As I recall from your expense accounts, you insist on investigating locations before a decision is made. A location in the Caribbean might require a little more investigation than a location in New York, but even so." Mavis shrugged casually. There was nothing casual in the way she fixed her black eyes on Alix.

"Oh, well. I was just getting carried away," Alix floundered about.

"Of course, we would have to go there, take Polaroids, and hold a meeting."

Perhaps it was out of pity for Alix. Perhaps it was out of unmitigated pride in my new home. Whatever it was, I was suddenly prompted to invite both Alix and Mavis for dinner at Hoek House, adding, "It can't be for a couple of weeks yet," shuddering inwardly at the state of the kitchen. Despite my cleaning attacks, it still remained stubbornly dingy. Yes, I told myself, it would have to be painted.

"Well, then," said Mavis. "Let's say two weeks from next Saturday, the first Saturday in March. That should give you enough time to settle in?" She raised her thick black eyebrows questioningly. I nodded. "Naturally, we'll be more than understanding if you don't feel that you're organized. These things take time. We won't be shooting the August issue until"—Mavis consulted her calendar— "the beginning of May, end of April, so there's plenty of time. But I do think that it's a splendid idea." She beamed at us both in turn. "That's all, ladies, thank you and enjoy your evenings." We were officially dismissed.

As we left Mavis's office, I glanced down at my watch: 5:20. Ten minutes left in the workday! Meetings were a waste of time.

"Very successful, don't you think?" Alix asked as we walked down the hall.

"In many ways, yes. But why didn't you give me any warning about using my house? Dirty Tricks Department that one."

"Oh no, Gretel. Really. It came to me in a flash," Alix protested.

"Uh-huh. Well, you've cadged a dinner, but it's up to Pieter whether or not it happens," I said.

"Admit it, Gretel, it'd be fun to do a shoot at your house."

"It would, true. But Pieter might not think so," I replied with a dim sense of foreboding. Although, I thought to myself back in my office, there wasn't any reason why Pieter should object. I'd keep everyone away from his studio. He might be amused by the shenanigans of a fashion shooting. He might even enjoy having the models about. Meanwhile, however, I had a dinner party to get through. I immediately called Melissa and made certain she was free for dinner that night, the second of March. I had no intention of going through with it without her help.

Five-thirty and time to go home. I felt strangely exhausted by my first day back, even though I really hadn't worked all that hard. But, as I surveyed my office before locking the door, it felt good to have my identity back.

In a few short minutes, I was plummeting down in the elevator, dashing out of the World Trade Center and walking the short distance to the private pier. Yes, there was my *Silver Fox*, bobbing gently where I'd left her. I clambered down, and began to unhook the tarpaulin I had put over her, then stopped. There, lying in the center of the tarp, was a rectangular piece of white cardboard. In the middle of the board the sign of El Condor was crudely printed—the large, winged bird hovering over New York City, its wing just touching the World Trade Center towers. Always a threatening image, the graphic now took on new meaning. It seemed to be personally threatening me. I worked in the World Trade Center.

Wait a minute, Gretel, I said to myself. Why would El Condor be threatening you? No reason, unless . . . I remembered the man I had seen Pieter talking to in Puerto Rico. Then the encounters had been mysterious, now they seemed ominous. Could that man have been connected to El Condor? Then, could Pieter? Wait a minute, I said again. Just because Pieter's half Puerto Rican doesn't mean that he would have anything to do with a Puerto Rican terrorist group. There is no reason for El Condor to know who he is, or who you are. It's a coincidence that this poster was put on the *Silver Fox*. It's probably stuck on every boat and wall in the area. New York graffiti. I threw it into the river, where it slowly sank, but not before I had seen the words "Car Service" printed on the other side. Another coincidence? There, that's the end of that, I thought, folding up the tarpaulin and climbing into my boat. I couldn't let a little thing like that bother me or I would start being afraid. Weird things happen in New York and you can't let it get you down. You forget quickly. You don't look back. I started up the motor and eased the *Silver Fox* out into the harbor.

It hadn't registered until now that I would be going home in the dark. I sat for a moment, letting the motor idle, accustoming myself to the gloom. Although I blamed my apprehension on my nervous state, I wished I had practiced driving the boat at night. But I couldn't sit here worrying. I couldn't be afraid. I sighed, pulled on the boat's headlights, and slowly started for home.

Once my initial fright passed and I relaxed, I quite enjoyed the trip. The harbor was lovely at night, not dark really, more gray from the lights of the surrounding buildings and the other ships. As I passed the ships anchored off Governor's Island, I automatically scanned the decks for a sign of Ensign Dragon, but there was no way to tell if he was there or not. I crossed the harbor without incident (the trip taking little more than a quarter of an hour), docked easily at Hoek Land, put the *Silver Fox* cozily in the boathouse, and headed eagerly up to the house. I decided not to mention anything to Pieter about the poster. It was silly, after all, and he would only fret about my safety.

"Hel-lo," I called out as I reached the courtyard. Pieter was working in his studio, I could see him silhouetted against the light. He waved and came to open the door for me.

"Welcome home. How was your day?" he asked. We both laughed at the reversal of roles. "I've even started dinner for you," he added.

"You're kidding," I said, delighted. I was ravenous. It seemed a long time since lunch.

"I'm a good cook," Pieter replied, kissing the tip of my nose.

"Apparently, there are still some things I have to learn about you," I said, taking off my jacket and—finally—my boots. I would definitely have to remember to carry a pair of shoes with me tomorrow.

I went to hang up my jacket, while Pieter busied himself at the stove. When I returned, he was bending over a casserole, the lid held delicately in his left hand, a wooden spoon in his right, stirring intently.

"Here," he called. "Taste this." Pieter thrust the wooden spoon at me.

I tentatively licked at its tip. "Good," I said.

"Hmmm." Pieter tasted it in turn. "I don't know. I think a few drops more lemon juice. There, that's much better. Don't you agree?" I tasted again. I couldn't tell any difference, but I shook my head yes. "Then, we're ready," Pieter announced. "Table set?"

"Oh, no. Just a minute." I scurried into the dining room. I hadn't expected Pieter to take charge of the meal like this. At best, I had expected a couple of hamburgers set to broil. I quickly set the table, lighting the two cream-colored candles we kept in the center. The highly polished candlesticks had been a wedding present from Melissa's parents. Pieter entered, bearing a steaming tray.

"What are we having?" I asked, sitting down to let him serve me.

"*Suprêmes de volaille à blanc.* With a few tender asparagus tips and"—Pieter lifted the cover off a serving dish—"some risotto. But first . . ." He disappeared back into the kitchen, returning with a bottle and two glasses. "First, a toast. To you, my lovely bride." Pieter poured the wine, and we touched glasses and drank.

"Well, I certainly am impressed," I said, surveying the table.

"A little something for your first day back at work," Pieter replied casually.

"But, but . . . all this! I didn't know you could cook."

"What, this? Anybody can cook chicken. With a little help from Julia Child." He winked.

"But you never said you could *cook*." I felt somewhat betrayed.

"You never asked. I enjoy it. It is a nice change after working."

We ate in companionable silence. It was delicious. I served myself a second, huge helping.

"Well, you can cook at our first dinner party," I said, smiling at him over my wineglass.

"What?" said Pieter, only half paying attention.

I sighed. "Two weeks from Saturday. My editor in chief, Mavis, and my fashion editor, Alix, whom I believe you already know. And Melissa, of course."

"Lot of women," Pieter muttered.

"You're right. I'll tell them that they can bring dates. That would be fun."

"What's fun about eating with a bunch of people you don't know?" asked Pieter.

"Oh dear. To be honest, I was sort of tricked into it. I was praising Hoek Land to everyone, and it just evolved." I hadn't expected Pieter to be ecstatic, but I hadn't expected him to be dismayed, either. "You can always spend the evening in the kitchen. How many women can brag of a live-in chef?" I teased.

"No more bragging to anyone, please," said Pieter, shaking his head, chuckling, "or they'll write me up in that magazine of yours."

* * *

I soon settled into a routine. By Friday, it seemed as natural to soar across the harbor in the *Silver Fox* as it had once to step from my apartment building to hail a cab. And it was definitely more fun, no matter what the weather.

That morning, I finally saw Ensign Dragon again on a ship circling Governor's Island. I waved cheerily, then slowed the *Silver Fox* to identify myself, calling out his name. He ordered the engine stopped on his own boat, blushing slightly when one of the crew said something with a glance at me. I decided definitely that Ensign Dragon was quite young.

This impression was confirmed shortly. We chatted for a few minutes, Ensign Dragon leaning over the railing of his boat—which, he told me, was an icebreaker, one of half a dozen assigned to keep the Hudson River free of ice. He was a recent graduate of the Coast Guard Academy in New London, Connecticut; he had only been on active duty a few months. This assignment to the headquarters on Governor's Island was his very first. He spoke of the Coast Guard with pride, saying it was a unique military service in that its goals were humanitarian ones. I decided that Ensign Dragon was quite nice.

"My only regret so far," he added, "is that I haven't seen very much of the city, other than the insides of a few bars when we've been off duty. I suppose you know New York well?"

"Oh, yes," I said. "I've been coming to New York all my life, and living in Manhattan for the past seven years. It's really very easy to find your way around. Where are you from?"

"South Dakota," Michael Dragon said. "But I'm sure it's more fun to go around with someone. I'm on duty most nights, but I can easily arrange something, if . . . if," he stuttered slightly, "that is if you'd . . ."

"Oh!" I exclaimed, interrupting him. I had just remembered Pieter's remark about too many women at our upcoming dinner party. "Would you be free on Saturday, March the second?"

"Sure. We trade off on weekends." Michael Dragon's smile rivaled the early morning sunshine.

"Good. I'm giving a dinner party then, and I'm a bit short of men. It will be fun. And that way you'll get to know Pieter, though you've probably seen him cruising about the harbor."

"Oh. You have a brother?"

"Two in fact, but Pieter's my husband. It's his family that owns the island. I only came to live there when we got married. It's been almost a month now," I added proudly.

"Oh. You're married." Michael Dragon's smile had vanished completely. Oh no, I thought, he didn't . . . oh dear. I felt a slight pang of guilt. Had I been flirting with him?

"Yes," I said. "But you will come, won't you?" I urged, starting up the motor. I was going to be late for work. Michael seemed to be turning things over in his mind, but finally he nodded. I felt relieved, we could be friends.

"What time?" he shouted, cupping his hands about his mouth to be heard over the engine's noise.

"Eight," I called back over my shoulder, waving as I gunned the *Silver Fox* for Manhattan. In another twenty minutes, I was at my desk, answering the first of my morning phone calls. Pieter called me midmorning. He had to come to Manhattan to deliver some drawings to a gallery in Soho, they wanted them sooner than he had expected. As his appointment was in the afternoon, he suggested we have lunch.

"Great!" I answered, hoping to show him off to the office. "Do you want to come here?"

"No, meet me at, uh, at Fraunces Tavern," said Pieter.

"Fine. I've never been there. I can be there in about half an hour."

"Make it forty-five minutes," said Pieter, and he hung up the phone.

I chuckled as I replaced the receiver. If Pieter and I spoke to each other in the mornings like other, more normal young marrieds, our lunch plans would have already been arranged. But Pieter was already in his studio by the time I made it down to the kitchen for my first cup of coffee, and I had made it a rule never to disturb him while he worked. As a result, unless we called each other, our first conversation of the day was usually over dinner. Lunching with Pieter would be a real treat, a perfect ending to my first week back at work. I hurriedly called my lunch date (a semi-business meeting with a color retoucher that I was considering canceling anyway), and tried to finish up my morning's work in the next twenty minutes. I certainly didn't want to keep Pieter waiting.

An hour later, I was being led through the boisterous lunchtime crowd, ducking around business-suited diners, following in the wake of a nimble-footed waiter who presented me with a flourish to a small table tucked away in a relatively quiet corner. A table at which sat Pieter, looking slightly out of place in his paint-spattered jeans, already halfway through a beer. He brushed aside my profuse apologies with an impatient gesture.

"No matter, no matter. An interesting place to sit. All the Wall Street flunkies soothing their ulcers," Pieter said between sips. He ordered another beer and one for me. I noticed he had his sketch pad on his knees. A large manila envelope (his drawings, I assumed) was leaning against the wall behind him.

"More victims for your collection?" I asked, remembering his caricatures of the tourists in Puerto Rico.

"Nothing much, just a few doodles," Pieter answered, moving the pad to the floor beside his chair, out of my reach. I had moved my hand toward the pad. A few minutes later he seemed to think better of it, and picked up the pad to slide it underneath him. He sat on it for the remainder of the meal.

"Boy," he muttered, looking about us. "Another big bang is what's needed here."

"What?" I was surprised by the bitterness in Pieter's tone. I knew he thought little of "fat, capitalistic cats" as he termed New York City's lawyers and bankers, but I had always thought it an abstract reference—directed more at the monolithic institutions they worked for, not the men themselves. "What *are* you talking about?"

"Don't you remember?" asked Pieter.

"Oh, right." I did recall something. "There was an explosion here several years ago."

"January of 1975, to be precise. Four people were killed and fifty-three injured. It was complete chaos. People were hurled from their seats in the middle of lunch, others staggered into the streets. The blast was so powerful that one victim was decapitated," Pieter said calmly.

I shook my head in disgust. The historic landmark restaurant, where George Washington had bade farewell to his officers in 1783, had lost some of its charm.

"The Puerto Rican liberation movement, the F.A.L.N., took credit for the explosion," Pieter continued. "That was what brought the organization national attention. After that, everyone knew they were a force to be reckoned with."

I was even more disgusted. I recalled the explosion of the oil barge last fall, which had introduced the city and the nation to El Condor.

"El Condor is supposed to be an offshoot of the F.A.L.N.," I mused aloud.

"What a preposterous idea. Nothing could be further from the truth." Pieter suddenly stopped, as though realizing what we were talking about. "What do you know about El Condor?" he asked sharply.

"Nothing," I admitted, shrugging my shoulders. "Just what they had on the news after that barge explosion. Why?"

"No reason," Pieter said, smiling again. "Don't take offense, but I've never thought of you as having an interest in things politic. Here comes the food."

"Gretel? Gretel Drew?" A firm hand grasped my shoulder just as I took my first bite of my hamburger. Still chewing, I looked around and up.

"John Cotton! My God! It's been years!" I hurriedly swallowed my food to greet him.

"Seven, to be precise. I don't think I've seen you since I went off to law school. Actually, I've just moved back to the city. I spent a couple of years in Washington after taking my degree," said John, leaning casually on the back of my chair. He was attired in the perfect lawyer's uniform: three-piece gray pin-stripe suit, blue- and red-striped (not too wide) tie, but the broad smile on his ruddy face was as mischievous as it had been the summer I was ten and Johnny Cotton had dared me to climb the oak tree in his back yard. And then left me there for hours (it seemed), when I was too scared to climb down.

"I'm delighted you're back in the city. Oh, excuse me. Pieter, this is John Cotton. We grew up together. John, this is my husband, Pieter Van der Hoek." Pieter half rose and John leaned over to shake hands.

"Congratulations," John said. "When did this happen? Mother usually keeps me up to date on the latest neighborhood gossip."

"Oh," I smiled, "we're newlyweds."

"Wonderful!" said John, beaming at us. "Speaking of neighborhood gossip," he continued. "You wouldn't happen to have Melissa's phone number, would you? Someone said she'd gotten a divorce. Is that true?"

"A year and a half ago. It was a mistake from start to finish." I shook my head. "Oh," I said suddenly. "That's right!" John blushed slightly, and I turned to explain to Pieter, saying, "Melissa and Johnny were the perfect high school couple. She was captain of the cheerleading squad and John was our star soccer player."

"They should definitely be reunited," said Pieter. "My wife is engineering a dinner pary, the first Saturday in March. Melissa will be there, and it seems as good an opportunity as any for a reunion."

"Great!" John exclaimed. "I'm free that evening and would be delighted to come."

"Then, it's settled," said Pieter, and proceeded to tell John where we lived. ("An island?" asked John. "An island," said Pieter. I nodded in confirmation.) We exchanged a few more pleasantries, and then John left, pleading an appointment at his office.

"Whatever possessed you to do that?" I asked.

"I like bringing people together. It does my romantic soul good. Besides, I like John. He's perfect for Melissa. She needs someone strong and stolid. And he's obviously adored her for years. Why on earth did she ditch him for her ex-husband?"

"It's a long, long story, and hardly worth the telling. I hope Melissa wants to be reunited with John as much as you both want her to be."

"Of course she does. And don't you go telling her, either. It should be a surprise," said Pieter.

"You're kidding! What an awful thing to do!"

"Trust me. It will be a disaster otherwise. Promise?" said Pieter.

"Okay. Promise," I muttered. I resumed eating my lunch. I was exceedingly hungry. I had Pieter order an extra plate of french fries.

"Considering how slim you are, it's amazing how much you eat," said Pieter.

"Oh pooh. I'm just hungry now because I didn't eat any breakfast. I had an upset stomach. I didn't even have any coffee."

"Something you ate yesterday?" asked Pieter.

"No. Who knows? Maybe I'm pregnant."

"Why do you say that?" said Pieter.

"Oh, no reason." I had said it casually, as something unlikely, a joke. Yet now I wondered—no, I couldn't be. Pieter was looking at me speculatively. I felt uncomfortable, and fished around for a new topic of conversation, saying the first thing that popped into my head.

"Did I tell you what Alix wants to do? Shoot the August fashion section at Hoek Land, using our house as background," I blithered.

"What?" said Pieter.

"It's not definite, it's just an idea. . . ." I faltered.

"It's a terrible idea," said Pieter.

"Oh, I don't know. It might be fun. We would do everything outside, so the house wouldn't be disturbed. It would be a lovely location."

"What's 'lovely' about having hundreds of people trampling the place?" said Pieter.

"Oh, silly. There wouldn't be hundreds, just me and Alix and her two assistants. The photographer and *his* assistants. And five or six models. Wouldn't you like having pretty girls around?"

"I've got my pretty girl," said Pieter.

I blushed like a schoolgirl. "Seriously, Pieter, you aren't going to forbid us the shooting, are you?" I thought of how embarrassing it would be to tell that to Mavis and Alix. "I could probably wrangle a location fee, say, a hundred, hundred and fifty per day."

"That's not necessary, Gretel," Pieter replied, his dark eyes twinkling under their heavy lids. "Money is the least of our worries."

"Oh?" I replied. Although he certainly was not starving, neither was Pieter one of the top illustrators in New York whose work was in such demand that they could command outrageously high fees for their paintings. Pieter's drawings were popular, however, and he was able to earn a comfortable living. But I certainly would have thought that an extra few hundred dollars would have been welcome, especially after the major expenses (the honeymoon, the *Silver Fox*, the washer and dryer, the new couch for the living room) we had recently incurred. Of course, there was now my salary, too. . . . I should really sit down with Pieter one night to plan a budget. I looked at my watch. "Oh, dear," I sighed. "Two-thirty. I really should be getting back. And I wanted to look upstairs, too, at the Revolutionary War museum on the third floor."

"Another time," promised Pieter. We paid the check. Pieter ushered me through the still-crowded restaurant. We stood for a few moments outside the handsome brick structure, savoring the bright sunshine. It was one of those false warm winter days that makes one long for spring. I decided to take full advantage of it and walk back to the office. I had hoped Pieter might walk with me, but he regretfully shook his head.

"Sorry, but I've goofed off long enough. I've got to deliver these drawings and get back to work. I promised the agency that I would have the whole job done no later than ten o'clock Monday morning, and I've been having difficulty finishing them up. See you tonight." Pieter turned, gave me a quick kiss, and hurried off.

I glided north on Broad Street, turning left on Wall Street, skirting the tiny dark cemetery of Trinity Church. I turned for a moment to look down Wall Street before cutting over toward the World

Trade Center towers. It was as though I was peering down a canyon. The sun's rays barely penetrated to the thick, dark, crowded buildings that housed the world's finances. I shivered, and not only because of the pale winter sun.

* * *

All weekend long I fought it, but by Monday morning, I surrendered. I did not feel well. I wasn't sick enough to stay in bed, but I felt tired. Though I could eat heartily, certain foods repelled me. And I couldn't eat anything in the morning.

The tiredness was easily explainable. I was continuing with a demanding full-time job while taking care of a house, and a husband, in addition to a bizarre commute. As soon as I had adjusted myself to this new schedule and new demands, I thought, I would return to my usual high-energy level.

My upset stomach was less easily rationalized. It could be nerves, a result of maintaining my new hectic pace. It could be that certain foods were beginning to disagree with me (old age, I moaned). It could be a lot of things.

"Of course you're run down," Melissa said at lunch a couple of hours later. "You're busy night and day. You might be developing an ulcer, and that's what it sounds like. Honestly, Gretel, it's depressing to sit across from you and watch you eat cottage cheese!" Melissa paused to eat a few mouthfuls of her highly seasoned eggplant parmigiana. "Maybe you picked up some weird stomach parasite in Puerto Rico. San Juan's Revenge. That would be interesting."

"Oh, very," I replied, sipping my milk.

"Well," Melissa continued. "I've exhausted my supply of medical knowledge. See your doctor."

"It's nothing, really," I protested.

"Maybe. Maybe not. You're better off knowing. If it is something, you get better. If not, then you'll get better anyway. You should check it out. I know someone who felt draggy for months, then finally she went to the doctor, and do you know what she had? It was a . . ."

"Please." I held up my hand. Melissa liked telling ghoulish tales. She was a catalogue of carcinogenic calamities.

"Well, anyway," she sniffed. "She recovered. But it took *years*. Not that I think it's anything serious like, uh, that. You're basically too disgustingly healthy. If I didn't know, *I'd* say you're preggers."

"God! I haven't heard that word since . . ."

"Miss Black's home room, seventh grade."

"Yeah, that was Mary Ellen DeVito's favorite word. Remember how she went about saying it all the time?"

"Until old Blackie told her what it meant." Melissa shook her head. "There's always one in every class."

I agreed. A tender memory: "preggers"—like a cat. It was silly, yet Melissa's idle remark moved my hand to the phone once I'd returned to my office. I misdialed Dr. Weiss's number twice before I got through. His receptionist, as always, was concerned, but once she'd had me admit that it wasn't exactly an "emergency"—just a checkup —the earliest she could squeeze me in was Friday noon.

Which meant that for four days I avoided the obvious with everyone, especially Pieter. I actually threw up only once and told myself that it was seasickness. I tried to lose myself in cleaning and applying the finishing touches to the kitchen's paint job (Was I allergic to paint fumes?) in preparation for my dinner party. Lord knows, there was certainly enough work for five women for five years. But on Friday morning there was no way to pretend my queasiness was anything but what it seemed—morning sickness. Usually, I avoided Pieter in the mornings, but that morning he chose to sleep late. As I went in and out of the bathroom, he looked at me curiously enough so that I had to change the atmosphere quickly.

"Heigh-ho, off to the salt mines," I said once I had finished dressing. "I hope I see Ensign Dragon this morning. His ice boat's been clearing the Hudson River all week."

"Who?" asked Pieter, poking his head through his sweater and wrestling it on.

"Oh. Haven't I told you?" I flicked off the bedroom light and led the way downstairs to the kitchen. "He's my friend in the Coast Guard. He's stationed at Governor's Island. At first, we just waved. Then one day we chatted. He's very nice and *very* young. I invited him to dinner with Alix and Melissa and Mavis. I'd thought it'd even out the man-woman ratio you were complaining about."

"You what?" asked Pieter.

"I invited Ensign Dragon to dinner. His first name's Michael, by the way." I finished tying my scarf about my neck and looked up to smile at Pieter, hoping that this conversation had distracted him from any curious concerns about my health. It had, only too well.

"You invited an ensign of the Coast Guard to dinner at Hoek House? We're going to have the Coast Guard here?" said Pieter.

"Well, well, uh," I stammered.

"The Coast Guard? Hah!" Pieter crashed off to his studio, slamming the kitchen door behind him.

Two minutes later I crashed off to the dock, slamming the door behind me. I was furious. If Pieter thought I was going to become a recluse like he had once been, he had another think coming. I had every right to invite whomever I pleased whenever I wanted. Pieter would just have to learn to like it or . . . or what? I couldn't answer that. Really, he had been too silly, slamming doors. And I had been equally childish, not telling him about not feeling well and my appointment that day with Dr. Weiss.

I had decided by ten-thirty, while discussing with the food editor which recipes were more photogenic, that I would level with Pieter as soon as the doctor had told me I was a healthy hypochondriac. By twelve, sitting anxiously on the examining table in Dr. Weiss's Park Avenue office, I had also decided that I would behave myself forever and never lie to Pieter again, as soon as the doctor stopped inspecting me so seriously and told me I was a healthy hypochondriac. He didn't.

"Well, Gretel, you're a very healthy young lady, as always," said Dr. Weiss, slowly straightening up. He smiled, the fine lines about his eyes deepening. "Marriage has definitely agreed with you in that respect. But"—he glanced at me over his glasses—"this complaining of being tired and some stomach problems."

"Yes, I've been having upset stomachs, especially in the morning."

"Well, I don't think you're anemic, though of course we'll test for it. There's not the slightest chance of an ulcer. The nurse will be in to take some blood, then, get dressed and come into my office."

After the nurse had left, I dressed quickly, shaking as I did so. Using the doctor's white-framed mirror, I brushed my hair vigorously and decided to reapply my rouge. I did look awfully pale. Suppose it wasn't the beginning stages of pregnancy, suppose it was something more. . . . Oh, stop it! You're as bad as Melissa and her horror stories.

"Young lady," said Dr. Weiss as soon as I was seated before him in his dark-paneled, thick-carpeted office. "My guess is that you are pregnant."

"I thought it might be that," I said, "but it didn't seem likely. I mean, I do practice birth control."

"How many weeks are you overdue?"

"Only a week, a week and a half, I guess. I've never been regular," I answered.

"You've never been married, either," said Dr. Weiss with a smile. "I'm a father seven times over and a grandfather of two. I think I know a pregnant woman when I see one. But the tests will say for sure. The results will be ready by the middle of next week. Though I can rush them if you want."

"That's okay. I really don't think I am. I don't feel pregnant. I've always thought I would." I smiled confidently, continuing, "My mother said you could tell almost from the very moment of conception."

"You do feel different. It's called morning sickness. Miss Henley will be calling you with the results either Wednesday or Thursday. Have a good day." Dr. Weiss made some more notes, put them in a file, and put that to one side. My visit was over.

A week, I thought as I caught a cab back downtown to my office. It was inconvenient having a doctor on upper Park Avenue, but I had been going to Dr. Weiss for seven years, since I had first moved to the city. He had nursed me through a severe case of chicken pox without ever teasing me about catching a childhood disease in my mid-twenties, or scolding me about not getting an inoculation. That consideration had earned my undying loyalty and trust.

A week. Perhaps I should have had him rush through the tests. No, if I was pregnant, I didn't want to know. And if I wasn't, then it didn't matter. The time would pass quickly enough. One thing was for sure; now I couldn't mention my visit to Dr. Weiss to Pieter until I knew the results. I hadn't liked the look on Pieter's face when I had joked about pregnancy the week before at Fraunces Tavern. He apparently had enough to fret about just getting used to being married. That was why he'd been so irritable this morning, I thought. He isn't used to a woman doing what she wants. And Gretel Drew Van der Hoek does what she wants. And now I was caught by my own stubbornness. I hadn't told Pieter about being ill because I didn't want to worry him, and now I couldn't tell him about it because I didn't want to worry him. A mess. But I resolved, as the cab pulled up to the World Trade Center, that I would apologize to Pieter first. It seemed the least I could do.

But Pieter outmaneuvered me. There was a message to call him waiting for me on my desk.

"I called to apologize for this morning," said Pieter when he answered the phone. His voice was both cajoling and charming. "I didn't mean it. I had no business berating you for inviting your soldier friend."

"Coast Guard," I corrected quickly.

"Coast Guard. Whatever. A uniform's a uniform. One's just like another. Anyway, it's your home, too. I'm sure that, uh, whoever, is very nice."

"Dragon."

"*Ridiculous* name. Really, what I'm trying to say is that I had no right to criticize your choice of guests. This is your home, you have as much right to invite anyone here as I have. I've become a hermit and a good thing it is that I married you. To save me from a lonely life."

"Well," I responded, mollified. After all, Pieter was only confirming my own thoughts. "If Ensign Dragon offends you in any way, just say the word, and I shall have him thrown off the place. Bodily." I blew him a kiss over the phone and rang off.

Yet once off the phone, I resumed my brooding. This dinner party already promised to be complicated, what with Pieter reuniting Melissa with her childhood sweetheart, and with Mavis always turning the conversation to her only topic, *Milady* magazine. Alix would undoubtedly try to bewitch poor Ensign Dragon. Pieter would sit silent, sipping whiskey, watching us all through hooded eyes. And now I wouldn't know until almost the day before whether or not I was pregnant.

Pregnant! I repeated the word so many times to myself that it completely lost its sense. I couldn't decide if I was happy or not. We wanted to have children, naturally, but we hadn't planned on having them so soon. I placed my hand on my stomach. No, it wasn't possible. I resolved not to think about it.

Yet I couldn't concentrate on my job. I was completely out of touch with the day. I broke off phone conversations, misplaced memos, and almost broke the slide projector. I was so befogged that in the midafternoon I didn't pay attention to a sudden burst of activity in the halls. There was a great scurrying, and I heard a whistle being blown several times. But I ignored it all, until Maggie rushed into my office, a panicked look on her face, and grabbed my arm roughly, saying,

"Come *on*, Gretel! What are you still sitting here for?"

"What are you talking about?"

"Someone set off a bomb on the floor above! There's been an explosion! Can't you smell the smoke?" said Maggie. She was on the verge of crying.

I sniffed. I smelled smoke! I could even see it. I grabbed my coat and purse and followed Maggie out of the office. The smoke was thicker in the hallways. We both choked as we made our way to the fire exits.

As I later learned, only the ten floors above the explosion and the ten floors below were evacuated. Once at the fire exits, we joined the line of people making their way down the stairs to the forty-first floor. From there, the elevators would speed us to safety. We were an orderly group, there was little panic displayed. I, for one, was too scared to talk. I concentrated on putting one foot in front of the other, never taking my eyes off the steps. My left hand slid along the railing, my right hand clutched my purse. Then we were on the forty-first floor and being herded by undemonstrative policemen into the elevators. Curiously, the descent in the elevators seemed to last two hours, while our much longer march in the stairwell seemed to last only a few moments. Once on the ground, I gulped fresh air as though I hadn't breathed for the past hour and my legs shook so much I nearly fell to the ground. I held onto an equally shaken Maggie for support. We staggered our way into the main plaza.

There was a large crowd gathering; everyone buzzed with their version of what had happened.

"There's a guy up there with a machine gun. Says he won't leave until he gets a million dollars!" "Nyah, it's that crazy guy, that toymaker from Queens climbing up the building again." "It's a real fire! I saw the flames myself. I thought I'd have to jump!" "And a good thing, too!" "Aw, it's just a movie!" "Yeah, I was here when they made *King Kong*. Got paid, too, for just standing around." "Yeah, well I better get paid for today. Remember the blackout? They called us up and told us to stay home. And we got docked a day's pay. I'm staying right here till five o'clock." "Yeah, well if they start shooting, I ain't sticking around, I tell you." "There ain't gonna be no shooting, how many times I gotta tell ya? This is just some stunt. Them crazies always pick on the Trade Center. It's good publicity. Tell me, ya see anything happening?"

I looked up at the tower. No, I couldn't see anything. The concrete and glass structure was as implacable as it always had been. But I had seen the halls fill with blue smoke. Who knew what was going on inside? I was still shaking, however. What had happened, I wondered? That one guy had been right, people did pick on the World Trade Center. Whether for fun, like that tightrope walker or the mountain climber, or profit, like the disgruntled employee who had taken hostages because he was dissatisfied with his pay. We spotted Alix in the crowd.

"Hi," she said, slightly out of breath. "What a nuisance this all is. From what I've heard, it's only a smoke bomb. But they're searching for others. And clues, of course. Isn't it exciting?" she asked, her almond eyes dancing. "Now that we know no one was hurt, of course," she added hastily. "I say, Gretel, you do look pale. Are you all right?"

"I feel pale," I admitted. "Listen, this has been a hell of a day. They're undoubtedly going to close the building, but I can't wait for that. If Mavis asks, just say I didn't feel well."

"You aren't well," said Alix, suddenly concerned. "Can you get home all right, by yourself?"

"I'll be fine," I assured her.

"Okay. Get plenty of rest this weekend," she said. I hugged both her and Maggie and then headed toward the *Silver Fox.*

* * *

Pieter wasn't home. Just as well, I thought. I wanted to take a nap. I went upstairs, undressed, and climbed into our huge, four-poster bed, disturbing Samantha of course. She looked unsettled for a few moments (it was too early for me to be at home) and then she licked herself and recurled, adjusting to the contours of my body. I fell asleep instantly.

"What's all this?" asked Pieter, coming into the room to sit on the bed beside me. "You aren't sick, are you?"

"No, I . . . what time is it?" I asked.

"Six-thirty," said Pieter.

I had slept for three hours. I sat up quickly.

"Well, if you're not sick, why are you in bed? You've never taken a nap in the afternoon before." Pieter looked at me intensely. "Gretel, you look awful. Like this morning. Are you all right?"

"Yes, yes. We had some trouble at work." Briefly, I told him of the afternoon's events.

"No one was hurt?" said Pieter.

"No, thank God. There should be something on the news tonight. Oh no!" I said suddenly.

"What?" asked Pieter.

"It's my turn to cook dinner," I said. "I am sorry. I was going to make a casserole, but maybe there's some meat defrosted." I frowned slightly. I couldn't remember what we had and didn't have in the refrigerator.

"Forget it. I'll throw something together. You relax with the tube."

I settled myself in front of the small black and white TV set we kept in the kitchen, while Pieter busied himself at the stove. It was just seven—Walter Cronkite was reporting the world news. There was one story about the Mideast situation, and then he turned to the national news.

"A terrorist smoke bomb exploded in the northeast tower of the World Trade Center today, while several other bomb threats forced over 100,000 people to vacate their offices in Lower Manhattan. The smoke bomb was set off on the fifty-first floor of the tower. The ten floors above and below were evacuated safely. The radical Puerto Rican terrorist group El Condor took responsibility for the explosion, believed at first to be a genuine detonation." While Cronkite chatted, scenes of the crowds outside the World Trade Center flashed across the screen. I tried to find myself in the shots, but it was impossible.

"The evacuations caused traffic jams throughout the area, as entire streets and sidewalks were closed. All the buildings involved closed early, sending their workers home. Millions of dollars were lost to business.

"El Condor gained recognition last fall with the alleged sabotage of an oil barge. In a prepared statement read over the phone to a reporter from the Daily News, El Condor said that today's incident was the second warning. No lives have been taken so far, but the next time El Condor struck, there could be casualties. A list of demands was then read off, including independence for Puerto

Rico, and the freeing of all Puerto Ricans held as political prisoners." Mr. Cronkite paused, looking directly into the camera and saying,

"El Condor's claim that it has taken no lives is disputed by New York authorities. The body of Starr Mills, the heiress turned radical, was found washed up on Liberty Island after the oil-barge explosion. Although no connection has been made between Starr Mills and El Condor, police officials believe that her death was related to the explosion. FBI officials investigating Starr Mills's death, however, have refused to comment."

"Dinner's ready," said Pieter, smiling, setting plates down on the table. I flicked off the television and shifted my chair to face the table.

"Poor Starr. Why can't they leave her alone?" said Pieter between bites. He seemed sad.

"You knew her?" I choked on a piece of meat.

"Years ago. The summer she came out. I went to a few of her parties, including that one in Newport that finished her career. The papers made it out to be more than it was actually. But then, Starr always got bad press."

"I never would have guessed. I mean, you don't seem the high-society type," I said, trying to be glib. It didn't work.

"The Van der Hoeks are one of New York's oldest families. I was once a sought-after 'extra man.' But that was a long time ago. It's no longer my style. It really wasn't back then, either. But Starr's parties were always wild." Pieter chuckled at the memory. For some strange, silly reason, I was jealous.

"Why did she end up like that?" I asked.

"The usual. Too much money, too little brains." Pieter shrugged. "She stopped coming back to New York for summers, and then, of course, after college she went underground. No one saw her then. Officially anyway. You really interested in this old gossip?"

"Well, not really," I said. "Melissa's cousin came out that same year, so we heard lots of stories. I saw Starr once, she was gorgeous."

"That she was," Pieter agreed. "All that golden hair falling straight down her back." He raised his glass as if in a toast. We ate for a few moments in silence.

"Pieter," I said suddenly. "What do you think of children?"

"Which children?" he asked.

"Well, ours, for example."

"We have the most wonderful children in the world," he answered. "Because they don't exist."

"Pieter!"

"Well, I guess it's hard to imagine myself a father."

"Never?"

"No, of course not never. Why are you asking all these silly questions anyway?" said Pieter.

"Oh. We have to talk about a family sometime," I said, hoping I was keeping my voice casual.

"Yeah, but later." Pieter winked at me. "Samantha is all the child you and I can handle right now."

The meal finished abruptly with the ring of the phone. It was my mother, making sure I had been properly terrorized by El Condor. I assured her all was well. The minute I hung up, Melissa called. Like it or not, I spent the rest of the evening talking about terror and El Condor.

7

Blizzard

"How could you do such a thing to me?" Melissa hissed in my ear as she stepped inside Hoek House. We were using the front entrance for the first time. I felt elegant as I greeted our dinner guests.

"Whatever do you mean?" I said, helping her off with her coat. The silver fox was beautiful, but heavy.

"I thought I would choke when *he* turned up at the pier," she replied, jerking her head backward to John Cotton grinning broadly at us both.

"Oh," I said, laughing. "That was Pieter's idea."

"I thought Pieter liked me," Melissa muttered, pulling off her boots to slip on a flimsy pair of black-satin sandals.

"We ran into John at Fraunces Tavern a couple of weeks ago. Pieter liked him, especially after he learned you were once childhood sweethearts. Now, you'll have a wonderful time. Admit you're glad to see John."

"Humph," Melissa said sulkily. She adjusted the wide sleeves of her flowing chiffon blouse, smoothed out her close-fitting black-velvet slacks, and went over to charm John Cotton.

"Gretel, I must say that I admire you tremendously," said Mavis, coming over to hang up her coat in the closet. She was dressed in a knee-length, red-print dress that wrapped loosely to form a deep vee at her neck, where a single strand of large pearls gleamed softly.

"Why?" I asked in surprise.

"For making that boat trip twice a day. Rugged, very rugged."
Mavis paused to light a cigarette. "Though it was gorgeous. We
loved it."

"Darling, it's absolutely wonderful." Alix came over to hug me,
enveloping us in clouds of heavy perfume. "And you look absolutely
wonderful," she cooed, holding me out at arm's length to survey my
white-wool dress. "That creamy color sets off your tan perfectly."

I murmured something equally complimentary about her own
outfit, a deceptively simple confection in scarlet and peach char-
meuse that was slit in the most improbable places; a ruffled stole
added the finishing touch. Alix informed me it was from Saint
Laurent's new fall line. My wool dress was three years old. I sighed,
and as soon as everyone had divested themselves of their coats, I
herded them into the living room where Pieter was toying with a fire
in Adrian's chimney. Just then, Ensign Dragon arrived, looking
boyishly handsome in his dress uniform. As I opened the door, he
presented me with a large bouquet of a dozen perfect red roses, well
wrapped against the evening's chill.

"Oh, Michael, thank you. They're lovely. Ummmm." I sniffed
deeply. "They smell heavenly. Oh, Pieter, look," I said, as Pieter
came up behind me. "Look at these wonderful roses Ensign Dragon
brought. Michael, this is my husband, Pieter Van der Hoek. Pieter,
this is Michael Dragon."

"Pleased to meet you, Michael," said Pieter evenly. "Here, let me
have those. I was heading into the kitchen anyway, I'll get a vase for
them." Pieter leaned over to take the roses from me, whispering, "I
told you he had a crush on you" in my ear before disappearing. I
glared after him.

I escorted Michael into the living room and introduced him
around. As I had foreseen, Alix's eyes lighted up the moment she
spotted him, and so I handed him over to her.

Pieter was the chef for the evening. As he had planned to serve a
Puerto Rican menu, the drinks and hors d'oeuvres had to follow suit
I was just pouring the first of the mango daiquiris, while the other
were exclaiming over the *avisperos* (plantain fritters), when there
came a sharp rap at the front door. Surprised, for we were expecting
no one else, I waited before going to answer it. It could have been a
branch tapping. No, it was definitely a knock. I went to see who i
was.

"Good evening. Mr. Pieter Van der Hoek, is he in?" A lean dar

man, dressed in jeans and a dirt-stained down jacket, stood just outside the door. He spoke in a thick Spanish accent. His black eyes
darted from side to side—a prowling cat seeking its prey.

"Uh. Why, yes, he is." I gestured the man inside. With a click of
his heels, he bowed deeply and entered. Then he cocked his head toward the living room.

"But no, you have guests. I am disturbing you, I think." He turned
as if to go.

"No. No," I said hurriedly. "Let me go get Pieter." Pieter at that
moment entered the hallway, the vase of roses in his hands. "Oh,
Pieter, this gentleman came to see you. You should ask him to stay
to dinner."

"Oh, no, no, no," the man began, but Pieter silenced him.

"An excellent idea, Gretel. Gretel, this is Jesús de la Ponce. An old
friend. He teaches at Queens Community College. Latin American
Studies. Isn't that right, Jesús?"

"Oh yes," said Jesús, agreeing offhandedly. I thought him an interesting combination of courtliness and cunning.

"And this is Gretel, my wife. Oh yes, my wife," Pieter said, in response to the man's obvious surprise. "I gave up bachelorhood over a
month ago."

"Forgive me, I did not know. Felicitations upon you both." Jesús
bowed low at the waist, seizing my hand to kiss it.

"Enough," said Pieter. "It'll go to Gretel's head. She's been
spoiled enough tonight already."

"Oh, I like it," I said.

"In any case. Jesús, come into the kitchen with me, we've a few
things to catch up on. I'll bring him in in a few moments, as soon as
I've checked on dinner." Pieter kissed me briefly, handed me the vase
of flowers, then led Jesús off. I stood for a few moments, watching,
then turned and went back to our guests.

"What was all that about?" Melissa came over to ask me.

"I don't know. Some old friend of Pieter's. I've never met him.
He'll be staying for dinner." I settled the vase on the sideboard, turning it till the roses showed to their best advantage. I poured Melissa
another drink and urged some hot fritters on her. She looked at
them dubiously, but took one.

"Gretel, they're fabulous! What are they?" she said between
mouthfuls.

"These are plantain and the one you just finished codfish," I answered.

"You've really become quite a cook since your marriage." Melissa reached for another as I moved away to pass the tray to the others.

"It's not me, it's Pieter who's the chef," I confessed.

The cocktail hour passed pleasantly. Our guests commented favorably on the view of the harbor from the living-room windows and on the house itself. I spent a good twenty minutes closeted in a corner with Alix, listening to her describe how she saw the fashion pages we could shoot in this marvelous location. Her enthusiasm was infectious, and I cheerfully resigned myself to the fact that we would indeed photograph the August back-to-school clothes at Hoek Land. Mavis agreed heartily, suggesting that perhaps a feature on Dutch New York could be included in the issue.

"We could center our whole issue around it," continued Mavis, as if we were sitting in her office and not in my living room. "We could have Dutch recipes, German-American. Our travel feature could center on Amsterdam, and the home decorating could . . ."

"Excuse me." I smiled. "I think I'll see what Pieter's up to in the kitchen." I made my escape gracefully.

As I passed through the dining room, I could hear the murmur of voices, but when I entered the kitchen, all conversation stopped. Pieter was standing over the stove, alternately stirring and sipping. Jesús de la Ponce was seated at the table, piling chunks of lettuce haphazardly into a large glass bowl.

"How's it going?" I asked cheerfully, breaking the strangely uncomfortable silence.

"Fine, darling. Everything should be ready to serve presently," Pieter answered, peeking through the oven's glass door. "Are they getting restless?"

"No, not really. Drinking and nibbling happily. Your fritters, by the way, are a great success," I said, adding, "I just came by to see if you needed any help."

"None whatsoever," said Pieter.

"I could do the salad," I suggested, looking over at Jesús's handiwork.

"Jesús can handle it," said Pieter. "Now, Gretel, this is your party and I want you to relax and enjoy it. What if you spilled something on that lovely dress?" Pieter came over, took me by the elbows, turned me around, and headed me toward the door. "Now, away," he said firmly. "Go and enjoy your guests, even get a little drunk if you want." Pieter kissed the top of my head, opening the door and guiding me through at the same time. The door shut behind me. I stood in the darkened dining room for a few moments, slightly indignant. I wanted to say that they were *our* guests, and that I couldn't get drunk because it . . . I sighed and turned to survey the dining room. It looked lovely. The long table was covered by a heavy linen tablecloth that had been my mother's; matching linen napkins were softly folded at each place. Oh, my God! There were only seven places, and now we were eight. I hurriedly went to the table and made room. There. Pieter and I could use the unmatched silver. I put an extra water glass on the table and, straightening one of the chairs, I left the room. As I did so, the conversation in the kitchen started up again. Oh well—I shrugged—they're probably catching up on each other's news. I paused for a moment; no, I could catch none of the conversation. They seemed excited. I distinctly heard Jesús's voice raised. I listened harder, but he was speaking in Spanish. I was certain that he had said "Dirk." As always, any chance to learn more about Dirk attracted me and I turned to tiptoe back to the kitchen door. I caught myself. Really, Gretel! Eavesdropping on your own husband! I scolded myself, hurrying into the hallway before temptation could overcome me.

When I entered the living room, everyone was standing at the window, gazing intently at the harbor view. "What's going on?" I asked, noting that John Cotton rested his hand on Melissa's shoulder and that she was behaving as if it were the most natural thing in the world that it should be there.

"We're fascinated by the snow," answered Mavis without turning around. "It's glorious the way snow falls on water."

"Romantic," added Alix. Ensign Dragon blushed. Oh, my, I thought. Whatever was Alix doing to that poor boy? I joined them at the window.

A light silvery snow was falling so gently that one could make out the individual flakes. It was a gay, caressing snow which couldn't last more than an hour at the best. Well, we'd enjoy it while it lasted, I thought, amazed at how a group of adults could be stunned into silence by a small act of nature.

"Dinner is served," intoned Pieter. I turned to see him make a low bow. Then he straightened and laughed, asking (as I had), "What's going on in here? It was so quiet I thought everyone had left."

"Look at the snow, Pieter," I said, holding out my hand to him. "Isn't it wonderful?"

"About time, after predicting it on the news all week," Pieter said, draping his arm over my shoulders. "It is lovely, but so is dinner. A sensitive chef gets quite cross if his food isn't eaten at the proper temperature. Otherwise, it upsets *all* the flavorings," he sighed with mock dismay. Everyone laughed, and we all followed Pieter into the dining room.

Pieter and I sat at the ends of the table. Jesús sat at Pieter's right, then Alix and Michael Dragon on my left; Melissa sat to my right, then John, and, finally, Mavis. The grouping had evolved naturally: John Cotton was as determined to have Melissa beside him as Alix was to have Michael beside her (though she seemed anxious that he was beside me as well). Conversation ceased for the moment as Pieter served the first course, an avocado soup. When that was finished, I cleared the table while Pieter carved the main course, roast suckling pig stuffed with a rice and pigeon pea mixture. I poured the wine, a full-bodied Côtes du Rhône that had been uncorked (according to Pieter's direction) a few hours before. There was an appreciative silence while everyone tasted. Then the compliments were made to me, and I passed them back to Pieter.

It was inevitable, I suppose, that after a few preliminary remarks about the meal, the Coast Guard, and New York City, the conversation then turned to *Milady*'s staff's adventures during the recent smoke-bombing. Alix gave a harrowing description of how she had been almost overcome by fumes, only just being dragged to safety. I politely refrained from reminding her that she was out of the building before I was.

"Well, I, for one, found it a pain! I lost almost a whole day's work," said Melissa, shaking her head. Even though her office was on a lower floor, they, too, had been sent home. The whole northeast tower had been closed. "I had to go into the office last weekend, just to finish cleaning up," she continued.

"Just think what a nuisance it would have been if it had been a real bomb," said Mavis sarcastically.

"Well, of course," said Melissa, embarrassed. "But still, it seems to me that there should be better ways for terrorists to call attention to themselves."

"An ad in the *Times*?" said Pieter brutally, causing a stir at the table. I felt that it was time to steer the conversation more generally about the table, so I said:

"Jesús, tell us. You probably know more about this than any of us, what do you think of El Condor?"

Pieter's friend raised his sharp eyes to mine in apparent surprise. He looked quickly sideways at Pieter. It seemed to me that Pieter shook his head slightly. Jesús cleared his throat, and said, "But, señora, I know only what you all must know. What is in the papers."

"But surely, because of your work," I continued determinedly, "you must realize that revolutionaries play a significant role in Latin America's history. Apparently, the quest for Puerto Rican independence is for some a revolution. El Condor claims to be a freedom fighter, a one-man revolution . . ." I stopped short, realizing that I was pompously lecturing a teacher.

"Yes, señora. You are correct about Latin America. Revolution is for many, not just some, a tradition. For myself, I was born and raised happily in Puerto Rico, in the countryside just outside of San Juan. Which, I understand, you and Pieter visited a short time ago." I nodded yes. "I came here to attend Yale University, where I met Pieter, and I have stayed on to teach. I hope to return to San Juan within the next few years and take up permanent residence. So, while I wish a happy life for my country, I also wish for it a peaceful life. What happens anywhere that concerns Puerto Rico concerns me very much."

"You favor independence for Puerto Rico?" asked Melissa eagerly.

"It may come to that. It may not. I want whatever is best. Statehood is another possibility. Whatever is fair." Jesús shrugged noncommittally and added, "What has happened to Puerto Rico so far has not been fair."

"I would say that Puerto Rico has been treated very fairly," interjected John Cotton. The conversation was now committed to this topic; I felt powerless to change it. I could only hope that Pieter would not say something cruel again. "Every year," John continued, "the United States Government pours three billion dollars into Puerto Rico without collecting one cent in income tax from the island residents in return."

"A regrettable situation," agreed Jesús, "that the government itself created, señor."

"While creating a middle class with the highest standard of living in Latin America," John added.

"With over sixty per cent of the population on food stamps, and an unemployment rate of at least seventeen per cent," finished Jesús.

"True, true, sad but true. Still, Puerto Rico will never become a state," said John.

"Why do you say that?" asked Melissa.

"Because, it has little to offer the other states in return," he answered, proceeding to tick the answers off on his fingers. "It has few natural resources. Its naval base is of little military importance. It is vastly overpopulated. Its language is Spanish, as is its culture."

"You've left out the most important reason why Congress won't vote for it," Pieter said quietly, speaking for the first time.

"What's that?" said John. I began to feel as if we were participating in a seminar.

"If it were to become the fifty-first state, Puerto Rico would have a congressional delegation of two senators and seven representatives. A delegation that would put it ahead of, I believe, twenty-five states."

"That does seem a little out of proportion," said Alix.

"There are a lot of Puerto Ricans, five million in fact," stated Pieter. Alix must have remembered that Pieter was half Puerto Rican, for she blushed. Pieter continued, "And although the Puerto Ricans, both here and on the island, are natural-born U.S. citizens and are governed by the United States, they now have no say or active representation in Congress. They are citizens and foreigners at the same time. A paradoxical situation that's hardly happy."

"That, señora, is one reason for your revolutionaries," said Jesús, turning to me. "The Puerto Ricans have no political power, their options are limited. Some choose violence."

"The question of the future of Puerto Rico is a difficult one," said Pieter.

"It's one that Puerto Ricans themselves can't agree on," added Jesús. "There are many who reject statehood because they feel that it is an American solution being forced on their country. If statehood comes, there will be violence," he added quietly.

"Is El Condor among those who oppose statehood?" I asked quickly, since it seemed that Jesús's remark was double-edged.

"I think, Gretel, that enough questions have been asked," said Pieter gently, but firmly. "Politics threatens to become a boring topic of conversation."

"But politics, especially the politics of terrorists, has become so much a part of our lives," interrupted Alix. "I mean, every day we read of kidnapings, hijackings, there are explosions where we work, where we eat . . ."

"Yesterday in the papers there was a report of a large theft of explosives from a dockside warehouse in Brooklyn," said Mavis. "The terrorists again."

"Did it say that in the papers?" asked Pieter.

"No. But who else would have need of such things?" said Mavis.

"Was it a large amount?" I asked. I had missed the item in the news.

"Enough to blow up half of Brooklyn," Mavis answered.

"Don't worry about that," said Michael Dragon calmly.

"What makes you say that?" asked Pieter.

"Because the harbor is being watched constantly. I probably shouldn't say this, but the main theory is that it was an Irish terrorist group. Every ship out of this harbor is being monitored over the next few weeks, especially those carrying cargo to Britain. By the police and the Coast Guard," Michael finished, a trace of pride in his voice.

"Why do you suspect the Irish?" I asked, seeing a way to steer everyone away from Puerto Rico.

"Because the type of explosives stolen are the type favored by the I.R.A.," answered Michael.

"Perhaps it was El Condor," said Melissa. I sighed to myself, looking at my plate and pushing the food about.

"This El Condor, whoever or whatever he is, is not organized enough to pull off a major robbery," said Pieter.

"He's pulled off two daylight explosions that could have been serious ones," said Melissa.

"That's what's so frustrating about these terrorists," said John. "They're smarter than ordinary criminals, more rational. And the police can't infiltrate their gangs, because the terrorists deal only with people they've known and trusted for years. They are highly intelligent, dedicated. The police can't cope."

"That's right," Michael said. "And I did read in the paper that this El Condor was planning something else. It wouldn't hurt to check into this further."

"I think you'll find," Pieter said, somewhat condescendingly, "that your superiors have already considered and rejected the possibility."

"El Condor is not known in Puerto Rico," said Jesús. "He could have no reason to send explosives home."

"Home," repeated John, obviously bemused by Jesús's choice of words.

"Perhaps he just wants to get them out of New York," said Alix, coming to Ensign Dragon's defense.

"I think you're right, Pieter," I said hastily. "Dinner and politics don't mix well. I think, that if everyone has had enough, then it's time to bring out dessert and coffee. And tea, if anyone prefers." Mavis and John took tea. Melissa helped me clear. Pieter obviously thought he had made more than his contribution to the dinner, and remained in his seat.

Melissa had brought a wonderfully rich chocolate-orange torte from my favorite bakery in Greenwich Village. As I served the paper-thin slices, poured the coffee, and (eventually) offered liqueurs, the table resumed its former good humor; the conversation returned to the safely trivial as everyone told of *their* favorite bake shop. I listened in a well-fed stupor, regarding Pieter, thinking how handsome he appeared by candlelight.

"Oh, look," said Alix suddenly, pointing to the window. "It's still snowing. Can you imagine?"

"It's still lovely," agreed Melissa, turning in her chair to gaze out.

"Oh, let's all go for a walk," Alix said eagerly.

The others murmured their agreements. I demurred.

"But, Gretel, why?" asked Alix. "You don't think you're going to clean up while we're all outside, do you?"

"No," I said.

"Well?" she persisted.

"I don't feel like it," I answered.

"It'll do you a world of good. Help work off some of that dinner," added Melissa.

"It's bound to be very slippery. I have to take care of myself," I said.

"Why? You're not really sick, are you?" asked Melissa with sudden concern.

"Oh, no. As a matter of fact, I've never felt better in my life," I said, suddenly, recklessly exhilarated.

"Well?" said Alix.

"Oh, all right. Pieter, forgive me, I didn't plan to tell you this way, but . . ."

"What?" interrupted Melissa, narrowing her eyes. Pieter showed little interest in the conversation.

"Well, I'm, we're . . . Oh, Pieter and I are going to have a baby," I finished quickly before I lost my nerve, yet blushing as I did so.

"Oh, my goodness."

"Oh, how wonderful."

"Congratulations to you both."

"Oh, how exciting."

I sat in silence, accepting their well wishes, finally answering them, "Yes, uh, the doctor confirmed it yesterday. Probably late September, early October. Well, yes, it is a little early to be announcing it. But I've been so excited, and couldn't keep it to myself any longer. Well, no, we haven't discussed that yet." I looked to the opposite end of the table. Pieter stared at me in stunned silence. Then, before I had a chance to apologize, he nodded to Jesús, and they both left the room.

In the end, it was Melissa and John, and Alix and a somewhat reluctant Michael Dragon who went out for a walk. Mavis elected to sit by the fire with me. We talked idly of office business, which was just as well. I had no desire to talk further of my pregnancy. I felt miserable. I was convinced that I had deeply offended Pieter. I should have told him privately and specially, I thought. The way I had meant to. This way, the emphasis had all been on *me*, not on *us*. I had grabbed all the glory I could get. No wonder he had disappeared immediately afterward. He had been humiliated.

I sat bolt upright by the fire, panicking. Suppose he doesn't want this baby? Suppose he thinks it's too soon after our marriage? Suppose he fears we can't afford it? That would definitely explain his pique. Oh, why didn't I tell him first? Why didn't I ask what *he* wanted? I slumped down in my chair, staring into the fire, paying no attention to Mavis's attempts at conversation.

The front door banged open. I jumped up, thinking Pieter had come back. But no, the others had returned quickly from their walk.

Melissa came in first, shaking the snow from her coat to crouch before the fire. "Whew!" she sighed. "It's really beginning to be a blizzard out there! We could barely see where we were going! It must have snowed six inches since we arrived." She looked up at the others for confirmation.

"At least." Alix shivered.

"I hesitate to suggest this, as it's still early, but I think we should talk about getting back to Manhattan," said John.

"Is it really that bad?" I asked. I wanted them all to stay. I wanted to put off being alone with Pieter.

"Not yet, but soon," John replied. "It seems best to leave before it gets impossible."

"All right." I stood up and yawned sleepily. "Give me a chance to change my clothes."

"Wait a minute, Gretel. Let Pieter take us in," said Melissa.

"Pieter is . . ." Oh dear, what should I say. "Pieter left while you were out walking. He had to take Jesús home. He had to be somewhere or something like that." There, that sounded vague enough. And God knows, Pieter could very well have gone off someplace with Jesús.

"Wait, I'll take you all home. I have to motor back to the base anyway," Michael said. Then he stopped and counted. "Oh no. I can't. My launch isn't big enough. Well, I can make two trips."

"Now, *that's* ridiculous. Why I'd be home safe and warm before you were ready to start your second trip. And by that time, the snow probably will be heavy, and there'd be more danger. No, I can fit everyone into the *Silver Fox.*"

"Then let me come with you, so I can make sure you get home safely," said Michael.

"No. I can't carry six. And I don't think that tonight's the right night to try to carry an overload. Now, really, it's sweet of you all to be so concerned, but I make that trip at least ten times a week. We'll go slowly. There's little traffic at night. And Michael, I appreciate your worry, I do. The boat has a heater. We'll all be very comfortable. Now, the longer we discuss it, the later we set off. All right?" I looked at them all inquiringly. Everyone shrugged. No more arguments could be thought of. "Good," I said, satisfied. "Now, it won't take me more than a minute to change."

I ran quickly up the stairs to our bedroom. Samantha, who didn't like visitors, of course, was curled up in the exact center of the bed. She stretched a paw out in greeting.

"Samantha," I said, bending over to kiss her pink nose. "You haven't seen Pieter, have you?" A slow blink was all the answer I received. I slipped out of my dress, hung it in the closet, and rummaged for my long underwear, my jeans, and a bulky turtleneck. I pulled them quickly on, scratched Samantha between the ears, and raced back downstairs. Everyone was ready. I put on my down parka,

my yellow rubber boots, grabbed four large flashlights, and opened
the door.

The snow seemed intense. But it was a light snow. Even though it
reached mid-calf, I pushed through it easily. I should have no trouble
getting to Manhattan and back, I assured myself. We went single
file, Michael Dragon leading, then Alix, Melissa, John, and Mavis. I
followed last, moving my flashlight from side to side to help light the
path.

The pier was slippery, and I was glad of the thick tread of my
boots. Alix nearly slipped off it into the water because of her leather
soles. A glance into the boathouse seemed to prove my theory that
Pieter had gone off with Jesús. The *Stuyvesant* was gone. The *Silver
Fox* bobbed alone. We piled in, arranging seats, life vests, and feet.
With a full load, and everyone straining toward the heater, the *Silver
Fox* became quite cozy. I started the motor while Michael untied the
moorings. I eased out, Michael calling directions. Then I gunned the
motor and we powered up, Michael waving behind. A few minutes
later, I heard the motor of his small launch start up. He pulled
alongside, we drove together for a while, then he veered off to the
right with much waving and shouts of good-bye.

It was an exciting, beautiful ride through the harbor. The snow
affected visibility, of course, but not badly. New York City loomed
ahead of us, a make-believe city of mist and snow, its lights twinkling
merrily. All about us was a comforting quiet. There was little traffic
on the rivers. The only boat we passed was the Staten Island Ferry,
chug-chugging sturdily through the slate-gray waters. After the first
few minutes of adjusting to the snow whipping around us, the trip
became as routine as any of the others I had made, and I relaxed to
join in the general conversation.

"You know, Gretel, now that I've seen it, I can't wait for the fashion shooting. It'll be easy, with so many locations to choose from.
We can shoot by the water, even use this boat! The trees—it'll seem
like the country. That brick-patio area, and of course, all around the
house. The details are marvelous—the door frame, the quaint diamond-paned windows. So picturesque. I'd like to come out during
the daytime and ·really scout around—after the snow's gone, naturally." Alix laughed. "That would be all right, wouldn't it?"

"Of course. We'll do it during the week, on company time. A
most pleasant working day," I answered.

"Hmmmph," snorted Mavis. "I've always suspected you two. All those times you claimed to be out scouting locations."

"Those times you claimed to be working at home," Alix retorted cheerfully.

"Now you've really confirmed my suspicions," Mavis chuckled. "Gretel, thank Pieter again for us. A fabulous dinner. Wherever did he learn to cook like that?"

"He said it was living in Hoek House with his father. They both enjoyed good food, and it was either learn to cook well, or eat in town every night. So Pieter learned. He claims eating his mistakes is the best way to learn." I laughed. "They couldn't afford to throw food out, so they always ate it—ruined or not."

"Tremendous foresight on your part, marrying a good cook," sighed Alix. "I'd give anything not to have to cook all the time."

"I didn't plan it," I confessed. "I didn't know until after we were married."

"Sure, Gretel," Alix said teasingly. "Oh. Doesn't the World Trade Center look pretty tonight. I'm glad it snowed. I wouldn't have missed all this!"

"Your conquest, you mean?" I said.

"Who? Michael? He's a sweet boy. A little young. Maybe in five years . . ."

"Just think, Alix," interrupted Mavis. "You could train him properly."

"Hmmm. He does have potential," said Alix, then she laughed. "Oh, Gretel, don't get huffy. Your little ensign is safe from me. Besides, I'm determined to follow your example and marry a cook next time. Pieter wouldn't happen to have an older brother by any chance, would he? You know the old joke—are there any more at home like him?"

"Does Dirk cook also?" asked Melissa. I glared at her over my shoulder, but by then we were nearly at the pier. That particular topic of conversation was forgotten.

"I hope it's all right," I said, "but I'd like to drop you off here, at the Battery Pier. It'd save me the trip up the river. The subway stop's not too far. It may be hard to find a taxi in this snow." I brought the *Silver Fox* gently alongside the floating buoy. John Cotton jumped out to fix the bow line, then the aft. He set to sweeping the snow from the planks with his feet.

"Heavens, Gretel," said Alix. "We'll all get home all right. But what about you?" She peered out into the night. The snow was a little heavier than before, but it was still pretty, not threatening.

"I'll be fine," I reassured them.

"Gretel. Why don't you stay over with me?" said Melissa. "Pieter will understand. Especially now that you're carrying excess baggage around with you."

"Thank you, Melissa, really. Thank you all for your concern. I'll be fine. There's no traffic on the harbor, I'll be home in bed in half an hour. I'll never get home if you all don't get out of my boat. Scoot," I said, thumping my dashboard for emphasis.

One by one, they clambered out of the *Silver Fox*, and onto the floating buoy tied along the pier. A ladder led up to the wharf. All the good-byes and thank yous were said. John untied the ropes, pushed me off, and I started the journey home.

After five minutes, I could already tell that it would take me longer than I had predicted. The snow gusted intermittently. I could see no more than a few feet in front of me. The world had gone gray-white. I didn't worry, though. I knew the route well, by keeping track of the familiar lights and of my compass, I felt confident of my path. I eased as much to my left as I dared, checking in that direction for the channel markers. Keeping the Statue of Liberty to my far right, the green sparkling lights of the Verrazano-Narrows Bridge dead ahead, I pushed toward home.

It was quiet, eerily so. The only machine sounds I could hear were the dull roar of my heater and the steady humming of my motor. The whir of the wind and the gentle splash of the water surrounded me. Then I heard a flutter, a cough, and nothing. The motor had stopped. Calmly, I turned the ignition again. I had been going slowly, probably too slowly. The motor wheezed, straining to turn over. Then it hiccuped apologetically and died. I turned the key again, and again. Still nothing, and nothing. I sat for a minute, gripping the steering wheel tightly. I refused to panic. I counted to ten very slowly, and turned the key again. The motor still wouldn't start. I flicked on the small, battery-operated light over the dashboard and scanned the dials anxiously. I couldn't believe it. The *Silver Fox* had run out of fuel. The indicator needle rested solidly on "E."

"Impossible," I said. One thing that I never did was to get into the boat without checking. The gas tank had been more than half full when I had left Hoek Land. More than enough to get me to Manhattan and back. Unless the indicator was faulty, I thought. I hadn't checked it all that carefully and perhaps I'd just thought it'd said half full. I had been in an agitated state.

"Damn, damn, damn, damn," I said, hitting the wheel each time. Then I stopped, shaking my stinging hand in the air. Whatever I did, I was not going to panic. I counted slowly to ten again.

I considered my position. I was protected from the elements. The heater ran on the battery, not the motor. I turned it to low to preserve power. Fortunately, I was warmly dressed. I also had lights, since they ran on batteries as well. Another ship could see me easily. If one passes, I thought. No one but a damn fool would be out on the harbor on a night like this. "The Staten Island Ferry," I said. On the way into Manhattan we had passed her. It shouldn't be too long before she made the return trip. Unless they shut the service down because of the weather. No, they wouldn't do that. I rummaged in the storage lockers for my signal light. It blinked a strong red light on and off. Any ship that saw it would immediately know that . . . I paused. It wasn't there! I frantically felt about again. I always kept it within easy reach. It should be on top of the blanket. Shivering, but not entirely with cold, I pulled the blanket out to wrap around my shoulders. I continued to search all the lockers. No light. But I did find another blanket. I pulled it over the vinyl seat. Lying flat on the floor, underneath the blanket, was a canoe paddle. I had forgotten it was there. In one of my first conversations with Michael Dragon, he had recommended that I always have a paddle with me. When I had laughingly defended my boat, he had answered, "It has nothing to do with how good a boat you've got, it has to do with common sense."

I tried to determine my position. I had been traveling for about twenty minutes when I ran out of gas, but I had been traveling at about half normal speed. I should be abreast of the Statue of Liberty, I guessed. I should also be able to see Hoek Land's pier light. I scanned the sky and water nervously, but could see nothing but snow, now thicker than ever. Damn snow! I thought bitterly. Who ever heard of this much snow in early March? I found myself staring at my own forward light, shining whitely off the bow. The flakes of snow now danced around it hypnotically; it was fascinating. With difficulty, I tore my eyes away.

For the first time I realized that this could end badly, that I might not be rescued at all. "I won't think about that," I said, still forcing my gaze from the forward light.

I considered the paddle in my hands. It would be slow going with the wind and the weight of the *Silver Fox*, but if I just drifted with the current, I'd miss Hoek Land and head for the sea. Doing something was better than doing nothing. If I sat around and thought about what might happen, I would go completely to pieces. Besides, I reasoned, because I was drifting with the tide, I probably wasn't where I had guessed I was. Suddenly, it occurred to me that I didn't know if it was high tide or low tide. Would I be drifting back to Manhattan? Or out to sea? I had no idea. One thing was reassuring: according to my compass, I was still pointed vaguely in the direction of Hoek Land.

Taking the paddle, I moved stiffly to the back of the *Silver Fox*, out from under the shelter of the vinyl cover. I brought one blanket with me, to kneel on and wrap around me. I left the other on the driver's seat, where it would remain dry. Fortunately, the wind had died down. The snow fell gently, but thickly. I positioned myself as comfortably as I could on the side of the boat, leaning over to dip the paddle into the inky water and pulling. Nothing happened. As far as I could tell the boat didn't move at all. Pull harder, Gretel, I urged myself, placing the paddle deeper in the water and pulling back. I watched the swirls it made. Was it my imagination? Or had the boat shifted direction slightly? I did it again, with even more force. Yes! The boat had definitely reacted. "Okay, Gretel," I said aloud, "we know that you can move the boat. The question now is, where are you going to move it?" I peered into the distance, but there was no clue there. I continued to paddle. It gave me a feeling of accomplishment.

Ten minutes later, exhausted, I decided to stop for a while, to save my strength. Also, I was beginning to feel numb. I crawled back underneath the protective cover and huddled under the dry blanket. Then I heard a faint sound. I couldn't see anything, but I listened all the same. I saw a faint shining. It was a light—and coming closer. After a few minutes, I could see that it was the Staten Island Ferry on its return trip. I grabbed two of my flashlights and went to the back of the boat. I pointed the torches in the ferry's direction, flicking them on and off—three shorts, three longs—the international code for help—SOS! But the ferry kept her course. It couldn't see me! The flashlights weren't strong enough! I groaned with frustration, throwing one of the torches against the dashboard. If only I had the red light. That would have been noticed, snow or no snow. I jumped up and down, waving my arms, crying at the top of my voice. But it was useless. The ferry was too far away. Sick with disappointment, I watched her lights disappear.

I glanced at my watch. It would be at least an hour before the next one passed. There was no guarantee that that ferry would see me, either. Yet there was one thing I could do. I now had a definite sense of direction. I could row in the direction that the ferry had come from, then I would be heading in the direction of Staten Island and, more important, Hoek Land. At the least, I would be closer to the ferry's route, so that when the next one came it would be sure not to miss me. Filled with new hope, I snapped up the paddle and went to the back of the boat.

I rowed steadily for what must have been an hour, if what I was doing could be called rowing. I dipped the paddle into the water a few feet ahead of me and pulled it back until I could reach no more. Then I lifted the paddle out of the water, slid it horizontally through the air, dipped and pulled again. I crouched at the side of the boat, leaning awkwardly to reach the paddle deep enough into the water to be effective. My legs had the soft vinyl padding to cushion them, but my hands had no such protection. I banged them repeatedly against the side of the boat. Soon, however, I was too numb to feel them. Every so often, I took a break, crawling onto the front seat under the vinyl roof to get out of the snow, to huddle against the heater, to rub my hands together fiercely to bring back some feeling.

I dipped and pulled, dipped and pulled, dipped and pulled to dip again. I had no idea if I was doing any good, but I had to try. Why wasn't the ferry coming? Where was it? I looked about me frantically, but nowhere could I see a sign of it. I paddled until I could barely lift my arms, then stopped to look at my watch. I dragged up my left arm, pushing back the sleeve of my jacket. The delicate dial framed in silver was smashed; one of the thin black hands was gone; the other uselessly, cryptically, pointed straight up to twelve. The witching hour—the moment when it was neither one day nor the next, the moment when one's soul could be snatched away. What silliness, Gretel, I thought, smiling at my fancy. It couldn't be midnight now, but I had no idea if it really was midnight, past midnight, or before midnight. I couldn't even tell, peering at my ruined watch, if it was the big hand or the little hand that was there. I twirled it with my finger, breaking it off easily. I unsnapped the watch from my wrist and tossed it over the side of the boat into the water. It made no sound when it hit the water. I lay back against a snow-crusted cushion, huddled with the sodden blanket. I was totally exhausted. I cried for a long time, quietly and sincerely. Then, for no reason, I sat up with a jerk and stopped crying. I wiped my face with the backs of my hands, blinking away the last tears to clear my vision. Still it snowed. Yet I would not cry any more. I stared straight ahead into the thick gray curtain of snow.

Was that a flicker? I closed my eyes wearily. I opened them again. No, there was something. A blue flash in the distance, straight ahead. It seemed more surreal than real—could it be a mirage? If one wanted something badly enough, one could will it. I wanted that light. I willed that light. The blue flash appeared again. It blinked on and off several times, at regular intervals. It seemed real. I grabbed up my paddle again, ignoring the pain that shot through my shoulders. Real or not, I was going to do my damnedest to get to it.

I pulled and pulled and pulled like a mad woman, pausing only to wipe the snow from my face, keeping my eyes fixed on the blue light that flickered on and off, and grew larger and clearer. Oblivious of all else, of cold, of pain, of wet, of sound, I rowed for my life.

"Gretel!"

I jumped, startled. That was Pieter's voice. And it was very close by. I turned my head from side to side.

"I'm right behind you," said Pieter, raising his voice above his boat's engine.

I turned around. Pieter maneuvered the *Stuyvesant* deftly alongside. He grabbed the mooring ropes and pulled my boat to his.

"Oh, Pieter," I said, as soon as he was close enough to touch. I fell gracelessly into his arms. We tumbled backward over the *Stuyvesant*'s gunwale into the cockpit.

"Hey!" said Pieter, pulling us upright, laughing as he hugged me. "I've been behind you for a good five minutes, calling your name. Old Gretel keeps paddling away."

"I was determined to get to the light," I answered.

"What light?" asked Pieter.

"That light." I turned to point. But there was no light.

"I don't see anything," said Pieter.

"I don't understand. It was right over there. In the direction I was heading."

"You were heading for the open sea. I think it was your imagination."

"It blinked off and on so regularly."

"Maybe it was that Cellar Ghost you're so fond of." Pieter laughed, stopping when he saw my expression and adding hastily, "Don't let's worry about it now. The important thing is to get you warm and dry. Here"—Pieter thrust a flask of brandy at me—"drink this."

"Ahoy, *Stuyvesant!*"

I looked out, and saw a large boat in the dimness. It was a Coast Guard outboard. Michael Dragon leaned over the side, a bull horn in his hand.

"All's well?" he asked.

"Aye-aye," Pieter shouted back. "Thanks for your help." Michael waved a cheery salute and the outboard roared off into the snowy mist. We watched it until its flashing headlights disappeared.

"I think there's your mysterious blue light," said Pieter, securing the *Silver Fox* to the *Stuyvesant's* stern. "You saw Dragon's searchlight."

"The light was blinking on and off. Like a signal. The searchlight is a steady beam," I said.

Pieter said nothing, starting the motor. I huddled next to him, sipping the brandy. I didn't care what Pieter said, my blinking light had led me to safety.

"How did Michael come to search for me?" I yawned, exhausted unto sleepiness.

"Melissa called," said Pieter. "Then your young ensign called. Still no Gretel. So, we organized a search party."

"How long were you looking?" I asked.

"About an hour or so," Pieter said. "What did happen to you?"

I told him quickly enough. Pieter listened with a sad, serious look until I was finished. I'm not sure, but I think, at the time, I wanted Pieter to seem more upset.

"You're sure you ran out of gas?" he asked, frowning.

"Positive."

"It was more than half full when you started out."

"True, but maybe the dial was wrong."

"I had that boat thoroughly checked out before I bought it."

"I'm just thankful I had that paddle."

"Yes," Pieter agreed. "That was lucky. I didn't realize that we'd equipped your boat so completely."

"*We* hadn't," I answered, explaining how Michael had suggested the safety precaution.

"Ensign Dragon again. *I* should have thought of it."

"This was just one of those freaky things," I sighed.

"Ha! I was terrified. One of those freaky things, she says," muttered Pieter, pulling up to our dock. We were home. "Especially now," said Pieter, leaning over to kiss me on the very tip of my nose.

"Then you don't mind about the baby?"

"*Our* baby," Pieter corrected gently. "I might have preferred to wait," he continued, "but now that it's here, I love you more than ever."

I smiled sleepily. With Pieter's help, I climbed out of the *Stuyvesant*. He lifted me in his arms and carried me through the swirling snow up the hill to Hoek House.

8
Shooting

"Gretel, peel me a grape," said Melissa lazily from across the patio. I sat up in my chair, and looked over the novel I was reading to where she lay stretched out full length in the late April sunshine. She had rolled her jeans up above her knees and pulled up her T-shirt to expose as much of herself as possible to the sun. I reached into the fruit bowl, scooped up a handful of grapes, and hurled them at her stomach.

"Hey!"

"You want grapes, you get grapes," I said.

"You're just jealous of my flat tummy," said Melissa.

I lifted my book and regarded myself. In another week, I would be exactly four months pregnant. And although I hadn't gained more than two pounds (a fact that surprised Dr. Weiss), my shape had definitely changed. That very morning I had discovered that I could no longer wear my close-fitting jeans. I had slipped into a pair of Pieter's castoffs, belting them with one of his ties. The result, Melissa had assured me (laughing) was *tres chic.* I would have to go shopping, and soon.

"Junior is due October?" said Melissa.

"October the fifth," I said.

"Then I hope Junior's a girl," she replied, turning over onto her stomach.

"Why?"

"You wouldn't want to get stuck with a male Libra, would you?" said Melissa, her blue eyes round with astonishment. I threw another grape at her. "Though I suppose," she continued, sighing, "though I suppose that Pieter wants a son and heir."

"I don't think it matters. As long as it's healthy."

"All men want sons," she replied firmly. "I think that's why Ed didn't fight the divorce. Because I refused to get pregnant."

"Pieter hasn't said a word about it," I said. Actually, I reflected, that was true. We had hardly talked about our baby except for the automatic "How do you feel?" that Pieter asked me every morning.

"You staying on at the office through the summer?" asked Melissa.

"As long as I can," I replied. "Through most of the summer, anyway. Maybe only going in once or twice a week in September. My doctor doesn't like the idea of a very pregnant lady motoring through the harbor twice a day."

"I should say not! You know, Gretel," Melissa propped herself up on her elbows. "I'm surprised that you can still go out in the boat by yourself."

"Nonsense."

"After what happened? It would take a lot to get me into a boat after that night in the middle of the harbor in a blizzard, powerless and drifting out to sea. My God! Did you ever find out for certain what happened?"

"Oh, I thought I told you," I said, pointedly picking up my novel. Melissa ignored my hint to drop the subject.

"I don't think you'd have ever told me anything ever again if it weren't for me calling to make sure you got home safely."

"Yes, you're probably right."

"So . . . why did it happen?"

I sighed. Good old persistent, nosy Melissa. "It seems there was a leak in my gas tank."

"A leak? What caused it?"

"Who knows? It could have been anything."

"I don't like it. Things like that don't happen in new boats. What did Pieter say?"

"He was furious, of course. He took the Silver Fox back to the marine center in Brooklyn where he bought it and demanded they repair it for free. I gather he nearly punched out the salesman. His temper gets the better of him sometimes," I said.

"Did they tell him what went wrong?"

"No. Too intimidated, I guess. Actually, I don't remember."

"So nobody knows why the gas tank suddenly sprung a leak?"

"Well . . ." I paused, remembering what Clyde had said a few days after the incident.

"What?" demanded Melissa, coming to sit on a chair beside me.

"We have this handyman, Clyde. I've told you about him. Anyway, he was the first one to look over the *Silver Fox*. It's really crazy. He said, that if he didn't know better, his first thought was that someone made that leak deliberately."

"No!"

"Of course, it's an impossibility. Even Clyde admitted that."

"Huh? Oh, I quite agree," answered Melissa, obviously forcing herself to change the subject. "You know, it's really hot out here."

"Yes, it's wonderful. I hope it holds," I answered, glad of the change of subject, even if Melissa was doing it melodramatically.

"That's right," she said, disinterested but polite. "You're doing your fashion shootings next week." Obviously, Melissa would prefer to continue discussing the boat accident, but I couldn't talk about it any longer.

For almost a month afterward, I *had* been afraid and not just of using the boat. I had actually been scared to go to work. Too many things had happened, too close together: my near disaster, the smoke-bombing at *Milady*. I had even recalled my first day at work after my honeymoon, when I had found the El Condor poster attached to the *Silver Fox*. I had dismissed it as a harmless prank at the time, but in light of recent events, it had taken on an ominous meaning. El Condor had acted twice, both times in the area where I worked, the second time actually at *my* office. A week later, *my* boat had mysteriously run out of gas. It seemed as if I were being warned.

I had stayed at home the first few days after my accident, but I soon grew annoyed at myself for giving in to my fears, for hiding. I had forced myself to go back to work. And, eventually, as nothing happened, my confidence returned. I had told no one of my fears, not even Melissa, and certainly not Pieter. It was a private struggle. I had to work it out for myself, no one could help me. And I had won. But, still, I preferred not to discuss that time. I eagerly seized on this new topic of conversation.

"On Tuesday and Wednesday," I continued. "It should be fun. Alix and the photographer came out on Thursday," I said enthusiastically, determined to snare Melissa's interest. "We tramped all over, took lots of Polaroids, discussed the various places to shoot. Mostly, we ate and drank."

"You hard-working magazine people," sighed Melissa.

"Trust me, it's work. Dismondi is not the easiest person to get along with. He's a great photographer. But he has to be humored. Pieter joined us for a drink before I took them back to Manhattan. Dismondi was wearing a gaudy Hawaiian-print shirt. Pieter hated him on sight. I'm sure Dismondi felt the same. Alix and I were *desperate*. What an ordeal!" I laughed at the memory.

"Taking my name in vain, eh?" said Pieter, suddenly beside me and kissing me on the neck.

"I was telling Melissa about your new friend, Dismondi," I said, squealing as his kiss became a playful nip.

"Oh, that fop." Pieter dismissed him with a wave of his hand. "I came out to announce that I'm hungry. You girls had enough of sunning? Interested in food?"

"I certainly am," said Melissa, sitting up and inspecting her arms. "Do you think I got any tan?" she asked.

"Scorched," said Pieter.

"Oh—you!" she said, wrinkling her nose.

"Anyway, I thought I might grill some hamburgers on the hibachi," Pieter said. "And dine out here, *alfresco*."

"Wonderful!" said Melissa. "What a life."

And it was, sun and sea and good friends. We giggled through lunch, helped along by red wine. Afterward, Melissa and I decided to stroll the island to work off our stupor. Pieter begged off, pleading work.

"Pieter does work a lot, doesn't he?" Melissa said, as we headed off toward the dock. The wind had come up, and I was glad Pieter, suddenly protective, had insisted I wear a jacket. I thought it unnecessary, but had obediently tossed my red windbreaker over my shoulders, tying the arms loosely about my neck.

"Constantly," I said, tying and retying the sleeves until I was pleased with the effect. "Even when he doesn't have an assignment, he works in his studio."

"That must take a great deal of discipline. Whenever I try to work at home, I eat."

"Pieter's disciplined all right," I answered, laughing. "Of course, he loves it. A true artist. He hardly thinks of it as work."

We reached the dock, moving along the water's edge, taking care to avoid the marshy areas. Even so, our sneakers were soaked through before a half hour had passed.

"This island is bigger than it looks once you start walking around it," said Melissa, pausing to pick a burr from her jeans. We were halfway through a hopeless tangle of budding vines. "You can't even see the house from here."

"I know. A very private place. Look." I pointed ahead of us. "There's a couple of rocks. Let's sit and rest there in the sun."

"What a life," sighed Melissa, again saying what was virtually her chorus for Hoek Land. She lay flat on a large rock, eyes shut dreamily, one hand trailing in the water. "I think I shall come here every weekend this summer. If you don't mind, of course. This has it all over Fire Island."

"Of course. You should bring John the next time."

"I don't know. This place is too romantic. He'd probably think I was angling for a proposal."

"Worse things could happen," I said.

"The trouble with you married women is that you can't bear to see your friends single." Melissa sat up to stretch.

"I do seem to remember . . ." I started.

"All right, all right. I did it, too. It's just that it'd be funny, after all these years, to end up with the boy next door." She paused and looked about. "Hey, what's that? Over there."

"Oh." I looked where she pointed. "Oh, that must be the other boathouse."

"Where Dirk lives?"

"Uh—yes."

"Oh, good. Let's go visiting."

"Melissa!" I cried, but she had already slid from the rock and was skipping off toward the boathouse. I called her name a few more times, but she ignored me. I could only follow her warily.

Melissa had already circled the structure by the time I caught up with her. "How disappointing," she said. "There doesn't seem to be anyone home." Good, I thought. Curious as I was about Dirk, I felt that this was not the correct way or time to meet him.

"Let's go back," I said.

"Not so fast, Gretel." Melissa held up her hand. "This is an interesting building."

"Why?" It seemed an ordinary boathouse to me, and a rather ran shackle one at that. I again turned to leave. I had a prickly feeling that Melissa and I were being watched.

"This lock, for example." Melissa went up to the door. "It's a very impressive one." She was right. The stained, weather-beaten door was fastened by a shiny overlarge padlock. The lower windows were boarded up. The upper windows were shut and rough curtains were drawn. Was it my imagination or did one of the curtains move? No, I was imagining things. They were as still as before. It was only my feelings of guilt that made me think we were being observed.

"I wonder what's in there," mused Melissa. "It must be awfully valuable to warrant this padlock."

"I imagine Dirk doesn't like people nosing about," I said.

"It's odd that you've never met him," Melissa said bluntly.

"Dirk and Pieter don't get along."

"Do you know why?"

"No. Not really."

"Doesn't Pieter talk about it?"

"Every time I've tried to bring it up, he gets angry. I gather that they disagree on many things. Look, Mel, I've told you all this before." I fidgeted nervously, anxious to be away.

"Lots of brothers don't agree on many things. That's normal. What isn't normal is that Pieter's brother lives on this island, just a few hundred feet from your house, and you haven't met him. You've got to make Pieter talk about him, Gretel."

"If Pieter thought I should know about Dirk, he'd tell me," I insisted loyally.

"I wonder." Melissa turned to stare at the boathouse. Melissa was right—it was odd that such a decrepit building should have such a magnificent lock.

"What do you wonder?" I asked, smiling.

"I wonder if there really is a Dirk," she said flatly.

"What?"

"You've never seen him. Never seen his picture. Right? There's no evidence that he exists."

"Why should Pieter lie? Oh, Melissa, what silliness."

"It is a puzzler," she admitted. "Perhaps it started off as a joke. Now he's embarrassed to admit it."

"Stop it."

"Whatever the answer is, the whole thing is very strange," she said flatly again. We turned to pick a path to Hoek House. We walked in silence.

* * *

That night, I had a nightmare. I dreamed that Pieter and I were sailing on a calm lake, with the gentlest of breezes wafting us along. Then slowly, steadily, the wind rose and the boat went faster. We both laughed, enjoying the gathering speed. But then the winds became a storm. The sky turned dark. I grew silent. But Pieter, if anything, became joyous, lifting his face to catch the rain that fell. I was afraid. I clutched desperately to the sides of the boat, screaming as each wave washed over me.

Then I noticed that Pieter was wearing a mask. He was only pretending to be Pieter. He lifted one hand from the tiller to untie the mask, working it off with his fingers. "I'm not Pieter," he said, flinging off the mask. The mask was gone, but in its place was Pieter's face!

I sat up. I was entangled in the bedclothes. I was alone. I listened, but could hear nothing. I lay back, breathing deeply, coming out of my dream, wishing Pieter was there to comfort me. I turned over on my stomach, snuggled into the pillow, and, cursing Melissa's fancies, fell back asleep.

* * *

For the first day of shooting, we had an unusually warm April day, but then, it was also May Day Eve. The deep-blue sky laced with puffy white clouds reminded us all that summer's heat was not far away.

Alix had chartered a large Chris-Craft to ferry everyone and their equipment to Hoek Land. I was up and brewing coffee and slicing Danish for them promptly at seven, but they didn't dock at our pier until nine, with vague stories of "unaccountable" delays, which I knew to be Alix's jargon for tardiness. And even though we were already an hour behind schedule, it took "unaccountably" long to set up. The four models, Mona, Doreen, Robin, and Wendy, came ashore soon enough with the makeup artist, Tony, and the hair stylist, Martin. But Alix and her two assistants, Carrie Ann and Buffy, took their time unloading and then unpacking and hanging up the clothes. Worse, Dismondi and his two assistants, Dickon and Sammy, fussed at length over their equipment as it was carried up to the house. By ten o'clock, I felt as though I'd already put in a full day's work.

We'd planned to take most of the fashion shots on the patio and by the front entranceway, using one of the smaller living rooms for dressing and making up. The rest of the house, especially the kitchen and Pieter's studio, was strictly off limits. I'd tried to make this clear, but Alix was soon gossiping to the others about how charming Hoek House was and so on, and, one by one, the girls asked me if they could just slip upstairs "for a quick peek." I sighed, smiled, and agreed, turning my attentions to hurrying up Alix and Dismondi.

Pieter was on his best behavior. He watched the arrival from his studio window, shaking his head at the inefficiency and general clutter. While we were setting up on the patio, Pieter emerged from his studio to eye Dismondi's photographic equipment and, I suspected, to eye the models in their various abbreviated costumes, showing their lean bodies nonchalantly as they scampered from house to patio and back again. Momentarily, I was jealous of their lithe, leggy good looks, but then Pieter laughed to himself as if watching a schoolyard full of children. He turned to return to his studio, but I caught his arm.

"Well, what do you think?" I said.

"It's definitely a circus," he said. "I had no idea this was what really went on. You do this all the time? What nonsense."

"It's really hard work," I said.

"So's the circus," said Pieter, smiling down at me. "No, really, everything seems fine. Even Dismondi. Just make sure no one wanders off. The last thing we need is a lawsuit. If someone got hurt on a rock or wading along the shore, well, just keep an eye on everyone, okay? There are parts of the island that seem inviting but are a bit tricky."

"Yes, I know. Melissa and I wandered over some on Sunday."

"What?" said Pieter.

"We walked to the other end of the island."

"On Sunday?" said Pieter.

"You don't mind, do you?"

"I don't think it was very safe."

"We were fine. We looked out for each other. We had proper shoes and everything."

"You shouldn't be wandering about in your condition," said Pieter, and then he walked away abruptly. I was annoyed by his bullying (there was no other word for it), though to be sure, I was more annoyed by the mystery of why he should be bullying me on such a seemingly insignificant matter. But I couldn't sulk for long. Alix and Dismondi both screamed for my attention. Life at Hoek House was never dull, I thought to myself, deciding that Pieter was out of sorts because of the invasion and not because of anything Melissa and I had done.

"Gretel!" Alix called again.

"Gretel!" Dismondi called again.

We had divided the August fashion pages into two sections, roughly ten pages each. (Although Alix would beg and barter for additional pages right up until the last minute.) We were doing two fashion "stories." First, the wardrobe for a young girl, just going off to college. The second, how that girl should translate the college look, four years later, into the clothes a young woman just starting her career should have. We had divided the shooting into two sections also. Today—the first day—we would photograph the back-to-school/college clothes. Tomorrow, we would photograph the working woman's wardrobe. Even with the beauty and accessory shots being done in the photographer's studio later in the week, it was a lot to accomplish in two days. There would be, I reflected, no more time for "unaccountable" delays.

Alix, Dismondi, and I had determined that there would be five major shots, with some close-up, detailed shots to be added for emphasis. The first one—all four models in various campus casual clothes—was the most difficult. The others involved only one or two girls at a time, with the last shot being an evening "look." The organizational work was done. Now it was just a matter of it all running smoothly and quickly. I bounced back and forth between all the elements during the preparations.

The first photograph was to be done on the patio, squarely in front of the house. Dismondi had already set up his lights, and was now testing.

"Ah, good, Gretel. Do me a favor, doll, and go stand over there. No, a few feet to your left. Good, turn, face the camera. Now profile. Do something interesting with your arms. Fine. Now, go to the other side of the terrace, and do exactly the same thing. Wait, hold it. Fabulous. Thanks, Gretel." He paused to examine the Polaroid shots he had just taken. I came over to look at them. The front of the house looked fantastic. The model less so. "I think we've just about got it," Dismondi said. "Of course, the girls won't be over as far as you were, but I just wanted to make sure. Dickon"—he turned to address one of his assistants—"I think maybe that one on the far left can be turned in a little more. And a white card against it, no, turn it in a bit more. Good. Tape it. And the fans go on the right. How are we going to do it?" Dismondi turned back to me. "Two and two?"

The photograph was going to run as a double-page spread. "No," I answered. "Three and one. Alix says that grouping works best for her in terms of the clothes. And it's good for me, too. I can run all my type on one page."

"Okay. Then look in the camera and tell me if this is good for you. The gutter can run down the side of the doorway, one girl can be standing in it, the others grouped in front of the windows to the right. I'll crop out the bay window entirely. We can use it in another shot."

"That'll be fine. Just be sure not to get too far away. I want the girls to pretty much fill the frame. I really don't want to be too aware of the house."

"But it's so lovely."

"And we're going to see some of it in every shot." I laughed. "By tomorrow afternoon, we'll be tired of it."

"All right. I'll move in a little closer, and then just give you some cropping room to play with."

"Fabulous," I replied. "How much longer will you need?"

"Oh, I'll want the models on the set in about fifteen minutes," said Dismondi. "Makeup and hair can still be worked on while I'm doing my final tests."

The living room designated for the models' use was in cheerful confusion. Clothes were everywhere, dangling on hangers from an impromptu rack, slung over the back of every chair in the room. Jewelry and accessories were spread out on every available flat surface. An ironing board was set up in one corner, and Carrie Ann was busily smoothing out any wrinkles and creases that had occurred in transit. The models were in various stages of readiness. Doreen, completely dressed in a tunic and pants outfit but makeup-less, was pulling on a pair of close-fitting, highly polished, low-cut burgundy leather boots. Her fashionably frizzed dark-red hair was a mess, but she would be wearing a hat in this picture. Mona was still in underwear, yet her blond hair was smoothed back and her face was immaculately made up. Alix was helping Robin into a loose-fitting, hooded jacket, no easy task, as Robin had just had her long nails lacquered and was waving her hands about madly to dry them. Robin's hair was done up in electric rollers. Wendy was sitting near the window, two lights trained on her upturned face, while Tony daintily mixed colors on a palette and applied them to her closed eyelids. Martin was brushing her long silky brown hair (Wendy refused to cut it, no matter what the fashion) into two artfully casual braids. He paused over his collection of hair ribbons. "What's Wendy wearing?" he asked.

"Brown and gold sweater, brown velvet knickers, the taupe textured stockings she has on, and ankle-length chocolate lace-up leather boots," Alix replied without turning around, tying and retying the sash of Robin's multicolored jacket until she was satisfied with the way the ends fell. Then she reached into her pocket and pinned them to hold them in place.

I cleared my throat and entered. "Fifteen more minutes," I announced in a most authoritative voice. There was a collective groan. "Sorry, guys, but we've got to do two shots before lunch. And that's only so Dismondi can make his test shots. Hair and makeup can be adjusted on the set. Tony, I think you're going a bit too dark. Wendy's supposed to be a college freshman, not a disco queen." Tony glared, but he dabbed at Wendy's mouth with a Kleenex.

"Is it windy?" asked Martin. He was threading thin gold-velvet ribbons through Wendy's braids. The effect, though stunning, was hardly what I thought of as a casual campus look. I said as much to Alix.

"You may be right, Gretel, but it looks so divine with Wendy's dark hair. It's just that extra touch. And college girls these days take more care with their appearance than you did. After all, who dressed up to burn it down?"

"She's right, Gretel," agreed Wendy, getting up to step into her knickers. "My sister's a sophomore at New York University, and she spends at least an hour in the morning getting ready for classes. I swear, she wears more makeup than I do!"

I looked enviously at Wendy's clear skin and dark long eyelashes and sighed. "All right, you know what you're doing. Just do it quickly, so we can get to work!"

"We'll get back on schedule," said Alix. "This one's the longest, because of the hair and makeup. The other shots will only require touch-ups. This is the only picture with all four of the girls."

"I know, I know," I laughed. "Twelve minutes."

Half an hour later, everyone was on the set. Dismondi was behind the camera, arranging the positions of the models, checking with me to see if it was "all right." Tony and Martin applied the finishing brush strokes. (I had to admit that Wendy's makeup looked more natural in the strong sunlight.) Alix and her two assistants were constantly darting in and out, giving a pull to a garment here, pinning a blouse so that it fit better, taping a stubborn lapel so that it lay in place properly. Then Dismondi yelled, "Action!" All four girls walked toward the camera, not stopping until they had, in fact, walked past. Dismondi stopped to reload, the models repositioned themselves, and Alix and her crew rushed in to repair the damage. The next time, the girls jumped, then they twirled; finally, they just lounged as though bored with classes. All the while, Dismondi fired off roll after roll of film, murmuring encouragements and giving directions.

"Fabulous, Mona, now an even bigger smile!"

"Wendy, for God's sake! Stop flinging those braids around!"

"Robin, honey, move to your left a wee bit. You've gone out of the picture entirely. Good. Now, fondle that hood—you love it madly. That's it!"

"Fabulous, girls, just fabulous. We've got it!"

The rest of the day went by at the same hectic pace. Either we were setting up a shot or we were actually shooting. While one picture was being taken, the models for the next one were being dressed and made up. We had planned it so the models rotated. There was no actual lunch break, but at around one o'clock, I began to set up a picnic table at one end of the patio, recruiting free hands at various moments to help me carry out the sodas (diet soda for the models) and beer, the sandwich makings and countless bags of potato chips that I had bought the day before. We snatched a bite whenever we could. At one point Pieter wandered out to make himself a sandwich. I was eating mine at the time and he ambled over to join me, sitting on the ground at my feet.

"How's it going?" he asked, pulling open a beer.

"Better than I thought," I answered. "We've just started on the third shot. Of course, I can't let Alix know we're on time. She'd slacken the pace."

"Boy, if that's the way college girls look, maybe I should go back to school for a refresher course," said Pieter.

"Silly, we're showing them how they should look."

"I sure don't remember any girl at Yale wearing a skirt on campus."

"I have been informed that times have changed," I informed him.

"Hey, look!" Pieter pointed at Wendy, who had turned so that her back was toward us. "Is that a new style—the dinosaur look?"

"Oh no." I laughed. "The dress looked terrible on her, so we tightened it with clothespins for a more fitted look."

"That's the way the dress is supposed to fit?" said Pieter.

"No. It hangs straight. But it didn't look good that way. Not on Wendy. But the other girls are too tall to wear it."

"So what about the customer who likes the dress and finds out it hangs on her funny?" said Pieter.

"A bag of clothespins free."

"I always knew you fashion people were dishonest," said Pieter, finishing his sandwich and retreating.

We finished at six o'clock. Everyone was exhausted. I longed for a nice hot bath. My back ached with standing all day, but I went around congratulating everyone, insisting they stay for a few minutes and have some wine. I had no trouble persuading them. It was the last thing I wanted to do, but the day had gone very well and it was important for morale that I show my appreciation. It was also good to unwind together.

Alix came over to join me. "You did pretty well for a pregnant lady," she said, sipping the imported mineral water she preferred to wine.

"I'm not that pregnant," I protested.

"Don't you feel it?"

"Right now the only place it bothers me is my clothes. I can't fit into any of my pants, and only a few skirts."

"Oh, don't worry about that," said Alix. "A friend of mine designs maternity clothes. Set aside a day next week and I'll take you up to his showroom. Chances are, if it's a discontinued item, he'll let you have it for practically nothing."

"That'd be wonderful," I said. "I'd hate to buy a whole new wardrobe for just a few months."

"You're so practical." Alix shuddered. "Have you decided when your last day at *Milady* is going to be?"

"Not really. That depends on what the doctor says and how I feel. Of course, commuting by boat complicates matters."

"Hmmm. You know, Madame is petrified you're going to quit completely," said Alix.

"Mavis hasn't said a word to me."

"Of course not, she wouldn't dare. She'd prefer to ignore the whole thing, hoping it would go away. You don't intend to quit working, do you?"

"No!" I answered. "I'll have to take a leave of absence, of course, but certainly not a permanent one."

"Good," said Alix, reaching over to hug me.

The photography equipment was packed up and stored in the front entranceway for the next day. Many of the clothes and accessories were also left behind for the morrow. The chartered boat was due promptly at six-thirty. I went down to the dock to see them off, hugged and kissed them all once again, then waved as they speeded back to Manhattan. I climbed wearily back up to the house, sinking into one of the soft canvas chairs on the porch. I had every intention of watching the sunset, but I fell fast asleep.

"Here you are." Pieter bent over to kiss me on the mouth.

"What a lovely way to wake up," I said. It was dark. "How long have I been asleep?"

"Couple of hours I didn't disturb you because I figured you needed the rest. It's getting chilly. How about a thick steak for dinner?"

"Sounds fabulous," I answered, using Dismondi's favorite word. "I'm starving!"

"Good," said Pieter. "Because I've already cooked it." He lifted me to my feet and we walked through the debris-strung rooms to the kitchen.

"Pieter," I said, speaking only after I had stuffed myself. "I've been wondering."

"What?" said Pieter.

"Why the boathouse at the other end of the island has such a wicked-looking padlock on it."

"You'd have to ask Dirk that," Pieter answered, not looking up.

"I never see Dirk," I said, poking through the salad remains for cucumber slices.

"Well then, you can't ask him."

"All the windows are boarded up. Melissa and I walked all around it. Everything was boarded up. The only door was thoroughly padlocked. It seems a peculiar way to live, as though Dirk had something to hide," I said.

"Look, Gretel," said Pieter, wiping his mouth with a napkin and laying down his fork to look straight across at me. "I have nothing to do with Dirk. How he chooses to live his life is no concern of mine, nor should it be of yours. I don't think you should prowl around down there. Ever. Stay away from that end of the island. If it's locked and boarded up, that means that Dirk doesn't want people nosing about. Now, I don't want to hear any more about it. I hope we don't have to have this discussion ever again. I thought I had made that clear, but apparently I hadn't. I hope I've made it clear now. Now, if you'll excuse me, I want to work some more. You look tired, Gretel, and you have another long day ahead of you. I suggest you go to bed. I'll take care of the dishes."

Pieter got up, leaned over to kiss me on the cheek, and went into his studio. Feeling like a small child sent to its room without dessert, I slowly went upstairs to bed.

* * *

The second day of the shooting began smoother than the first. The clothes and photography equipment were already at the house, so there was not the "unaccountable" delay in unloading. And, because we had gotten half the job successfully out of the way, everyone seemed more relaxed. We were using different models of course —the clothes to be photographed today were aimed at the young woman just starting her first job. They required a slightly more sophisticated look than the fresh-faced, junior models we had used the previous day.

We had used these four models for *Milady*'s fashion pages often. (Mavis preferred to stress maturity rather than just youthful prettiness.) I knew them fairly well. I sat with them as they were being made up and dressed in order to catch up on their lives. Elise, a wispy though dramatic blonde who had just done her first movie role —a small part as one of the star's girl friends—was full of Hollywood gossip, and peppered her conversation with celebrities' names. Alison was getting married in two weeks. Whitney had discovered est. She was convinced we all must try it. Only Hazel seemed to have little to say, regarding herself dreamily in the mirror.

"So, what's your news?" I said, sitting down beside her and handing her a cup of coffee. "You haven't said much of anything."

"The same old stuff." She smiled. "Actually, if you must know"—
she dropped her voice to a whisper—"I'm in love," she finished dramatically. "Sssh," she said, as I began to exclaim. "I don't want the
others to know. They'll tease me. I couldn't bear that." She blushed
furiously. Though she was one of the highest paid fashion models in
New York, Hazel was extraordinarily shy.

"Anybody I know?" I said. I was fond of Hazel. She had had several love affairs in the few years I had known her, all of them pas-
sionate, all of them tempestuous, all of them brief. Several times she
had asked my advice, and though I doubted she ever followed it, I
had been flattered. Hazel was just twenty, and she respected my
opinions. It was like having a younger sister. In fact, Hazel and I
resembled each other more than some sisters I knew. We were the
same height, with the same shoulder-length dark hair, with even the
same pale complexion. Yet Hazel's delicate bone structure and start-
lingly blue eyes gave her face an ethereal beauty I could never hope
to equal.

Hazel blushed again. "Yes, it's Dickon," she said, giving the name
of one of Dismondi's assistants. "That's why I was so eager to come
on this job. I canceled a booking." Hazel giggled a little. "I suppose
that was awfully unprofessional."

I smiled at her enthusiasm. "Just so long as it wasn't *my* booking
that got canceled. How long have you two been together?"

"Oh, a long time," she replied. "Two wonderful weeks."

"Well"—I paused—"enjoy yourself. Dickon's a sweet boy." At
twenty-eight, I felt very old. "Now, hurry up and finish dressing.
You're in the first shot."

"Oh, damn!" wailed Whitney from across the room. "I've broken
a nail!" Winking encouragingly at Hazel, I went over to help Whitney repair the damage.

The weather, which had promised to be as sunny and warm as the
previous day's, began to change as we took the first pictures. Large
clouds appeared, blocking the sun. Also, much to the dismay of Martin, the wind, which had been no more than a gentle breeze, began
to gust. Dismondi won't need his wind machines today, I thought;
the clothes will move about quite naturally. Perhaps too naturally, I
added to myself as Elise's wool cap almost blew away. The models,
in their fall woolen clothes and sweaters, were quite comfortable.
They had been too warm the day before. But the rest of us, dressed

for spring, shivered. I scrounged about for jackets and sweaters for everyone.

"Some May Day," Alix muttered, slipping into one of the jackets we had already photographed.

"It doesn't look like it's going to rain," I said. "It may be better this way. It'll look more like fall with this light."

"Light. Phooey. I don't like it," said Alix, rubbing her hands vigorously along her arms.

"Alix, it's not *that* cold. If you like, I'll break out the brandy bottle later."

"Bless you," said Alix.

We moved smoothly into the second shot. As we worked, I noticed that Hazel, who was not in this photograph, had changed back into her jeans and a faded denim workshirt and was hovering near the cameras, either holding rolls of tape for Dickon as he worked, or just sitting to one side, long legs curled underneath her. I sat beside her.

"The first shot went well," I said.

"Oh thanks. The pages should be lovely. This is such a fabulous place. How lucky you are. To have a whole island to yourself."

"Actually, it's not that big." I laughed.

"But it's yours," Hazel said, smiling. Then she shivered slightly.

"You're freezing!" I said, touching her arm.

"I'm fine."

"Here, take this." I pulled off my red windbreaker and arranged it over her thin shoulders.

"What about you?" asked Hazel.

"I insist. I don't want to be responsible for your being sick next week." Hazel laughed and did as I ordered, admitting that she was more comfortable.

At lunchtime, I repeated the menu of the day before, only this time making sure there was lots of coffee and hot chocolate. I was disappointed that Pieter didn't join us. I wondered if he was still annoyed about my expedition to Dirk's boathouse, but I decided not. He had seemed his usual amiable self at breakfast that morning, although neither of us had lingered over our coffee.

We took a real lunch break; even Dismondi paused to sit down to eat his sandwich. We were ahead of schedule and everyone looked forward to a relaxing afternoon. With the sudden cool, I opened up the living room and even started a small fire in Adrian's chimney

We chatted and relaxed, turning the half-hour break into a raucous picnic. When we did get back to work an hour later, it was in fits and starts, neither organized nor serious. We were a very casual crew. It wasn't until the midafternoon then that anyone noticed Hazel was missing. We were setting up the last shot, in which both Whitney and Hazel were to wear evening clothes. I was with Dismondi, discussing the lighting, when Alix came over to pull me to one side.

"Uh, Gretel, I can't find Hazel anywhere," she said.

"Maybe she was tired and wanted to lie down," I suggested. "Come on, let's look in the house." Alix and I went from room to room, but Hazel wasn't napping on any of the couches or beds. In fact, save for Samantha lapping water in the kitchen, the house was empty.

"Maybe she went for a walk," Alix said. "Pieter's not here, maybe they went for a walk together. Oh, Gretel."

"What? Oh, don't be silly. Hazel's madly in love with Dickon. This week anyway," I said.

"Maybe he knows where Hazel went," said Alix, going outside.

"I'm ready, my crew is ready, Miss Whitney is ready," Dismondi announced as soon as we reached the patio. "The light is beginning to go. Where is Miss Hazel?"

"Uh, let's see, uh," stammered Alix. "Dismondi, we'll do the dresses singly, not together. Dismondi, start shooting with Whitney, and then, Carrie Ann, go and tell Elise, no, Alison to get into the black velvet. We can't have two blondes in evening dress."

While Alix rearranged the details of the shooting around Hazel's absence, I questioned Dickon. He said he knew nothing.

"I saw you talking together before lunch, Dickon," I said. "Didn't she give you any clue? I know about the two of you," I finally said in desperation.

"All right," said Dickon sheepishly. "We agreed to meet during the lunch break. You know, to be alone for a while." Dickon's blush was as deep as Hazel's had been earlier. "We were going to meet in the woods. Hazel left first. Then I went to join her."

"What happened?" I said

"I couldn't find her. I thought she was playing a game, you know. Hide and seek or something. But then I began to feel pretty foolish, you know? So I figured she had changed her mind. Or something. I knew Dismondi would be looking for me to set up, so I came back. I didn't see her, but I was still pretty mad, you know? You don't think anything's happened to her, do you?"

"I don't know, Dickon." I didn't like this. Hazel could be giddy at times, but she was not irresponsible. Alix came over and I repeated Dickon's story to her.

"So, what do you think?" she asked, sitting down as though I'd hit her in the stomach.

"She may have fallen and be lying hurt somewhere," I answered. "There's no way she could have gotten off the island without us knowing."

"Maybe we didn't hear the boat," said Alix.

"She wouldn't take one of the boats without asking."

"Maybe she and Dickon had a fight. She wasn't thinking clearly," said Alix.

"Look, finish up the shooting here and I'll go down to check." I hurried off toward the dock. There was someone down there. Thank God, I thought. Hazel had just gone for a joy ride. I called, waving my arms. But it wasn't Hazel tying up the *Stuyvesant*, it was Pieter, looking up at me dumfounded.

"My God, Gretel. You gave me a scare, charging down here, screaming your bloody head off," said Pieter.

"Oh. I'm sorry. What are you doing here?" I said.

"I live here," said Pieter.

"Sorry. It's Hazel!" I blurted out.

"Who's Hazel?"

I told Pieter the problem. He considered for a moment, then shook his head. "No, I haven't seen her. I ran out of pipe tobacco and went over to Richmond."

"I guess we should search the island thoroughly," I said glumly. I waited while Pieter finished tying up the *Stuyvesant*. We walked slowly up to the house.

Dismondi was packing up his equipment. Alix was packing up the clothes. Hazel was still missing. We decided to organize a search party, in three groups. Pieter would lead one to the south side of the island working toward the boathouse. I would take the second off to explore the north side with Alix and Whitney in tow. Dickon volunteered to lead another to the grounds immediately below the house. We searched diligently for a good hour, without turning up even a footprint for a clue. As we neared Dirk's boathouse, I saw Pieter and his group. They, too, had been unsuccessful. Together, we all solemnly trudged back up to the house.

Dickon's group had failed also. There was nothing to indicate that Hazel had ever wandered over the island, and certainly nothing to give a hint of how she had left it. Her purse and her makeup kit were at the house. All her identification, her money, even the keys to her apartment—everything had been left behind. It was frighteningly mysterious.

To keep my thoughts off my worst fears, I busied myself making a fresh pot of coffee and serving drinks. Finally, with all the theories as to where Hazel could be proposed and rejected, a dreadful silence fell over the group. Everyone waited for everyone else to speak. No one wanted to be the first to voice what we all were surely thinking.

Pieter broke the silence. He stood up to knock his pipe against the fireplace, contemplating the ashes as they fell softly "We've done all that we can. It's time to call in help."

"The police?" gasped Alix, her hands twisting nervously.

"Yes," Pieter answered.

"That seems so final," said Alix.

"Alix, we have to face, uh, we should assume that the worst has happened. We should have called in the police immediately," I said.

"We've behaved correctly so far," said Pieter.

"Maybe Ensign Dragon could help," I suggested. Alix visibly brightened at the idea. "That way it would seem less official, less harsh."

"We shouldn't call on him every time we have a crisis," said Pieter.

"Michael wouldn't mind," said Alix quickly. "And isn't that what the Coast Guard is supposed to do? Find people lost in the harbor?"

"All right." Pieter threw up his hands. "We'll call in the Coast Guard." He went off to telephone.

"Look here," said Dismondi irritably, sitting up and stretching noisily. "Is it necessary that we *all* remain here? I mean, now that the authorities have been called in?"

"Well, I guess not," I said. I had no idea of what was proper, but I did know that the fewer people I had to cope with, the better.

"I'd like to stay, if that's all right, Gretel, until, well, until we know something definite," said Dickon.

"The boat's already down at the dock," said Alix, looking at her watch. "It is silly for everyone to stay. I'd like to stay, too, though, Gretel," she added softly.

"Of course," I answered, taking her hand. Just then Pieter entered the room.

"The Coast Guard is on the way," he announced dramatically.

* * *

It seemed better once everyone had gone. In one sense, though, it was worse. Without the noise and confusion that a group of anxious people generate, I could think over the day's events, on Hazel's disappearance, of what I should have done that I didn't, of what I shouldn't have done that I did. Alix did her best to keep up a lively stream of idle chatter, but she, too, soon fell gloomy. She could barely muster a flirtatious smile when Michael Dragon arrived.

"We've a boat out prowling the waters," he said, accepting the cup of coffee I handed him. "I thought I'd come up and see if there was any information you could give us that could be helpful."

Alix and I told him what we could, but it was precious little. We had both been so busy during the day that we hadn't paid attention to anyone's particular movements.

"The last time I remember seeing Hazel was before lunch. She was chilly and I gave her my jacket to wear," I finished.

"What color is it?" asked Michael.

"Red."

"What else was she wearing?"

"Blue jeans, a blue shirt. I don't remember her shoes," I answered.

"How about a general description?"

"She's a very pretty girl," I began.

"She's Gretel's height and size," interrupted Alix. "With long dark hair."

"Okay," said Michael. "That should be good enough. This will help us and save some time when the police arrive."

"Are the police coming?" asked Alix.

"Yes," he answered.

"Michael," I said, walking him to the door. "I really do appreciate your help in all this. It seems that we're always asking you to help out in our moments of crisis." I sighed as I repeated Pieter's words.

"I'm more than glad to be of service." Michael smiled down at me. "I enjoy it. And besides, it's my job."

I returned his smile. "Thank you anyway. You will let us know the minute you . . ."

"Yes." And Michael Dragon went out into the darkness.

It was a dreary evening. Alix and I sat alone in Hoek House, in front of Adrian's chimney, staring at the flames. But the fire did nothing to take the chill from the night. Only Samantha, curled up purring in my lap, seemed relaxed. Every once in a while Pieter, or Dickon, or one of the others tramped wearily up to the house, but there was nothing to report. I sent them back with a fresh thermos full of hot coffee. It began to rain mid-evening, and it soon was a steady downpour that made the searching very difficult. I thought I should scream with the waiting.

"They also serve who stand and wait," Alix reminded me, pouring herself another brandy.

"That's a stupid thing to say," I replied sulkily.

"So's that," Alix snapped back.

"This waiting is driving me crazy!" I screamed, upsetting Samantha. Alix ignored me, but I did feel better. "Isn't there anything we can do?" I asked.

"We're staying by the phones," said Alix. "We're making fresh coffee and sandwiches and . . ."

"Being typical women," I finished bitterly. "Sit and wait, make coffee. Ugh!"

"It's a lot better than standing about out there, getting drenched and dirty," said Alix.

"At least they're doing something! They're helping!"

"Gretel, be sensible. You're four months pregnant."

"I wouldn't miscarry."

"How do you know?"

"I can't take it anymore," I said, standing up. "I'm going down there."

"Then I'm coming, too," said Alix, looking slightly relieved. "Have an extra coat?" she asked, peering into the closet. I found a poncho of Pieter's; we belted it around her as best we could. Picking up a flashlight, I led the way outside.

I had no idea where the search party was, but I guessed them to be at the opposite end of the island, where the harbor was deeper and there were more rocks. I was right. We found them easily, following the blue flashing light of the Coast Guard cutter. Briefly, for an uncomfortable moment, I was reminded of another night when I had followed a blue light, but I pushed the memory from me.

A group of men was standing at the water's edge while a boat went back and forth. A searchlight was trained on the water. A couple of men were standing in the back of the boat, leaning over the stern, pulling something along. Alix and I joined the group on shore.

"Go home at once!" said Pieter, shining his flashlight on my face.

"No," I replied, surprised at my temerity. Alix was right. We had been better off in front of the fire. It was horrible weather. We sank ankle-deep into the marshy ground.

"Then stay out of the way," growled Pieter.

"Who's this?" a man standing next to Pieter asked.

"Detective, this is my wife, Gretel Van der Hoek. This is Alix Silverstein. Gretel, this is Detective Abramowitz. He's in charge of the search."

"Hello," I said automatically. "Detective, what are those men doing?" I pointed toward the boat.

"We're dragging for the body, ma'am," he answered in a flat, bored voice.

"Are you sure that . . . that Hazel is . . . is there?"

"We can't be sure of anything, ma'am," said Detective Abramowitz. "She's not on the island. Your husband says there's no way she could have gotten off without swimming."

"That's right," I whispered.

"So," he said in the same deadpan monotone.

"I suppose," I whispered again. "Why should she be in the water?"

Just then, one of the men on board gave a shout. Something was pulled in. It wasn't a body. Someone went out in a launch to retrieve the object. A few moments later, Detective Abramowitz held it out in front of me.

"Can you identify this?"

"Yes." I took a deep breath. "It's my windbreaker. I lent it to Hazel to wear. She was cold."

"Seems we were right." The detective turned to one of his men. "Keep searching, Casey." He turned back to me. "What condition was the garment in when you lent it to the young lady?"

"Fine, I guess."

"No tears, stains?"

"Nothing. I'd just had it cleaned. I'd only worn it one other time since then."

"All right. Thank you, ma'am." The detective handed my jacket back to Casey. As he did so I could see that it was ripped badly. The jacket was made of strong material. It had taken a hard pull to rip it that jaggedly. I felt funny and clutched at Pieter's arm.

"Alix, take Gretel home," he commanded, ignoring my protests.

"I'm fine, I'm fine," I insisted.

"Get up to the house and stay there," said Pieter angrily.

Alix led me back up the hill. We stopped twice along the way, for I was indeed sick. Once we reached the house, however, even though I felt weak, I refused to be put to bed. I did allow Alix to lead me to the couch in the living room, and wrap me snugly in a quilt.

"You know, Alix," I said, once I had got my breath back. "We've never considered the possibility that someone could have hurt Hazel. That her disappearance could have been caused by someone."

"Of course not. Who'd want to hurt Hazel? She was just a sweet kid. Oh, my God. I didn't mean to use the past tense." Tears began to well up in Alix's eyes.

"Maybe," I said, "there was a psychopath lurking on the island."

"How could someone come on the island without your knowledge?" said Alix.

"Hazel disappeared without our knowing," I answered. We sat for a while, contemplating the worst. Suppose it was some crazy man, I thought, who motored to the island for some crazy reason, and came upon Hazel as she waited for Dickon. It could happen. Pieter was right to scold me for wandering about the other end of the island, even though I had had Melissa for company. I thought about that expedition, thought about our conversations, thought about Dirk's boathouse.

"Alix," I said aloud, "Hazel was wearing *my* jacket."

"So?" she asked, blowing her nose.

"So, suppose someone thought it was me. From a distance we do look alike." I spoke slowly, unsurely.

"There being so many thousands of people who are just waiting for the chance to bump you off," teased Alix. "No, Gretel, no way. Normal people don't go around getting murdered. If something happened to Hazel, it was a terrible, freaky accident, but an accident just the same. Now, stop being morbid, and have some brandy."

I wanted to tell Alix about the other "freaky" accident that had happened to me in the harbor. I actually started to tell her. I abruptly changed my mind. I didn't want to start being afraid again. And it was ridiculous, really, to assume the events could be connected.

* * *

It was long past midnight when the men returned to the house. I was dozing. I woke to hear them report to Alix. No further trace of Hazel had been found. The search had been called off till morning. They were widening the area to be searched, however. The tide had turned.

9

El Condor

"What story?" I asked sleepily, turning over to look at the alarm clock—7:00 A.M. I had been asleep only four hours. I readjusted the pillows. Pieter snored softly beside me. "Melissa, it's awfully early," I hissed into the receiver, but she interrupted.

"I couldn't believe it," she said. "There, in the New York *Times* no less. A missing model! From *your* island! Is it true?"

"Well," I said.

"Who is that?" asked Pieter, groaning as the light hit his eyes.

"It's Melissa. Hazel's disappearance has made the morning papers," I answered.

"Damn!" Pieter sat up, paused to stretch his back, then climbed out of bed and went into the bathroom.

"Are you there?" said Melissa.

"We were up late last night"—I yawned—"this morning."

"How terrible!" said Melissa.

"What does it say in the paper?" I asked, pulling the blanket up around my shoulders. Pieter liked to sleep with the window open.

"Not much, really. It's all in a boldface caption. That a high-fashion model vanished from Hoek Land during a fashion shooting for *Milady* magazine. 'The model, Hazel Breen, is known for her work in television commercials.' There's a picture of the June issue of *Milady* with Hazel smiling on the cover. Then there's a picture of the island."

"What's she say?" called Pieter.

"That there's a picture of the island in the *Times*," I answered.

"Damn!" said Pieter, throwing his towel on the floor as he came back into the bedroom.

"It doesn't show the house," said Melissa.

"Melissa says you can't really see anything," I said. Pieter went on dressing.

"Were the police there?" asked Melissa.

"And the Coast Guard," I said, sighing.

"What happened?"

"I don't know. No one knows," I answered. I really was not in the mood to gossip about yesterday, even with Melissa. "Melissa, I'm sorry, but I really am exhausted."

"Of course. I wasn't thinking. Listen, I'll speak to you later in the day," said Melissa, ringing off. I snuggled back into the pillows.

I had just drifted off to sleep when the phone rang again. I groaned, and reached my hand out for the receiver, but it stopped after two rings. Pieter must have answered it downstairs, I thought, relaxing. Then the phone rang again, and again Pieter answered it on the kitchen extension. Not five minutes had passed before it rang a third time. This is ridiculous, I thought, sitting up in bed, rubbing my eyes. I was now thoroughly awake. I got up, slipping on my robe, and went downstairs.

Pieter was sitting at the kitchen table, sipping coffee. He started as I entered the room. "Well, good morning," he said. "I didn't expect to see you up so early. Want some coffee?"

I nodded wearily. "I didn't expect to be up so early, either, but I had no choice with all those phone calls. Nobody ever calls this early. Who was it?"

"Someone kept dialing the wrong number," said Pieter. "Have a cruller."

I dunked it in my coffee, watching the sugared icing float. I picked out the bits of sugar with my spoon. "Whose idea was it to have an extension in the bedroom?" I said.

"Yours," said Pieter. He was grumpy this morning.

"I suppose that now I'm up, I might as well go into the office. I guess I . . . oh, I'll get that," I said, as the phone started to ring once more.

"I will," said Pieter. He picked up the phone, listened for a few moments. Then he said, "No, no," and hung up the receiver.

"What was that?" I asked. It was obviously *not* a wrong number.

"The Free Press," Pieter said, banging his fist on the table. "Newspaper, television—everybody wants to know about the disappearing model. The vanishing beauty. Innocence lost. You know."

"I hadn't thought of that. I suppose it is good copy that someone vanishes during a fashion shooting. In the middle of New York harbor. On a private island."

"I suppose you're enjoying this?" said Pieter.

"How can you say that? I'm sick over Hazel. She's a friend of mine."

"That damn phone's getting on my nerves," said Pieter in apology, bringing his hand up to touch my cheek.

"We're both nervous," I said, kissing his fingers. We both winced as the phone rang again.

Pieter let it ring until it stopped, but then it started again and again. Finally, Pieter yelled, "Enough!" and, jumping up, he ripped the phone from the wall and threw it across the room. It fell crashing against the dining-room door. Then he dashed upstairs, returning with the white phone we used in the bedroom. He dumped them both in the garbage can. "There," he said. Half-amused, half-annoyed, I decided it was time for me to leave for work, and I went quickly upstairs to dress. A few minutes later, as I untied the *Silver Fox* and motored out into the harbor, I caught a glimpse of police and Coast Guard boats already searching the waters at the far end of the island. I speeded up the boat to startle my head awake with salt air and spray, thinking to myself: things have to get better. Of course, they got worse.

There were three dark-suited strangers looking like trouble around the receptionist's desk at *Milady*'s offices. I turned away and sneaked in through the back entrance to the art department, locking the door behind me.

"I didn't expect to see you today," Maggie said as I stopped by her desk for my messages.

"What's been going on here?" I said, fearing the worst.

"What hasn't?" Maggie moaned as her phone rang. I shook my head. "No, no, she's not in yet. No, no, I don't know when she will be. Good-bye." She replaced the receiver, grimacing. "All morning long."

"Why don't they hold the calls at the switchboard?" I asked.

"Because, Nancy's overloaded," Maggie answered, running her

fingers through her boyishly short, curly black hair. "And Miss Hollosoll hasn't made up her mind what *Milady*'s official position is."

"Well, I'd better go in and see Mavis then," I said. "As soon as I take care of a few things."

I first called the telephone company, to report our out-of-order phones. Not wanting a lecture on the wanton destruction of New York Telephone's property, I glossed over the details. The *earliest*, I was told, the earliest a repairman could be sent out was sometime next week—Thursday. Typical, I thought, hanging up. I then tried to do some work. But it wasn't easy, as my staff slipped in questions about Hazel. I finally gave up and chatted for a few moments, looking over the account in the *Times*. To my relief, Melissa was right. The caption was brief, almost vague; the picture of the island didn't show our house. That should calm Pieter, I thought, folding the paper and putting it in my briefcase. Then, after asking Maggie to send a messenger to Dismondi's studio for the film, I went into Mavis's office.

Alix was there already, looking as fresh in her silk tunic and pants as though she had slept for a week. Unfair, I muttered to myself. I knew I looked as exhausted as I felt.

"I really didn't expect to see you, but I'm glad you're here," said Mavis flatly, stubbing out her cigarette in an ashtray already overflowing with lipstick-stained butts. It was unlike her to be untidy.

"The phone started at seven," I answered, flopping onto one of Mavis's brightly colored sofas. I told them what Pieter had done with the phones. Alix shook her head, smiling at his madness.

Mavis obviously disapproved. "The phones have been ringing here all morning. Some calls I've taken, the others I put off. I've been trying to come up with some official stance, but it's not easy." Mavis paused, looking down at a memo pad on which she had been scribbling.

"Do we need an 'official' position?" asked Alix.

"Of course we do," Mavis snapped back. "Something like this reflects badly on *Milady*'s image."

"Not to mention Hazel's," I said.

"All right, you're right. I apologize. It's easier for me because I don't know her. I'm sorry. But I am worried about *Milady*. I can't have the public thinking that kinky things happen in our office. What a mess!" She shook her head. "Is there any news?"

"They've extended the search to include more of the harbor," I said. "It could take some time."

"If they ever find her," Alix added morosely.

"Let's pray she just wandered off with a boy friend," said Mavis. "Now, I think our best bet is to co-operate with the press. But not too eagerly. Refer them to the police. Of course, we shouldn't endure harassment. But we can certainly *talk* to them. We're all journalists, after all."

"Mavis," I began, but she cut me off.

"And we should continue working, and not let anything upset the routine of *Milady*. Business as usual." She smiled briefly.

"You're the boss," Alix said, looking over at me.

"Good," said Mavis, pleased with herself. "I know this is going to be the hardest on you, Gretel."

"And Pieter," I said.

"Yes. Well, just try to be polite and not antagonize any of the reporters. What shall we do about Hazel's family?"

"I don't know," said Alix.

"She's from Boston," I said. "Her real name is Brenski."

Making another note on her memo pad, Mavis said, "I should call to express our concern. I guess that's about everything. Gretel dear, why don't you go home early? You look terrible."

"Thanks," I said.

"What does she expect you to do?" asked Alix, once we were out of Mavis's office and in the hallway. "Throw a big party and invite the boys from the press to Hoek House?"

"Pieter'd kill me," I said, leaning against the wall. "How can you look so good on just a few hours' sleep?"

"I didn't get any sleep at all." Alix sighed. "By the time Michael got me back to Manhattan, it was really late. And then I felt so sorry for Michael. I invited him up for some coffee. We got to talking, and before I knew it, the sun was up. Then I made us breakfast."

"Alix, you and Michael, uh, you . . ." I trailed off.

"For heaven's sake!" laughed Alix. "Here, come into my office. Everyone is looking at us." I followed her into her clutter, pushed a jumble of mismatched shoes and stockings off a chair, and sat down. Alix perched behind her desk, peering at me over bottles and jars of various lotions and notions. "Michael Dragon is a very nice boy," she said. "We just talked. Matter of fact, we talked mostly about you."

"Oh?" I said.

"Michael adores you," said Alix, examining one of her long, sculpted nails. "And he is very concerned."

"Oh?" I said. I could see what was coming, and I didn't feel this was the proper time. My head was too foggy.

"It seems that last night was the second time he's been called to Hoek Land on an errand of mercy," said Alix, tapping her nails on her desk.

"Oh," I said. I was not about to elaborate.

"Is that all you have to say about it?" Alix said slowly. "Michael worries about you being alone in your boat so much, especially now. The baby and all."

"That's very sweet of Michael. And of you. But I am careful, and I've got a husband to take care of me," I said cheerfully.

"Yes," agreed Alix. "You're lucky there. Well, scoot home in your little boat and I'll see you tomorrow. Don't get excited about the reporters. Ignore them. No matter what Madame says. What you need is sleep."

"What I need is peace of mind," I said. Which, if I had hoped to find at home, I didn't.

Our little dock was no longer ours. There were several boats drawn up, one with the legend "WCBS NEWS" painted starkly on its side. I realized that the reporters had not been put off by the absence of a phone. They'd flocked to Hoek Land. I thought of turning around, but I had to go home eventually. Ignoring their shouts, and maneuvering around their boats, I slid into the boathouse. I was relieved to see the *Stuyvesant* there. As I stepped from the boat, it began.

"Are you Mrs. Van der Hoek?"

"Do you have any idea why the girl disappeared?"

"How well did you know her?"

"Have you spoken to her family?"

"What about drugs?"

"What's the name of this island?"

"How long have you lived here?"

"Is it true the girl's family is suing *Milady* magazine?"

"Is the magazine going to sue you?"

"Please, please. Be quiet," I yelled. "I'm afraid I really can't answer your questions. I'm very tired, and, yes, the girl was, is, a friend. Now, if you'll excuse me. No." I held up my hands. "No, you can't come up to the house."

"Shove off!" Pieter's voice thundered from out of nowhere. "Get off my island. All of you! Neither of us have anything to say. Now, get out of here!" Pieter descended like a mad bull. He finished grandly, drawing me to him in a protective gesture. It was a frighteningly melodramatic performance. The reporters retreated to the dock, albeit unwillingly. Their photographers snapped pictures as they went. I turned my face away, but I could hear the familiar whirring click-clack of the Nikons. Mavis won't like this, I thought. Even though I agreed wholeheartedly with Pieter, I wished he had been a little less brutal. "Thank you," I said as I snuggled in his arms.

"The way I feel, I could tear them to pieces!" We hurried up to the house and slipped inside.

"It's not that bad," I laughed, going to the cupboard to take out a bag of chocolate-chip cookies. I handed one to Pieter. "They're just doing their job," I reminded him.

"They're beasts! This is my island!" said Pieter.

"Oh, Pieter," I said. "Maybe we should talk to them. Give them what they want. Then they'll go away and leave us alone."

"Never," Pieter replied. "They're vultures. They smell out and create scandal. The police are ghouls enough for me."

"Mavis wants us to co-operate," I said, trying to explain why I was being so tolerant. "She thinks it's best for *Milady*."

"*Milady!* You know what you can do with *Milady!* God, give a woman a career and she thinks she's Kissinger. *Milady* magazine got me into this. I never should have agreed to that shooting. Do you have any idea what a lawsuit could do to us? And *you're* worried about *Milady!*" Pieter flung the remains of his cookie at me, missing me (I presumed) on purpose. Then he retreated to his studio, slamming the door. He always did that in a temper, but this time I was too tired and cranky to complain. But, what had *I* done wrong anyway? I went up to sleep, waking sometime after dark to discover that Pieter hadn't come up. I crept downstairs to discover also that Pieter was still in his studio, the FM radio blaring while he clumped around behind the shut door. I decided to keep my pride. I put some food out for Samantha and went back to bed in a sulk. As I feared, I spent the night alone.

Worse, the next morning, as soon as I'd sat down at the kitchen table, Pieter, dressed up and cheery-looking, told me he was going away for the weekend.

"But where?" I said, wanting actually to ask "why?" I wasn't for a moment fooled by his calm manner. Pieter was punishing me.

"Boston. I've been asked to judge an art show," he said.

"What art show?" I persisted.

"My old college roommate, Robbie, is an art director at Little, Brown. He's also an officer of the illustrators' club up there. I'm sure I told you," Pieter added patiently.

He hadn't. "How long will you be gone?" I said.

"I'll go up this afternoon to look over the entries. There's an awards dinner on Saturday night. I'll be back Monday."

"Can't I come with you?" I asked.

"You've got a job, remember?"

"I can take off." I was not to be put off.

"No," said Pieter, looking into his coffee.

"I really don't want to stay here by myself," I burst out, deciding enough was enough. I would beg.

"Why? They'll have forgotten all about us by Saturday. Somebody else will disappear, or die, or, you know, another catastrophe."

"It's not the press. I don't want to be here alone. I don't know why," I confessed, which was true. It was a feeling I had. "Especially without a phone."

"Then have Melissa over. I'm sure she'll jump at the chance to visit the scene of the crime. There are so many police about, you couldn't be safer. And your ensign, of course. Nothing to worry about." Pieter got up, poured me another cup of coffee, and went into his studio, shutting the door. I stared at the door for a few moments, hating it. Pieter spent more time in there than he did with me.

"Okay," I said aloud. "I'll be just fine. I hope Melissa doesn't have a date this weekend. I certainly don't."

Thankfully, neither did Melissa. "John's away on business," she said when I called her (Aha, I thought, so it's only John Cotton that Melissa dates now) from my office later that afternoon. "He had to visit a client in Miami Beach. Miami Beach, I ask you? Mighty suspicious. Anyway, I'm just dying to find out the gory details."

"Not funny," I said. We arranged to meet after work for a quiet dinner in the Village ("Just like old times," Melissa said), Melissa returning with me to Hoek Land afterward. She was on her best behavior, and didn't once tease me about the case of the "Missing Mannequin," as the *Post* had termed it. I was certainly glad to have her with me. A night alone in bed with Pieter locked in his studio had left me unnerved. I understood why he blamed me, and, in one sense, I blamed myself. Still, I felt he was being extreme. He had not even said a proper good-bye. But with Melissa listening sympathetically, I began to be glad for Pieter's trip. Things would surely get better once he'd returned. We both needed time apart.

Melissa, of course, thought I was thinking foolishly. She thought I was totally right and Pieter totally wrong. In fact, she elaborated on her theory during the ride back from Manhattan, during the "Late Show," and through most of the "Late Late Show," until we fell asleep on the couch. Melissa continued to preach over breakfast the next morning.

"Newlyweds," she said. "If you'd talk to each other instead of trying to guess what the other is thinking, you'd be better off."

"Regardless. Pieter is upset. But it seems to me it's more than Hazel's disappearance," I said, putting my innermost thoughts into words for the first time. "Oh, he's sorry about her, of course. But he didn't even meet her. There's something else."

"If there is," said Melissa, carrying the breakfast dishes over to the sink and turning on the faucet, "you'd do well to talk to Pieter about it Monday night. I just think you're being sensitive. You're overreacting because you're pregnant."

"My pregnancy has nothing to do with it," I said defensively, perhaps stridently.

"The best thing is to relax," said Melissa, condescendingly patient as if speaking to a child. "Here, lazy, come and dry these things. Don't let your guest do all the work." I joined her and we worked in silence, until the kitchen was spotless. "There," said Melissa. "Now I'm ready for lunch. No, no, just kidding. But what are we going to do this afternoon? My plans for sitting in the sun are shot," she added, nodding at the window. A light rain was falling, hitting the glass with a soft pitter-patter.

"A good day for snuggling before a fire, eating chocolates, and reading romantic novels," I said, stretching.

"I did not come here to eat and read. Let's explore," said Melissa, jumping to her feet.

"Explore what?" I asked, suspicious.

"The house. It'll be fun. And relaxing," she said. "I bet there's lots you haven't shown me."

"Actually, no. The other bedrooms are empty," I said. Melissa refused to be daunted.

"Well, the cellar, then. You do have a cellar, don't you?"

"There's a cellar."

"What's it like?"

"I've only been in the laundry room," I confessed.

"It's time you went. Come on!"

"All right." I laughed, getting up to lead the way to the stairs in the hallway. "As long as you're not afraid of ghosts."

"Ooooh, your family ghost. Is this the place?" Melissa said delightedly.

"This is where he fell. And," I said dramatically as I opened the door to the cellar, "he swore revenge on all women who set foot on Hoek Land. So beware!"

"Hooray!" said Melissa. She bounced down the cellar stairs.

I followed more slowly, wishing I hadn't told the story. Although I knew that these were not the same steps that that long-ago Van der Hoek had fallen down, they seemed the same. They were brick. I had no difficulty in picturing that accident—a few bricks carefully loosened, a man losing his balance to fall and hit his head, his wife coming to enjoy her success, her lover inspecting the body to make sure the neck was broken. I imagined it intensely, down to the starched ruffled collar on the woman's dress. Then I remembered the blue light that had saved me that snowy night in the harbor. Perhaps it was a friendly ghost after all.

"Hey, Gretel!" Melissa's voice broke my trance. She came over to touch me on the shoulder. "Seen a ghost?"

"Remembering one," I said, shaking my head to stop my silliness. "It's just damp down here."

After my first feelings of uneasiness, I began to enjoy our expedition. The cellar was filthy, of course. Complicated cobwebs hung in the corners. Scratchy scurryings hinted at mice. The single naked electric bulb cast eerie shadows over the ancient brick walls. The cellar was the oldest part of the house (after Adrian's chimney), Pieter had once told me, having been part of the original structure built in 1661. Some of the dust looked equally old, yet there were some areas that were relatively clean. Melissa and I kept mostly to those. Sometime, I thought, I would have to come down here to clean. But today was for exploring.

There was an old trunk against one wall. Its rusted lock gave way easily, yielding a wealth of Van der Hoek memorabilia—the sort of memorabilia I had looked for in vain in the bedrooms upstairs. There were old-fashioned baby clothes—perhaps a christening dress; hats with outrageous plumes that Melissa snapped up; high-heeled, many-buttoned boots too dainty for my feet; and faded, worn kid gloves. There was a velvet box filled with jewelry that I put aside for later. But, best of all, there were pictures—tinted daguerreotypes of severe, bearded men and placid ladies looking scared to death of the camera. And finally, slipped down along the side of the trunk as though just recently put away, was a picture of a man so like Pieter, and a woman, with such glistening dark hair and glittering black eyes, that I knew immediately they were Pieter's parents. Nicholas wore a dark suit. Isobel wore a light-colored, flowered chiffon dress, carrying a small bouquet, with some more flowers in her hair, which, in defiance of the style of that time, hung straight to her waist.

"Pieter's parents. It must have been their wedding day," I said.

"Mr. Van der Hoek looks smitten. She's gorgeous," said Melissa.

"She still is. Wait, there's more. Look at this," I giggled as I pulled out the next photo, taken a few years later. Isobel's hair was braided now, wrapped in shining coils over her ears. She was smiling, but not at the camera. In her lap, struggling to free himself from her hold, was a pouting child with dark-blond hair, dressed for the occasion in a sailor's suit and shiny, black patent-leather shoes.

"That's Pieter?" asked Melissa, looking over my shoulder. "But how funny! Look at those curls. Imagine having a blond baby."

"There don't seem to be any more," I said, disappointedly peering into the trunk.

"These are priceless," said Melissa, picking up the wedding picture again. "Do you know why they divorced?"

"If you believe the legend, it was the ghost who drove her away."

"No more ghost stories."

"Okay." I laughed, sitting back on my heels. I surveyed my dust-stained denim jumper. Melissa was equally dirty. There were black streaks on her forehead from brushing the hair out of her eyes with grimy fingers. "You're a sight," I said.

"We both are," she agreed.

"I want a bath," I said, getting awkwardly to my feet, stiff from kneeling. I picked up the pictures, and the jewelry box. Melissa grabbed a floppy hat. We shut the trunk and headed upstairs.

A short while later, scrubbed and shining, we dined before a small flickering fire in Adrian's chimney, busily licking the meat from chicken bones with Samantha prowling between us awaiting her share.

"This is the life," sighed Melissa, stretching wide in Pieter's old terry-cloth robe. I had finished eating and sat regarding the two pictures we had found in the trunk.

"I'll have to get these framed," I said, holding them out in front of me, sighing. "I was hoping for more. I suppose Isobel took them with her."

"Pictures of Dirk?" Melissa asked coyly.

"There don't seem to be any. It's peculiar," I admitted.

"You've looked everywhere?"

"Everywhere but the cellar, where we were today."

"Yeah," Melissa yawned. "There's a lot more places to look down there."

"True," I said, jumping to my feet.

"What are you doing?"

"Let's look right now!" I said.

"Don't be ridiculous. We're cleaned up. Besides, that cellar is spooky. Let's go back down there tomorrow, when it's light out."

"It'll still be dark in the cellar."

"Please?" Melissa recurled herself in her chair and poured herself another glass of wine.

I flopped down on the floor, pulling my velour robe close, absentmindedly scratching Samantha's tummy. "Peculiar," I repeated to myself. Everything about Dirk was peculiar, but not half so much as —wait! There was still one place I hadn't looked. On sheerest impulse, I jumped up—scaring Samantha and Melissa—and ran from the room.

"Gretel, what are you doing?" said Melissa, following slowly.

I didn't stop until I was in the kitchen. Then I paused, took a deep breath, put my hand on the glass doorknob, and turned it. To my surprise, it opened easily. I flicked a light on and stepped inside Pieter's sacrosanct studio. Melissa followed me inside, squealing:

"What is this? What's in Pieter's studio? My goodness, it's messy." Melissa held the sides of her robe closely lest she brush against wet paint. As I picked my way over jars and cans and rags, I did the same. "This place is a firetrap," Melissa muttered. I ignored her.

This was the first time I had been in Pieter's studio when he wasn't here, perhaps the tenth time I had been in it at all. I had no idea of how he organized his work—by subject? by material? or just in order of completion? Canvases were stacked against each wall. There was a large filing cabinet, its drawers filled with drawings. I looked them over casually. I had no idea what I was looking for, nor would I until I found it. Perhaps not even then.

I went through one stack of canvases quickly, then one caught my eye. It was a portrait of a beautiful golden woman. She sat on a rock, her feet dangling to the water below, one long tanned leg kicking up a glittering spray. She wore a colorful tunic that matched her exuberance. But the most striking thing was her hair—long and gold, it swirled about her like a cloud. I glanced at the lower right-hand corner. Pieter had signed his name, dating the painting the previous August. "Melissa, should I recognize this girl?" I said tremulously.

"Who's that?" said Melissa, coming up behind me. "That's Starr Mills."

Of course. Starr Mills. I had seen her only once, ten years before. Then she had been wearing a Chanel suit, white gloves, and a pillbox hat atop her neatly coifed bouffant hair. She'd been taking tea at the Palm Court in the Plaza, very demure and ladylike. Yet, as I (then a sophomore in high school) had passed by with my mother, I had spied a twinkle in her eyes and had liked her instinctively. I liked the girl in the painting, too. She seemed too sprite to be the infamous radical terrorist on the FBI's most-wanted list. The years had not dimmed her warm smile.

"Why should Pieter do that?" asked Melissa. "And aren't those the rocks where we were last weekend?"

They were. What was Starr Mills doing on Hoek Land? Last August, when she was supposed to be underground. Maybe it wasn't Starr. "Pieter knew Starr," I said to Melissa absent-mindedly. "He went to her deb parties in the sixties."

"Oh." Melissa fell silent. We looked at the painting a little while longer. "Still," she said, "it is peculiar."

"There's a lot peculiar, Melissa," I said, returning the painting to its place against the wall. "It's chilly in here, let's get back to the fire." "Peculiar," I muttered to myself, as I switched off the light, and closed the studio door behind us. Too many things were peculiar. I didn't speak again until we were in the living room.

"Melissa, remember last weekend? When we went exploring? When we found the boathouse and walked around it?"

Melissa nodded as she poured herself another glass of wine.

"What was I wearing that day?"

"Jeans, I guess, and, oh, you were wearing that bright-red wind-breaker."

"Do you know what Hazel was wearing when she vanished?"

"No, why?"

"Hazel and I were, are, similar in appearance. Oh, hardly identical, of course, but to someone who didn't know either of us well, to someone who was only judging by the clothes, we could be easily confused. And she was wearing my red windbreaker."

"What are you saying?"

"I could have been the intended victim."

"Victim?"

"Someone either saw us or knew we had snooped about the boathouse. Someone was afraid I had found out something, or that I would continue snooping until I did find out something. As we just did."

"You lost me," said Melissa.

"I told Pieter we had been to the boathouse. He was very angry. Out of all proportion."

"So?"

"There's more." I was surprised at my composure. I again told Melissa about my accident in the harbor, but this time, I emphasized the details of how the tank had leaked gas.

"A hole on purpose?"

"Clyde said that's what it looked like," I said slowly. "Of course, I didn't pay him much mind. Now, I'm not so sure."

"Pieter loves you," said Melissa.

"I never did know why Pieter and that Jesús person left the party early," I said, mostly to myself.

"Gretel, make sense," said Melissa.

"You've been right all along," I said.

"I have? About what?" said Melissa.

"About there being no Dirk," I announced.

"I was teasing you," said Melissa.

"Pieter invented Dirk as a convenient excuse. The boathouse is padlocked, says Pieter, because Dirk keeps it locked up. I hear a boat in the middle of the night? Well, it must be Dirk returning from some escapade, says Pieter. Of course Pieter doesn't like to talk about Dirk! Dirk doesn't exist! That explains his anger when I ask questions. You know, old Clyde didn't seem to know who Dirk was, and he's known the family for years! Even Isobel looked a bit strange when I mentioned Dirk. It explains so much more!"

"Gretel, I really think this is too much," Melissa began, but I waved her into silence. I was thinking about Puerto Rico, and the strange man I had seen with Pieter—I told Melissa about him.

"What an odd business," she said.

"They were definitely talking together. And if he were only asking a question or trying to sell Pieter something, there was no reason not to tell me. If it had been an innocent encounter, Pieter would have told me."

"I see what you mean. Perhaps it was a family matter. Pieter didn't tell you because he had wanted to surprise you about his mother?" Melissa said hopefully.

"That's more far-fetched than anything *I've* said," I scoffed. To convince her, I finally told her about Pieter's gambling, and the large amounts of money he had won.

"Wow! I didn't know Pieter gambled."

"He doesn't. That was the only time. He doesn't even buy lottery tickets."

"Maybe he just gives in to the urge once in a while. Gets it out of his system."

"Some system. He won thousands! Too much for the occasional gambler. No, I think it was some kind of payoff."

"What?"

"It was a clever way to transfer money without anyone noticing," I said.

"Pieter wouldn't have any reason to obtain large amounts of money," protested Melissa.

"No, but El Condor would." There, I'd said it. My wildest, grimmest theory.

"What?" Melissa choked, almost screeching the word.

"I think that Pieter's mixed up in some way with the El Condor terrorists," I said.

"Uh, why do you think that?" Melissa was still choking. She poured herself a generous amount of wine, sloshing it over the glass's rim. "Look, Gretel, I know you're miffed about Pieter going up to Boston, but that's no reason to suspect he's El Condor."

"I don't think he *is* El Condor, just involved in some way. Look, it explains *everything*. That man in Puerto Rico, the money, why

Pieter didn't want the fashion shooting here, why he didn't want a Coast Guard officer coming to dinner, his weird friend Jesús. Pieter was on the harbor during the barge explosion last November, and, as we just saw, he was still in touch with Starr Mills. She was probably hiding out on Hoek Land. Of course! She worked with El Condor and somehow was killed during that explosion!"

"Phew! What circumstantial evidence," said Melissa, slurring her words slightly. "Wow! But, but, Pieter rescued you that night you were stranded. And he certainly wouldn't mistake Hazel for you."

"True, but maybe someone else was trying to scare him into co-operating. Pieter might be forced to work with the El Condor gang. That could explain the smoke-bombing at the office! That was just before Jesús's visit. Jesús realized it hadn't worked and planned my accident. Of course!"

"Now you're really getting outrageous." Melissa sloshed some more wine in her glass. "You're tired, overwrought, in a snit because Pieter went off this weekend. Oh! You're silly!"

"Well . . ." I began.

"So you want Pieter to be El Condor?"

"No, of course not," I quickly replied.

"Then stop trying to convince yourself that he is El Condor and let's go to bed. You need a good night's sleep."

I obeyed Melissa's good, motherly advice, but it was a long time before I could fall asleep.

My late-night theories did seem far-fetched as Melissa and I sat over breakfast the next morning. I was slightly embarrassed to remember them. Imagine—thinking Pieter a terrorist! Thankfully, Melissa didn't mention it and neither did I. It was best forgotten. I had been overwrought. Yet I was determined more than ever to find some proof of Dirk's existence, for that would erase the last lingering doubt. I rushed Melissa through breakfast (much to her annoyance) and into the cellar without even pausing to do the breakfast dishes. "They'll keep," I assured her. "This won't."

We rummaged diligently for an hour. We found nothing. Just dirt and more dirt, old papers, some more books, some more clothes. But nothing to either prove or disprove that Dirk Van der Hoek had ever existed.

"You know," Melissa said, sinking down on the brick cellar steps. "This is pretty much nonsense. Two adult women playing girl detectives. We're not going to find anything. Ever. No matter how long we search. I've got a bad headache."

"Well, go upstairs then. I'll look by myself."

"No, no. As long as you're here, I'll stay here, too." Sighing loudly, Melissa pulled herself upright. She yawned again, then stopped abruptly. "What's that?" she asked.

I lifted my head to listen. "It's Samantha. She's followed us down here. She must have gotten into something."

Directed by her meowing, we found Samantha soon enough. Getting her out was something else. She had crawled underneath and then between some heavy wooden boxes. She had panicked.

"Oh, Samantha," I sighed, starting to lift some of the lighter boxes. The others required Melissa's help. Samantha cowered farther back against the wall. She wouldn't come out on her own. I leaned down to pick her up with my left hand, leaning against the wall with my right for support. As I did so, I suddenly fell over. The wall had given way.

"Gretel!" said Melissa, helping me back on my feet. Samantha scampered up the cellar steps.

"What happened?" I asked, stunned. My cotton dress had ripped and I was covered with plaster dust.

"You fell over . . . look, Gretel, a door!"

What had seemed a part of the brick wall was really a cleverly concealed door. Somehow, I had pressed the hidden catch that made it spring open. I pushed at it, and it swung wide easily, revealing an underground tunnel.

"Did you know your house had secret passages?" said Melissa.

"I'll have to ask Pieter where it leads," I said cautiously.

"Let's find out now," said Melissa, plunging down into the tunnel.

"Melissa! Melissa, come back here!"

"It's perfectly safe. And solidly built," said Melissa, slapping her hand against the stones for emphasis. "Matter of fact," she continued, peering at the walls, "I'd say it's better built than that cellar."

"All right," I said, giving up. It was like we were children again, Melissa leading us into trouble while I followed. I even had a skinned knee. I grabbed up the flashlight and followed.

"I don't like it," I said, once I had caught up with her.

"Where's your spirit of adventure?"

"Upstairs."

"It is kind of chilly down here," said Melissa, "but it's not too bad," she added, taking the flashlight from me. She led the way deeper into the long passageway. It curved slightly, it narrowed, it went down and then uphill. But it was always damp. The stone walls were water-stained, with patches of mildew.

"We must be walking to Manhattan," I said finally.

"It just seems that way because you don't like it," said Melissa.

"You're right," I said.

Then, all of a sudden, the tunnel stopped. Or, at least Melissa stopped. I crashed into her. We were standing on a dirt, not stone, floor.

"This is as far as it goes," said Melissa, flicking the flashlight about. We were surrounded by stone. It was a roundish room of some kind, with no way out other than the tunnel.

"What is this?" I said.

"Maybe it was a storage area," said Melissa.

"For what?" I asked.

"I guess there's nothing for it but to go back. What a shame," said Melissa. Truth to tell, I, too, was somewhat disappointed—but also relieved. We had turned to go, when I heard a noise. I stopped, clutching Melissa's arm. She started to speak, but I stopped her, listening for the sound again. Yes, there it was. I took the flashlight from her, and shined it on the ceiling. It was a wooden ceiling, made from rough-hewn planks. Someone was pacing across it. That was the noise I had heard. Slow deliberate steps. I crouched down to concentrate better; Melissa joined me. Now there were two people walking up above.

"What do you . . . ?" Melissa started to whisper, but I put my fingers across her mouth, shaking my head. I stood up and took her back with me into the stone tunnel.

"If we can hear them, then whoever that is can hear us," I said.

"But where do you suppose this is?" asked Melissa. "We're not back under your house, are we?"

"No. We don't have floors like that, and besides, no one is there. I think that we're under the padlocked boathouse we saw last weekend."

"Dirk's boathouse," said Melissa. I nodded. "And you think that might be Dirk walking around up there?" I nodded again. "Oh, Gretel. Then he does exist after all!" She turned back for the little round room. I caught her arm.

"Where do you think you're going?" I asked.

"To eavesdrop."

"We can't do that."

"Why not?"

"What if we're found out?"

"How else are you ever going to learn about Dirk if you don't snoop?"

"I don't like it," I insisted.

"*I'm* going to listen," said Melissa, shaking free of my arm. More curious than I would care to admit, I followed her. We crouched together on the floor, listening intently.

For a long while we heard no more than footsteps or a scrape as a piece of furniture was moved along the floor. Occasionally, someone would say a word, but it was muttered and impossible to understand. Then a third joined those in the room, and there was lengthier conversation. I realized then why we hadn't understood. They were speaking partly in Spanish. Melissa and I stared at each other. But then, it did make sense. Dirk, like Pieter, was half Puerto Rican.

There were four men now, and they seemed to be waiting for someone else. I heard one of them, called Carlos, ask for the time repeatedly. Another one cursed repeatedly. "*Basta!* Enough!" another kept muttering. I shifted my position slowly, so as not to make even a rustling sound, but to ease my cramped legs. Melissa was curled against the wall by the tunnel, her eyes closed. She gets us into this, I thought, then goes to sleep.

Then, someone new entered the room. Melissa opened her eyes in anticipation. The conversation became intense and muddled, partly in English, partly in Spanish, but mostly in what Pieter had once told me was called Spanglish, that is, New York City street Spanish. We could only hear snatches, but that was enough.

"*Que pasa*, Jesús?"

"Hey, brother."

"He's late, man."

"So," the newcomer said. I pictured him shrugging his shoulders.

"Well, hey, we ain't got all day. Tonight's the night."

"Hey, you don't think he knows that? And the way you guys work, this is it."

"It wasn't our fault, man."

"Who's then?"

"Ease off, Jesús."

There was the name "Jesús" again. I poked Melissa, raising my eyebrows to ask the obvious question. Could it be the same Jesús who'd come to my dinner party? Melissa shook her head "no," hard, then stopped and made a "perhaps" face, putting her fingers to her lips.

"You messed up just the same," said the one they called Jesús. "He's furious. The timetable's trashed. You better be ready."

"We're ready."

"At least we didn't get nobody killed, Jesús."

"Yeah, man."

"You got a complaint?" said Jesús.

"It's cool. It's just that we got just as much to lose as him. They bust us, they bust all of us, not just El Condor."

Melissa and I fell together. I was stunned, turning clammy, breathing hard and shallow, just like Melissa. We were out way too far, and we were too shocked to even try to get back.

"*Silencio*, Carlos. Here he comes," said Jesús with melodramatic authority. Chairs scraped as the men in the room shuffled about anxiously. Whatever they felt privately, it seemed as though they didn't dare confront their leader openly, especially since their leader seemed to be the deranged terrorist El Condor. Of course! Our island! Dirk! Dirk was El Condor. I wanted to run to Pieter immediately and tell him. But then, I thought, Pieter must have already supposed as much—*that* was the reason for his peculiar behavior. No matter what, brother could not turn on brother.

The conversation above us raced even faster. We missed a lot. They discussed an "operation." Everyone gave a report. Something seemed to be very wrong. Their plans were confused. Their timetable, as Jesús had said, was off.

"Carlos, have you got enough?" said Jesús.

"More than enough for this. It's just a big bronze statue, man, it's hollow inside. There'll be plenty left over," said Carlos nonchalantly.

"No," said a completely new voice, whom I supposed to be Dirk, that is, El Condor. "That's not what I said. I said to use it all. This time. There won't be a next time. This is to be spectacular. I want the TV cameras to show there's nothing left of Miss Liberty but her pedestal. We will make the maximum effort. Is that clear?"

Oh, God, I thought, I know that voice. I looked into Melissa's face. She was blank. I know that voice, I wanted to scream at her. I said nothing.

"Hey, it's too much. We don't need it. It's too heavy, too much to carry. One boat can't handle it," whined Carlos.

"Then get another," said El Condor.

"How?" said Carlos.

I never heard the answer. Melissa had snapped out of her daze enough to grab me roughly and pull me toward the tunnel. She was hysterical. I fought her. I didn't want to leave yet. I had to be sure about that voice. No, I already was sure; I hoped that something would happen to make it not so. Oh, please make it not so, I thought. I *had* been right. El Condor was my Pieter.

"Gretel!" blurted Melissa in her panic, loud enough to be heard back in Manhattan, let alone five feet above us. There was pounding and scraping above. Melissa froze at that, still clutching my arm. I thought fast. They knew someone was down here. One of us had to be caught, but not both. If it was me, they wouldn't think to search for Melissa, since they probably didn't know she was on the island. I resolved to sacrifice myself, foolishly but bravely, I thought. Irrevocably, I knew. I gathered my strength, seized Melissa by the shoulders, and threw her as hard as I could back into the tunnel. Then, before she could react with a scream, I yelled:

"Oh! My ankle!" up toward the ceiling. It opened, a trap door, as I'd suspected. I sat down on the floor.

"There she is!" yelled one of the men, reaching down, but I didn't want them down here just yet, since Melissa still hadn't gathered herself together to escape. Glaring at her, I moved away from the tunnel entrance, picking up the flashlight Melissa had dropped. I held it out threateningly. "Don't come any closer," I warned. Laughter greeted this announcement, but it had worked. Melissa had disappeared into the tunnel's blackness. But for good measure, I hurled the flashlight at the trap door. "Damn!" someone said, and I smiled in satisfaction, hoping it was Jesús I had hit. "Okay, that's enough, bring her up." Long rough arms reached down, and, knowing I had no other alternative, I allowed myself to be pulled up.

But I was hardly grateful. I screamed, kicking at them, anything to keep them from going into the tunnel. I was grabbed at haphazardly. Then someone tackled me. I crashed to the ground very hard, falling on my side. Whoever had tackled me was very strong, because he then lifted me, carried me upstairs, and, with one brutal motion, threw me into a small dark room. The door slammed shut behind me. I lay there, gasping for air, more stunned than hurt, listening for

Melissa's screams. I breathed easier as I heard only men, muffled by the door and the distance.

"Who . . . what do you want?" a female voice asked sleepily from the corner. What I had thought to be a rolled-up blanket turned over to reveal a pale face.

"Hazel!" I stepped to her side and embraced her. I was no longer terrified now that I was no longer alone.

"Gretel? My God," Hazel giggled. "What are you doing here?"

Briefly, I told her of my capture and the events leading up to it. Everything, in fact, that had happened since she had vanished.

"Too much," Hazel said, shaking her head. "My parents, flying in from Boston. They must think I'm dead." She giggled again. "Just think, my picture on the front page of the *Times*."

I was glad to see that her spirits were high, although her giddy mood puzzled me. She looked pale, and there were bluish smudges under her eyes; her hair had probably not been combed since Wednesday, and she could do with a long hot bath. But she hadn't been starved (the remains of a meal were scattered on a tray near the door), and she showed no signs of maltreatment.

"Are you all right?" I asked.

"Yeah. 'Cept for my leg," she said, grimacing slightly. I pulled back the blanket to see. Her blue jeans were rolled up and I could see that her right ankle was swollen and badly bruised. Instinctively I reached out to touch it, but Hazel stopped me. "No, it's all right. It doesn't hurt. They give me these little pills," she said, giggling again. That was it, I thought, they've been keeping her drugged.

"The worst thing," said Hazel, "is being bored to death. The only thing to do is sleep. Do you know where we are?"

"On Hoek Land," I answered.

"Far out. But the wildest thing is that I don't even know why I'm here. Who are these people? Nobody tells me anything. All I want to know is why I was kidnaped."

"It was a mistake," I said.

"You can say that again."

"No, Hazel, really a mistake." I told her my theory, omitting an reference to Pieter. I didn't want to talk about him. Hazel listened in amazement.

"Far out. I've read about El Condor. To think all this time they've been hiding out on *your* island. Wow. Oh, Gretel, I'm real sorry, but I lost your jacket."

"We found it," I said.

"Far out. You must have thought I was dead. It tore off when they caught me. I twisted away and fell against a tree trunk. That's when I hurt my leg. My shirt, too." She turned to show me her blouse. It had been ripped down one side. Hazel had knotted it at the waist. I saw the fading yellow trace of a large bruise.

"When they brought me here," Hazel continued, "one of them looked at me. He seemed real surprised. He asked me what my name was. He started cursing. He was real mad."

"What did he look like?" I asked, knowing that Hazel had never met Pieter.

"Puerto Rican," she said.

"Oh," I said, wondering why I felt relieved. "It must have been Jesús."

"Yeah, that's right. That's what they called him. Oh." She moved stiffly. "They better bring me some more of that stuff soon. I'm beginning to ache."

I patted her shoulder sympathetically. Then I got up from the dirty floor and walked about the small room, feeling its walls, pushing against the door and against the one window, which was boarded up.

"If you're thinking about escape, forget it," Hazel said. "I picked at those planks for a whole day. I worked one of the nails loose, got the board out about half an inch, but when they brought in my supper, they noticed it. He just laughed, got a hammer, and pounded it back in. Three nails broken. For nothing!" Hazel held up her hands to show the chipped and broken remains of her manicure.

"We've got to try something, Hazel," I said.

"I would, but . . ." She gestured to her leg.

"We can't just sit here while those animals blow up . . . oh!" I waved my hands in frustration.

"What are they going to do?"

"They're going to destroy the Statue of Liberty," I said. "I think tomorrow morning. Maybe tonight."

"Wow." Hazel giggled.

"They really are," I said.

"It's impossible. They can't do that."

"They're no dummies. They wouldn't try it if they didn't think they could succeed."

"There are guards at the statue."

"True, but I remember a few years ago, a group of Puerto Rican nationalists took an early morning excursion boat over to the island, walked right by the guards, chased the tourists out, and locked themselves in the statue. They occupied it for eight hours," I added, remembering the news photos I had seen at the time showing the Puerto Rican flag hanging from the Statue of Liberty's crown, covering her brow.

"What happened to them?"

"The Park Police charged them with trespassing on federal property."

"So why do these guys want to blow up the statue?" said Hazel.

"I have no idea," I said.

Hazel and I sat in the dingy room for several hours, mostly in sullen silence. All I could hope for was that Melissa had escaped and was summoning help. But after chatting cheerfully to Hazel about our imminent rescue, I remembered that there was now no phone in the house. Had Pieter pulled it out on purpose? I then wondered if Melissa would drive the *Silver Fox*, if she *could* drive it. Melissa was resourceful if she wasn't too scared to think.

I could hear our captors stirring restlessly in the other rooms. The conversation was punctuated with occasional raucous, nervous laughter. But I could make out none of it. Once, our door was opened long enough for a fresh tray of food to be substituted for the empty one. I tried to peer around the guard, but the hallway was dark. I could see nothing. Our dinner consisted of cold chicken, a couple of hard rolls, and cheese. Hazel ate eagerly, but I was too upset to be hungry. I took up a roll and crumbled it nervously between my fingers. I noticed that the plates were paper. The food we had been given could easily be eaten with our fingers. There was no silverware. Our captors had thought of everything.

It was about an hour later when the door opened again. I scarcely looked up, assuming it to be someone collecting our tray. But this time the door opened wide to reveal two men. One went over to Hazel, giving her something, then standing over her while she swallowed it. She curled up in the blanket, turning her back to the room. The man, who I thought to be Carlos, came over to me, saying:

"Mrs. Van der Hoek, please come with us."

"Do I have a choice?" I asked, rising stiffly to my feet and smoothing out my wrinkled and dirt-stained cotton dress. "Where are you taking me?" I said, smiling bravely. But I knew where they were tak ing me. I squared my shoulders, preparing to look Pieter defiantly in the eye.

"Come on," the other man said, pushing me into the hallway, down the stairs, and into a large, bright room.

For the first few moments, I blinked against the light, shielding my eyes from its glare. Several people were in the room—all talking. Jesús was there, studying a piece of paper.

"Everything's fine," Jesús said to no one in particular. "We're slightly ahead of schedule, actually. One half hour."

"I suggest we relax," said another voice, Pieter's, from across the room. My eyes adjusted slowly to the light. Pieter was sitting down, slouched in a high-backed armchair, with his back to me and the others, consulting a large map of New York City's harbor crookedly tacked to the wall. An old baseball cap was pushed far back on his head.

"Why don't we leave now?" Jesús asked.

"Organization, careful planning," said Pieter. "No need to rush. We're due to set off at eleven-thirty, and at eleven-thirty we will set off."

Jesús mumbled a reply. He was ignored. The chair started to swivel around and I straightened up to meet Pieter's hooded eyes.

10

Heart of the Harbor

El Condor was not my Pieter. He had Pieter's voice, Pieter's mannerisms, and the Van der Hoek eyes. But he was younger than Pieter by at least five years, shorter than Pieter by at least half a foot, and broader, squarer, more solid-looking than Pieter. He had a swarthy complexion, a neatly trimmed black mustache and beard, a wide nose, and Isobel Van der Hoek's full, sensuous lips curving gently now into a sly smile as he said:

"Welcome, sister."

"Dirk," I whispered. He existed. I stared at this mystery who was no stranger.

"I apologize that we have to meet again under such difficult circumstances," Dirk continued, waving his hand at the five other men in the room. "Dear Gretel, you are persistent. I admire that quality. You want to know. You go after it. Now you know it all. Please, sister, come and sit." Dirk rose to sweep several books off another chair, catching my hand nimbly to lead me to sit beside him. I obeyed, regarding him intensely all the while. Where had I seen him before?

"No, we don't look alike, do we?" said Dirk.

"No," I said. "I mean, yes, some."

"Half-breeds that we are," said Dirk, smiling broadly. "I am the darkling, true. I am the Cain to his Abel. Do you follow me?"

"Perfectly, only this time I don't think Abel is so pure," I said with as much contempt as I could manage, given that he charmed me despite myself.

"Pieter? Oh, he's pure all right. He wouldn't have anything to do with me, with all this. He doesn't approve." Dirk sneered, arranging his features to look uncannily like Pieter. Pieter's face gone wrong. "Not that I didn't try—here and in San Juan, but he shunned us. The best he could manage, I suppose, was to pretend I didn't exist. Perhaps El Condor would vanish!" Dirk spat on the floor. "Until now, I've never thought much of Pieter or his taste. Especially his pretty pictures, his 'work.' But then, he says as much for my prose. We've never agreed on anything. Sharing only this island Eden. But I do admire the pluck of his wife."

"Thank you, I'm sure," I said. "What's to happen to me? And to Hazel?"

"Good, difficult questions," said Dirk, his mood changing abruptly —sad now. "We've been discussing the subject."

"You wouldn't dare hurt us!" I said, suspicious of his tone.

"Let's not talk like that," said Dirk. "Perhaps it's best to say that I haven't made a decision yet."

"Hah!" said Jesús from the side. I glared at him. He glared back, frightening me so deeply that I didn't dare breathe lest I give myself away with a scream.

"I don't like it when you rattle women, Jesús," said Dirk, low and angry. "Ultimately, I take responsibility for your conduct. I don't like your conduct."

Jesús shrugged.

"Well?" said Carlos, glancing at his watch.

"Yes, both of them, then," said Dirk to Carlos and another one, named Tony. "The boathouse has outlived its usefulness. We won't be coming back."

They were taking us with them. Dirk left the room with Jesús, while Tony, a short ugly boy of about nineteen, bound my hands behind me. He then tied a gag around my mouth. Not knowing what else to do, I followed like a model prisoner.

Tony walked me out the door, down to the pier, where we waited for the rest of the party. I turned to see two members of the gang whose names I didn't know carrying Hazel between them. She looked unhurt but unconscious, or near to it, from those drugs they'd given her. I didn't like this. How easy it would be for them to throw Hazel into the harbor to drown. Oh, God! I thought, my imagination leaping ahead. They could then do the same to me. If I was ever found, it would look like I had gone searching for Hazel on my own. But, I thought, trying to calm myself, they don't know about Melissa. Melissa will upset their schemes. Oh, Melissa, where are you? Have you figured out how to drive the *Silver Fox* yet? What's taking you so long?

I heard engines. A large launch motored up along the pier, towing a small engineless boat like a barge, heaped with crates mostly covered by large pieces of canvas secured with rope. Those must be the explosives, I thought, admiring the cleverness of the affair. If they'd been encountered out there in the harbor hauling the explosives, or if we were encountered on our way tonight, they had only to cut the barge free. The evidence would float away.

Another engine approached. My heart pounded. I knew that sound. It was the *Silver Fox*. Not here, Melissa, I thought. But my fancy was short-lived. It was the *Silver Fox*, all right, but as it bumped along the pier to a halt, I could see Jesús at the wheel. He was alone in the boat. As Tony moved me into the *Silver Fox*, and as the others handed Hazel's inert body down beside me, I groaned aloud. Now Melissa was without a boat and a phone. And the fact that they had the *Silver Fox* either meant she'd done nothing all day long, or that they'd found her earlier and . . . I let that go. I turned to make Hazel as comfortable as possible.

We pulled away from Hoek Land in the wake of the larger motor launch towing the barge. There was a crescent moon above huge clouds. From the lights in the city, I guessed it to be before midnight. I looked back as long as I could at Hoek Land. The only light was at the end of our pier. Hoek House was completely dark.

We maintained a slow, but steady, pace. As we neared the uneven oval of Liberty Island, the men began to smear black grease over their faces, so that their skin would not reflect the light. They were already dressed in black turtlenecks and jeans. Tony smeared some on my face, too. It smelled and felt terrible. The breeze blew a strand of hair onto my cheek and the grease made it stick. I rubbed my face against my shoulder to rub it away.

The Statue of Liberty loomed three hundred feet tall before us—grandiose in the darkness with her torch and crown aglow, the statue itself illuminated by spotlights about the island.

First the launch, then the *Silver Fox*, slowed, cutting their motors to the barest whisper as they pulled up between large boulders. W were on the northeast side of the island, well away from the pier and the guard house, just beneath the ramparts of an old fort that served as the statue's base. Dirk and his men scrambled up the slimy rocks to the mossy ground alongside the ramparts. Then, slowly, carefully, they began to unload the barge, passing the heavy crates to shore. They seemed to have brought enough to blow up all of Manhattan, I thought, as I watched them strain. They worked quickly, but it was some time before Dirk called a short rest. Then they began the more strenuous task of moving the explosives up on the ramparts. Then men moved swiftly to Dirk's hoarsely barked commands. I watched him as he ordered his gang. He stood at rigid attention, his square shoulders thrust back, his powerful hands cradling a large rifle of some sort, his feet in perfect alignment. In his dark clothes, blackened face, and baseball cap, he was an eerie figure—a short, dark specter who spoke with Pieter's voice.

In a way, what I had suspected was true. I had thought El Condor represented Pieter's dark side, Pieter's angry, mad side. He did. Dirk was a dark, angry Pieter. So similar and yet different—the "darkling" he called himself. I studied him—a parody of every military movie that I, and I suspected Dirk, had ever seen. Dirk was acting out a role, but for whose benefit?

The unloading was finally done. It must be long after midnight, I decided, shifting in my seat. Hazel was still curled on the floor of the *Silver Fox*, breathing softly, a gag stuffed in her mouth.

"C'mon, lady, let's go," Tony hissed in my ear. I looked at him in amazement, finally realizing where I had seen Dirk before. He had been driving the gypsy cab I had ridden in so many months before. And Tony had been in the back seat. Pieter must have told him about me, about our late-night expedition to Hoek Land, and Dirk had been curious about me. Using the flowers to identify me, he had given me a ride home. A bit bizarre, perhaps, but obviously typical.

Tony grew impatient with me. "C'mon," he growled again. I needed no further urging, for I saw metal in Tony's right hand. I climbed out of the boat as best I could, slipping about on the wet rocks, and joined the others on shore. Led by Dirk, we advanced in single file, Tony and I last in line.

Frustrated by my helplessness, I wondered what I could do. There should certainly be Park Police on duty. I slowed my step. The members of the gang were preoccupied with carrying the explosives. With my hands bound behind me, and the light wool jacket I had been given to wear slipping over my arms, I found it awkward to crouch down—the pressure on my stomach made it uncomfortable. I was walking more or less erect. Would I be able to dash off into the dark protection of the trees? I decided to try it, jumping away—one step, two, three, but then I tripped, landing heavily on my knees, unable to break the fall with my hands. Tony came up quickly behind me, grabbing hold of my shoulders, forcing me upright. I walked with knees bent, like an overgrown crab.

Jesús bounced over to us, muttering, "Just try that again. Give me an excuse."

"I've got her," said Tony.

"Make sure you do. Bring her up here," said Jesús. "Close to us."

I was miserable. I had botched it. There'd be no second chance. Tony pushed me roughly forward.

We reached the structure's redoubts easily enough. Following whispered commands, the men divided the crates among them. One crate was broken open. I recognized sticks of dynamite, long wires for fuses, but there were objects I didn't know—long metal tubes and plumbing pipes that the men handled gingerly. Seven of us, Dirk and Jesús in the lead, entered the underground passage that runs under the sloping walls of the old fort. There was one lone guard nodding at his post just inside the entrance. We waited in the shadows (a firm hand held me fast) while Jesús crept up and around, surprising the guard from behind. Jabbing something into his ribs, Jesús commanded the man to lead us—past the souvenir shops, the snack bars, and the American Museum of Immigration—to the base of the statue, and then to open up the elevator that would take us up ten stories to the top of the mammoth concrete pedestal.

It was close in the corridor. I closed my eyes rather than see the guard's face. I was scared, but in control. Seeing someone else's fear might send me over the edge. With the elevator set, the guard became dispensable. He was forced to lie down. His hands and feet were bound tightly, his mouth gagged. Then they began to load the elevator with the explosives, making ten trips before it was my turn. It was a brief ride. We were now at the foot of the statue. Opened crates were everywhere, wires dangling loose. The men worked by flashlight, and by the red glow of the EXIT lights.

Jesús then sent three of the men up the circular staircase that threaded up through the body and head of the statue to its crown.

The rest of us proceeded outside to the observation platform that runs about the top of the base, on all four sides.

It was windy on the platform, so I kept as close to the walls as possible to keep out of the worst of it. I had to keep tossing my head to keep my hair out of my eyes. I would have preferred to huddle in a corner until it was all over, but Tony made certain I kept up with him. I watched him as he took a few sticks of dynamite, attached a fuse, deftly bound it, and fixed it to the stone wall with gray putty. He repeated this process every few feet. It seemed to me that they were going to blow up parts of the pedestal, as well as parts of the torso, so that the statue would topple over and smash to the ground.

Suddenly, I looked away from the statue. I could feel my tears. They were really going to do this. It was breath-taking madness. I blinked rapidly to clear my vision as I felt my way along the wall, keeping the required number of paces behind Tony. I was feeling the exhaustion of a long night. I leaned heavily against the shoulder-high wall. As I did so, I felt a twinge in my stomach. I bent forward in response, almost losing my balance. The feeling stopped as quickly as it had begun. What was wrong? Then I felt a series of soft, slow strokes in my lower abdomen, and I nodded in relief. I was fine. The baby was fine. Because of my exhaustion, I had misidentified the first tentative movements of my unborn child as trouble. Yet I was being taught a lesson. There was nothing I could do about El Condor's crime. But there was plenty I could do to protect myself. I decided to concentrate on my own safety.

I looked over the wall down to the star-shaped redoubts surrounding the statue's base, where on a usual summer's morning hundreds of tourists would be strolling. It was empty now—no, not completely. One of Dirk's men dashed across. Then another. They must have finished their task of laying explosives about the base of the pedestal. Tony and the others were almost done here at the top. Soon, all would be ready, and Dirk would give the order to leave. Then, it would be time to deal with Hazel and me.

It was lighter now, sunrise not far off. There was a golden glow in the east, though it would be some minutes before the sun actually appeared. It would probably be a beautiful summer day. I wondered how much of it I would see.

I continued to look down at the base. Another of Dirk's men streaked across, darting from the protection of one wall to another, so as not to be seen. The man's coattails flapped as he ran. I paused to look again. None of Dirk's men wore jackets—sweaters only. But this man was definitely wearing a jacket. I glanced over to Tony as he wrapped the last of the fuse about the dynamite. He was too intent on his task to have noticed anything. I looked back down. I saw several other men on the grounds. I studied them carefully in the dim dawning. They were definitely not part of El Condor's gang. But who were they? Then one stepped forward, pausing in the light for a moment before disappearing from sight; but not so quickly that I didn't recognize the dark-blue and white Coast Guard uniform. I gnawed at the rough gag in my mouth, scanning the waters of the harbor. Yes! There, to the south, a little way off the island was a Coast Guard cutter. I stood as close to the wall as I could, raising myself on tiptoes, shaking my head to let my hair blow free in the wind. I was helpless and unable to signal my would-be rescuers. But, at least, I hoped that one of them would look up and see me. Then I sank back down on my heels. At this distance, and with my grease-smeared face, it was too much to think I could be recognized. The Coast Guard could well think I was a female member of the gang. I suddenly realized that there might be shooting. Bending my knees, I crouched down lower against the wall. Think of yourself, Gretel, I reminded myself.

"We're all finished here," said Tony. I opened my eyes. Jesús and Dirk had come up to us. They were apparently making the rounds, to be certain all was in order. How long would it be before they realized they had failed?

"All right, then," said Dirk. "Let's get out of here. Jesús, you and Tony take her down. In the elevator. I'll get Carlos and the others and go by the stairs. We'll meet by the boats." Dirk nodded and was gone.

Shuffling between Jesús and Tony, I entered the small elevator. I slumped against the wall as Jesús pressed the button. The ride lasted less than a minute. The door slid open. I looked out, expecting to see the Coast Guard, but, in the dark hallway, there were only empty crates.

Jesús and Tony stepped out into the hall, their sneakers padding on the marble floor. The elevator door slid shut behind us.

"Halt right there." A command echoed out of the shadows.

Jesús stopped so abruptly that I bumped into his back. Reaching behind him, he grabbed me by the arm, pulling me roughly in front of him. He pulled something from his pocket, bringing it against my neck. I felt cold metal press uncomfortably just below my right ear. I shifted my head, but he pressed harder. Tony crouched low next to us, like a cornered animal desperate to flee.

"Okay," said Jesús, "come out where I can see you. Slow and careful."

I held my breath as a man stepped forward, his hands held away from his body at shoulder level. I didn't recognize him. Several more followed, all dressed in the Coast Guard uniform. Then I caught a glimpse of Michael Dragon. He was almost out of my sight, far to our left. When he noticed me looking at him, he broke into a cheerful grin. His greeting was more suited to a casual dinner party, but it made me feel better. I tried to smile back, but I couldn't.

There was a commotion in the back of the hall. Jesús jerked up slowly, turning slightly to face in that direction, bringing me with him. More men were entering the hall. Some members of the gang seemed to have already been taken prisoner. Michael took a few steps toward us.

"That's far enough," said Jesús. Michael stopped a few feet away.

"Let Gretel go, Jesús," Michael said calmly. His voice had a steady confidence to it.

"If I don't get out of here, she gets it. And that goes for you! Get in my way and I'll shoot!"

"Let Gretel go," Michael repeated. "You won't get away. Give it up."

"I'll get away," said Jesús.

Michael's expression remained impassive. "There are a lot of charges against you, including kidnaping. If you give yourself up things may go easier for you."

"No way, man. I'm not falling for that. I'm getting out of here, and she goes with me. It's up to you how this goes down."

I closed my eyes, not daring to look at Michael. Nothing more was said. Jesús shoved me forward so brutally that I stumbled as I walked. Jesús kept jerking me upright. We must have made a curious sight as we moved through the helpless Coast Guarders, bouncing along like awkward children. Tony followed behind, turning around constantly to make certain no one followed us too closely. Oddly, Tony whimpered. Jesús kept telling him to "Shut up!"

We seemed to walk forever. Numb with disgust and fear, I concentrated on placing one foot in front of the other. Jesús grew impatient, urging me to walk faster. I couldn't. The others of the gang must be captured by now, I thought, Dirk surely among them. Jesús's chances of escaping were hopeless. But he kept on. I knew he was desperate enough to do something crazy and violent.

We came out of the dark hall into the full of the morning. We went down some steps. Unaccustomed to the light, I tripped, losing my balance. I twisted to the side trying not to fall on my face. Cursing, Jesús loosened his grip on my arm to keep from falling himself. Somehow, I managed to sit down hard on the steps with Jesús standing straight up over me. He yelled—a high-pitched scream. Tony leapt over me to run. I closed my eyes, and all was confusion. The events jumbled together. I heard several loud cracks that I guessed to be gunshots. They echoed loudly in the cavernous hall. Free for the moment from Jesús's grasp, with my eyes still tightly shut, I hunched down, sliding myself along the steps, pulling myself with my feet until I had reached the bottom. There, I crouched low, pressing my body into the steps, keeping my eyes closed. Several more shots were fired. Then all stopped. Someone came over to me, his footsteps thudding.

"Aren't you going to thank me for saving your life?" Michael Dragon said. I opened my eyes to see him sitting beside me. His eyes twinkled as merrily as ever. He slipped the gag from my mouth; it hung loosely around my neck. I wet my lips and swallowed.

"Oh, I . . . oh," I tried to say something. The tears stinging my eyes welled over, spilling onto my cheeks. Michael, suddenly embarrassed, patted my shoulder awkwardly as I unashamedly wept. After a few moments, I composed myself and began to apologize, which only seemed to embarrass him more.

"Gretel!"

"Melissa? Melissa?" I said, turning.

"She wouldn't stay away," Michael explained with a shrug.

"Gretel!" Melissa screamed again, running pell-mell up the path, flinging herself at me. She, too, was crying. "You're all right! You're all right!"

"Why are you here?" I said.

"Miss all the fun?" She twinkled through her tears. "Oh, Gretel, I just had to see for myself that you were all right. They wanted to leave me behind, but I put up such a fuss. Well! Didn't Pieter tell you?"

"Pieter's here, too?" I asked.

"He's the real hero," said Michael, untying my hands. I rubbed my wrists hard for circulation.

"Sorry to interrupt, but we've rounded up everyone," said a young Coast Guard officer, coming quickly up to Michael. They conferred for a few moments, then he and Michael went off together, leaving Melissa and me alone temporarily.

"But where's Pieter?" I asked, looking about. I couldn't see him anywhere.

"He's here," said Melissa. "He was frantic about you. God, what a night!"

A Coast Guard sailor and a man in a green uniform, whom I guessed to be a Park Policeman, then came over to escort us away from the explosives, walking us to the other side of the island, to the Park Police building. Liberty Island was a bustle of coastguardsmen, policemen, and flashing lights. Someone was shouting something about waiting for the "Bomb Squad." The commotion made me dizzy. The Park Policeman told us we'd be questioned later, but, for the moment, we should make ourselves comfortable. We collapsed at one of the picnic tables outside the refreshment building, which had been opened to provide coffee. Another very nice Park Policeman brought us each a cup, telling us we were "brave young women" and that "the Old Lady had been saved from a fate worse than death." Melissa and I laughed till we choked. It wasn't that funny, but he had said it so seriously. And we were so happy. Finally, once we were alone again, Melissa told me what had happened to her.

As I had thought, she had panicked when we'd been discovered. She hadn't fully comprehended that I had sacrificed myself so that she could get away. She had remained cowering in the tunnel for what might have been hours, waiting for them to find her, too. Then, collecting herself, she had cautiously made her way back to the cellar and up into the house. There, she had discovered that the phones had been ripped out. Forgetting, in her panic, that I had told her Pieter had done it three days before, she had assumed that it was El Condor's men, that they had been there before her, that perhaps they were searching the house for her. Creeping upstairs, she had hidden herself in one of the back bedrooms. Although she hadn't heard anything, she was sure that the house was being watched, and that El Condor's men might re-enter at any moment. Therefore, she hadn't even tried to get to the *Silver Fox*, although—as she admitted —she had no idea of how it worked.

Then (about eleven o'clock, she guessed), she had heard a motor-boat at the dock. She'd waited, but nothing had happened. No one had come up to the house. An hour or so had passed. Melissa had gathered up enough courage to emerge from her hiding place and make her way down the stairs. Suddenly, she had heard someone entering the house. She'd frozen again, and had stayed in the hallway, crouched on the stairs, clinging to the banister, waiting for "them" to come and get her.

There, Pieter had found her.

"I'm sure he thought I was deranged," said Melissa. "I jumped up and threw my arms around him, shrieking that El Condor had taken you away and that it was all my fault."

"Oh, heavens," I said.

"Well, I was the one who insisted on knowing about Dirk. Anyway, he calmed me down until I made sense. I told him everything. Except the part when you thought he was El Condor."

"But what about Boston? He was due back Monday! Today!" I said.

"He said he'd been feeling guilty about leaving you. So he came back early. He'd just gotten the last shuttle out of Boston. Imagine if he'd missed it!"

"Where is Pieter?"

"I don't know. Don't you want to hear this?" she asked, piqued, proceeding with her story.

Once she had finished telling Pieter what had happened, they had headed for the tunnel. They had followed it to the end, but the boathouse was deserted. Melissa had begun to cry, but Pieter had made her go over everything we had overheard. Melissa had been foggy about it, but she had remembered enough to make Pieter certain of El Condor's target: "Miss Liberty."

Pieter had grabbed Melissa's hand and led a wild dash back to the *Stuyvesant.* Pieter had driven across the harbor like a madman, pulling into Governor's Island with no thought for his or the others' boats. The guards had challenged them, and Pieter had threatened them. After much shouting, Melissa had managed to communicate that they wanted to see Ensign Michael Dragon. Michael had arrived (still buttoning up his uniform) just in time to save Pieter from arrest. Pieter then told Michael everything. Michael had called his superior officers and organized a rescue operation. After much Coast Guard militarism and expertise . . .

"Here we are," said Melissa, finishing triumphantly, hugging me again.

"Come on," I said. "Let's go find Pieter."

We walked over to a group of coastguardsmen. They told us they were still checking the statue to make certain all the explosives had been found and disconnected. They pointed us toward the area where the members of the gang were being questioned. We walked there, but I still didn't see Pieter. Nor did I see Dirk. We went back to find Michael, who was talking intensely with the Park Police.

"Are those all the prisoners?" I asked him abruptly, pointing to the gang.

"Yes," said Michael, surprised.

"But—Michael!" I said.

"What?" said Michael.

"The leader, El Condor, he isn't here," I said.

"Are you sure?"

"Of course, I'm sure. I know him."

"Maybe you're confused. It was dark," said Michael, escorting me closer. There was Tony, and Jesús clutching a bandaged arm, and Carlos, and the three others whose names I didn't know. No Dirk. And no Pieter.

"I wouldn't confuse Pieter's brother," I said to Michael as I turned away. Even though he was under guard and wounded, Jesús still frightened me.

"Pieter's brother?" said Michael. Briefly, I told him all I knew of Dirk and his activities.

"But I can't be sure of Pieter's true feelings," I said, shrugging my shoulders helplessly. "He's never spoken of Dirk really, though he must have known, or at least *guessed*, about El Condor. I'm worried that he may have gone to find Dirk. He's not here. Melissa, did Pieter come with the Coast Guard, or in the *Stuyvesant?*"

"Why, he came in the *Stuyvesant*," said Melissa. We raced onto the pier. There were many boats of all sizes, with more arriving all the time, but no *Stuyvesant*.

"What do you think?" said Melissa.

"I think that Pieter's gone after Dirk," I said grimly. "Abel has a score to settle with Cain."

"What?" said Michael. "Gretel, this is serious."

"I am serious. Dirk was too clever for you. He counted on Jesús losing his head. It gave him time to escape."

"Stay right there!" said Michael, who ran back to the policemen, to tell them, I supposed, that the man they really wanted had slipped their net. I was surprised by my calm, considering how much danger there might be for Pieter. But somehow, I felt the two brothers would never really harm each other. Their dispute was deep-seated. No violence could settle it.

Melissa and I waited in silence until Michael came back. He told us that they had already determined the leader, El Condor, was missing. Michael said they wanted to question me now. I told him I was much too tired and that I wanted to go home to rest and to wait for my husband. I would answer questions later. When Michael started to object, I reminded him of my pregnancy, and that I was sure if he informed the police of my condition, they'd let me go home. I was right.

"Can Melissa and I be taken over to Hoek Land?" I asked, once Michael had returned.

"I'll run you home myself," said Michael. He walked off again to confer with his fellow officers, asking permission, I assumed. Then, he came back to me. Yes, he would escort Melissa and myself back to Hoek House (Hazel had been taken to a hospital in Manhattan), and he and his crew would stay with us. I started to protest that it wasn't necessary for him to stay, but Michael assured me it was not out of consideration for me, but orders. Someone must be on duty at Hoek Land waiting for Pieter to return. He had to be questioned as to Dirk's whereabouts and his own part in this affair. Michael apologized profusely for acting as our guard, but, of course, he had no choice. I nodded my acceptance. The nightmare was not over. Nor would it be for some time.

We rode in a Coast Guard cutter (the *Silver Fox* had been impounded by the authorities as "evidence"). It must have been a beautiful early morning ride, but I sat with my eyes closed, letting the wind blow over me. Every inch of my body ached with weariness. My arms were so heavy I could scarcely lift them.

Already, there were two strange launches at our pier, which I guessed, correctly, to be the press. They must have raced right here after they had heard the name "Van der Hoek" from the police. I had to admit it was quite a story, but, even if it was their "ghoulish" job to harass us, I had no obligation to help them. I told Michael I had nothing to say. He asked me if I wanted to be taken somewhere else, to Melissa's apartment in Manhattan, but I said no. This was my home, where I would wait for my husband.

We stepped off the cutter gingerly. The two reporters and their photographers jumped at us, but Michael and his men pushed them back. There were other strange launches heading for Hoek Land out in the harbor. It seemed so inevitable and so foolish. Michael escorted us to the boathouse, where, when one of the photographers assaulted me with his camera, Michael lost his temper. He told us to wait while he and his men cleared the press from the pier. As I leaned to rest against the boathouse, something caught my eye through the tiny window. I looked. The *Stuyvesant* was there!

"Melissa," I whispered, pulling her to me. "I've got to get up to the house. Pieter's there."

"What?" said Melissa, turning back to Michael, who was officiously ordering his men about, and yelling to the reporters to stay clear.

"No," I said. "Don't tell them. Not yet. I'll go up now. Let me have five minutes before you tell Michael. Okay?"

"Are you sure you'll be all right? What if Dirk's up there? What if . . ."

"Pieter's there," I interrupted. "And he's by himself. I'm certain. I'll be fine. Give us five minutes alone." I squeezed her hand, edging away from the pier. Preoccupied with the press, Michael didn't notice. I raced up the path, all exhaustion forgotten in my passion. The door was locked, of course, but the spare key was where it should be. I opened the door and stepped in, shutting the door firmly behind me and locking it again. The kitchen was empty, but there were two half-empty cups of coffee on the table, a white envelope between them. I walked to the stove to find the coffeepot was still warm.

"Pieter?" I said, moving immediately to where I knew he'd be. I didn't knock. I just opened his studio door and stepped in. "Pieter!" I said again, racing to him. He stood up from his stool. I jumped into his arms.

"Gretel, you should be in bed," said Pieter finally, squeezing me tightly one last time and then holding me back at arm's length.

"In a minute," I said. Pieter looked exhausted, too, showing the strain of the past night, and something more. Pieter looked very sad. His face had settled into the harsh lines I had seen at the gaming tables in San Juan, and had not seen since.

"You're all wet," I said, looking at his clothes. His jacket was damp from the sea. His shirt was soaked from sweat.

"What?" said Pieter, looking at himself, adding, "It's you that matters."

"I'm fine," I repeated stubbornly. Why was it so hard for us to talk?

"Gretel, it's not just you I'm thinking about."

"Oh," I said, blushing at Pieter's earnest display of concern for the child I was carrying. So I had been wrong about that, too. Pieter wanted this child, our child. "Oh," I repeated, remembering. "The baby moved today, for the very first time. It was scary, but it was wonderful." I beamed at him. We stood quietly together for a moment. Then, I had to ask:

"Where's Dirk?"

"Dirk," said Pieter, turning from me back to a trash can he'd been toying with when I'd entered. I looked down to see, surprised, that it was half full with ashes and charred wood. The room had a lingering smell of fire above the usual odor of paints and turpentine.

"Yes, Dirk," I repeated. I was determined, finally, to know as much as I could.

"We were very different as children," said Pieter, kicking the can away. He took me by the arm and led me back to the kitchen. I sat down at the table. He paced behind me. "Oh, there was the difference in age, of course. I was five years older. But it went deeper than that. I was very aware of the disagreements between our parents. Dirk was not. He worshiped our mother. He was fascinated by her. She became one of the creatures in his fairy tales—the beautiful princess from a distant garden land across the sea. We spent several summers there, and, for Dirk, it was a magic time. The sun, the flowers, the beautiful lady—totally different from our life in New York. Puerto Rico became all that was warm and bright in his life. New York all that was cold and morbid. Unknowingly, my father reinforced Dirk's alienation from America. Dirk reminded him of Isobel in looks. My father resented him for that. Father was a moody artist, Gretel, and not always careful of others' feelings. Also, Dirk had the misfortune to be *my* younger brother. I was the perfect son. I looked like a proper Van der Hoek. I behaved like one. I did well at school. I was polite. I liked to draw. Dirk did none of those things. Father was always on edge when Dirk came to the island, for he had to be watched constantly in case he might drown or do something wild, like set the house afire. He tried that once. I don't know. I should have done more for Dirk."

"You did all you could," I said lamely.

"I don't know. You do what you can. Dirk was not a likable child. He nicknamed himself 'Cain' and me 'Abel.' I was more than relieved when he went to spend several years with Isobel. By the time he came back, I was at Yale. We led separate lives after that."

"Did you suspect he was El Condor?"

"Yes and no. It fit in perfectly with what Dirk is. He had recently moved to the island, renovating the boathouse. Starr Mills stayed there for a while, hiding out. Such a child she was then. Her 'crime' was jumping bail. I painted her portrait that summer. That's what I was doing in there, burning it on Dirk's advice. Just in case, he said, the FBI start sniffing about. Starr never said anything then about El Condor, of course. She'd known both of us for years. But I should have been more suspicious. Her death shook me. Meeting you helped. I wanted to forget Dirk. But I knew for certain Dirk was El Condor when we went to Puerto Rico."

"That man I saw you talking to at El Morro."

"He asked me to carry money," said Pieter. "I refused, of course, but he was persistent, even following me to the casino. I was sure he'd ruin my luck."

"Then you really did win all that money," I said.

"What?" he said.

"Does Isobel know?" I asked, chagrined that he might catch me having doubted him.

"Good God! No! El Condor isn't known in Puerto Rico. I think Dirk is a disappointment to her, though she'll never admit it. She's never been able to refuse him anything. He's constantly asking her for money. She always gives it, she feels guilty. Dirk was a baby when she left. He ran through his inheritance years ago. He gave it away. Dirk's got a wild, generous heart, but he's inconsistent. His politics are a good example. He's right about Puerto Rico, the way the Puerto Ricans are abused and cheated. But he gets confused. And when he's confused, he turns violent and mean."

"Couldn't you have stopped him once you knew about El Condor?" I asked.

"What could I do? I had no *real* proof. I knew Dirk. I knew he would make sure no lives were lost. The burning of an abandoned barge in the harbor, a smoke bomb—frightening, yes, but strictly showmanship. Starr Mills's brand of glamorous, but introductory, guerrilla warfare. I'd hoped Dirk would tire of it. I tried to talk with him, but he cut me off. His reply was that smoke bomb—a stupid, collegiate prank, hyped up by the press. I did manage a meeting with his second-in-command after that."

"Jesús," I said.

"He showed up unexpectedly the night of our dinner party. I begged him to stop Dirk. I thought I had convinced him, but then something happened that made me realize I was wasting my time. And that they were idiots."

"My accident?"

"That was a warning from Jesús, not Dirk. What might happen if I interfered. I don't think he planned to really hurt you. It was just a scare tactic, though I'm sure the outcome didn't matter to Jesús. He's ruthless in his bitterness. And just plain stupid. As Starr found out."

"Starr?"

"From what Dirk told me, she grew quickly impatient with El Condor. She didn't want just symbolic gestures, or mere media games, but a demonstration of revolutionary warfare. There was a parting of the ways. According to Dirk, she and Jesús were showing off after they had fired the barge. They drove their boat into the flames. She didn't come out."

"When did you talk to Dirk?" I asked.

"He left an hour ago. I knew he'd come here. I followed. We talked."

"Where's he gone now?"

"I have no idea," said Pieter. "Gone. Gretel, he's my brother. Remember that. Whatever else he is, he is my brother. And," Pieter continued sadly, "I know that for Dirk, El Condor is finished. It couldn't last much longer. He knew that, so he's off to something else. He left me this." Pieter scooped up the envelope on the table and waved it.

"What?"

"A statement to the effect that I was ignorant of his actions. Something which I'll need very shortly. Dirk said to tell you 'The shadow of El Condor will no longer darken New York.'"

Corny as it sounded, it made me shiver slightly. I had been too long in that "shadow." "Where do you think he'll go?" I asked.

"Ultimately, I think he'll go back to Puerto Rico. It's where he's the happiest. But . . . what's that?" Pieter jerked his head up. There were shouts, coming closer.

"The reporters," I said. "They were at the dock. And Michael Dragon. The police are very interested in anything you might know. I asked for a few minutes alone."

"It's not over, is it, Gretel?" said Pieter, slipping the envelope into his pocket.

"No, but I can bear anything if you're there," I answered with my whole heart.

Pieter bent over to kiss me tenderly on the lips. Whatever happened now, I thought, we would face it together. As I looked into Pieter's eyes, calm, confident, and loving, I knew that our life together would be as happy as any life could be. We had come safe to our harbor.

Michael and Melissa knocked on the kitchen door.